To the Bacon.

# A MURDER AT THE FLOWER SHOW

Neal Sanders
May 2017

**Neal Sanders**

*The Hardington Press*

### Also by Neal Sanders

*Murder Imperfect*
*The Garden Club Gang*
*The Accidental Spy*
*A Murder in the Garden Club*
*Murder for a Worthy Cause*
*Deal Killer*
*Deadly Deeds*

*To the volunteers — amateurs in name only —*
*who lend their time, talent and expertise;*
*and whose passion is the heart and soul of any flower show.*

# A MURDER AT THE FLOWER SHOW

**Chapter 1.**
**Saturday**

It was the quacking of the ducks in the darkness that first caught the night watchman's attention. The yellow glow from his flashlight played across the treetops and onto the lush plantings below. The trees were heavy with blossoms, the shrubs and perennial borders dense with colorful blooms. Everywhere there was the scent of lilac, jasmine, honeysuckle and other, more subtle perfumes. His torch passed across the pond from which the noise emanated, its rim edged with iris and moss.

*A hell of a sight better than last month,* he thought as he walked slowly across a gracefully arched wooden bridge to get a better view of the pond. *Auto parts,* he mused. *Can't make 'em pretty no matter what they do. Acres and acres of damn auto parts.* He heard a rustling sound over his head and turned his flashlight upward. In the steel trusses of the roof, thirty feet above him, sparrows caught inside the cavernous exhibition hall fluttered at the unexpected interruption of their nocturnal privacy. Below him on the pond, ducks continued to make noise.

He turned the flashlight back to the pond below. Two ducks paddled away from the light, giving an un-landscaped white island in the middle of the pond an especially wide berth.

The night watchman studied the island more closely. White, yes, but seemingly covered in fabric while everything else in the exhibit was draped with plant material. Also, the island bobbed slightly as the ducks paddled. It appeared to float rather than being anchored.

He retraced his steps across the bridge and walked thirty feet around the perimeter of the exhibit, then stepped up on the wooden risers three feet above the concrete floor. The thing – whatever it was – was now about ten feet away. The flashlight revealed no further details beyond what he had seen from the bridge. Whatever it was, though, it didn't belong. It had likely been thrown into the pond in the past hour or so because the cleaning staff had done a thorough job of picking up the area after the party, and he hadn't seen it on his first or second pass through the area.

The night watchman remembered a long pole in the maintenance area. He retrieved it, returned and poked at whatever was floating. It was heavy but not solid. Pushing at the object, he slowly guided it to the edge of the exhibit, about ten feet down the artificial shoreline from where he now stood.

He walked the few feet, playing the flashlight across the object and the adjacent water. When he was five feet away, he began to see what the light refraction had previously hidden, and he involuntarily drew in a gulp of air and felt the resulting sourness rising in his throat.

Arms and legs, also clad in white, extended away from the body in a loose 'X' formation, the hands and feet sinking toward the bottom of the two-foot-deep, man-made pond.

He did not turn over the body, even to make certain the person was dead. Sixty years of watching television told him you never disturbed a crime scene.

The night watchman reached for his cell phone and dialed 911.

* * * * *

The cell phone chirped in the dark, a tinny fragment of the William Tell Overture that served as the theme to *The Lone Ranger*.

Victoria Lee opened an eye, looking for the blinking red LED that would betray the phone's location. Once she spotted it, she would try to remember where she left her shoes, and then, regardless of how many months remained on the service contract, she would smash the phone into oblivion with a heel.

But the red light did not blink from anywhere in the room even though, by its volume, the phone was probably within ten feet of her. She looked at the clock beside her bed.

3:37 a.m.

She reached out and bumped her hand into the lamp on the table beside the bed. She placed one hand over her eyes, closed her lids tightly and turned on the switch.

Muttering a slow, steady stream of random obscenities, she got out of bed and walked in the direction of the telephone's music. It was in her jacket pocket, the jacket, in turn, thrown haphazardly across a chair tucked neatly under a dressing table that collected books and files rather than cosmetics.

Adjusting to the bright light, she looked for the incoming number, though she knew by the idiotic, distinctive ring that it was one of her detectives. She stabbed at the 'answer call' icon.

"This had had better be good," she said.

"We're at the Harborfront Expo Center," a male voice said. "A guard found a floater in a pond at the flower show."

"Who is this?" Lee asked, simultaneously and unsuccessfully trying to absorb the words and identify the caller. "Mazilli?"

"It's Alvarez. Jason Alvarez, Ma'am. The night watchman found him. The guy has probably been in the water less than an hour…"

"And you're calling me because… why?"

"I thought you'd want to know. The last time I didn't call a higher-up on something like this, I got reamed…"

"You did the right thing…. Jason." The fog in Lee's head began to lift, ever so slightly. "Jason, it's three-thirty. The middle of the night. Isn't this something that can keep until morning?"

"Mazilli said I shouldn't bother you. In fact, he was fairly adamant about it. But the guy…" Alvarez trailed off.

"The guy…" Lee prompted.

She heard Alvarez exhale. "It's the head guy for the flower show. He's in a white tux. They say he's also the head of the society that puts on the show.  Maybe it's an accidental drowning but, from my initial look at the body, I'd say we need the full team."

Lee sighed.  "Call the M.E.…  And give me twenty minutes."

* * * * *

The towering illuminated sign blinked its message in the nighttime sky:  127th ANNUAL…NORTHEAST GARDEN AND FLOWER SHOW… FEBRUARY 15-23…DOORS OPEN 10 A.M…

Lee pulled into the Harborfront Exposition Center's vast parking lot and drove across the macadam toward the flashing lights. Red and blue lights from one ambulance, two police cruisers, and a detective's car all rotated pointlessly, wearing down batteries.  Three other vehicles were parked haphazardly in front of the entrance.  Lee parked her Honda Accord carefully within the lines of a parking space.

The Harborfront Exposition Center was a sprawling structure that, despite remodeling over the decades, betrayed its roots as a failed cargo port and warehouse.  Once a premier site for trade shows and conventions, its exterior now looked dowdy, the façade dated.  Three of the ten floodlights that illuminated the building were not working, and the balance were mismatched in color, leaving the face of the building a patchwork of yellow, blue, white and gray.

Inside, all lights were on, the building interior as bright as midday. Masses of flowers were everywhere, spilling out of containers and bordering pedestrian walkways.  To the left was a cavernous area of vendor booths.  To the right were display gardens.  Lee walked toward the voices in the gardens, all the time sniffing hopefully for the aroma of coffee.  She ought to have put on her dark blue jacket and skirt to show deference to whatever grieving family members might show up later.  Instead, she had slipped into jeans, a sweater, sneakers and her ski parka.

*Fine,* she thought.  *It's my third day on the job, and it's four o'clock in the morning.  Let them think anything they want to.  Just get in, evaluate, get out, and be on the train at eight.*

A hundred feet in front of her were a clutch of people. A young detective she assumed to be Jason Alvarez moved briskly from point to point, indicating places a police photographer should record. Nearby, Alvarez's partner, Vito Mazilli, leaned against a column, taking notes on something being told to him by one of the crime scene technicians. Neither saw Lee enter the building. But a white-haired security guard, seventy years old if he was a day, spotted her and ambled over.

"You can't come in here yet, Miss," he said. "No vendor set-up until six o'clock." He said the words in a kindly, grandfatherly way, as though shooing away errant vendors without annoying them was one of the main bullet points of his position description.

"Actually, I'm with the police," Lee said, fumbling in her purse for the leather case that held her badge.

"You're Lieutenant Lee?" he asked, squinting and his brow furrowing with doubt.

"Surprise," Lee said and smiled.

"Sorry, I expected…"

"Yeah, yeah, yeah. You expected petticoats and mint juleps," Lee said. "I get that a lot. My parents should have changed our names to something really oriental like 'Ming' before we emigrated. It would have cleared up a lot of awkward moments like this. I see Detectives Alvarez and Mazilli and a couple of techs. And, what's your name?"

The guard recovered sufficiently to nod. "Walter O'Brien."

"How long you worked here, Mr. O'Brien? I'm guessing a long time."

He nodded and pushed back his cap an inch or so with the fingers of one hand. "Thirty-two years."

"Seen a lot of flower shows, I guess."

He nodded again. "And boat shows and car shows and everything else."

"Anybody ever turn up dead at one of them on your watch?"

"Found a vendor dead of a heart attack once. Home Show. Nineteen…. eighty-eight. Yeah. The year Dukakis ran for president. Died back in his holding area and nobody noticed. Never had a chance."

"They say the same thing about Dukakis," Lee grinned. "You found the body this morning?"

O'Brien nodded. From the look on his face, it hadn't been a pleasant experience.

"You had met the victim?"

"Oh, yeah," O'Brien said. "I remember him from last year, too. He's been around here all week, and I saw him tonight. Ought to have figured out it was him right away. He was strutting around in that white suit…"

"What time did you come on?"

"Midnight," O'Brien said. "Same as every night, show or no show."

"And there was a party? The sign outside says the show opens today… this morning."

"Oh, they've been in here for a week, setting up. The 'load in' they call it. Last night was their big party for all the money people. The 'Gala'. Everyone in tuxes. All the ladies in gowns and fancy jewelry. But St. John was the only one…"

"I'm sorry," Lee said. "Sin Jin?"

"His name is spelled 'Saint John', but everyone pronounced it Sin-Jin. His full name is something long. Two last names with a hyphen between them."

"Sounds like a mouth full," Lee said.

"That's why everyone called him St. John," O'Brien said, nodding. "Saved a lot of words."

"English was he? Spoke with an accent?"

"I suppose so. Sounded like that guy who used to be on Masterpiece Theater."

"Alistair Cooke," Lee offered.

"If you say so."

"So, St. John-two-last-names-with-a-hyphen was the only man in white tie and tails last night as far as you were aware."

O'Brien nodded.

"And what time did the party break up?"

"One-thirty, quarter to two."

"Lot of people?"

"Place was full. Close to fifteen hundred, I heard."

"And everybody drinking, I imagine," Lee said. "Liquor and Champagne free for the asking. Any chance he got drunk and fell in?"

O'Brien shook his head. "I walked the same area at two and two-thirty. Didn't see him then."

"So, after the party, everybody went home and you had the place to yourself?"

"Then the cleaning crew went to work," O'Brien said. "'Bout a dozen of them. Picked out all the glasses from the bushes, cleaned up the spilled food. They worked fast. They were out of here by a quarter past two."

"And what were you doing during the party and the clean-up?"

"Same as I always do," O'Brien said, a hint of a smile creeping across his face. "Stopping people from going into the vendor area. Even rich people get light fingers in a place like this."

Lee looked past O'Brien at the vast expanse of vendor space. Then, from the corner of her eye she saw Vito Mazilli lumbering toward her. Five minutes of talking with a useful witness was all she was going to get. Twelve hours from now, O'Brien's recollections would be tainted by his conversations with other people. He would begin repeating what he had heard others say, believing it was what he had seen.

"Just a minute, Mazilli," Lee said, waving him off.

"I've got a couple of people lined up for you, Lieutenant" Mazilli said, oblivious to the tone of Lee's voice. "Plus, we're about to fish the guy out of the pond." Mazilli had drooping eyelids, as though he were about to nod off.

"Give me another minute," Lee said, firmly.

This time, Lee's words got through. Mazilli sighed and turned around. He shuffled off to a spot twenty feet away where he roosted, his face showing annoyance, impatiently waiting for the allotted minute to be up.

"When the cleaning crew was finished, it was just you in the building, is that right?" Lee asked.

O'Brien nodded. "Just me. I walk the entire center every half hour."

"You understand that if this was a murder, someone had to kill St. John, dump his body in the pond, and get out without being seen," Lee said.

O'Brien rubbed his chin with his hand. "Wouldn't be that hard. I can only be in one place at a time."

"But the outside doors are all locked?"

"They're locked," he agreed.

"And alarmed?"

O'Brien paused. He started to say something different, then stopped himself. He shook his head. "Not really. Not anymore. Maintenance is part of it. Owners have been wanting to tear this place down for a couple of years and, at this point, they're not doing anything except plugging holes in the roof. All the big shows are over at the Convention Center now; the mid-sized ones at Seaport. Back when the alarms worked, if there was a malfunction and somebody responded, it used to be two, three hundred bucks as a fine. Got to the point where there were four, five false alarms a week. The owners got tired of paying. So, now the alarm signs are just for show."

"Security cameras?"

O'Brien made a chuckling noise. "Not for a long time. They got me. They got three people on days and more when shows come in."

Lee had a dozen other questions, but Mazilli had wandered back. "Lieutenant, there are some people I really think you're going to want to talk to."

Lee grimaced. She plunged her hand into her shoulder bag and came up with what she hoped was a card. "Please stay close by, Mr. O'Brien, and don't talk to the media. You're the guy who saw the crime scene first. Your recollections are very important."

Mazilli walked Lee back into the heart of the exhibit area. It was a series of islands of greenery, some more than a thousand square feet in size, others just a few hundred. All were lush, imagined landscapes, with everything in bloom simultaneously. Outside, it was mid-February and massive piles of ugly, brown snow were everywhere. Inside, it was a balmy, late spring day.

"What have we got?" Lee asked.

"St. John Grainger-Elliot, age forty-two," Mazilli said. "Executive Director of the New England Botanical Society, which sponsors the Northeast Garden and Flower Show. We're about to take him out of the pond. Thanks to young Alvarez, the ME is on her way, with some choice words about being dragged out of bed at four in the morning."

"I know just how she feels," Lee said. "And our little group up there?" Lee indicated three people talking with Alvarez, thirty or forty feet away.

Mazilli took out his notebook and read. "The tall one is Linda Cooke. She runs the flower show." Mazilli indicated a thin woman, probably six-one in flats. She looked to be in her mid- to late thirties, with black hair pulled back in a ponytail. "To her left is Winona Stone. She's Cooke's assistant." Stone was of medium height, slender with long, red hair. She appeared to be in her mid-twenties. "The big guy is Tony Wilson. He runs the physical plant at Botanical Hall – that's the society's headquarters – and he's more or less in charge of making everything go smoothly at the show." Wilson was an African-

American in his fifties who looked as though he might have played tackle for the New England Patriots. His neck was as large around as his head.

"Who called them?" Lee asked. "And how did they get here so quickly?"

"After the security guard called 911, he called building management," Mazilli said, referring to his notes. "Building management called Cooke, which Cooke says is policy. Cooke called the others. They're all staying at that hotel across the parking lot."

"Any of them look guilty?"

"They look tired," Mazilli said. "They were here until around two. They thought they'd get at least four hours of sleep."

"So did I," Lee said, yawning involuntarily.

"The lieutenant had a social obligation?" Mazilli asked.

"The lieutenant had classes until ten o'clock and then a study group until one in the morning. The lieutenant needs a cup of coffee. Strong and black."

They reached the crime scene. Grainger-Elliot still floated face down in the pond. Four technicians were removing their shoes and rolling up their pants legs in preparation for retrieving the body.

"The floors were all washed as part of the clean-up after the party," Mazilli said. "Crews went through the exhibits looking for cigarette butts and glasses. The brown stuff in the exhibits is mulch, not dirt, so it doesn't hold shoeprints very well."

Mazilli indicated a spot a few feet down a three-foot-high timbered retaining wall. "The security guard said he climbed that wall to get a better look at something floating in the pond. Otherwise, he left the scene alone."

"Good man," Lee said. "I knew there was a reason I liked him."

Lee saw Jason Alvarez meticulously bagging and tagging mulch fragments from the floor. Mazilli and Alvarez comprised two of her four night-shift detectives. Mazilli, she knew primarily by reputation;

Alvarez, only a few months on the detectives' squad, was a name she knew only because she had read his personnel jacket her first day on the job. While Vito Mazilli was heavy-set and in his late fifties, Alvarez was probably about thirty; her own age give or take a year. He was good looking, lean with a dark complexion and short, black hair and sideburns just below the middle of his ears. *Mutt and Jeff*, Lee thought.

"Any evidence?" she asked him.

"Good morning, Lieutenant," Alvarez said. "We've tagged everything we can find. What we especially don't have are any shoe prints on the floor, so there isn't much to go on. I'm getting one of the techs to sift the mulch around the edge of the pond. We might get something. I've had the filter for the pond turned off, and we'll comb the bottom and check the filter cage as soon as the victim has been pulled out."

*Well, at least he's organized*, Lee thought. *Bright, and attentive to detail.*

O'Brien, the night watchman, approached Lee gingerly. "Lieutenant Lee, there's a TV news truck that just pulled up at the door and a reporter who says he wants to talk to the person in charge."

Lee, distracted, asked O'Brien to wait a minute. There was a splashing sound behind them as the crime scene techs waded into the pond, unfurled a plastic tarpaulin underneath Grainger-Elliot and carefully lifted the body out of the water. Mazilli directed four EMTs, who took the body from the techs and laid it on the concrete floor, still on its plastic sheet. Lee noted that Mazilli carefully avoided getting himself wet.

"Let's roll him over," Lee said. "Gently."

Grainger-Elliot now lay face up. He might have been handsome if he weren't dead. Slender build, perhaps five-ten in height. Blonde hair, blue eyes, a fair complexion and a small moustache.

Three things were immediately evident. First, the telltale broken capillaries around the nose and cheeks were missing. Grainger-Elliot had not drowned. Second, there was a four-inch-long, oval-shaped red mark on the right-hand side of his forehead, indicating he had been struck with something. Third, there were ligature marks above the collar indicating something had been tied around the man's neck before he died.

Lee donned latex gloves and, from the pocket of Grainger-Elliot's tuxedo jacket, she extracted a wallet. It held half a dozen credit cards and a hundred dollars or more in cash. From another pocket she pulled an iPhone. From the wrist of his left arm, she took a Piaget watch worth, probably, twenty thousand. She handed those items to Alvarez to be bagged.

"Mazilli," she said, "call headquarters and tell them to wake up someone in public affairs. Tell them to get their ass down here in ten minutes. This area is sealed until further notice, and tell that P.A. person that if I see one reporter or a camera in this building, I'm going to hand them their head in an evidence bag."

Lee took a long breath. "Gentlemen, this is now officially a homicide."

## Chapter 2

Linda Cooke poured the coffee. They were in the Expo Center's VIP lounge, a twelve-by-twelve room with muted lighting where the New England Botanical Society – 'The Society', she kept calling it – brought wealthy, would-be contributors to relax away from the hustle and bustle of the show. Here, prospective donors could rest up in comfortable chairs and admire the antique, hand-tinted botanical prints adorning the walls. They could hear, first-hand in one-on-one sessions, from earnest experts from the fields of horticulture and botany. Depending upon the time of day, they could sip coffee or wine or something harder. And here, they could be encouraged to show their appreciation for the hand-holding by writing large checks to the Society.

At 4:30 a.m., the beverage was coffee, hot and caffeine-laden. Lee was on her third cup, consumed from an ivory-colored mug bearing a Botanical Society logo.

On closer inspection, Lee judged Cooke to be in her forties. Her hair was pulled back to minimize facial lines, and her makeup was carefully applied. She was not an especially attractive woman; her mouth was too small and her nose too prominent. But Cooke used cosmetics to minimize those flaws and to pare years from her appearance. Lee noted that even coming on a few moments' notice with the news of her employer's death, Cooke had taken the time to add eyeliner, blush and lipstick. There was also a rigid quality to Cooke's brow and chin. Lee wondered if Botox might be part of Cooke's regimen and, if so, how far along in her forties Cooke was.

"St. John was the savior of the Society," Cooke said for possibly the fourth time. "He appreciated talent. He understood marketing. He understood botany. He talked about a two-hundred-year plan for the Society and what it could accomplish. He was a man of vision."

"Who would want to kill him?" Lee asked.

"Nobody," Cooke said emphatically. "That's just it. Everybody liked St. John. Everybody respected him. We would do anything for him and vice versa. He had breathed life into a moribund organization."

"Nevertheless, somebody killed him," Lee said. "Strangled him, carried him to one of the exhibits and dumped him into a pond."

"I can't imagine who would do something like that," Cooke said, shivering. "It strains credulity."

Lee wondered how, two hours before sunrise and on one or two hours of sleep, someone could work words like 'moribund' and 'credulity' into a sentence.

"He was married?"

"Cynthia. Beautiful woman. Very supportive," Cooke said, emphasizing 'beautiful'.

"Has anyone called her?" Lee asked.

A pained look passed across Cooke's face. "No. It isn't something I'm looking forward to... I thought the police..."

Lee nodded. "We'll take care of it. Was Mr. Grainger-Elliot also staying at the hotel here?"

"Of course," Cooke said. "The whole Garden and Flower Show staff – ten of us -- have to be available around the clock."

"What about Mrs. Grainger-Elliot?"

Cooke shook her head. "It isn't really a lot of fun for spouses. We're here up to eighteen hours a day. And, for whatever it's worth, Cynthia uses her maiden name, Duncastle."

"Not even for the big party last night?" Lee asked. "I would have thought that would have been fun... like a reward."

"St. John worked the crowd," Cooke said. "It was be nice to trustees, be nicer to prospective donors, be nicest to people who just wrote checks. Besides, St. John and Cynthia have three children, all under the age of ten."

"Three children, "Lee said. "I take it they live out in the suburbs."

"Oh, no," Cooke replied. "The Society owns a townhouse adjacent to Botanical Hall. St. John and his family live there."

*Which would make the Grainger-Elliot/Duncastle residence just three and a half miles from where they now sat*, Lee thought. *Not exactly a hardship to get from Point 'A' to Point 'B' and back. And Mrs. Executive Director would pass up the opportunity to put on a fancy dress and pull out all the family baubles because it wasn't 'a lot of fun'?* It didn't sound right.

On the whole, Lee decided, Cooke's answers were too perfunctory, too defensive of her boss and not especially forthcoming. But cases were built fact by fact. She would come back to Cooke when she knew more, and when she could ask better or more intelligent questions.

\* \* \* \* \*

Tony Wilson blew on his coffee incessantly. Because only two of his huge fingers would fit through the mug's handle, he also held out his pinkie finger when he finally deemed the mug's contents to be the right temperature, though perhaps his un-masculine grip could be explained by the fact that his hand was several times the size of the cup. Unlike Cooke, who had arrived at the Expo Center in an impeccable camel-colored suit, Wilson was in a plaid shirt and mulch-smeared jeans. He also possessed an easy demeanor that invited trust in what he said.

"Enemies?" he said. "Hell, last night the man had a list of enemies as long as your arm. You got fifty-one exhibitors who dropped anywhere from a couple of thousand to nearly a hundred thousand bucks putting together a landscape for the show. Every one of them expects a board full of ribbons out in front of the exhibit to impress potential customers. Instead, one guy runs the table and gets forty-two awards while the other fifty exhibitors get to share thirty-nine. And a lot of those are made-up things that everyone gets, like the

'Botanical Society Award of Merit'." Wilson spoke with a slight trace of a southern accent. Lee decided his family must have moved to Boston when he was a child.

"Would that be enough for someone to commit a murder?" Lee asked.

"These guys here," Wilson said, blowing on his coffee again. When he spoke again it was in a lower voice. "This is their lifeblood. They've got this and the Boston Flower and Garden Show next month to showcase what hot stuff they are. Every big nursery, every fancy landscaping service, every landscape architect is here. They've got nine days to write a year's worth of business based on being able to showcase their skills in a twenty-by-forty-foot space. They plant themselves on stools, ready to waylay people who look like they've got a couple of hundred grand to spend on landscaping."

"And the ribbons validate their skill and imagination?"

Wilson grinned and wagged a finger at Lee. "You understand. The more ribbons and trophies, the more prestige. The more prestige, the more business."

"People come here looking for a landscaper?" Lee asked.

Wilson laughed. The sound was deep and hearty and filled the room. "They come here because it's February and fourteen degrees outside and it's the middle of May in here. Anyone with twenty bucks can come here and get a day-long dose of spring. They don't come in expecting to have someone re-do their property, but they're the right age, they linger by an exhibit, the wife is carrying an expensive purse, and all of a sudden some guy walks up to them and says, 'I'm pleased you like my design'. Ten minutes later, the guy knows they live in Sherborn on three acres but nothing on their property looks like what they see in front of them. The guy starts sketching and, an hour later, the people from Sherborn are in love with an idea and well on their way to spending a hundred thousand bucks for a pond, a waterfall, and some new specimen trees."

Lee nodded, absorbing the image.

"Now, everybody gets some kind of an award but, like I said, most of those are kind of like kindergarten sports," Wilson continued. "You get a blue ribbon just for showing up. But there's a world of difference between the 'Mary Chase Wilson Award for Best Use of Dahlias' – Mary Chase Wilson being my wife -- and the 'Award of Merit' that's on every single exhibit." He finished his mug of coffee and poured another for each. "Now, when you get past the exhibitors who wanted to tear apart St. John…"

"Wait a second," Lee said. "Who decides who gets the awards? Can't the Botanical Society divvy them up equally?"

Wilson held up a stubby finger. "That's the problem. There's a separate group of judges to keep the whole thing honest. Now, St. John names the people on the panels for the Society awards. It's three people – usually one hot-shot designer who doesn't have a display this year and two little old ladies with lot of money who are *thrilled* to be asked to judge. But the 'real' awards are picked by the groups that sponsor the trophies. And, believe me, those people take it seriously."

"I got it," Lee said, having heard enough to understand. "Did he have other enemies?"

"Well, then there are the vendors," Wilson said. "More than three hundred of them spread over five halls, each an acre in size. Linda Cooke and St. John will promise every vendor who signs up for next year and puts down their deposit now that they'll be right on the concourse outside of the exhibit hall – what we call the 'gold coast'. Instead, they show up here on Thursday morning and find out they're back in Siberia with the foot massage people. That tends to make them cranky."

"But those people wouldn't have been at the party last night?"

"The exhibitors get comped for the Gala because they're the star attractions, but the vendors have to pay their own way in – two hundred bucks a head, so they don't show up," Wilson conceded.

"But believe me, the exhibitors were here yesterday afternoon making plenty of noise, plus there were about three dozen vendors who were screaming for St. John's or Linda's head yesterday because they didn't get the space they were promised."

"The exhibitors," Lee said. "They were angry just because they didn't get enough awards?"

"Awards, plants missing from their displays, having an exhibit space away from the heavy traffic areas, being locked out of the exhibit hall on judging day and not having access to their exhibits until four hours before the Gala… you name it, they were bellyaching about it. But it's the same old stuff every year."

* * * * *

Winona Stone was a fresh-faced twenty-five. On a different morning, Lee decided Stone would have been judged beautiful by anyone who saw her. She had translucent skin and soft red hair that fell in waves like a pre-Raphaelite model. But at that moment she looked as though her world had fallen apart and could never be put back together. Her face was drawn and pale. She was horrified at Grainger-Elliot's death. Far more than Cooke or Wilson, she was visibly shaken by the event. Her hands shook as she held a mug, the coffee in it offering both warmth and a distraction from the night's events.

She said her official title was Assistant Garden and Flower Show Director. "But it's, like, just a title. My job is to do whatever Linda tells me to do. I'm supposed to, like, watch her and learn. This is, like, my second show. Linda is, like, awesome."

Lee was ready to strangle Stone after the tenth iteration of 'like' in the woman's responses. Instead, she mentally screened the word out of the woman's vocabulary.

"Did you see Mr. Grainger-Elliot spend a lot of time with anyone in particular at the party?"

"I think St. John talked with everyone there. He shook a million hands. I don't believe he spent more than a minute or two with any one person."

"Did he drink?"

"I suppose so. I mean, he had a glass in his hand most of the evening."

To Lee, the answer sounded tenuous. But there would be a tox screen. If Grainger-Elliot was sloshed when he died, it would be quickly known.

"To your knowledge, did he have any enemies?"

Stone shook her head. An even sadder look came over her face. "He must have," she said. "Someone killed him." Stone put her head down and, when she raised it again a few moments later, her eyes were filled with tears.

"Tony Wilson told me some vendors and exhibitors were angry with Mr. Grainger-Elliot. Did you see him with any of those exhibitors last night?"

Stone thought for a moment. "No. In fact, I guess he was avoiding exhibitors. He told me they'd get over it after a day or two. He said they were like little children who didn't get an A+ on their homework."

"When did he tell you that?"

Stone started to speak but then closed her mouth. A few seconds later she said, "Um, yesterday evening sometime, I guess. St. John wasn't there when the exhibitors were let back in. So it must have been after seven. I guess some exhibitors said something to him."

*A lie*, Lee thought, *and not a very good one.* She wrote a note on her pad. *Where was G-E between 3 and 7 p.m.?*

"Whose exhibit was he found in?" Lee asked. "I didn't really know each one was created by a different designer."

"That's Blue Hills Gardens' exhibit. They're the one that won more awards than anyone else."

"Who runs Blue Hills Gardens?"

"Oscar McQueen."

"He must have been all smiles last evening," Lee said.

"He was getting a lot of congratulations. He was very happy."

Lee wanted to follow up but was interrupted by Jason Alvarez. "Lieutenant, the M.E. wants to talk to you. It's pretty interesting."

Lee excused herself and walked with Alvarez to where the body was now on a gurney. The Medical Examiner, Lois Otting, waved as Lee approached. Otting was a bowling ball of a woman, not an inch over five feet and tipping the scales at over two hundred pounds. She was, despite her orders-of-magnitude variation in appearance from the doctors who inhabited network television shows, the best M.E. Lee had ever worked with.

"Hey, Vicki, you got a live one here," Otting said.

"He didn't look that way when we fished him out of the pond," Lee responded.

"Well, this guy was a triple threat," Otting said. "If I were looking for a sequence of events, I'd say first he was hit over the head. Didn't break the skin but it was a good whack."

"Like a pipe?" Lee asked.

"A pipe would be good. Or something wooden, like a baseball bat. Give me some time in the lab. One good hit intended to knock him out or at least incapacitate him. The fact that it was just one indicates your perp had something more in mind for the guest of honor."

"Hit from the front?" Lee asked, tracking a circle around the bruise with her finger.

"More like from above," Otting said. "The bottom of the bruise is deeper than the top. Someone could have been holding him from behind and whacked him to keep him from struggling. So, unless your boy had his eyes closed or was asleep, this started with an assault."

"Did he put up a defense?" Lee asked, picking up one of Grainger-Elliot's hands."

"Smooth as a baby's bottom, no evidence of a struggle. And the man liked his manicures. I'll get under the fingernails, but an hour in the water may have washed off anything useful. If you look at the wrists, there's evidence that his hands were bound with duct tape. There's also tape residue over his mouth and his moustache. Both areas are still sticky. The tape was removed before he went in the water, though. Find the tape and you'll find your murderer. That stuff collects DNA like there's no tomorrow."

Lee made a note to send the techs out to look for duct tape.

"The cause of death, however, was asphyxiation," Otting said. She traced her finger along the ligature marks on the neck. "Judging from what I see here, I'd say nylon rope, wound around a couple of times. I'll look for traces when I get him on the slab but, while you're looking for that duct tape, keep an eye peeled for a length of nylon rope."

"Time of death?" Lee asked.

Otting looked at her watch. "It's 5:45 now, I'd say time of death was sometime between 1:45 and 2:15 a.m. based on body temperature and adjusting for having been in the water."

"So, just about the time the party was breaking up," Lee said.

"I don't know," Otting replied. "I wasn't there. Nobody ever invites me to those kind of shindigs."

"Can you tell when he went into the water?"

Otting scratched her chin. "After two. Maybe as late as three. But he was definitely dead. No water in the lungs as far as I can tell. I'll be certain when I open him up."

"So, somebody stashed a body for a while," Lee said.

"Looking at it that way, yeah. Somebody stashed a body."

"Do me a favor, Lois," Lee said. "Give me a blood workup as soon as you can. I need to know if Grainger-Elliot was intoxicated when this happened." As an afterthought she added, "Also, pay careful attention to his genital region. Give me a call when you're done."

"You think our boy was high and dipping his wick and got whacked for it?"

"I don't know," Lee said, shaking her head. "You've got the head of the New England Botanical Society on the biggest fund-raising night of the year. As the party's breaking up, someone grabs him from behind, clobbers him with a pipe, then strangles him, hides his body and then tosses it in a pond where it's sure to be found."

"Not your average murder," Otting said. "At least you got me out of bed for an interesting one."

"Why the extra steps?" Lee asked. "Why not just smack him three or four times and cover him up with a sheet?"

"You're thinking degradation," Otting said. "Make the bastard suffer."

"Or make him talk," Lee replied. "That's one reason I want a blood alcohol level. As for the sex part, I just want a more complete picture of the guy than I'm getting from his staff so far. I'm getting a lot of guarded responses."

Lee called over Mazilli and Alvarez. "Mazilli, get more uniforms in here. Have them go over every square inch of every back room and every trash can. They're looking for duct tape. Grainger-Elliot's wrists were bound with the stuff. They may also find a length of nylon rope. We need to move fast. As soon as they've got their instructions, you're going into Back Bay and break the news to Grainger-Elliot's wife. I want to know if she got a good night's sleep."

"What are you going to do about the reporters?" Mazilli asked.

"Isn't the public affairs person handling them?" Lee asked.

"Well, yeah," Mazilli said. "But the gal said she's got nothing to say. She sounds pretty upset."

Lee chafed at the casual use of the word 'gal' by Mazilli but said nothing. "She's going to keep on saying nothing until we're finished in here. And don't you talk to them on your way out."

To Alvarez she said, "Get me the complete workup on Grainger-

Elliot. Newspaper articles, profiles, résumés. Be prepared to educate me in an hour."

Alvarez dashed off.

"Mazilli, why are you still standing there?"

\* \* \* \* \*

Linda Cooke hovered outside the door of the VIP lounge as Lee spoke by phone with Mazilli, who had just broken the news to Grainger-Elliot's wife. Mazilli had offered to send a patrol car for the woman once arrangements were made for the care of her children. He said Cynthia Duncastle sounded suitably grief-stricken and accepted the offer of a ride.

As soon as the call was completed, Cooke entered the room. "I have a show that opens in less than three hours," Cooke said, impatience in her voice. "May I assume you'll have made all the measurements you need to make by then?"

Lee looked at her watch. It wasn't on her wrist. She had forgotten to put it on in her haste to get to the crime scene. She picked up her cell phone which displayed the time as 6:17. She'd never make the 8:10 Acela. Was there one every hour on Saturday?

"The big sign outside says 'Doors open at 10'," Lee said.

"That's for the general public," Cooke said. "Members have a preview hour from nine to ten. And, at ten, I have more than thirty buses scheduled, with sixty more before noon. This is always our biggest day. Fifteen thousand people, easily."

Lee shrugged. "I hate to put it to you this way, but your boss was murdered a few hours ago. Would you like me to catch his killer or not?"

"You've already examined the crime scene," Cooke said, her voice testy. "You photographed every inch of it. What more do you need?"

"I know where your boss was *found*," Lee said. "I don't know where he was *killed*. The moment your hordes of people come into this building, I lose any chance of finding that place and whatever evidence was left behind."

"What about the vendors?" Cooke asked, her voice rising with annoyance. "I've got three hundred people in the lobby who need to get their booths ready. The vendor area was sealed off last night. Surely, you can let them in."

Lee thought for a moment. "Find me the night watchman… O'Brien."

Cooke took a walkie-talkie from her pocket and paged the security guard. As they waited, Lee and Cooke eyed one another warily. O'Brien appeared a minute later.

Lee asked, "Mr. O'Brien, you said that from midnight until you started your rounds, you kept people from going into the vendor area. How sure are you that no one got around you?"

"I'm sure. I've been doing this a long time. I know all their tricks."

"When did you start your rounds?"

"Right at two. All the guests had left." He indicated Cooke with his chin. "Miss Cooke was the last one here."

*Except for the murderer*, Lee thought.

Lee looked at Cooke. "Your vendors can come in at seven and not a minute before. But *no one* comes into the exhibit area."

Cooke began to protest. "But the exhibitors…"

"*No one*," Lee repeated. "And the first time I see someone who doesn't have a badge in the exhibit area – and I mean a *police* badge – I shut this place down. All day, if I have to."

To the security guard, Lee said, "Mr. O'Brien, I would be grateful if you would take me on your rounds just as you did them last night."

Lee and O'Brien left, leaving Cooke to begin furiously making phone calls.

"Show me what's behind the scenes," Lee asked. "Not the vendor halls and not the exhibits. What else is here?"

O'Brien guided her through areas behind black curtains – 'pipe and drape' he called it -- that separated the public from the non-public areas of the show. Most were rooms filled with show supplies or designated for judging or meetings. Lee peppered O'Brien with questions. When asked if anything looked different from the evening before, the invariable answer was 'no'.

"There are offices up front – where the VIP lounge was set up," Lee said. "Can we go there?"

O'Brien led the way. What he called the 'show office' was a triangular-shaped warren of tiny rooms accessed through a set of double doors.

"You looked in every one of these rooms on your rounds?"

O'Brien shook his head. "Don't have to. I just made certain the master door is locked when I start each of my rounds."

Lee went back to the double doors and felt their edges. There was no evidence either one had been jimmied or taped open.

"I noticed some windows that open out into the exhibit hall," Lee said. "Which offices are those?"

O'Brien walked a few feet and opened a door on the left. Beyond it was a neat office. Two doors farther on, he opened the entry to a second room.

The room was a shambles. The desk was bare. Papers were strewn on the floor along with a desk lamp. A chair lay on its side.

Lee's heart raced, and she reached for her cell phone to call Mazilli. Then she looked more carefully at the floor and said, "Crap."

Amid the papers on the floor was a pair of black panties.

O'Brien followed her gaze and smiled. "We get that with every big party."

"There were three windowed offices," Lee said.

O'Brien led her past two doors. He opened the third and turned on a light.

The first thing Lee saw was a coil of nylon rope. The second were drops of blood on the carpet.

She opened her cell phone. "Mazilli, if you're not already back here, then step on it. Get yourself and the crime scene techs over to the management offices. I think I found where our guy was killed."

* * * * *

The office was ideal for a murderer, Lee thought. There were nine rooms in the building's management center. Two were used full-time; one by the maintenance workers union rep and the other by a representative of the building's owner. The other seven, including this one, were given over to whomever was holding a show at the facility. Keys were readily available, and the double doors had been open throughout the evening, locked only when Linda Cooke left at 2 a.m.

The murderer – or murderers – could have lured Grainger-Elliot to this room on any pretext between 1:30 and 2:00 a.m., killed him, then watched the exhibit area through the office's window until the guard made his rounds through that zone. Once the guard left the area, there was a twenty-five-minute window to drag the body to the pond and dispose of it. Leaving the building was a matter of using any of the emergency exits. Alarms did not function, lights did not flash, and no camera recorded the departure.

The night guard, O'Brien, returned a few minutes later, ashen-faced. "Somebody taped open the emergency exit door off the management offices," he said, shaking his head. "The tape's not there now, but the door jamb is all sticky. All I do on my rounds is check to make certain it hasn't been propped open…"

"Get a fingerprint crew on the door," Lee said to Mazilli. "Anyone smart enough to do that was probably smart enough to wear gloves, but we may get lucky."

"It's my fault, then," O'Brien said. "If I had checked the door…"

"I'd guess the person who did this was already in the building when you came on duty," Lee said. She had no desire to berate an old man. The building's owners would likely fire him if they weren't too busy defending themselves from a negligence lawsuit from Grainger-

Elliot's family.

But the taped-open entry also was a clue. Someone inside the building had rigged the door in order to allow someone from outside the building to come in undetected. Whether the crime was committed by one person or two, someone involved had both knowledge of the building's weaknesses and unfettered access to the management area.

Alvarez, having completed his research assignment, joined Lee. He carried an iPad in one hand. Lee filled him in on the taped door.

"So we know how our guy got in and out without being spotted by anyone," Alvarez said. "But it means the perp also knew the alarms didn't work."

"Which was probably common knowledge to everyone working the show," Lee countered. "This place ought to have been torn down years ago, and it isn't being maintained. Tight security is the first thing you let lapse because it doesn't matter unless something bad happens."

"It's also possible that the show staff taped open the door to make it easier to get stuff in and out," Alvarez said. "I'll ask everyone and assume someone will give me an honest answer if that's the case."

Lee nodded agreement. "But, why leave the body in an exhibit?" she asked, more of herself than of Alvarez. "If Grainger-Elliot's body was left in the office, it's possible his body might still not have been discovered."

The office was being gone over for every scrap of evidence. Crime scene techs were pulling equipment down the hallway. Lee and Alvarez left the murder scene and returned to the VIP lounge.

"You were going to tell me about Grainger-Elliot," Lee said.

Alvarez brushed his fingers against the iPad's surface and began reading from a document. "Educated at Oxford in botany, according to the Botanical Society website," he said. "Three years at Kew Gardens as an exhibit manager. Four years at the Royal Horticultural Society, three of them as an assistant manager for the Chelsea Flower

Show. Came to the U.S. five years ago to be Executive Director of the Atlanta Horticultural Society. Hired two years ago for the same role with the New England Botanical Society."

"A stellar resume," Lee said. "What doesn't the website say?"

Alvarez tapped the screen. "Government Center Plaza. Right after he got here, Grainger-Elliot came up with his 'master vision' – a plan to 'green up' all those dreary eight acres of brick around Boston City Hall. He was going to turn it into a destination…"

"That was his idea?" Lee said. "The 'garden for the city on the hill' or something like that?" I remember it. What happened?"

"The formal name is 'The Gardens at Government Center'," Alvarez said. "Apparently, Grainger-Elliot never raised a dime toward it, and the New England Botanical Society is broke. So broke they've been selling their glass flowers."

"Glass flowers?" Lee asked. "That one you're going to have to explain."

Alvarez tapped the screen again. "Between 1887 and 1936, a German glassmaker and his son made more than five thousand botanically accurate glass flowers that were used by universities as teaching tools. Harvard's Museum of Natural History has three thousand of them, the Botanical Society has – or more accurately had – the rest. Late last year, twenty five of them showed up for auction in New York. It turns out that Grainger-Elliot had been selling them to raise operating funds. Not capital funds like for the City Hall project, but day-to-day stuff."

"Don't they sell memberships?" Lee asked.

"When Grainger-Elliot came to the Botanical Society it had a staff of ten," Alvarez said. "It's now close to thirty. When the Boston *Globe* asked for an exact head count, Grainger-Elliot refused to provide one. The article said the nickname for Botanical Hall is the 'estrogen palace' – practically all women except for Grainger-Elliot, all young and all cute, with a lot of them working in 'donor development'."

"That's a lot of people," Lee mused. "Why on earth would he build such a large staff?"

Alvarez shrugged his shoulders. "I'm just compiling data right now. This is what I got in an hour. If there's this much in the press and on blogs, you can only imagine what else is going on out of sight. I'd say St. John Grainger-Elliot was a very complex man who didn't have anyone telling him what he couldn't do."

"He had to have a boss," Lee said. "A board of directors, overseers, something like that."

More taps on the screen. "There's a Board of Trustees. The chairwoman is Mary Ellen Dawson."

"Get hold of Ms. Dawson and ask her to make an early appearance at the show this morning," Lee said. "I'll make the rash assumption that, this being the Botanical Society's big deal for the year, she's planning to drop in. I've got an hour before the widow Grainger-Elliot makes her appearance."

Lee started ticking off instructions on her fingers. "Tell Mazilli to get every bit of evidence the two of you have collected over to the lab for processing, and have him sit on them until they get results. While he's there, he can also start filling in the background on the physical evidence – catalog what was found and what's missing. He can pull phone records, credit card charges, and call other trustees to get information on people who were unhappy with Grainger-Elliot. Your job is to interview everybody on the show staff, and give me a chart of who left the party and when – and if someone taped open that door yesterday or last night. Get a list of guests and be prepared to tell me when they left. Who do they remember as still being here? What was the last time anybody remembers seeing Grainger-Elliot? Did anybody seem to drop out of the party? Give it to me in as fine a detail as you can, and not just staff but guests and exhibitors."

"Where will you be?" Alvarez asked.

Lee looked at her cell phone again. It showed 8:00. "There's a train for New York leaving in ten minutes but, thanks to you, I'm not going to be on it. I'm going home to shower and change."

**Chapter 3.**

Cynthia Duncastle, a widow of perhaps six hours, was attempting unsuccessfully to keep her composure. She had come to the interview in a black wool suit that smelled heavily of cedar. To Lee, this was fairly substantial evidence that either Grainger-Elliot's wife did not have forehand knowledge of her spouse's death, or else was the kind of person who thought detectives were aware of and made note of such subtle things.

Duncastle was an attractive woman, perhaps five-eight with glossy, auburn hair worn shoulder length. She appeared to be in her mid-thirties.

"I told him he should never have accepted this position," she said. "I had a premonition." Duncastle spoke with a decided British accent, saying 'pre-mon-NISHUN', Lee noted. It was like listening to the BBC World Service from her childhood.

Duncastle took a sip of coffee. Tears streamed down her face again.

"I'm terribly sorry to have to ask these questions, Ms. Duncastle," Lee said. "But time is the enemy of finding your husband's murderer. Did your husband confide in you? Did he talk about his work at the Society?"

Duncastle nodded, suppressing a sniffle. "We had no secrets. He would come home evenings, ranting and raving at the small-mindedness of the people he dealt with. I helped where I could. I was his sounding board."

It was an answer Lee liked. "From what I've learned, your husband was someone who wasn't afraid to think on a grand scale."

Duncastle nodded. There was a small smile and a gratified look on her face that someone understood. "The Garden at Government

Center," she said. "It should have been the monument to his vision. It's the reason we came here."

"Yet funds weren't raised," Lee prompted.

"Funds *were* being raised," Duncastle corrected, with a sharp note to her voice. "St. John had pledges in hand for more than ten million toward planning and construction with another fifty million in the wings. Those dreadful articles in the newspapers are the lone reason we've not broken ground. The *Globe* singlehandedly cost the Society tens of millions. St. John was furious and was preparing to file suit for slander and defamation."

"Did he have a figure in mind?" Lee asked.

"Fifty million dollars," Duncastle said. "St. John was certain he would win."

"But the suit was never filed…"

"Because the trustees dawdled," Duncastle said. There was evidence of distaste in the way she said 'trustees'. "They were hesitant to offend the press, as though the *Globe* had not sufficiently offended the Society. The trustees weren't even interested in an apology."

Lee shook her head. "This is new information for me. I think the *Globe* ran an article about the sale of the glass flowers…"

Duncastle gave Lee a withering look. "The Blaschka Collection…"

"Those are the glass flowers?"

"Yes, those are the glass flowers." Another withering glance. "The Blaschka Collection is the least of the *Globe's* slander. The heart of their crime was in their allegation that St. John mismanaged the Society. Spent money recklessly. Personally profited from ventures. None of that was true."

"The *Globe* knew your husband was going to sue?"

"Of course they did. And the newspaper did everything in its power to stop the suit. Lobbied the trustees. Made threats that there were more sordid details." Duncastle paused and sighed. Her eyes again moistened. "And now he is dead."

"I'm sorry for your loss, Ms. Duncastle. My goal is to catch the person or persons who killed him. To do that, I'll need your full cooperation."

"Catching the killer will not bring him back to life," Duncastle said stiffly.

"But it will ensure the person who killed him will be punished."

\* \* \* \* \*

Lee knew she had only half-concentrated on the conversation with Duncastle. Instead, her mind was still filled with the resentment of her phone conversation with Frank Abelson, chief of detectives.

*"Come on, Frank, I've had this weekend on my official calendar for a month,"* she had explained. *"One of my junior detectives got me out of bed at three in the morning, and I got the ball rolling. You've got a dozen favors you can call in…"*

*"You caught it, you're on it,"* Abelson had said, without a trace of sympathy in his voice. *"This is your first big case, and it's luck of the draw that you caught it on a Saturday morning. It doesn't matter if you've been on the job three days or three years: the case comes first. Be resourceful. Figure out a work-around. But I'll make some calls and let you know later today…"*

All because I answered the phone, she thought.

\* \* \* \* \*

"Please, call me Mel," the woman said. "'Mary Ellen' is for annual reports and formal invitations." Dawson was attired in slacks and a jacket that, to Lee, looked as though it has been cut from a medieval Flemish tapestry and sewn by cloistered nuns. On her wrist was a wide expanse of gold bracelet with a Parthenon-like frieze of overlapping Greek gods and goddesses. The ring finger of her left hand held a muted, tasteful blue-white diamond of perhaps five carats. Somewhere in her early fifties, she possessed a tan that indicated she had not spent the past month huddled indoors in New England. Her hair was brunette, worn shoulder length. Dawson crossed her legs and sipped the coffee, nodding approvingly at its flavor.

"Yes, St. John's death is a shock. I liked him. We all liked him." Something in her voice sounded less than convincing.

"I hear a 'but'," Lee said.

Dawson exhaled and thought for a moment. She uncrossed and re-crossed her legs. "We didn't do our homework when we hired St. John. This will all come out at some point so there's no point in beating around the bush. He was about to be terminated and, by 'terminated', I mean fired for cause. It starts with his résumé, which was, to put it mildly, padded. He *is* British, or at least we're willing to concede that much, but as to his degrees, his association with the RHS – the Royal Horticultural Society – and Kew, it's all fiction."

"You didn't verify his education or prior employment?"

Dawson grimaced and flicked her hand in the air. "He produced all the right certificates and wonderful letters from previous employers – all of whom had conveniently retired or moved on. I guess it goes to show what you can do with computers."

"How did you learn the truth?"

Dawson sighed. "We've had bits and pieces over the past year," she said. "My first inkling was when I bumped into a visiting Fellow from the RHS at a meeting down in New York a few months after St. John was hired. I mentioned that our new Executive Director had been one of the assistant managers at the Chelsea show. I gave him St. John's name. The man must have thought for about thirty seconds, then came back and said, 'I think I know everyone in management at the show going back five years, and his name doesn't register. How long ago was he there?' I said it has been just a little over three years since he had come over from the U.K., and the man was startled. He had never heard of anyone named Grainger-Elliot."

"Why didn't you do something then?" Lee asked.

"Well, the man I was talking to was relatively young, and he could have been wrong," Dawson said. "Or so I convinced myself. And St.

John was doing a terrific job at the time. He was full of ideas and really lit the place on fire with his energy."

"But something else happened," Lee prompted.

Dawson nodded. "Lots of little things at first, then bigger things. We announced the Government Center project with great fanfare. I assumed – the entire Board of Trustees assumed – we had buy-in from the City. We did, but only at the very lowest levels. Boston is a city where you don't surprise the politicians, especially the mayor and the city council. They came around, but only because the newspapers – and the public – thought it was a wonderful idea to finally acknowledge that all those acres of bricks had been an awful idea for more than four decades. St. John convinced us that it was his strategy from the start: to make public support for the Garden at Government Center our anchor rather than relying on buy-in from the politicians. It worked, so who were we to complain?"

Dawson took another sip of coffee before continuing. "He had asked for a free hand in staffing Botanical Hall. He gave us financial reports that showed we were in the black and that everything going forward looked fine. But we never got an audit of the books – not that we pressed him for one. Then, the middle of last year, we got the first reports that things were being checked out of the Repository. That's where we keep the especially rare items."

"The glass flowers – the Blaschka Collection?"

"It started with rare books," Dawson said. "Our curator, Linda Beckett, said St. John would pore over books for hours, then pick ones to take out overnight. They'd come back the next day. We couldn't imagine what was happening at first. All we knew was that it was odd behavior. Then, a few months ago, we examined those books and found that pages had been cut from folios – though we couldn't determine when it had happened. The pages that had been cut contained hand-colored botanical prints. Very old and very, very rare."

Dawson indicated the prints on the wall. "Like these, but one of a kind and infinitely more valuable. The book in a complete form might be worth, oh, twenty thousand. But an individual page with a rare, hand-tinted print might fetch two thousand all by itself. We couldn't prove anything, and no one wanted to think that St. John was stealing. But then prints that we suspected were part of those folios would show up at auction. Still, we had no proof because we had never microfilmed or digitally scanned the books."

"That's when the business with the glass flowers began. We have nearly two thousand of them, all very carefully catalogued, and we almost never loan them out. Then, a clutch of twenty five of them showed up in a Sotheby's catalog, being offered by an area antiques dealer. We confronted St. John."

"What happened?" Lee asked.

"He told us he 'had' to sell them to keep the cash coming in to support the Society's staff. He had every dollar accounted for – at least for the glass pieces. Every dollar was going to pay for new hires to cultivate donors for the Government Center project. Otherwise, he said, the Botanical Society was effectively bankrupt. You can believe me that was the first time we had ever heard that word – *bankrupt* – from anyone on the Society's staff. That's when I hired a private investigator. On my own nickel, without going through the trustees. I got the report back ten days ago. Nearly two hundred pages including supporting evidence."

Dawson poured a fresh cup of coffee. She stared at the contents of her mug for several seconds, watching the reflections of the light on the surface of the liquid.

"St. John Grainger-Elliot is – was – a complete fiction," she said. "His real name was John Spense. He was from Brighton – the one in England, at least – where he was enrolled at but did not graduate from a trade school. He certainly did not attend Oxford. He did prison time for forgery in the U.K in the late nineties. Cynthia Duncastle may or may not be his wife. There is no marriage license on record for anyone by that name to anyone named Spense or Grainger-Elliot in the U.K or the U.S. I assume she's fully aware of his schemes."

"St. John – it's easier to call him that – showed up at the Atlanta Horticultural Society five years ago with the Grainger-Elliot résumé. They hired him. It's a fairly sleepy organization, and people down there are enamored of anyone with a British accent, so all he had to do there was show up for work every day. Well, he showed up for work all right. And, after a year or so on the job started charging things to them. Big things, like plasma TVs, works of art and a leased Mercedes. They were just about to show him the door when our crack search committee contacted him and asked if he would like to be considered for a move up to the New England Botanical Society."

"St. John, of course, said he'd be delighted to speak to us, but only on condition that we didn't speak to the Atlanta Hort people because he didn't want them to know he was open to other offers. Like idiots, we didn't do a post-employment check. My investigator did. The Atlanta Hort people were the happiest people in the world because we had relieved them of the onerous task of firing St. John and paying out his contract. They didn't believe their good luck."

"Did St. John know any of this was happening?" Lee asked. "Did he know that you had hired an investigator?"

"Inevitably, he almost certainly did," Dawson replied. "He had a five-year contract with us but we had an 'out' because of the credentials falsification. The trustees met privately on the subject after I got my report from the investigator. I talked them through the high points, though I confess I didn't read all of it… it was too depressing. The investigators gave me a written synopsis of the worst parts, and I handed it out at the meeting. My suspicion is that someone among the trustees was his pipeline, and they gave him a head's up that the roof was about to cave in."

"When were you supposed to meet with Grainger-Elliot?" Lee

asked.

"This morning," Dawson said. "At ten o'clock. Myself and two other trustees, both of them lawyers."

"But as far as he was concerned there was no specific agenda?" Lee asked.

Dawson shook her head. "It was expressed as 'a critical meeting about the future of the Society' but I was careful to say nothing about his employment contract, and he didn't press. But, if he had a mole among the trustees, he may well have put two and two together."

"I spoke with Cynthia Duncastle this morning," Lee said. "She said St. John was preparing a slander or libel suit against the *Globe*."

Dawson smiled. "Certainly, he was. We told him two months ago that, if he filed suit, he would be doing so entirely on his own, and that the Trustees would have nothing to do with it, including finance it."

"And what about the big donors she said were scared away by the articles?"

"*What* big donors?" Dawson replied. She shook her head slowly. "That was our biggest failure as trustees. He'd give us a list, but it was always, 'a major philanthropist', 'a hedge fund manager' and 'an extremely wealthy North Shore couple'. He told us they were all people he or his staff had cultivated, and he didn't want their names used until he had the complete funding in hand. We were stupid. We believed him."

"Can you think of who might have killed him?" Lee asked.

Dawson was silent for several moments. She took a sip of her coffee and pursed her lips, apparently having lost her taste for it. She returned the mug to the table in front of her, then appeared to study one of the botanical prints on the wall. "I started wondering that as soon as I heard the news," she said. "What we – the trustees – learned over the past ten days is that St. John was essentially a con man. He utterly fabricated a background tailor-made to get him the executive director's job, and he fooled us. Let me be blunt -- he made fools *of* us. We told ourselves that, when we fired him, we could do it all quietly and that he would just disappear. The two trustees who are lawyers quickly disabused us of that notion. They said that, based on their previous experience in similar cases, St. John was not going to go quietly. He was going to threaten to take everything public."

Dawson looked directly at Lee. "I don't expect you to understand this, but there are reputations at stake in this. The New England Botanical Society has been accused for several decades of being... exactly what it was. A group of wealthy dilettantes who played at overseeing a venerable major Boston institution. We attended Trustees meetings but never bothered to read the documents in front of us. We were more interested in what wine was being served before the meeting than in questioning why the Society ran at a deficit every year. Instead, we just opened our checkbooks and made up the difference. Meanwhile, the rationale for the Society was slipping away. We stopped sponsoring research, and we stopped holding important symposia. We had the Northeast Garden and Flower Show. Period."

Dawson twisted the gold bracelet on her arm as she spoke. "A few years ago, a group of us set out to change that. We wanted a vision. We wanted to make a difference. We hired St. John, and all of a sudden we had this marvelous project called the Garden at Government Center. We congratulated ourselves on our business acumen in hiring St. John. We gave him a free rein. We gave a *con man* free rein of our Society." Her hands went to her lap.

Dawson looked away from Lee for a long moment. She took a deep breath, her eyes closed. She exhaled, and her hands shook slightly. When Dawson looked back at Lee, her eyes were moist. "Do you have any idea of what the media is going to do with this? We're going to be crucified. We're going to be held up as blithering idiots with trust funds who shouldn't be given any responsibility more important than choosing china patterns. Whatever we get, we deserve it. We deserve it for not demanding answers to the most basic questions like where the money was supposed to be coming from and why it was going out the door so quickly."

"So, who could have killed St. John? Any of us. Any one of us who felt like they had been used for the past two years. Any of us who hated the idea of being raked over the coals by the newspapers and television stations. Murdering St. John isn't the answer to anyone's prayers, but it means that, when it comes out – today, tomorrow – it's over and done with. The lawyers had prepared us for a three- to six-month fight with St. John selectively leaking something to the media every few days. With St. John dead, that isn't going to happen. We'll look like the fools we are this week, but then it will be finished. We can try to clean up our mess and do it right the next time. I hate to say it but, if you're looking for a murderer, you've got a terrific bunch of suspects among your trustees."

The coldness of Dawson's statement took Lee by surprise. All she could muster by way of a response was, "I'm sorry for what you're going through." She added, "Does anyone on the Society's staff know about this report?"

Dawson shook her head. "No. We've kept it very quiet. We didn't want anything to threaten the flower show before it opened." Dawson rose from her chair. "I'm going over to Botanical Hall this morning, and I'm going to start going through his office," she said, determination in her voice. "And I'll bet there's not a scrap of evidence of any of those donors."

"You can't," Lee said. "We've got to find out who murdered him. The answer may be in those files."

Dawson looked annoyed. "What if I'm there while you go through it?"

"It won't be me," Lee said. "But you can have access to the office and see the files *after* my detectives finish their search."

The two women stared at one another for a moment, defiant.

Finally, without acknowledging defeat, Dawson picked up her purse, a vintage crocodile Kelly handbag.

"Call me as soon as I can have access," Dawson said.

＊ ＊ ＊ ＊ ＊

Lee walked out of the VIP lounge, stretching her arms and back muscles, attempting to make sense of what she had heard while clearing away the general body discomfort that came from lack of sleep.

She was immediately caught in a whirl of people. Thousands of people crowding and standing on tiptoe for a better view. The flash of cameras was everywhere. Sometime while she met with Mel Dawson, the show had opened.

The faces she saw were full of joy. Here, inside this dilapidated building with its leaking roof and non-functioning alarm system, was a respite from yet another horrid, unending New England winter. Hordes of people were willingly paying money to experience a few hours of ersatz springtime. Families lined up to cross the bridge over the pond from which Grainger-Elliot's body had been lifted a few hours earlier. People pressed against one another and craned their necks for a view of an artificial waterfall and waited patiently for the opportunity to walk, single-file, through a glade of gloriously green bamboo. They contemplated imagined back yard gardens with implausible concentrations of flowering plants and shrubs.

Children shrieked with joy, adults gasped with awe at displays. The Northeast Garden and Flower Show was proof that winter would eventually have an end, and that the few fleeting weeks of pleasant weather that was spring in New England was worth the interminable wait. Despite the crush of people, the crowd was orderly, without pushing or jostling.

The polite throngs took Lee back to her earliest memories of her childhood in Hong Kong, walking densely packed streets holding her mother's hand. There, too, people were cognizant of the need for, and willing to provide, that extra fraction of an inch of space, and there was an unspoken patience about getting from point to point.

Her family had emigrated when Lee was four. Her father began liquidating his businesses as soon as the Sino-British Joint Declaration was signed in 1984, the year of her birth. Ardent Anglophiles with a deep mistrust of the mainland's promises, the very notion of being under Beijing's rule was something her parents could not even begin to contemplate. By 1988, their holdings had been converted to Canadian dollars, and the Lee family moved to Vancouver; a wet, chilly city that nevertheless welcomed Hong Kong expatriates. When the formal transfer came nine years later, Hong Kong was a distant memory for Victoria Lee.

By the time Lee graduated from high school, she knew that Vancouver was only a way station for her. Her parents had a plan for their only child: an undergraduate degree in biology, medical school, residency, marriage, and three children. *Chinese* children to be raised in a house near their grandparents. Lee wanted to chart her own course.

Armed with a full scholarship, she had fled across the border to Northwestern and then to Boston University. There, three thousand miles from Vancouver and eight thousand miles from Hong Kong, she made the final break with her parents' plan, graduating *cum laude* with a degree in criminal justice. That she had added a degree in public administration from B.U. and was in her second year of law school at Suffolk University was of little interest to her parents. Any conversation with them inevitably included the question, *"Which part of 'medical school' didn't you understand?"*

These thoughts were in Lee's head when she found herself in front of a forest of Lucite stands. Attached to the stands were ribbons and certificates. *The Mrs. Edward Marsh Cup for Distinguished Use of Annuals, The Winslow Trophy for Imaginative Display of Rhododendron, The New England Hosta Society Award for Best Display of Hostas.* Each certificate bore a separate, succinct statement, such as, *'Seamlessly integrates horizontal and vertical elements into a pleasing whole'.* The recipient of each was Blue Hills Gardens *Oscar McQueen*, Linda Cooke's assistant had said.

Ten feet away from her, perched on a stool, was a large man in his fifties with a bushy beard. He wore a blue work shirt, and he carefully studied people, especially couples, who paused at the exhibit. Lee, being a lone woman in her early thirties, was ignored by the man. She walked over to him.

"Oscar McQueen?" she asked.

The man's head swiveled, a practiced, professional smile on his face. "Yes," he said.

Lee took her badge from her purse. "I'm investigating the death of St. John Grainger-Elliot."

McQueen glanced at the badge and started to say something, then changed his mind. "It's mostly busloads of seniors right now. How can I help you?" He indicated a stool beside him.

Lee declined. "I've been sitting since before dawn," she explained. "Tony Wilson said you were the person who, in his words, 'ran the table' on awards."

McQueen gave a toothy smile. "I did all right. But then I've been doing this a long time." He threw his hand out toward the surrounding exhibits. "Most of these guys won't put the money or the thought into the process, and you can see it in the result. They fill a greenhouse with exactly enough material for what they think they'll need for their display and then get surprised when things don't force. You can't do that and expect to win awards. It doesn't work that way. You need to start with three times as much plant material as you think you'll need."

Lee indicated the Blue Hills Gardens exhibit with her arm. "May I ask what all this cost?"

McQueen shrugged. "Round numbers, seventy-five including labor."

"Mr. Wilson said you could write a year's worth of business here."

McQueen smiled, coy this time. "A slight exaggeration. But I can get to know people and start a relationship that builds over several years. He probably told you that someone might come in here and be prepared to drop a quarter million on a project. That isn't the way it works; or at least it isn't the way it works these days. The 'whales' are few and far between. I work out a master plan with someone, and we start with one or two elements – a wall, a pond, a small garden. It might take five years to truly see its shape and, by that time, the client's tastes will have evolved. No, what I do here is, I meet people. That's enough for me."

"All these awards," Lee said. "Is there a trick? Do you know what the judges are looking for?"

"There *is* a trick," McQueen said, "but it's no secret. Every exhibitor gets a list of awards and the criteria months in advance. The Hosta Society gives an award. OK, include some interesting hosta in the exhibit and make it look attractive. Then check off that box to make certain the judges know you're eligible. There are more than a dozen cultivar-specific awards. I made certain to include every one of them in my landscape, and to put the plants out where the judges will see them."

McQueen eased himself off his stool and walked half way around the exhibit. He pointed to a clutch of shrubs with colorful spotted leaves and delicate pink flowers. The plants were easily seen but just out of reach of anyone. "This is weigela hortensis 'Seurat'. I have eight of them here. This is a brand new cultivar, and it has never been seen at any show. It got me a trophy for best display of a plant not previously exhibited."

"The leaves are almost like a Pointillist painting," Lee said, admiring the small shrubs. "How did you come to have them?"

McQueen laughed. "Believe me, it wasn't an accident. I've been working with the breeder for two years, and this is her big introduction, too. There are about fifty of these plants in existence right now, eight of them are here, and these are the largest and the only ones in bloom. She has tissue cultures underway to get the number up to a few hundred by summer, and they'll go to other shows. The big roll-out will be next year, and it will be a 'must have' plant for every landscape architect and garden designer. They'll pay hundreds for a small 'Seurat', thousands for ones this size, just so their clients can point to it and say they're the first people on the planet to have an entirely new – and gorgeous – plant. Five years from now, these plants will still sell for forty dollars for a gallon pot, in part because they won the Lucile Grassi Cup at the Northeast Garden and Flower Show."

"It's that prestigious?" Lee asked.

"It's that prestigious." McQueen nodded.

"What happens to the plants after the show?"

McQueen smiled. "Sonja Johanson collects them personally. She's the botanist who bred these."

"What happens if one goes missing?"

McQueen laughed. "They won't. I'm here every morning at six. I'm here until an hour after the show closes. This exhibit is my baby for the next ten days."

Lee nodded her understanding. "You knew St. John Grainger-Elliot, I assume. Tell me about him."

McQueen clenched his jaw for a moment. He looked off in the distance, perhaps wondering what to say, trying out words in his mind. Finally, he spoke. "Those guys are all pretty much alike. They beg money for a living, and that takes a certain kind of personality. I have to say I liked his idea about tearing up the bricks at City Hall. I guess that plan dies with him."

"Was he ethical?" Lee asked.

"Who knows," McQueen said. "I mostly deal with Linda – Linda Cooke. I know – excuse me, I *knew* – St. John from the awards banquets and galas. He hit me up for a contribution to the Society when he first got here. I told him that giving this show its classiest exhibit every year was plenty of contribution."

"Do you have any idea why his body was found in your exhibit?"

McQueen shoved his hands into his pockets. "I've been wondering that myself all morning. Luck of the draw, I guess."

\* \* \* \* \*

Her cell phone was blinking. There was a text message:

*R U on the train? Haven't heard anything…*

Lee walked back into the VIP lounge and stared at the screen. Matt was a late riser on weekends, but he would be up and have had breakfast by now. She should have called an hour earlier and told him something. Told him there was a delay. Told him she would skip the train and drive down as quickly as she could hand off the case. Told him to do the gallery hopping without her and that she would call as soon as she got to New York.

She could give the case back to Mazilli if Captain Abelson couldn't come up with someone sharp and available from another precinct. After all, it was supposed to be Mazilli's case. He was the senior detective. He had ample experience.

She composed a brief message: *Slight hitch at this end. Galleries aren't my thing, anyway. See you this afternoon.*

She re-read her message and added, *Sorry, midnight work call.*

She pushed, 'send' and thought to herself, *God, I need help.*

\* \* \* \* \*

The call from Medical Examiner Lois Otting came just before noon. "Get your scrawny ass down here, Vicki. This body has a story to tell."

Bleach, disinfectant and miscellaneous unidentified chemicals permeated the air of the Forensics Laboratory in the basement of the undistinguished Boston Medical Center building in the South End. Lee resigned herself to sending her suit to a dry cleaner before wearing it again.

Otting pulled back the sheet from Grainger-Elliot's body. She had made the initial 'Y' shaped incision to reveal internal organs but had not yet started the full autopsy. "The things you can hide under a white suit," she said.

Grainger-Elliot's body, from his navel to his upper thighs, was a mass of bruises.

"Either somebody was out for revenge in a big way or else they wanted information from your boy," Otting said. "They really kicked the crap out of him."

"Which explains why his hands were bound," Lee said. "It was an interrogation."

"You're ruling out revenge?" Otting asked. "That's not like you."

"This guy was the executive director of a non-profit society," Lee said. "I'm also learning that he was a fraud who may have been stealing the Botanical Society blind. I don't hear revenge in any of that. Not to have killed him like this. But information? That, I can see."

Otting nodded. "Then we'll do it your way. You've got a minimum of fifteen separate imprints. I'd say Grainger-Elliot was on his side and his back, his hands bound behind him. His mouth was duct-taped shut at some point but that may have been when he was first assaulted. I've also got cotton fiber in his mouth so he was probably gagged after they got him into the office. Whoever did this was strong and determined. You're looking at a mark from a big leather shoe. If you're right about someone wanting information, my guess is they'd ask him a question and, if they didn't get an answer they liked, they'd plug back in the gag and administer some persuasion. The rope around the neck most likely came at the end. There's a lot of internal bleeding, and the organs down there I've seen so far look like they went through a Cuisinart. Whoever did this was playing for keeps."

Vito Mazilli, who has accompanied Lee, said, "Jesus Christ."

"No, that was a crucifixion," Otting said. "This was getting your liver and kidneys pulverized." The medical examiner looked at Lee. "If you say it was to get information out of him, I'll go along. But you'd do the same thing if you were going to kill someone and enjoy watching him die." Otting pointed to the different colors and sizes of the bruises. "This went on for fifteen or twenty minutes. I've had bodies in here where someone didn't have a gun or a knife and used their shoe to kill someone. They did it faster. The bruising in those cases occurred within a very few minutes – basically as fast as someone could kick. Relative to those bodies, this was leisurely. The person who did this wanted your guy to suffer, and suffer he did. That's why I asked about revenge."

"We're still early in questioning people, but I'll keep revenge in mind," Lee said. "But, assuming we're talking about prying information out of him, we need to find out whether Grainger-Elliot didn't have the information the murderer wanted or else the information he had was more important to him than his life," Lee said.

"That's why you guys get the big bucks," Otting said. "I've got nothing better to do today so I'll do the full work-up and tell you more, but I thought you had to see this."

"Thanks, Lois," Lee said. "I've gotten some data that said Grainger-Elliot might have had something like this coming."

"Oh, and one more thing," Otting said. "I did the tox screen and a comb-out of the pubic region like you asked. The blood-alcohol level was negligible – definitely not drunk. But I did find some foreign pubic hair. Unless this guy was incredibly un-hygienic, he got some nookie in the hours before he died."

When they were outside the autopsy room, Lee asked Mazilli if the evidence collected had so far yielded any clues.

"Slim pickings, Lieutenant," he said. "Throwing the guy into the water was a good move on the perp's part. The white tux was basically clean of hair or oils. We've got some mulch on the floor but then the place is filthy with the stuff…"

"Did everyone supply their own mulch?" Lee asked, "Or did everyone get it from a central pile?"

Mazilli shrugged. "I don't know. I guess I'll ask. Also, we've got no DNA from the rope other than the vic's. The crime scene guys must have bagged fifty rolls of duct tape. They found it in every corner of the place. It will take a while to check them all for fingerprints, but I'll stay here until they're finished."

"What about the trustees?" Lee asked. "What did they have to say?"

Mazilli gave her a blank look.

"The Society's trustees," Lee repeated. "You were going to call them. You were going to pull phone records."

"I thought this was more important," Mazilli said, his face impassive.

"That's it?" Lee asked, stunned that Mazilli had accomplished nothing other than accompanying rolls of duct tape to a lab. "You're going to take a chair and read the newspaper until someone else has processed all the evidence? You can't think of anything else to do on this case while you're sitting here, waiting? You don't have a phone and something to write down information?"

Mazilli looked puzzled by Lee's ire. "Well, this is one of the things you asked me to do. I told them to put a rush on it. I check with them every half hour or so. I'm really on them."

Lee felt her anger rising. There was no way she could hand off the case to him. She wondered if the detective could be trusted to do anything important.

Like most large city police forces, Boston paired older, experienced detectives with younger ones. The idea was to transfer the tribal wisdom and cultural knowledge of the more seasoned detective to their partner. Mazilli was the senior half of the team but, in his case, all that could rub off were bad habits and a haphazard work ethic.

Mazilli, she knew, was in his late fifties and had been a detective for nearly thirty years. From his personnel jacket Lee knew he had no commendations in the preceding twenty years – making him almost unique within the Boston Police Department. He had numerous reprimands for sloppy work and one citation for use of excessive force, though that was more than a decade old.

He was on the graveyard shift by choice, itself a red flag. The handful of cases he caught were ground balls – the open-and-shut domestic squabbles that were part of any urban area – or else the late-night drive-by shootings that would be solved only when the gangbanger boasted of his exploits to the wrong set of ears. Mazilli had been part of no task forces and offered no insights that led to major arrests. Were it not for the Civil Service Commission, detectives like Mazilli would be eased out if not fired outright. Instead, he clung to his job, making certain he used the maximum number of sick days and personal leave days each year.

She had sympathy for the junior detective, Alvarez, who had earned his detective's shield just a few months earlier. From his personnel record, she knew that for him, the graveyard shift was both a consequence of being the new man at the precinct as well as a necessary function of having a working wife and a special-needs child that required at least one parent to be home at all times. The police department, unlike other employers, offered three shifts of work, seven days a week. The downside was drawing someone like Vito Mazilli as a partner. She knew Alvarez would learn nothing from his time with Mazilli, and Alvarez apparently sensed it as well. He had already made his written plea for a transfer.

Which, in turn, was likely the reason Lee was still here. For any other detective team, Lee would have listened to the detectives' assessment, offered advice, asked to be kept informed and then gone back to sleep. By now she would be pulling into Penn Station, having gotten a few more hours rest on the train so as to appear refreshed and ready for the long weekend with Matt.

Instead, Alvarez's lack of experience and Mazilli's well-earned reputation for sloth put Lee in the position of becoming lead investigator for what Captain Abelson had termed a 'high profile' case; and it had happened on her first week on the job. It was the long-established custom of the Department that detectives who caught a case followed it through to its conclusion. Unless Abelson made those calls as promised or she could get a quick, lucky break, she was stuck.

Being a detective was a role she had been loath to give up. She had gotten her shield at twenty-five, the youngest woman to do so and the first of Chinese ancestry to make detective in so short a period. Her rapid rise to detective had drawn the attention of the Boston Police hierarchy who saw in her promotion an opportunity to allay the mistrust of two under-represented constituencies. Her partner for those five years had been a senior detective of uncommon intuition and a solid link in a chain of custodial knowledge stretching back half a century. She had learned more from that partner than from any teacher in her life.

At thirty, she had taken and passed the lieutenant's exam. Three days earlier she had officially moved into a glass-walled lieutenant's office. Now, the death of John Spense, a.k.a. St. John Grainger-Elliot, gave her what she thought she had given up in return for her promotion: a complex case with ample suspects and multiple threads, each of which needed to be followed and unraveled.

It was eight hours since she first stumbled into the Harborfront Expo Center on two-and-a-half hours sleep. She realized she was wide awake and fully alert. Was her body telling her something? That she would rather be here than in New York? She shook off the thought.

Mazilli broke the silence that had descended between them. "Lieutenant, it's after noon and I've been off the clock for four hours now…."

"Fine, Mazilli," she said, allowing her annoyance to show. "Go home and get some rest. You're going to need it. Give me a call when you're ready, and I'll bring you back up to speed. Count on this being a twenty-four-seven case until it's solved."

The momentary startled look on the detective's face told Lee that Mazilli was going to come down with a virus between now and midnight. It might be a burden on her personal life. It would be no loss to the investigation.

As Mazilli shuffled down the corridor, Lee realized there was only one solution to getting this investigation done right: *bring in John Flynn.*

# Chapter 4.

The parking lot of the Expo Center overflowed with cars. Five buses disgorged passengers at the front entrance. Lee ignored the attendants frantically waving her toward auxiliary parking in a distant lot and drove directly to the main entrance. There, resorting to a tactic she disdained when used by other officers, she parked in a handicapped space and placed her Boston Police placard on the Accord's dashboard.

Inside, several hundred people waited in line to purchase tickets. Lee showed her badge and walked through the exhibitors' entrance.

She found Alvarez, who said he was still assembling his timeline of people attending and the times they departed last night's Gala. They agreed to meet in an hour's time.

"You've been on for twelve hours, now," Lee said. "You're under no obligation to keep plugging away. Mazilli just went home."

Alvarez looked at Lee with equal parts astonishment and gratitude. "I'm OK, Lieutenant," he said. "It's Saturday. I talked to my wife and she's fine with my working through the weekend. But I have to tell you, this is the first good case I've fielded since I made detective. In fact, this is the first time I've felt like I'm really a detective."

Lee smiled and nodded. "It's good to hear that." She was going to add that it was also good to know that Mazilli's bad habits weren't rubbing off on the young detective. But she knew her role as a lieutenant required that she keep to herself opinions of the detectives under her command, however valid those thoughts might be. What she also thought but did not say was, *in a few hours, I may have the kind of detective working with you that you so desperately need.*

A woman walking briskly toward the black curtains that separated the public from the non-public part of the exhibit hall caught Lee's attention. Lee had seen her several times that morning, moving among the exhibits and then disappearing behind the black curtains. She had not been corralled with the Botanical Society's staff, but her presence, hours before the show's opening, indicated that she was connected with it in some way. The woman went behind the curtains again. Lee followed.

Lee drew her badge from her purse. "Good afternoon, I'm Lieutenant Lee with the Boston PD. I've noticed you around this morning, but you seem to have escaped my detectives' dragnet."

The woman turned. She was somewhere in her fifties though well preserved, blonde, and slender. Unlike the Botanical Society staff, who had returned to the show dressed to impress, this woman was in slacks and a Garden and Flower Show sweatshirt. She held an armload of clipboards in one hand. She extended the other.

"Hi, I'm Liz Phillips," she said. Phillips paused, noting that the name didn't register an association on Lee's face. "I'm the chairman of the Judges' Committee."

Lee nodded acknowledgement. "You hand out all those awards," she said.

Phillips smiled. "I run the three-ring circus that hands out *some* of the awards. There's another group entirely who does the flower show."

Lee's face showed non-comprehension.

"There are really four shows going on here," Phillips explained. "There are the big landscape exhibits. That's the part that I chair. There's also a standard flower show – all those flower arrangements you see in the 'B' Hall – that's a garden club federation event. There's a photography competition. That's a different garden federation's event. And there's a big amateur horticulture section in the 'C' Hall with the photography. The Botanical Society runs that one. All of it gets judged, so we have lots and lots of judges."

"Do I want to know how many judges?" Lee asked.

"For the part I run? About two hundred," Phillips said. Seeing the surprised look on Lee's face, Phillips added, "We hand out ninety-one awards and each judging panel is three people. Two hundred is really just scraping by because I re-use panels for smaller awards."

"One exhibit got a lot of ribbons," Lee said. "Did... what's his name? Oscar McQueen have a lot of friends among the judges?"

"Actually, no judge had any idea of whose exhibit they were looking at," Philips said. "The first thing I did at five o'clock yesterday morning was to make certain no exhibit had any identifiable markings on it except the number that the judges go by. Exhibitors had to be out of the building by seven, and they weren't allowed back in until the awards were posted."

"Which was after three?" Lee said. "I remember someone saying exhibitors were angry that they couldn't get in until four hours before the party."

"They have the same complaint every year," Phillips said with no hint of sympathy. "They know the rules. The judges genuinely don't know whose exhibits they're judging. If Oscar McQueen is tidying up an exhibit when a judge is around, it's kind of a dead giveaway."

"You know I'm here investigating the death of St. John Grainger-Elliot," Lee said.

"I suspected as much."

"You worked closely with him?"

"Not really," Phillips said. "His job was to run the Society. To him I was just another volunteer. I doubt he even knew my name."

Lee considered the woman. Smart, self-assured and well-spoken. Clearly, no axe to grind. "I need someone who can take me through what happened yesterday. What time everyone got here, how did it work, that sort of thing."

"For that I'll need a cup of tea," Phillips said. "And I don't mean the dreck they serve out in the vendor halls."

"I know just the place," Lee said.

The two women walked over to the VIP lounge. As water for the tea heated, Phillips recounted Friday's schedule. "I got here at five. Tony Wilson was already here. I did my walk-through of the hall, made certain all signage was covered, and told all of the exhibitors they had to be out by seven. Most of them had probably worked through the night, putting finishing touches on their exhibits. At a quarter of seven, a couple of clerks and I went out and physically got the last of the exhibitors out of the hall. That was the first time I saw St. John — he was out in the hall talking with landscape exhibitors. He said he and Linda would make certain that everyone stayed out. I went back to the judges' office."

"Wait," Lee interjected. "How do you make certain exhibitors stay out of the hall?"

"Very simple," Phillips said. "If I see them in the building, their exhibits become ineligible for any award. It's a simple weapon but very powerful."

"And you say St. John was in the building at a quarter of seven?"

"Without a doubt," Philips said.

"When did judging start?"

"We allow judges to look over the exhibits before their panels formally go out. It gives them the opportunity to form an overall impression of the show. We give them their instructions over breakfast. St. John came in about eight-thirty and said a few words — nothing memorable. The first panels to be released to the floor are the ones with a lot of ground to cover — say, they've got twenty or twenty-five eligible exhibits. We let them out ten minutes early. At nine o'clock, everyone's on the floor. They stay out for anywhere from two to four hours. Then they come back and write up their comments. If judges are on two panels, then they repeat the process. This year, we were finished a little after three and had all awards posted before three-thirty. Then I collapse."

"Did you get out on the floor during judging?"

"I was out there quite a lot," Phillips said, nodding. "Each time was because a judging panel needed a clarification of a rule or couldn't find the material they were sent out to examine. It can be a problem in some of the larger exhibits. I traipsed through two exhibits to find the plant material the judges couldn't see. In three others, the material just wasn't there and, believe me, I looked for it. An exhibitor can make a last-minute change and delete something that makes them ineligible for an award. Maybe the material didn't force or it died. But they can't add material at the last minute and ask to be eligible for a new award."

"When do the exhibitors get to see the awards?"

"Yesterday, they got to see them at about three-thirty."

"Was St. John there when the exhibitors were let back in?"

Phillips thought for a moment. "Uh, no. In fact, I didn't see him between his talk to the judges in the morning and the Gala. He usually has lunch with the judges. But then I went to my hotel room, changed and checked out, so I'm probably not the right person to ask."

"What about the other staff members?"

"Oh, Linda was there. And I know Tony was there. They were getting the brunt of the exhibitors' screaming…"

"Because Oscar McQueen got all the awards," Lee said, nodding. "Was his exhibit that much better than the others?"

"Oh, it's excellent," Phillips said. "He's a master at staging. Plus, he was eligible for just about every award given, and if he could find a way to qualify as a first-time exhibitor, he'd check that box, too."

"But there's no pressure to spread around the awards," Lee asked.

"Of course, there's pressure," Phillips said. "Which is why we have the 'Botanical Society Award of Merit' type of ribbons. Everybody gets gold or silver, whether or not they deserve it. But if I allowed one of the 'real' awards to be taken away from one exhibitor and gave it to another one, it would be the last time that judge would ever agree to work with us. And, word would get around. One reason the show enjoys the prestige it does is that the awards – most of them, anyway – are real and the exhibitors have to earn them."

"I spoke with Oscar McQueen," Lee said. "He showed me his 'Seurat' plant."

"Weigela hortensis 'Seurat'," Phillips said, nodding with approval. "It's amazing. I could look at that plant all day. I want one. No, I want more than one."

"How many exhibitors were eligible for that award?"

"The Lucile Grassi Cup," Phillips said. "Ahhh, six, I think. No, actually, five. One exhibitor apparently pulled his plant material at the last minute. And it would have been a dandy, too. A blue daylily."

"A blue daylily?"

"*Hemerocallis*," Phillips explained. "Literally, 'beauty for a day'. Most of the traditional daylilies you used to see were orange. Since the 1970s, hybridizers have come up with white, pink, purple, red, gold and yellow. They've created repeat bloomers. But never a blue daylily. Stuart Wells – Sunrise Gardens – had it on his list. The judges couldn't find it. I couldn't find it. I gave up. Another exhibitor had checked 'annuals' and another had checked 'succulents' – both of which are award categories. I went over every plant in both exhibits. None of the plant material was annuals or succulents."

"Did you see the exhibitors that evening?"

"Most of them don't know me and, if I know them at all, it's mostly on sight," Phillips said. "It doesn't pay to get chummy with them."

"At the Gala," Lee asked, "was St. John behaving in any unusual way?"

"As far as I could tell, he was having a grand time. Lots of back slapping and clinking glasses of Champagne."

"When did you leave?"

Phillips laughed. "Remember, I was here at five on Friday

morning. I turned into a pumpkin sometime around ten. Plus, I had a fairly long drive home over back roads."

"Where's that?" Lee asked.

"Hardington," Philips said. "Forty-five minutes with no traffic."

"Ms. Philips, please stay close, especially tomorrow," Lee said. "I've got a world of people to speak with today, and I know a lot of that information is going to be conflicting. You understand how this place works, and I frankly don't trust a lot of what I'm being told."

"Well," Phillips said, "my work here was basically done once the awards were up. I was just in today to clean things up. But, if you'll let me take the rest of today off, I can be around all day tomorrow if it helps. Anyway, I'm on my own this weekend."

Phillips left, leaving Lee to ponder her cooling mug of tea. "*Be resourceful,*" Captain Abelson had said. "*Figure out a workaround.*" Liz Phillips would be part of it. So would John. She had a plan. She looked at her watch, now securely on her wrist. It was one o'clock. Alvarez should have his list ready.

\* \* \* \* \*

The chart was impressive, a *tour de force* of computer expertise. The fourteen hundred names of the Gala attendees had been downloaded from the Society's invitation list, together with the names of the thirty-seven Society employees. On Alvarez's iPad screen, the names of everyone who was believed still to be at the party after midnight was color-coded in red. From there, the departure time of each person interviewed was shown, together with a list of who that person believed was still at the Gala.

Alvarez tapped the screen and an inverted pyramid appeared. Fifty names represented the last hangers-on, and their names were coded in ten minute increments.

"Grainger-Elliot is last seen at between 1:40 and 1:45," Alvarez said, indicating a point midway down the screen. He was easy to keep track of because of the white tux. People saw him in the company of several donors in those final minutes but it was all very friendly, and he appeared to behave in an entirely normal way."

Lee leaned forward, peering at the diagram. "So the question is, who else disappeared at about the same time?"

Alvarez expanded out the view. "Here is the list of individuals that witnesses remember seeing at the party and talking to Grainger-Elliot after 1:20. None of these people were seen after 1:45, the last time anyone can say definitively that they saw the victim." The screen popped up six names:

*Richard Durant*
*Alice Shelburne*
*Donald Kosinski*
*Stuart Wells*
*Oscar McQueen*
*Robert Zimmer*

"Oscar McQueen, I've met," Lee said. "Stuart Wells was a name mentioned by someone a little while ago…"

"An exhibitor," Alvarez said. "Owner of Sunrise Gardens. Durant and Zimmer are trustees of the Society. Kosinski and Shelburne, according to Linda Cooke, are prospective big-money donors. And, no, I haven't spoken with any of them yet. But then, I've only had three hours."

Lee indicated the tablet. "You've already accomplished more than most detectives could do in a day. It's great work. I'll track down these people. What you need to do is prepare another chart – this one for Grainger-Elliot's last day."

Alvarez cocked his head, a puzzled look on his face.

"Here's what I know from talking to the head of the Society's trustees," Lee said. "Grainger-Elliot was a fraud – a con man. His real name was John Spense, and the trustees were about to fire him. They did a private investigation of him – two years too late – and found that he never worked for the U.K. groups on his résumé, never attended Oxford, and apparently hasn't raised a dime toward this Government Center Garden. He was almost certainly stealing fairly significant sums from the Society. He may or may not be married to Cynthia Duncastle and, to me, it's improbable that she wouldn't know about the fraudulent credentials."

"From the Medical Examiner, I now know that somebody repeatedly kicked Grainger-Elliot in the midsection before strangling him with the rope, and probably while his hands were bound. They did it over a twenty-minute-plus period. My gut instinct is that they were trying to get information out of Grainger-Elliot. Either he didn't have what they wanted or else he felt so strongly about it he was willing to take the beating."

Lee continued. "Mary Ellen Dawson told me some of the trustees were angry enough that they might have killed him. I don't put a lot of credibility in that statement, but I'm not going to rule them out either. I need to know a lot more. I also have a problem with donors killing him. If you don't want to give, just say 'no' and keep walking."

Alvarez broke in. "What if a donor gave money, but Grainger-Elliot somehow diverted it? What if it were a lot of money? A million dollars?"

Lee nodded. "That might do it. Remember, we're dealing with a con man. I would also look closely at exhibitors. The M.E. talked about the kicks as having come from someone with a big leather shoe. The power of the kicks almost certainly meant they were made by a man. I'd look carefully at the staff, but, except for Tony Wilson and a few maintenance people, the staff is uniformly women."

"What kind of information could Grainger-Elliot have that would be worth killing him to get?" Alvarez asked.

"That's the magic question," Lee said. "Answer that question and you have your murderer."

\* \* \* \* \*

As soon as Alvarez left the VIP room, Lee checked her phone for messages. There was nothing from Matt, which wasn't surprising. She had watched Matt scroll through dozens of messages, taking in screens full of data at a glance; deleting messages as fast as he read them and blasting back two- and three-word replies to a handful that required them. He would have read her simple message and then… what?

She was still here and no closer to leaving than she had been five hours earlier. She tried to compose a new message to him that would provide an update or an explanation. After half a dozen starts she put the phone back into her pocket.

* * * * *

The Sunrise Gardens exhibit covered more than a thousand square feet. A ten-foot-high waterfall tumbled from a massive stone block into a grotto that turned into a meandering brook winding seventy feet. At each turn in the brook a different color theme emerged; yellow, then red, then white, then blue, then gold. Large trees in full leaf dotted this landscape, and a hammock was slung between two of them. At the rear of the exhibit, the façade of the back of a luxurious home opened onto a brick patio, with all of nature within easy reach.

From a table and chairs set on the patio, Stuart Wells commanded a view of everyone who admired the exhibit. He was a husky man in his mid-thirties, someone who looked as though he worked outdoors and was at his most comfortable there. Dressed in jeans and a chambray shirt, he sat with a pitcher of iced tea and tall glasses on the table in front of him, a sketch pad in his lap.

He was, Lee thought, a good-looking guy with an intelligent face. Her gaze, though, kept going to his size-12 Timberland shoes. As they talked, Wells' eyes continually moved over the crowd, tallying interest and probable net worth of those who took more than a casual glance at the intricate patterns of plants. Lee noted that he seldom looked at her.

"He was a son of a bitch," Wells said. "But then, they're all sons of bitches. I was promised – personally, by St. John – that if I signed up for a thousand square feet, I'd be front and center in the exhibit hall. Instead, I'm back here next to the fill-in non-profits." He pointed to a neighboring exhibit which had a pair of small wind turbines and a row of black compost bins. "These people shouldn't be at the Garden and Flower Show. They should be at the Eco-Freak Convention."

"You saw a layout of the exhibit hall floor, didn't you?" Lee asked.

Wells snorted. "Sure, right up until the week before the show. Then, along came a revision that St. John 'forgot' to show me."

"Isn't that Linda Cooke's fault?"

Wells shook his head. "Linda runs the mechanics, and I have no complaint with her. She takes – she *took* – her orders from St. John. She apologized for him constantly. I think that was her main job at the Society."

"You spoke with St. John last night," Lee said. "What did you talk about?"

"Am I a murder suspect?" Wells asked, raising one eyebrow.

Lee gave her most disarming smile. "I need to get an understanding of the man. I'm going to talk to every exhibitor and ask them the same questions." It was a lie, but police were allowed to lie to suspects to keep them talking.

Wells body relaxed a bit. He nodded. "I reamed him out five days ago about the exhibit placement. He offered to help out with some ads and signage. It doesn't help the booth traffic, and it doesn't reduce my sunk costs, but it's a start. Plus, he said I'd get my placement guarantee in writing for next year. If I come next year."

"Placement is that important?"

Wells clenched his jaw and slowly nodded his head. Lee thought the physical reaction was much more intense than the question warranted. "I've got a hell of a lot of money in this landscape," he said. "Nothing in here except the stonework is recyclable. You can't take an azalea you've forced into full bloom for February and put it in the ground either in my own or someone else's property after the show. You mulch it. I've got two hundred shrubs that are going to be mulched in nine days. I'd better write one hell of a lot of business in that time. And, trust me, you don't write nearly as much business when the geeks next door are demonstrating their wind turbines."

Wells pointed toward the Blue Hills Gardens display, the most prominent in the hall. "And, if you think judges aren't swayed by where an exhibit is located, you need to re-read your psychology books. A big garden right up front implies prestige, and the judges automatically give it a higher score. I got five ribbons. I should have had twenty-five or thirty."

A thought occurred to Lee. "I spoke with the head of the judges' committee a little while ago. She said one exhibit was up for one award but she couldn't find the plant… a blue daylily."

Wells nodded. This time, he tried to show disinterest in the question, but Lee saw Wells' hands unconsciously tighten their grip on the pad on his lap, bending its edges. She had touched a very uncomfortable subject. "*Hemerocallis* 'Carolina Blue'," Wells said. "Unfortunately, when the hybridizer delivered them, they were all scape and foliage. Maybe three buds in the whole batch and nothing that was going to bloom during the show. I didn't use them. Which is too bad. That would have gotten me the Grassi Cup for sure." Wells shrugged in a gesture of resignation. "What can you do? Instead, the hybridizer will offer them to someone for the Philadelphia Flower Show next month and they'll get all the credit."

*Too much answer*, Lee thought. She changed tactics. "You said you were guaranteed a specific space on the basis of agreeing to a specific size exhibit a year in advance. That wasn't covered in what you paid for the space?"

Wells cocked his head. "You need a basic education in the economics of a show like this." He gestured toward the vast halls beyond the landscape displays. "The vendors out there pay for their space, and they pay a premium for location. We – the landscape exhibitors – don't pay anything. Instead, the Garden and Flower Show pays *us* to show up. It isn't a lot: six bucks a square foot. Which means the Society cuts me a check for six grand. But, without these exhibits, no one would come. Nobody wants to pay twenty bucks for the privilege of shopping. The landscapes we create are the draw."

Wells began doodling on his drawing pad as he spoke, sketching a plant, then other plants behind it. "Now, six thousand is a drop in the bucket compared to what it costs to build an exhibit like this. I've got more than fifty thousand in time and materials and, like I said earlier, in nine days all of this is mulch. My expectation is that I'll make that back in meeting prospective customers, but there's no guarantee."

Wells put down the pad, stood up, put his hands in his pockets, and paced around his display's patio, trying to end the interview.

*The man is holding back*, Lee thought. *There's something going on he's not telling me.* Lee leaned forward. "Who would have had motive to kill him?"

Wells looked up at the ceiling. "Vendors, if he was shaking them down – and I wouldn't put it past him. They're not exactly ladies and gentlemen back there. They have to hustle for every dollar, and if St. John did something to cross them, they'd repay him in kind in an instant. Who else? The husbands or boyfriends of whichever one of those young ladies on his staff he was… partaking of. And, believe me, when you hire exclusively women in their early twenties with long blonde hair and zero business experience, you've got something in your mind other than running a botanical society. How about donors? I read the pieces in the *Globe* about the fact that he hadn't raised squat toward that garden downtown. If I had ponied up money for that boondoggle and found out I was the only one, I'd want my money back. And I'd bet that St. John wouldn't give it back. Or else he'd give back part of it and keep the rest for himself."

"What about exhibitors?"

Wells shrugged. "I know these guys. They get angry. They may not be intellectual giants, but they understand that murdering someone doesn't solve the problem. Not even a slug like St. John. When you don't get what you want, you raise a stink. I didn't get the space I was promised, so I got ads. Whoever is running this show next year will know that I got shafted by St. John and I'm owed a better deal."

Having gotten through the lead-up questions, Lee took the plunge. "You were at the Gala last night. Did you speak to St. John?"

"He asked me if I was having a good time. I said it was a swell party. After that, we stayed away from one another."

"You said you were past the 'reaming out' stage," Lee said. "Why would you still be avoiding one another?"

"Because he isn't going to be a client, and I was at the party to meet prospective clients." Wells returned to his chair and, for the first time, faced Lee directly. "I'm the new guy on the block. McQueen has been in the business twenty-five years and has two hundred projects in a binder. I've got a degree in landscape architecture and maybe ten good projects so far. This exhibit is my fantasy land. I spent most of the evening parked right here on this stool talking with people who have a hankering to add a little magic to all those acres of grass around their homes. I didn't need to make nice to St. John, and he knew I can't afford to put anything into his tin cup for the City Hall garden."

*Too much information, too much explanation*, Lee thought, though she only smiled and nodded. "What time did you leave?"

Wells audibly exhaled, shook his head and looked up at the ceiling. "One o'clock or a little before. You have to talk to people when they're sober. I left when the crowd started to thin out and people's speech started getting slurred."

"I have you down as one of the last people to speak to St. John as the party was winding down."

Wells shook his head firmly. "They're mistaken. I know I was out of here by one in the morning."

Lee could have pressed the point. She decided this was not the time to do so. There had been moments of truth in what he said, but he had told lies during their talk. The timbre of his voice had changed at several points and there was the nervous doodling. She would seek corroboration elsewhere – perhaps from Liz Phillips – and, if need be, confront Wells at another time.

"You drove home?" Lee asked.

"I'm at the hotel across the parking lot. I was back here this morning at six, except that I was told I couldn't come into the exhibit hall."

"That's when you heard St. John had been murdered?"

"What I heard was that he had drowned. That he was floating face down in McQueen's pond."

\* \* \* \* \*

Linda Cooke said she could page several members of the development staff who were working the show and have them ready to interview at Lee's convenience.

"Not ones currently at the Society," Lee said. "I want ones who left in the past, say, six months."

Cooke's face showed surprise.

"I need people who have some distance between themselves and the Society," Lee said.

Cooke said she'd assemble the list.

\* \* \* \* \*

Robert Zimmer stood several inches over six feet, his height accentuated by a lanky frame that included long, dangling arms encased in a frayed, blue sweater. He was a man somewhere past seventy, a fringe of white around his well-tanned head. Lee and Zimmer were seated in the VIP lounge, a pot of coffee on the low table in front of them. It was nearing three o'clock and Lee, who had eagerly sought out coffee earlier in the day, now dreaded the social nicety of drinking yet another mug full.

"I think Mel overdramatizes the Trustees' position," Zimmer said. "St. John wasn't who he said he was. His idea of the Garden at Government Center was a good one, but he didn't execute on the fund raising. He would have been let go, naturally. But, 'making fools of us'? No, I don't think so."

Zimmer shifted his long legs, scrunching them under the chair as he balanced his mug. "And, I think he would have listened to reason. He could make things unpleasant for the Society, but we could have made things even more unpleasant for him. His family's presence at the Society's townhouse, for example. That was never part of his contract. The building was empty, he asked if he could use it, and we said 'yes'. If he made a fuss or said he was going to the press, we could just as easily have asked that he vacate the townhouse by nightfall."

"But he was going to be fired today?" Lee asked. "That's what Ms. Dawson said."

Zimmer nodded agreement. "We had reached that conclusion among ourselves. Once the show opened, there wasn't much he could do to muck it up. It's really Linda's show, anyway. At this point, St. John's was more of a… ceremonial position."

"Can you think of any reason anyone would want to have killed him?" Lee asked.

Zimmer was silent, nodding his head slightly, his eyes moving slowly over the artwork around the room. Thirty seconds went by. "A few people might have had motive, though I don't know that they were capable of murder. Raymond Brady is one. Alice Shelburne might be another."

"I know Ms. Shelburne is a large contributor to the Society," Lee said. "This is the first time I've heard Raymond Brady's name."

Zimmer sighed. "Raymond was the purchaser of a lot of twenty-five of the Blaschka glass flower pieces. He gave St. John a cashier's check for two hundred thousand dollars. He then turned around and immediately put them up for sale at Sotheby's. Which is how we came to know in the first place that they weren't in the archives where they belonged. Sotheby's had a pre-sale buyer – what we call a pre-emptive offer – for the lot at a price of something like a half a million dollars plus the buyer's premium."

Zimmer picked at a piece of lint on his sweater. "Brady agreed to the pre-emptive offer, then the Society stepped in and questioned whether St. John had the right to make the sale in the first place. Sotheby's, which having been burned publicly a couple of times never wants to get involved in a provenance squabble, backed away. They wouldn't broker the pre-emptive offer even though it meant giving up an easy commission. And, in any event, that buyer backed off as soon as the title issue was raised. Brady – who is an antiques broker and dealer, not a collector – said he wanted to return the pieces and get back his money plus some 'fees' he said he had incurred. St. John said the proceeds had already been spent. We couldn't give Brady back his money even though St. John had no right to sell him the pieces."

"Which left Raymond Brady owning twenty-five glass flowers he didn't want?" Lee asked.

"Which, until St. John's death, left Raymond Brady owning twenty-five glass flowers he *says* he couldn't sell except at a steep discount," Zimmer said. "He had been threatening a lawsuit for the past two months. The Society's position is that St. John had no authority to make the sale and that Brady should have known better. We'd love to take back the pieces but, as the books show, the money has been spent for 'fund raising'. We've offered him clear title, but the pieces are tainted now. Just last week he told us it would take years to sell them with that cloud hanging over them."

"How does St. John's death solve that problem?" Lee asked.

Zimmer's face took on a weary look. He exhaled deeply and pressed his fingers together in front of his face. "I don't pretend to understand the human mind, Lieutenant. I do know something about greed. Until two months ago, Mr. Brady had a sure-fire way to turn two hundred thousand dollars into five hundred thousand by doing nothing more than owning something for a few weeks and knowing how and to whom he could sell that something. St. John Grainger-Elliot was both the instrument of depriving Mr. Brady of that instant enrichment and of turning two hundred thousand dollars of Mr. Brady's ready cash into an illiquid asset."

Zimmer shifted in his chair, looking for a more comfortable place for his legs. "I have also heard, through people who know these things, that, as a result of that fiasco, Mr. Brady has found that his usual buyers are wary of dealing with him. He has a lot of merchandise and very few takers. Brady may have simply wanted revenge. He may also have had some plan to force St. John to give back that original investment in order to tide him over. Perhaps that plan didn't work out."

"Brady wasn't at the Gala last night?" Lee asked.

Zimmer laughed. "No, I doubt that very much. Raymond Brady has very little good to say about the Society right now, and I think that paying two hundred dollars to sip some Champagne with the trustees is not something he would consider money well spent. But he lives in Brookfield, maybe thirty miles from here, not in Timbuktu. He is probably worth talking to."

"And Ms. Shelburne?"

"She was here last night. I saw her with St. John more than once. She seemed rather distracted."

"Could you guess at what?" Lee asked.

Another pause to collect thoughts. "Alice is a great believer in the good works of the Society though she has several times turned down the opportunity to become one of its trustees. She was an early and enthusiastic supporter of the Government Center project. St. John never publicly identified any of the people who said they had pledged money, though Alice was almost certainly one of them – if there were any."

"And the reason for killing St. John?"

"Alice is the widow of Marc Shelburne…"

"Founder of Mass Biotech," Lee said, recognizing the entrepreneur's name.

Zimmer gave a tip of an imaginary hat. "Good for you, Lieutenant. "And Mass Biotech was sold for an unconscionable amount of money to Sanofi-Aventis. Alice prefers to make her charitable donations in the form of appreciated stock. She's very shrewd about that. Her cost is minimal but her charitable deduction is enormous."

"I still haven't heard a motive," Lee said.

Zimmer pressed his fingertips together as he spoke. "Like any non-profit, the Society immediately sells any stock it receives as a charitable donation. We are not seers. We cannot guess the direction of the market. But we also placed an unwise amount of trust in St. John. There is a possibility – and I readily acknowledge that it is only a possibility – that Alice made a gift of stock to the Society for the purpose of kick-starting the Garden at Government Center. But that stock never reached the Society because St. John wanted to be able – or so he may have said to Alice – to show all of the funding at once. It is possible that the stock left Alice's hands and went to St. John's, but went no further, with the idea that it was being held for his 'grand unveiling' of the full amount. You need to ask Alice what she did or did not do by way of contributing. I only know that she spoke to St. John several times last evening."

"When did you leave the Gala?" Lee asked.

Zimmer blinked. "I know I stayed up past my bedtime. After midnight, for certain. I live on Beacon Hill, and I have a long case clock that keeps excellent time. It 'bonged' once as I entered my home, but I cannot say if that single 'bong' was for twelve-thirty, one, or one-thirty."

"Would it surprise you to know that you were one of the last people to speak to St. John that evening?"

Zimmer's eyebrows went up. "It would surprise me very much."

"What did you talk about?"

"As I recall, I told him that if we didn't have straight answers for the trustees this morning, he was going to be in a world of hurt."

"And what did he say?"

"Oh, he lied to my face and said everything was going to be fine."

* * * * *

Alone once again in the VIP Lounge, Lee looked at her phone and saw the blinking red LED. The area code was Boston but the number was unfamiliar. Because few enough people had her cell phone number, the call was worth returning. She tapped the callback key and heard Captain Abelson's voice answer on the first ring. He had been calling from home.

"I've been doing some thinking," Abelson said in deliberate tones. There was a long pause. "Lee, there are a lot of eyes on you. Most of them – mine especially – are pulling for you to succeed."

*This is not going to be good,* Lee thought.

"There are a few people out there who want you to fail. They say you're too young and too inexperienced to have command responsibility. They resent that – at least in their eyes – you vaulted over two dozen more senior detectives to become a lieutenant. For them, this is the 'gotcha' opportunity. It's a high-profile investigation and, whether or not it was supposed to happen, you got the red ball." Another long pause. "You've got to see this through."

Lee gritted her teeth.

"Prove them wrong…" Abelson said.

"I need resources," Lee broke in. "I've got one detective who's wet behind the ears and another who is borderline… no, who *is* incompetent."

"And the department has a hiring freeze and a seven percent budget reduction mandate," Abelson said. "Be creative. Shuffle people. Get the resources you need."

*Just don't expect any help from me*, Lee thought. "Sir, I'd like to bring in John Flynn."

There was a moment's silence on the other end of the phone. Then, "I thought he retired."

"Not quite," Lee said. "He's taking a week to clean up case files. Strictly desk work."

"So, he's on the clock?"

"Technically," Lee said. "Just barely."

"Then ask him," Abelson said. "I don't think he'd say 'no' to you. Just get a quick resolution, Lee. You probably haven't had time to watch the news but the media is all over this. Make an arrest and make it stick, and you'll be a hero."

Hitting the 'end call' icon on her phone, it occurred to Lee that, despite his protestations, Abelson might be one of those people rooting for her to fail. It was time to pull a rabbit out of a hat. A rabbit named John Flynn.

Her old partner. The man who had taught her how to be a detective.

\* \* \* \* \*

The red in Alvarez's eyes showed the effects of being on the job for too many hours. He scrunched his eyelids several times over the course of a minute, a sure sign of a man who was pushing himself too hard.

But his presentation was ready. Lee leaned back, fascinated that a detective could be so completely comfortable with computer technology.

"I spoke with thirty people either in person or over the phone, and got from each of them where and when they saw St. John yesterday," Alvarez said. "And, by the way, none of them say they were aware that the emergency exit by the management offices had been taped open or had used it. Based on those interviews I can fairly well pinpoint St. John's movements over the course of the day and the evening with very few gaps."

Alvarez tapped the iPad screen. "St. John got here at 6:20 on Friday morning. He had a brief staff meeting at 6:30, then walked the landscape displays. Starting at 6:45, he helped Linda Cooke clear out the hall of exhibitors. He spoke to the staff again around 8:15, then he gave a talk to the judges at 8:30, popped in on the staff at nine and spent from then until 11:30 out talking to vendors in the other halls. He had lunch in his office and another staff meeting at 12:30. His wife dropped by to see him at about 12:45. He and Tony Wilson met with the Expo Center union rep at 1:30. At 2:30 he was in the back halls chatting up the vendors. He watched the ribbons go up from three until about 3:15 and then left the building, much to the disgruntlement of all. He said he was going back to the hotel to rest up before the party, but no one can confirm that he did that. He was back at 6:15 checking final arrangements. From 6:30 p.m. until 1:45 a.m. he made the rounds. At 1:46, he wasn't there. No one remembers seeing him go off with anyone. No one remembers any phone calls or arguments. He just vanished. Until the night watchman found him."

Next to each point on the timeline was an annotation with the name of the person or persons who had provided the information. The early morning and late afternoon and evening information contained the most names. Mid- to late-morning and early afternoon contained few confirming names.

Lee pointed to the 3:15 p.m. entry indicating Grainger-Elliot was going back to the hotel. Half a dozen names confirmed the time he left. "But none of these people know for certain where he went?"

Alvarez clicked on one of the names. A balloon read, *"SJ said he was going back to hotel to rest up for Gala and would return by 6:30."*

"They all confirm he said exactly the same thing," Alvarez said.

"How about phone calls?" Lee asked, hoping that Alvarez had performed the task that Mazilli neglected to do.

Alvarez gave a weary shrug and tapped on a tab. "I did a dump of the call for yesterday from the phone we fished out of his pocket. His first call was to his home at about 9:10. He made a cluster of calls while he was in his office around noon, mostly to nursery owners – six in total. He made or received calls sporadically over the course of the afternoon. The names tie to the Society's list of contributors. There was another call to a contributor in the afternoon and one a few minutes later to one of the trustees, Richard Durant, followed by one to his home. That was just before three o'clock and was his last call."

Lee looked at the data in the windows. "You did all this in three hours?"

"I just started downloading databases and then told the system to look for links," Alvarez said. "It's mostly automatic. Data mining stuff."

"Stuff," Lee repeated, amazed. "You realize no one else in the department is doing this."

"There's no reason why they can't." Alvarez yawned. "Lieutenant, I'm going to have to go home and sleep for a while, but I'll email you the spreadsheet so you can play with the information if you want."

Lee nodded her head, still stunned by the trove of information Alvarez had gathered. "Go home," Lee said. "Get a good night's sleep. Let's pick this up tomorrow morning bright and early. Consider yourself on day shift until we get this solved. I know you have a special-needs child at home…"

"It's a school vacation week," Alvarez said. "Terri and I can work around it." He paused, a look of uncertainty on his face. "Lieutenant, before I go, I want to throw a name at you. Call it a hunch, call it too many things not quite right."

"You have a suspect," Lee said.

Alvarez nodded. "Linda Cooke. She was the last person to leave – in fact, no one *saw* her leave, not even the night guard. Less than two hours later, and half an hour after she got the call from the guard, she's here looking like she *expected* to be dragged out of bed. Not a hair out of place and fully dressed. Then, you told me she gave you the stiff arm when you first questioned her: 'he's a man with no enemies and we all loved him.' Everyone else I've talked to has been a lot more honest."

"Do you have a theory about motive?" Lee asked.

"I'm working that one," Alvarez said. "She may have wanted his job. The people I've spoken to say she chafes at being pigeonholed. The only thing she does at the Society is run this show. She tells everyone she can do a lot more, and she bad-mouthed St. John behind his back."

"Jason, we never zero in on one suspect this early unless there's overwhelming physical evidence," Lee said. "Everything you're saying is true, and I'm not going to make any excuses for her behavior. I'm going to keep what you said in mind. For now, go home, get some sleep, and be ready for a very full day tomorrow."

Alvarez nodded, wordlessly. He collected his computer and rose from the chair. Lee watched him walk out the door of the VIP room. She wondered, *is it a rookie mistake, jumping to a conclusion; or it is an insight I missed?*

* * * * *

Linda Cooke sipped a diet soda through a straw. She pushed across a sheet of paper with the name and address of a woman who, Cooke said, had been part of the development staff until six months earlier. The woman was now training as a securities broker, and had agreed to meet Lee later that afternoon at her home.

"You weren't exactly forthcoming this morning," Lee said. "'St. John was a wonderful man with no enemies,' was what I think you said. "If I'm going to find his murderer, I'm going to need your full cooperation, not words from a Society script."

Cooke put down the can. "I can't help that I admired him. I knew what he was trying to do for the Society..."

"Did the two of you get along?"

Cooke paused. "We had some professional differences but, for the most part, we got along."

Lee pondered the woman. *Who gets a call in the middle of the night that her boss has been found dead and immediately does full-face makeup?*

"An exhibitor told me this afternoon that the design for the exhibition hall changed in the last two weeks," Lee said.

"The design changed continually," Cooke replied. "Exhibitors dropped out, exhibitors were added. Exhibitors went from twelve hundred square feet to five hundred because their plant material wasn't ready or a supplier fell through. We didn't freeze the design until two days before we started the build."

"Did exhibitors move from the back of the exhibit to the front or vice versa?"

Cooke thought for a moment. "Everyone moved at least once. But there's no such thing as a 'bad' spot. If you're in Exhibit Hall 'A', you get the same foot traffic regardless of whether you're the first exhibit everyone sees..."

"Was Oscar McQueen's garden always that first exhibit?"

"No, his space moved several times. He also agreed to nearly two thousand square feet this year."

"Who makes the final decision? How did the design finally get frozen?"

"Both St. John and I had the software on our computers. I'm not sure who did the final revision."

"What criteria did you use in making changes so late?"

"Our own judgment of what would please people. How well exhibitors had done in the past. Seniority, up to a certain point. Interesting plant material based on the plant list supplied by the exhibitor. Interesting water features or walk-throughs. McQueen's bridge over the pond is a huge draw. Every television station featured it. People wait fifteen minutes just to walk over it so that they can stand at the top of the bridge and admire the view."

"And you don't remember who had the final say over where exhibits were placed?" Lee said.

Cooke shook her head. "It gets crazy around here just before the load-in."

\* \* \* \* \*

Patricia Carlton was twenty-four, with long, strawberry blonde hair, and perfect skin. She wore a form-fitting sweater that accentuated a voluptuous figure. Her well-furnished, cheerful apartment in Jamaica Plain bespoke an allowance from mom and dad.

"I was there for ten months," she said. Outside, it was twilight and Carlton had pulled the cork from a bottle of wine, an overpriced but trendy Pinot Grigio. "It was fun at first. Exciting even. Everyone warns you that your first job out of school – if you can find a real one instead of making change at a Starbucks – is going to be something in a cubicle in a dreary office building."

"Instead, I was at this incredible place in the Back Bay – a castle – surrounded by artwork, with an office that faced out onto Comm. Ave. Everyone was nice. Everyone was pumped up. There was this beautiful model of the garden in the grand hall. It reminded you of what you were there for. And St. John was very nice. He worked with us, told us it was OK to make mistakes as long as we learned from them. He said that what we were doing was going to leave a mark on the city for the next hundred years."

"It sounds perfect," Lee said.

Carlton shrugged. "In a way it was," she said. "The pay wasn't great, but we were mostly there for the experience. It was like getting paid for an internship. We'd all go out for drinks after work and stuff like that."

"Something changed," Lee prompted.

Carlton shook her head and then had some wine. "No. That's just it. Nothing changed. I mean *nothing*. We'd have this list of people to call and we'd call them. We'd go out for appointments. I'd call, like, forty people a week. I'd meet ten people either at Botanical Hall or at their offices. They'd be polite. They'd listen. Most of them told me they would 'take it under advisement'. And that would be the end of it. If anyone expressed interest, St. John took over, and that was the last we'd see of them."

"You were there almost a year," Lee said. "How much did you raise?"

Carlton took another drink of wine and brushed back her hair with her hand. "As far as I know, not a dime. In ten months, I didn't get anyone to contribute. St. John took over every prospect who was even remotely a potential donor. There were fifteen of us when I left with more coming in the door every week. I think between all of us, we could total up maybe thirty or forty thousand that we knew we raised."

"That's why you left?"

"I figured I ought to leave before I got fired. Also…"

Lee waited while Carlton drank more wine.

"There was something in the atmosphere. I didn't see it at first. St. John was always very proper, very solicitous in groups. He wanted to hear everyone's ideas, he wanted to hear everyone's plans. But in private, he was always… touching us. On the shoulder, on the arm. He would take your hand while he talked to you. When he started touching my knee, I started avoiding private meetings with him. I also started looking for another job."

"Did everyone feel the same way?"

"Not everyone."

"Do you think he was having an affair with anyone on the staff?"

"Not that anyone admitted. But not everyone talks. We'd bring it up – the touching, the grabbing -- over drinks, and there were a few of us who just kept our mouths shut. It isn't like he was really old or ugly. But it wasn't going to look good on your resume – doing the boss."

"How did he get along with the trustees?"

"We were under strict orders never to talk to trustees. In fact, we were never to talk to *anyone* except him about fund raising. He was incredibly secretive."

"And that didn't strike you as odd?"

Carlton drank the last of her wine and refilled the glass. "It was my first job. I didn't know it was strange. I thought it was how these societies operate. I think that's why he hired only kids fresh out of school. We didn't ask questions. We just did what we were told."

* * * * *

Lee threw her jacket over the chair in her bedroom. She slipped out of her skirt and pulled on sweatpants and a cotton sweater. The clock read 6:18. It was now fifteen hours since she was jolted out of her sleep by the call from Alvarez.

She looked in the bathroom mirror and gave a deprecating self-appraisal. Growing up, Lee's mother had always called her 'my beauty'. It seemed to Lee that if there ever had been beauty it was slipping away. The classic, round Han face was still unlined but there were bags under her eyes from chronic lack of sleep. Years ago, she had adopted a no-nonsense brush cut that allowed her to shampoo her jet black hair, blow it dry and be out the door in less than ten minutes. Except that she would go six weeks between trims and too often, as now, her hair was too long and lacked body. Her face was, she observed, only one of her faults. She was sufficiently tall to intimidate most Chinese men, but her body was too boyish to merit second looks from westerners.

And now, she might be letting Matt slip away.

She didn't view Matt as some kind of 'last chance', but he was rare.

First of all, he was acceptable to her parents because he was Chinese, had never been married, and had the requisite financial resources and a prestigious job.

*Pleasing my parents*, Lee thought with grim amusement. Matt might be fourth-generation American but he was also the product of five thousand years of Chinese culture that worshipped sons. He had breezed through Carnegie-Mellon and Wharton and, at 32, was head of quantitative analysis at the largest hedge fund in Boston. He surrounded himself with computers and generated trading models that kept the fund a step ahead of the market.

She also knew that behind Matt's veneer of American customs was a Chinese mind. He professed to respect her career choice, but he had no patience with her hours or dedication. Meanwhile, the whole long weekend had been built around two factors: that the U.S. markets would be closed on Monday for the Presidents Day holiday, and that Matt was prepared to spend some fraction of his just-delivered bonus on art.

Which, in turn, meant that they would have spent all day today going from gallery to gallery looking at obscenely priced pieces of stone or metal being passed off as sculpture. Tomorrow, they would see *his* friends. By Sunday evening he would be sneaking peeks at the Asian markets. And, on Monday, holiday or no holiday, he would be back to his emails. That was how they had spent Thanksgiving and Christmas. Why should this weekend have been any different?

*Love?* Love was a cruel joke played on women with careers. Love was putting up with being berated for going to class and study group Friday night instead of flying down with Matt. Love was smiling through long, alcohol-fueled reminisces between Matt and his old college buddies that rehashed decade-ago conquests. Love was making a cheerful, one-sided conversation over breakfast while Matt surreptitiously checked the price of obscure commodities in London trading.

This had been going on for six months. Lee looked again in the mirror. *I need a better class of boyfriend*, she thought.

It wasn't for lack of trying. Lee readily acknowledged to herself that her degree in public administration had been pursued in some part in the expectation of meeting someone. Even in law school she hoped to find a potential partner. Her fellow students were other people her age, also with day jobs and many with city or state agencies. But as far as she could tell, her classmates had all paired off years earlier. The men wore wedding rings or looked at their watches as the study group sessions wore on, a sign someone was waiting for them at home.

Lightning would strike, she thought. She just had to be awake enough to notice.

In the kitchenette was a half-bottle of Scotch. She looked in the cabinet and found only a large tumbler. Everything else was in the dishwasher, and the dishwasher hadn't been run in three days. Dutifully, she added detergent and pushed buttons so that at least she'd have a clean cup for coffee in the morning. She poured a quarter glass of Scotch and turned on the computer on the coffee table in the living room. Alvarez had efficiently emailed her his multiple diagrams. All of their hidden layers were there for her inspection.

But she was too tired to look. The light was blinking on her telephone. It wouldn't be Matt. He communicated exclusively by cell phone. She pressed the message replay button and sat on the sofa, listening to voices. Her mother had called. Twice. *"Where are you? We're sick with worry. Your father had a traffic accident and nearly killed himself. Call me."*

A 'traffic accident' could mean something as simple as backing into another car while parking. By Lee's count, her father 'could have been killed' or 'had nearly been killed' four times in the past six months. That her father's 'nearly killing himself' was the third item in her mother's message indicated the 'traffic accident' was possibly imaginary.

There was also a message from Mazilli, who had wisely called her home number rather than her cell phone. *"I tripped going down the stairs and think I sprained my ankle. I'm going to the doctor in the morning. I let the duty desk know I'm out."*

*Yeah, and we're going to miss you something fierce*, Lee thought, erasing the message. Flu. Sprained ankle. It was all the same. Anything to dodge a case. No wonder Alvarez had been pleading for re-assignment.

On her kitchen counter, a green stick with a handful of thin, grass-like leaves sat upright in a glass, her 'lucky bamboo' which she watered meticulously despite its lack of growth. In the narrow living room window, a plant whose name she had never bothered to learn wilted either from a lack of water or, perhaps, from overwatering. She didn't know which. Another plant, on closer inspection, seemed to be covered in spider webs and had gnat-like creatures buzzing around it. She looked around for something that might hold water that she could take to the plant but was too tired to rummage through the dishwasher.

She took out her cell phone and typed out a message to Matt:

*I miss you*, her message said. *I wish I was there.*

She tapped 'send'.

There was one more task she had to do before she could go to sleep. She needed to call John Flynn. He would say yes, or so she hoped. He would revel in a case such as this. He would develop his own leads and likely be the one to find the murderer. She could trust him to be meticulous and to withhold nothing. *She could trust him.* That was the key. Everything else was secondary.

There were other reasons to choose Flynn. When they were first teamed she was obviously young to be a detective; almost certainly too young. It was equally clear that the eyes of the department were on her; most wanted her to succeed and to move up in the ranks. There was intervention in her career, some of it ham-handed. But in five years Flynn had never once said or done anything to lead her to believe that he thought of her as anything other than his professional equal. Though it was apparent that Flynn's career arc ended at the grade of senior detective, it was also evident that Lee would vault into police department management as quickly as her track record and exam grades permitted. Those realities never stopped him from chewing her out when she made a mistake. It never caused him to give her a false or undeserved compliment.

Flynn announced his retirement the same day Lee was told she had passed the Lieutenant's Exam with a grade of 97. Thirty-three years, he had said, were enough, and he had no desire to break in another partner. She accepted that statement at face value. She also knew that, in return for being her mentor for five years, Flynn had been offered his choice of assignments within the Boston PD including Major Cases. He had turned down that and other opportunities.

Three weeks later, Lee was informed she was being assigned to District C-6, working out of the nondescript two-story building that covered the city east of the Financial District, including South Boston. Flynn remained behind at their old precinct in the South End, saying he needed only to get his case files in order. Once that was done, he would take his accrued vacation and sick leave as a lump sum and officially end his police career.

In five years, Flynn had said almost nothing about his home life; an omission that told her much. She knew Flynn's wife was a nurse and that there were no children spoken of. Tellingly, there had never been a time in all the years they worked together when Flynn's wife called him while on duty.

Lee's watch read 6:45 p.m. She knew Flynn's cell number from memory. A few seconds later, she heard his phone ringing. He answered in his distinct baritone.

"I need your help," Lee said.

"You caught the flower show murder," Flynn said. "I heard."

"I've got one detective who is a computer whiz but whose shield is so new it hasn't left an imprint in its case..."

"And you've got Mazilli, who is probably already AWOL," Flynn said.

"He's already left a message that he sprained his ankle running away from the case," Lee said. "But I was going to ask you in anyway. This is going to be a hard case. Your kind of case. Can you put off retirement for a day or two?"

"Do you want to start tonight or tomorrow morning?"

"Tomorrow morning. I've been at this since 3 a.m. and I desperately need some sleep."

As she ended the call, Lee reflexively checked for messages that might have come in from Matt. There were none. She closed her eyes momentarily, contemplating the silence from New York and what it might mean, or not mean. There was nothing she could do about Matt tonight, and she had a job to do.

Sighing, she put down the phone and stared again at the computer screen with Alvarez's charts, leaning back on a sofa cushion.

Three minutes later, she was asleep.

**Chapter 5.**
**Sunday**


At 4 a.m., Lee was wide awake.  Coffee dripped into a pot, breakfast heated in the microwave oven.  Her dishwasher had been emptied, two weeks' worth of dry cleaning had been taken out of plastic bags and hung neatly in the closet, and a grocery list had been uploaded to PeaPod.

Fresh from a shower and wrapped in a favorite robe, Lee pored through Alvarez's charts.  The staff listing led to Facebook and blog pages that confirmed what Patricia Carlton had told her the previous evening.  The New England Botanical Society's 'development' staff was comprised exclusively of recent liberal arts college graduates, none with prior business employment experience.  They were uniformly female and attractive.

In short, these women were intelligent putty, Lee concluded.  They could be trained to deliver a pitch and, if the spiel fell on deaf ears, the 'development staff' would brush it off.  But, if there was interest, then all leads were fed directly back to St. John.  Lacking business experience, the staff wouldn't question why they had no further contact with prospective donors.  Being unschooled in the ethical niceties of non-profits, they would be unaware that St. John's admonition to have no contact with trustees was a fiduciary red flag.

Which, in turn, allowed St. John to have total control over fund raising.  He may have raised twenty million dollars.  He may have raised nothing.  He may have *collected* twenty million and given nothing to the Society.

*Task #1,* Lee wrote on a note pad.  *Find Alice Shelburne and ascertain what she gave for the Government Center Garden.*

'Follow the money.'  That was what Deep Throat had told

Woodward. Money was at the root of half the murders she investigated as a detective, though sometimes the amounts in those killings had been as little as a few dollars. Money might well be at the core of this one as well. How many donors had given and how had they been instructed to write those checks?

Every financial scam, in turn, required bookkeeping. When numbers grew large enough, no criminal could keep them in his or her head.

*Task #2. Go through St. John's office. Go through his home. Find his books.*

The links in Alvarez's charts took Lee to articles about the other people who were last seen at the Gala between 1:30 and 1:45. Richard Durant was a trustee of the Society but he was also a developer. His high-end condominium project in Lexington was languishing, with only fifteen units sold of nearly two hundred built, according to the *Boston Business Journal* link in Alvarez's spreadsheet. Was there a tie-in?

Robert Zimmer, with whom she had met Saturday, was also a trustee. Alvarez's links showed a more nuanced man. Zimmer was a retired lawyer laid low by the Madoff Ponzi scheme scandal. The *Wall Street Journal* reported that Zimmer had turned over millions of his own family's money plus twice that much of his clients' funds to Madoff. Those clients were suing Zimmer, even though he had lost a substantial part of his net worth to the scam. The article quoted him as saying that his life had been ruined because he had trusted a man he had met only once. Lee wondered why was he still a trustee.

Donald Kosinski was perhaps the most intriguing name. He was identified by the people Alvarez had spoken to as a prospective large donor. Yet, his name appeared in no listings of wealthy Bostonians. The matching name and address from the invitation list linked to that of a graduate student at Northeastern, and the address was in Boston's Mission Hill neighborhood, not exactly high-roller territory. Kosinski had a website offering freelance computer programming. Why had St.

John considered Kosinski a large donor?

The last item to catch Lee's attention was the police record for Oscar McQueen. The owner of Blue Hills Gardens had twice been arrested for assault. Though one arrest was nearly a decade old, both times were over money McQueen believed was owed to him. Both cases had been settled when the persons McQueen had assaulted had declined to go forward with charges. Lee thought back to the large man with the bushy beard and huge hands. He had been capable of assault. Was he capable of murder?

*Task #3*, Lee wrote. *Interview all persons with reason to beat information out of St. John.*

Which, of course, raised the question of Raymond Brady, the antiques dealer who had been conned into buying glass flowers with an unclear title – if, indeed, 'conned' was an accurate description. What information might Brady need from St. John?

*Task #4. Take apart Brady's business and finances.*

Lee thought back on Alvarez's suspicions about Cooke and her own unsatisfying encounters with the woman.

*Task #5, Look into Cooke's motives and background.*

She looked at the list and added a sixth item. Mel Dawson had said, somewhat cryptically, that Cynthia Duncastle might be as much a fraud as was St. John.

*Task #6, Determine whether Cynthia Duncastle was accomplice or dupe.*

Lee sighed as she wrote the last words. There was no question but that Alvarez was talented. But he was green and he was one person. John Flynn was indefatigable but he, too, was only human. It would take the three of them all day – and possibly all of Monday – to get through this list

New York was no longer in the cards.

\* \* \* \* \*

John Flynn listened intently as Lee and Alvarez brought him up to speed on the investigation. He had sandy brown, close-cropped hair with a sprinkling of gray. Despite three decades of close and continuing exposure to the worst of human behavior, he possessed an unlined face that made him appear a decade younger than his fifty-nine years. His body was lean and athletic. He professed no special training regimen but had, to Lee's personal knowledge, outrun physically fit perps half his age over half-mile-long distances.

They were at a table in a Dunkin' Donuts a block from the Harborfront Expo Center. Flynn sipped a large coffee. Alvarez drank orange juice. Lee enjoyed her fifth cup of coffee, and the sun was not yet lightening the eastern horizon.

"The thing we've kept to ourselves is that someone tried to beat information out of St. John before they killed him," Lee said. "To me, that's the key. I've found plenty of people with reason to want to see him dead, though none yet who had a strong enough motive to have committed the crime. But I also haven't seen anyone yet who needed to pound answers out of him before they killed him."

Lee pushed copies of her list across the table. "Six items, three of us. Jason has impressed me no end with his computer skills. I'd like him to focus on St. John's office." Speaking to Alvarez, she said, "Dig down deep. Take nothing for granted. And, keep me posted on anything you come across."

"John, I'm giving you Cynthia Duncastle to start with. Let on as little as you can get away with, but get me the truth. I don't think she killed him, but I don't think she's entirely innocent, either. She was married to a con man. She had to know that. What did he tell her about the Society? And, from that, find out how deep she is into his con. I also want you to talk to Cooke. Jason pointed out some oddities yesterday, and I'd like you to look at her critically."

"I'm going to get to know Alice Shelburne and a guy named Donald Kosinski who was supposed to be a high roller but who on paper looks more like an indigent graduate student. I'd like to know a lot more about him. John, I want both of us to see Raymond Brady.

I want to find out if he has two hundred thousand dollars that he can afford to tie up in glass flowers, and who was the buyer who stepped away. I suspect that, by the time we have this list checked off, there will be a new one, a lot longer."

Everyone nodded agreement. Flynn added, "I'd like to see the crime scene."

Lee grinned and nodded. "That's why I suggested we meet here. You always wanted to go back over the crime scene."

* * * * *

They started with the exhibit hall where, at six in the morning, crews were already watering trees and shrubs, checking kickboards for wear and replacing spent bulbs.

"Amazing," Flynn said, looking at the activity around them. "All this for just nine days."

"Exhibitors expect to generate a lot of business from this," Alvarez said. "Vendors expect to sell a lot of garden equipment and plants. Otherwise, none of this would exist."

As Flynn and Lee stood in the center of the exhibition space, Oscar McQueen approached them. He was clad in jeans and a plaid work shirt and wore heavy boots. With his girth and beard, he looked like a lumberjack. All three detectives' eyes went to his boots.

"Lieutenant Lee," McQueen said. "Either you've solved your murder or else you're fresh out of clues."

Lee gave a faint smile. "Bringing a colleague up to speed." She indicated Flynn. "This is Detective Flynn, who will be... providing an extra set of eyes on the case."

McQueen stuck out a huge hand. "Solve it quickly, Detective. I spent half of yesterday answering morbid questions from people who wanted to know where the body was found and whether my late friend, Mr. Grainger-Elliot, had on any clothing."

"This is Oscar McQueen," Lee said. "Owner of Blue Hills Gardens and the exhibit where St. John was found."

"Any thoughts as to why he was dumped here?" Flynn asked McQueen.

McQueen shrugged. "I've now asked myself that same question a couple of dozen times. I've got the biggest water feature of any exhibit. Maybe the murderer wasn't very smart and thought the body would sink to the bottom and not be found for days. Or, maybe the killer wanted me to be your prime suspect. Other than that, I'm out of ideas." The response came out sounding smug.

"What time did you get here this morning?" Flynn asked.

"Let's see," McQueen said, scratching his beard. "I left here about midnight. It's a ten-minute walk across the parking lot, and I think I got about five hours of sleep, so I must have gotten here this morning about half past five."

"Why so early?"

McQueen gestured at his display. "Look around you, Detective. There are more plants packed into my exhibit than there are in half a dozen average home sites. Every one of those plants has to be at the peak of perfection. Each one has to look like it belongs. I personally groom every plant here every morning." There was pride in his voice.

"What about Friday morning?" Flynn asked. "What time did you get here that morning?"

McQueen gave a wide, toothy smile. "I never left here. A couple of us did all-nighters. We got our sleep when the judges threw us out of the hall. Either you take this seriously or else you get trampled by those who do."

"You've got all the ribbons," Flynn said. "You must take it more seriously than everyone else."

"I'm in landscaping, Detective," McQueen said, putting a booted foot up on the exhibit's kickboard. "There's a foot of snow outside. What the hell else am I going to do? There's no excuse for coming here with some half-assed exhibit. Everybody gets the same show manual with the same listing of awards. There's no reason not to read it. This is as level a playing field as it gets."

"Except some playing fields are more level than others," Flynn said. "You're up here at the front of the hall. The guys in back get to watch you pick off the best prospects."

"Which is a load of crap," McQueen spat out. "A guy with a pickup truck and two lawn mowers can come in here, ask for a thousand square feet of space and put up a masterpiece of design that grabs the judges' attention. And, if he gets that attention, that guy will also book the business regardless of where he's situated. But I was assigned this location because I've been an exhibitor every year for the past twenty shows. I'm front and center because Linda knows I'll put up the best exhibit in the show, and she doesn't want to lead with some untested jackass who might back out at the last minute or put in some stonework and sod and call it a display."

"You also got a body in your pond," Flynn said.

McQueen folded his arms across his chest. "I've got work to do," he said. "Nice talking to you."

At the doors of the exposition center, Flynn and Lee spoke. Flynn shook his head. "Touchy guy. If McQueen is an example of the level of cooperation you're getting, this is going to be one hell of an investigation. Our problem is that we still don't know what questions to ask," Flynn said. "Until we do, we're playing our hand unnecessarily. Unless you get very lucky, you're still at the beginning of a complex investigation."

Flynn paused, his mind working. "I'll start with the widow and then move onto the show director," he said. "Then let's circle back. We've got a lot to accomplish."

Lee smiled inwardly. Flynn had said '*we*'.

* * * * *

Alice Shelburne occupied what was at minimum a fifteen-room home in Cambridge's Coolidge Hill neighborhood. Here, the exteriors of rambling old Victorians had been meticulously restored to turn-of-the-twentieth-century magnificence. The interiors had been brought forward a full century with contemporary, light-filled spaces and large rooms the homes' original architects could never have imagined.

The front parlor of Shelburne's home, where Lee now enjoyed a cup of freshly ground and brewed coffee, was a pictorial memorial to the late Marc Shelburne. One wall was given over to photographs and mementos. The biotech pioneer was shown talking and gesturing while presidents, prime ministers and other corporate and scientific legends listened intently. Plaques attested to his charitable generosity. Atop a credenza against another wall of the room was a scale model of the Shelburne Biotechnology Center at MIT.

Alice Shelburne was a silver-haired, diminutive woman of about sixty, which would have made her fifteen years junior to her husband. Her hair style was uncomplicated, and her face showed the lines that were natural to aging. She was attired in a nondescript sweater and slacks, and she wore bedroom slippers. This was not a vain woman, Lee thought.

Shelburne lightly tapped the edge of her coffee cup with her fingernail. It may have been unconscious or it may have been a signal that Lee was intruding on a Sunday morning that held things of greater interest than talking to the Boston police.

"You were one of the last people to see him alive," Lee explained. "I'm interested both in his state of mind and in what the two of you talked about."

Shelburne took a sip of her coffee. "St. John was preoccupied, if that's what you mean."

Lee arched an eyebrow. An invitation to continue.

"He seemed very upset with something though he was trying his best not to show it. He seemed very conscious of the time and looked at his watch rather quite a lot."

"And what did the two of you talk about?"

Shelburne took another sip of her coffee. "The usual. Money.

The Government Center project. It was what he cared about." There was disappointment in her voice.

"You had pledged money toward the garden?" Lee asked.

Shelburne nodded. "I had done more than pledged it. I've given the Society stock worth five million dollars."

"How long ago did you do that?"

"Two months ago," Shelburne said. "Almost three."

"Yet there had been no announcement of the gift," Lee said.

Shelburne nodded again. "At his insistence. He wanted to announce three gifts all at once. He said those gifts would be, collectively, twenty million or a quarter of the cost of the garden. Friday night, the last thing he told me was that he said he had the balance of the pledges in hand and that the donations would be announced this week."

"Did he name the other benefactors?"

"He held that information very closely," Shelburne said. "He said I knew them but he wouldn't say more than that. The total figure indicated the two other pledges were larger. He spent the evening trying to coax me into upping my number to match theirs."

"But the stock had already been turned over to the Society," Lee said.

"Yes," Shelburne said. "The transfer was done in mid-November. I wanted it to be reflected as a charitable contribution for last year. So, it has been almost three months exactly."

"Did you have any doubts about where the money would be going? What with the financial condition of the Botanical Society."

Shelburne shook her head. "No. I leave that to the attorneys and the accountants. The shares were transferred to an entity – something like the 'Government Center Garden Fund' or words to that effect. St. John had established it to hold all of the contributions until he was ready to announce the start of construction. I took his word that the account was registered as a charity and had the right exemption status.

After the first of the year, my accountants called him looking for the charitable ID number. To be tax deductible, an organization needs to have established eligibility under a particular section of the IRS code and received an identifying number. St. John said the paperwork was in progress. My accountants told him that, if he couldn't produce proof that the account had a charitable status by the first of March, they would ask that the contribution be rescinded."

"How did St. John react?" Lee asked.

Shelburne poured another cup of coffee. "He said he was confident he would meet the deadline. He told me Friday night that he would call the accountants on Monday morning. The papers had all been filed and approved."

"You believed him?"

"I wouldn't have transferred the stock in the first place if I had doubts."

"One of the people who saw you speaking with St. John after midnight said you looked concerned," Lee said.

Shelburne sipped her coffee. She would not be rushed into any answer, especially in her own home. "People who do not know me can easily mistake my candor for 'concern'. They shouldn't ascribe emotions to me unless they're well-acquainted with me."

"Were you aware that one of the trustees – Mary Ellen Dawson – had done a background check…"

Shelburne cut off Lee. There was anger in her voice when she spoke. "Mel Dawson is a fool. She has personally run the Society into the ground through a combination of interference in things she should leave alone and negligence of those things it was her responsibility to oversee. She should have resigned years ago. St. John pleaded with me to become a trustee, but I would not serve as long as that woman had any position of responsibility. So please don't tell me about some 'background check' she may have run. I'm certain it was performed as incompetently as everything else she does."

"Who would have motive to murder St. John?" Lee asked.

Shelburne did not hesitate before giving her answer. "Anyone who wanted to see the Society closed. Anyone who coveted one of the choicest locations in Back Bay. Anyone who believed that if St. John were gone, the Society would wither away. I would look at developers, and you know there are a couple of sharks on that board of trustees. I would look at buy-and-flip antiques dealers. The New England Botanical Society is a house filled with treasures that starts with its real estate and continues with its priceless collections. St. John was all that stood between greed and beauty."

"If you were to guess who the other contributors were, who would be at the top of your list?"

Shelburne rose from her chair; an indication that the meeting was over. "I said he kept that information close to his vest. There are a finite number of people who, in the current economic climate, can write checks for sums between five and ten million dollars. They shouldn't be hard for you to identify."

Lee also rose and collected her purse and coat. "But is there anyone else close to the Society who would be in that position?"

"I wish you luck in quickly identifying St. John's murderer," Shelburne said, her voice cool. "I don't care to be a party to a posthumous destruction of his reputation."

* * * * *

'The Castle', as Botanical Hall was informally known, occupied half of a long block on Commonwealth Avenue. Built, like much of the surrounding Back Bay neighborhood, of brownstone, its turrets with their flapping flags were a local landmark and a regular stop for tourists. Adjacent to Botanical Hall was a four-story, twenty-five-foot-wide, bow-front brownstone. It was the kind of structure that in recent decades had been carved into four or even six condominiums. But the single buzzer by the front door of this building held no panel listing multiple occupants. Instead, there was a simple brass plaque with the words, 'Botanical Hall Annex'. Flynn rang the buzzer. There was delay of several minutes before the door was opened.

Cynthia Duncastle was a woman in her mid-thirties and very attractive. These were the first things Flynn noted as he sat across from her in the small room that faced out onto Commonwealth Avenue. She was dressed in a black cashmere sweater and slacks that showed off a swimsuit-model-worthy figure. And, she had not been crying. These were the second things he noticed.

Flynn had gone through the formalities of the interview, offering his condolences and expressing his intent to find Grainger-Elliot's murderer as quickly as possible.

"Since your talk with Lieutenant Lee yesterday," Flynn said, "some difficult information has come to light about your late husband's background. I need to understand that information in order to proceed. The head of the trustees..."

"Mel Dawson," Duncastle said in her clipped, English accent, nodding. "The dossier her detectives compiled on my husband. Yes, I know all about that."

Flynn said nothing, but mentally noted that Grainger-Elliot had not been formally confronted with the report. There was, indeed, a leak from the trustees to its executive director.

Duncastle re-arranged herself in her chair. "My husband was the extraordinary child of very ordinary parents. His IQ, once it was finally measured, was in the 140s. But he grew up in an impoverished city in a poor part of England. In that city, the local comprehensive school trained children to work in factories, most of which were already redundant. They had no time for gifted children and no interest in them. In America, John Spense – and that was his given name – might have been spotted by a caring faculty and given the opportunity to advance via scholarships. In Brighton, he was simply ignored. His parents loved him but they could do nothing for him."

"The dossier says my husband spent time in prison. That is

correct. It was for eighteen months and the charge – to which he readily pleaded guilty – was for forgery. He did so to help someone who could not otherwise get work papers. His only crime was to aid a friend, a man who was a political refugee. John didn't even accept payment for what he had done. When John got out of prison, he chose to re-invent himself and knew that, to do so, he would need to leave the U.K."

"His logical destination was America. I will not bore you with the details of how we got here but, once in this country, he set out to build a new life. John's genius was his ability to grasp ideas and details. He understood the law, he understood science. He could not only quote long passages of literature, he also understood the author's intent. We chose Atlanta because it was a city full of people born elsewhere into which we could readily be absorbed. Atlanta also has a class of people who, frankly, have a special place in their hearts for those with English accents."

"John reinvented himself as St. John Grainger-Elliot. St. John had the proper upper-class connotation. Grainger was his mother's maiden name. Elliot was his father's given name. Five years ago, when he learned of the Atlanta Horticultural Society position, John made himself an expert on both the organization and the subject. He went into his interview with every fact and detail at his fingertips. And he was the ideal man for the position. It was a provincial organization that existed in the shadow of the larger and better-known Southeast Horticultural Society. It had a core of supporters but no discernible purpose. John gave it an ecologically relevant mission and began raising the funds to fulfill the promise he saw in the organization."

"We were happy in Atlanta. Our third child was born there. I was not in favor of uprooting ourselves from the South. I perceived, correctly as it turned out, that Boston was more of a closed society, unreceptive and suspicious of outsiders. But John felt it was a calling and that he could accomplish greater things with a more established organization. The New England Botanical Society, for its part, carefully hid the extent to which it was in precarious financial condition. In point of fact, the search committee lied to him."

"But John saw the potential for greatness. The Society had devolved into an entity that sponsored the Northeast Garden and Flower Show and did little else. Moreover, show attendance was shrinking and fund raising had become a matter of passing the hat among the trustees. John conceived the idea for the Garden at Government Center. It was his own vision; his own contribution to creating something of lasting value for the city. He dragged the trustees into supporting it, and single-handedly won over the politicians at City Hall."

Flynn interrupted Duncastle's flow of words. "There is considerable question as to whether funds had been raised for the garden."

Duncastle waved her hand dismissively. "The pledges were there. John's goal was to have at least half the money in hand before commencing construction."

"Had he reached that point?"

Duncastle was silent for several moments. "My husband compartmentalized his life to a great extent. There were times when he sought my advice, and I readily offered it. There were other times – and that was the more usual path – that he chose not to bother me with details or problems. Fund raising and the day-to-day workings of the Society were two areas that he did not discuss with me."

"Yet he told you that a trustee had done a background investigation on him," Flynn said.

Duncastle nodded. "That had the potential to affect our lives and especially our children's lives. Of course he discussed it with me."

"And, what was he going to tell the trustees?"

"What I told you just now," Duncastle said. "He would readily own up to not having the degrees or the background, but he would point to his current success and ask which mattered more: credentials or demonstrated competence. He was confident the trustees would see things his way. He was quite excited about Saturday morning's meeting."

"And the missing pages from books and the sale of the glass flowers?"

Duncastle's face showed distaste for the subject. "Every penny of the sale of the glass pieces was accounted for. John checked out books from the archives in order to better understand the evolution of botanical knowledge. He never removed a single page from any book nor did he ever remove a book without expressly signing for it. There is simply nothing to those allegations." Duncastle said these words emphatically.

Flynn said nothing in response, noting only that Duncastle's knowledge seemed extraordinary when it came to defending her husband's integrity yet non-existent on the subject of fund raising. He waited for Duncastle to say more. She sat silently.

"Time is the enemy of an investigation, Ms. Duncastle. Someone murdered your husband. You can help me narrow the list of suspects. I'm sure that, however compartmentalized he kept his life, he spoke of people who either threatened him or to whom your husband was a threat."

"Raymond Brady would be your first suspect," Duncastle said. "He saw the Blaschka Collection as his road to instant riches, and I'm sure he thought he was stealing them in the financial sense. When the trustees intervened, they made his ownership of the pieces a long-term proposition. For someone like Brady, owning something for more than two weeks constitutes 'long-term'. He was livid. He made repeated threatening calls. My husband explained that the money was spent – the Society had used it to pay its bills. Brady owned them but their provenance had been called into question. With my husband's death, I suspect their sale becomes considerably easier and now may even have the cachet of a mystery attached to them. I think Raymond Brady was quite capable of killing because it was about money, and money is the thing that Raymond Brady cares about above all else."

"Anyone beyond Brady?"

"I would also look carefully at Linda Cooke," Duncastle said. "She coveted my husband's position and worked continually to undermine his authority. John believed, though he could not yet prove, that she was stealing money from the Society. I would also pay attention to the trustees, especially the clever ones. They care so very much about their precious reputations, and my husband was in a position to make their oh-so-comfortable lives a little less so. John had already signaled that he would not be made the scapegoat for twenty years of poor stewardship by them. One of them might well have thought they could put off facing their own ineptitude by murdering John."

"What about contributors?" Flynn asked.

"What about them?" Duncastle responded.

"Were any of the people who had pledged money for the Government Center Garden angry or upset?"

"That question pre-supposes that I know who those contributors are," Duncastle said, a slight smile on her lips. "My husband didn't share that information with me. And he made no mention of any patrons of the Society who were angry."

"You weren't at the Gala Friday evening," Flynn said.

"No. There were times when I was useful to my husband in social settings and there were times when I was too much of a distraction. Also, Caroline, my youngest, was running a fever and had been in bed all day. I wouldn't have gone in any case."

The interview seemed to have run its course. As he closed his notebook, Flynn asked, "Do you know what you'll do now – where you'll live? Those kinds of decisions?"

Duncastle gave an audible sigh. "I'm going to take John home to bury him. I know that much. His father, Elliot, died some years ago, and it would be a comfort to his mother to have them buried together. I know that, sooner or later, I will be asked to vacate this house. Where I will settle is something that I will decide once John is at rest. The children are in school here, and they know no place except America. I'm not anxious to uproot them. Some friends have offered homes... It's just too early."

The answer caught Flynn by surprise. Few widows of twenty-four hours had any inkling of their plans. Most could not even think of their husbands in anything but the present tense.

Except the ones that had a hand in their spouses' deaths.

\* \* \* \* \*

The main entrance to the Castle was fifty feet away from the townhouse. Flynn surmised Jason Alvarez would still be hard at work in Grainger-Elliot's office. The entrance was locked, and it was several minutes before a security guard came in response to Flynn's ringing of the night buzzer. Flynn showed identification through the glass.

Alvarez was indeed still in the midst of his investigation. He was hunched over file drawers. On the large, antique desk at the center of the room, a small black box was toggled to a desktop computer via a cable.

"I'm copying St. John's hard drive so I can look at it later," Alvarez explained. "Some of the data files have security locks and encryption keys, but I have some fairly sophisticated stuff at home for unlocking those."

"What's in the files?" Flynn said, indicating the file cabinets.

"Mostly junk. Administrative things, personnel matters. Garden and Flower Show schedules and contracts. Nothing at all about fund raising, which is what I'm looking for."

"Pull out anything on trustees," Flynn said. "Also, everything about the sale of the glass flowers."

Alvarez indicated a small number of folders off to one side. Flynn opened the one on top. It contained a series of letters from Boston law firms. The letters – mini-briefs, essentially – told an escalating story of alleged duplicity and double-dealing by each side. Raymond Brady's attorneys charged that Grainger-Elliot had no authority to sell pieces from the Blaschka Collection and so the initial sale to Brady was void. Botanical Society lawyers gave no ground and countered that Brady had cherry-picked the collection at bargain-basement prices. Brady's law firm replied that press coverage of the controversy surrounding the sale had tainted the provenance of the collection 'beyond reconciliation' and asked for a full refund, plus damages appropriate to the sullied reputation of one of the region's most respected antiques dealers. The Botanical Society responded that Brady intended to own the pieces for less than a month, and that he demanded a refund only after Sotheby's noisily withdrew the pieces from its February sale and the pre-sale buyer backed out. Brady pressed on for a refund only to be told by the Botanical Society lawyers that the $200,000 he had paid had been spent, and that the Society had no funds to give him. The original sale agreement had required no escrow, and so the Society had used the funds as it saw fit.

There, the correspondence ended. It was acrimonious as only aggrieved parties could be when their affairs were placed in the hands of attorneys who billed by the hour. No case law was cited in these letters; that would be saved for the actual litigation if threatening letters did not resolve the issue.

To Flynn, it appeared that Brady was on shaky ground and that, in any event, there was no money to refund – unless Brady was angling for a larger number of pieces to sell in return for agreeing to drop a suit. It was, he thought, lawyers doing what they did best – muddying the waters. In criminal trials they created doubt. In these civil matters, they created fear of spiraling and never-ending costs.

Flynn turned his attention to the small black box next to the computer. "This gizmo will hold the entire contents of that computer?" he asked Alvarez.

Alvarez, not looking up from the files, nodded and said, "Fifty-nine bucks at your local Staples. The department ought to keep a couple of dozen of these for cases like this. They don't, so I brought one from home."

Flynn chuckled. "You're about two decades up on the department. The last I saw they were still storing things on floppy disks."

Alvarez stopped and turned. "That's what I don't get – the resistance to technology. It doesn't make sense. It drives me up the wall."

Flynn put his hand on Alvarez' shoulder. "You're what – thirty? I want you to remember this conversation and then think back on it twenty years from now. The department will have hundreds of these drives and the rest of the technology you take for granted right now. You'll be a captain and you'll think it's terrific stuff. And the thirty-year-old detectives coming up will call you a fossil or worse because you're using antiquated equipment that they have to supplement from home. It's the guys in their fifties and sixties who run the place and, what they're comfortable with is twenty-year-old technology. It's the way of the world."

Flynn paused, an idea forming in his head. "Jason, you know the current limits of the technology. Think back five years. I just talked with Grainger-Elliot's widow, and she said he 're-invented' himself once he was here in the States. She also said she didn't want to 'bore me with the details' of how they got here. To me, that's a red flag that says it was done some way other than waving a passport at an airport and applying for a green card. The report Mary Ellen Dawson commissioned said U.S. Immigration has no record of a Cynthia Duncastle or St. John Grainger-Elliot coming into the country. Yet they're here and apparently legal. Cynthia Duncastle also said that her husband went to prison for 'forging work documents' for a friend.

Can you forge a passport these days? Could you have done it five years ago?"

Alvarez nodded as Flynn laid out the problem. "There's pre-9/11, there's a period of a few years after 9/11, and there's, say, 2005 and after," Alvarez said. "Before 9/11, passport control was a joke. Things tightened up after that but the technology didn't exist to catch well-done counterfeit or altered passports for three years or more. Today, it's very good. A lot of money went into both creating better passports and scanning technology to catch switches. If St. John carried on his forging career after he got out of prison – and remember, he had all those degrees and employee references that turned out to be phonies, and they needed to be created to apply for that first job in Atlanta – then he and his wife may have gotten here on forged passports. They may also have arrived earlier than she claimed, in which case it would have been easier still."

"His passport is probably in his house or a safe deposit box," Alvarez continued. "I can do some basic analysis, and I have some friends who can really take it apart. My question is, why does it matter? We know where he came from and that he created a new identity for himself. Are the mechanics of how he did it really that important?"

Flynn grimaced. "Maybe. Maybe not. You get feelings. I'm fairly certain Cynthia Duncastle was up to her neck in whatever her husband was pulling off. Her claim is that he didn't share that information – that he 'compartmentalized'. I don't believe it. I'm also leery that she's only taking his body home to be buried. I'm not at all certain that she's coming back."

"What we've got going in our favor is that there's an autopsy and we – meaning Boston PD – control when the body is released," Flynn continued. "And Ms. Duncastle isn't going anywhere without the body. But she's a grieving widow, and grieving widows make for excellent TV news footage. That's why we need to get to the bottom of Grainger-Elliot's finances as quickly as possible."

* * * * *

A call to Mel Dawson's home produced the information that the trustee was at the Garden and Flower Show.

"Someone has to step into St. John's shoes," Dawson said as she and Flynn walked the aisle between vendor stalls. She took purposeful strides, stepping around shoppers. This was not someone who was wandering the halls attempting to look busy.

"What about Linda Cooke and Winona Stone?" Flynn asked, matching her stride. "Don't they actually run the show?"

"This show runs for nine days," Dawson said. "If it's run right, it shows a profit of nearly half a million dollars and sets the stage for an even more profitable show next year. Linda and Winona considered the bulk of their work done the morning the show opened because they spent six laborious months setting it up. St. John's job – which is now my job – is to see that the show is *run* right; not merely that it was set up right. This morning I pulled fifty thousand dollars of television advertising and put it on radio. I jettisoned a worthless, full-page ad in the *Globe* and told our PR firm to gin up two dozen exclusive features for TV reporters who are too lazy to find their own stories. I have found a Japanese interpreter for a bus load of tourists who were otherwise going to come in, look, be disappointed that nothing is signed in their language, and then go home and tell their friends not to bother with the Northeast Garden and Flower Show next year."

Dawson opened a small notebook. "By the end of today, I will have met with every exhibitor in the 'A' and 'B' halls, and they will not only have seen my smiling face, they will have been told what paid attendance was on Saturday and know that it is up five percent from last year. I will run interference with the unions, and I will personally supervise the gate count this evening. In the meantime, Miss Stone can't even replenish the water bottles in the VIP lounge because she is too upset over someone breaking into her room, so I suppose I will have to do that, too."

"What do you mean, someone broke into her room?" Flynn said.

"Just that," Dawson said, increasing her stride. "She was here all day yesterday from before dawn until after midnight. Sometime during those hours, someone broke into her room. It's a second-tier trade show hotel. People come and go at all hours. Security is poor at best. Any person with common sense knows if you must stay there, don't bring anything of value."

"Did anything get taken?"

"She didn't say. I think it was more a matter of violation of her space. I really didn't have time to do anything other than offer sympathy."

"Lieutenant Lee told me about your report from a private investigator," Flynn said. "I need that full report, and I need to get to the person or agency who prepared it."

Dawson took a phone out of her pocket, placed a call and spoke a few words. When she was finished she said, 'There's a copy at my home, waiting for you, together with the name of the agency that prepared it. They'll have been contacted and will expect your call this afternoon."

\* \* \* \* \*

Winona Stone, looking pale and very tired, sat in one of the cubicles in the warren of management offices. A stack of work requests – dozens of individual sheets of paper -- was piled on the desk in front of her.

"It wasn't like the room had been torn apart or anything," she told Flynn. "It was that someone had been in the room and had searched it. Things were out of place."

"You called hotel security?" Flynn asked.

Stone shook her head. "It was midnight, I was exhausted from everything that happened yesterday and I had been on my feet for more than eighteen hours. It was creepy but I wasn't up to explaining to anyone. This morning I checked and nothing seemed to be missing, so I let it go."

"There are a lot of people staying at the hotel from the show," Flynn said. "Did any of them talk about their rooms being entered?"

Stone shook her head again. She began sifting through the sheets of paper. "I haven't really talked about it. I only mentioned it to Mel because she was on my case for not getting these requests taken care of. I know that sounds lame…"

"Winona, there's no easy way to ask this question, but I'm trying to solve a murder." As Flynn spoke the words, he saw Stone shift uncomfortably in her chair, her body becoming tense. She knew what was coming. "We know where St. John was Friday afternoon up until about three thirty. Then, he was gone until a little after six. No one saw him. Was he with you?"

Stone's face blanched. She said nothing.

"Winona, it's really important. It's critical…"

"Yes," she whispered.

"How much of that time?"

She shifted in her chair again. "Almost all of it. He left at about six to get changed into his tux. That stupid white tux."

Flynn paused, connecting the timeline in his mind. "Who knew about you and St. John?"

"No one," Stone said. Her answer came too quickly.

"Please think again," Flynn said, his voice soft. "Who – either among the staff or trustees or anyone – knew about you and St. John?"

Stone turned her head and spoke, not to Flynn, but to some spot on the wall in the tiny office. "I never told anyone. St. John said he never told anyone. But a couple of people let me know they knew. Linda. Linda Cooke. I'm pretty sure she knew. Claire Cain. She's the receptionist at Botanical Hall, and it's hard to keep a secret from her about anything that goes on in this place. Sheri Timlinson on the development staff. She used to ignore me but, a few months ago, she started giving me this look like, 'I know something'."

"Any of the trustees?" Flynn asked.

Stone looked back to Flynn. "They never said anything to me. They never leered or winked, if that's what you mean."

"Donors?"

"I didn't really know any of them."

"Do you think Linda or anyone else on staff knew the two of you were together Friday afternoon?"

"No one said anything. After the awards went up, we all agreed we were going to get some rest before the Gala. St. John told everyone he didn't want to be disturbed and left Tony to handle everything. No one called me, and St. John turned his phone off."

"Thank you for your honesty," Flynn said.

"Does anyone have to know?" Stone had a pained look on her face. "Am I going to have to testify or anything?"

"I don't think so," Flynn said. "But it means the person who killed St. John was looking for something and, either he or she searched a lot of rooms or else that person knew you were with St. John Friday afternoon and thought he might have left something there. I'm going to have your room dusted for prints. I'll have some others done as well, including St. John's. I need to know who was in your room, but the world doesn't need to know why."

"Thank you," Stone said, her voice soft. The weariness on her face looked even more pronounced than when he had first started talking with her.

* * * * *

Lee and Flynn were in the Harborside Inn, a dowdy, 1960s-era relic that continued to exist and operate only because the adjoining Expo Center's doors were still open. Too many blocks from downtown to attract business travelers and overshadowed by the newer convention center hotels a mile away, it booked rooms only when the infrequent show came to the Harborfront Exposition Center across the crumbling parking lot. When demand re-emerged for ten acres of land on Boston Harbor beyond the Seaport District, both structures would vanish overnight, and no one would mourn their passing in the name of historic preservation.

Around Lee and Flynn, two crime scene technicians dusted Grainger-Elliot's suite for prints and bagged fibers that might have been left behind when his room was searched. That someone had been in the room was evident. Instead of the gentle search of Winona Stone's room, the person who had been in Grainger-Elliot's suite had not bothered to hide his or her intent. Drawers were open and the contents of two suitcases had been dumped onto one of the beds.

The brazenness of the room search, however, also decreased the probability of finding prints or other evidence. Just as Grainger-Elliot's body had not been hidden, so the person who killed him had made no effort to mask the search of the victim's room. It was likely that this killer had worn gloves.

While technicians looked for physical evidence, Lee and Flynn tried to see the suite through the eyes of Grainger-Elliot's killer. If Grainger-Elliot had told his killer what he or she wanted to know, and if the thing or things sought had been where they was supposed to be, the room would not look like this. If Grainger-Elliot had lied about its location, then whatever was at the bottom of the pile might represent where the killer started looking and would tell them more about the physical size of the object.

"We're looking for five million dollars," Lee said, surveying the two rooms. "Maybe as much as twenty depending on whether St. John was lying or telling the truth to Alice Shelburne."

"And it's probably not a passbook savings account," Flynn added, donning latex gloves.

"Shelburne turned stock over to St. John in December," Lee said. "Instead of depositing the funds with the Society, St. John had it placed in something like the 'Government Center Garden Fund'.

Shelburne will check with her accountants tomorrow and get the correct name. Her accountants were all over St. John because it lacked the proper charitable designation, which means it may have been a dummy account."

"So someone may have been trying to beat an account number or a password out of him Friday evening?" Flynn asked.

"It's the first credible motive I've heard," Lee said. "You don't kill the guy because someone got more ribbons than you, or you are dissatisfied with the way he's running the organization."

"So, what do think we're looking for?" Flynn said as he carefully moved items from one bed to the other.

Lee shook her head. "Anything that links St. John to his murderer. Something St. John told – or didn't tell -- his murderer before he died. Something St. John hid or that someone believes that he hid."

"Here's something to consider," Flynn said, continuing to sift the contents of the bed. "From talking with his widow this morning, St. John knew all about Mel Dawson's report on him, which means he also knew from his mole inside the trustees that he was about to be fired. St. John had the money from pledges for the Government Center project. He may have squirreled away other money or objects that he could convert to cash. So, consider this theory: St. John was getting ready to cut and run. He may have been days or hours from clearing out when he was killed."

"The person who killed him may have known he was about to flee or it may have been a coincidence," Flynn continued. "The person may have wanted their share of what St. John had stolen, or maybe St. John got greedy and tried to take one more bag full of loot. He wouldn't be the first thief to do that."

"I like your thinking," Lee said. "Anything in mind?"

"Perhaps more of those glass flowers or plates from old books," Flynn offered. "Perhaps there were other things of value down in the

Society's archives. Something portable that he could sell later. Maybe he got a check from one more little old lady Friday night."

"It would have had to be Friday during the day…" Lee said.

"…Because otherwise, he would have had whatever it was on him when his killer started working him over." Flynn picked up her line of thought. "Right. Which also explains why the killer went through Winona Stone's room. They figured St. John took something out of the building when he left at three o'clock. But Stone said only three people knew about her and St. John."

Lee gave Flynn an exasperated look. "John, you need to start living in the real world. If Winona was aware of three people who knew her 'secret', then it was common knowledge. It means everyone knew it because gossip about sex is legal tender for women, especially at that age. So, if the little darlings around the Society knew about it, so did the trustees. And, it spreads out in concentric circles from there. Every time Winona sashayed her little tush down the aisles, someone nudged someone else and said, 'there goes St. John's nooner."

"I knew that," Flynn said.

"No, you didn't," Lee said. "For someone who may be the smartest person in the world when it comes to catching bad guys, you don't understand women at all."

"So, did Cynthia Duncastle know her husband was seeing someone?"

Lee thought for a moment. "Patricia Carlton – the woman I talked to last evening – was part of the development staff up until six months ago. She didn't know about Winona although she said St. John hit on just about everyone there. So, the affair is less than six months old. Based on what Carlton said, St. John considered the staff to be far game, so it's unlikely Winona was his first. With Cynthia Duncastle living right next door, it's hard to believe that she didn't know."

Lee continued. "The real question is, did she care? Or, did she accept that her husband — and we still haven't established that she's married to him — is chronically unfaithful. If she didn't care, that's one thing. If she did care, then along with everything else, it's a motive for murder. And, if you're right and he was planning to cut and run, did his plans include her? If they didn't and she had figured it out, it's really a motive for murder."

\* \* \* \* \*

Raymond Brady's home was a small, but meticulously restored colonial in the historic district of Brookfield, a village thirty miles northwest of Boston that appeared unchanged since the Battle of Lexington and Concord, which had taken place less than ten miles away. The home fronted on the village green, or what would have been the village green had it not been covered with two feet of snow. A row of other structures of similar vintage lined the street. The building on one side of Brady's home was a bed and breakfast. To the other side was a smaller home, the first story sign indicating it was an 'Apothecary'.

"What do you buy from an 'apothecary' in the twenty-first century?" Flynn asked as they walked by the building. "Leeches? Eye of newt?"

"Candles," Lee responded. "And potpourri. Everyone needs candles and potpourri, so there will always be apothecaries. Isn't there a fair out here?"

"The Brookfield Fair," Flynn said. "I always had my choice of one fair a year when I was a kid. The three 'fields': Brookfield, Marshfield or Topsfield. I think we came out here three or four times. Good rides, lousy clam fritters."

Brady's house bore a discreet, oval sign on the porch saying, 'Uncommon Antiquities'. He appeared at the door almost immediately when Flynn knocked. Brady was a big man, pushing two hundred fifty pounds and more than six feet in height. His thinning, brown hair was partially and unsuccessfully disguised by a comb-over. Contrasted with the graying eyebrows, the brown hair looked dyed. He wore an ancient, herringbone sports jacket and a narrow black tie. In true country gentleman style, the jacket had patches on the elbows.

The interior of Brady's home was an un-cataloged, eclectic museum, with antiquities stacked in cases floor to ceiling in every room. Roman busts overlooked Louis XVI chairs and Ming vases served as bookends for hand-bound leather tomes. Some items bore price tags, most did not. Brady led them through several rooms to the rear of the building.

In the dark, cramped dining room where they sat, Sevres porcelain pieces filled the table. Incongruously, Lee, Flynn and Brady drank coffee from mugs emblazoned with the logo of the Harvard Coop.

"If I had it to do over again, I would never have met with that ignominious bastard," Brady said. His voice was a cultured New England bass, his pauses between phrases measured. "It was on the grapevine that the Botanical Society was looking for a buyer for a part of the Blaschka Collection. Of course, I was interested. So was every dealer in Europe and North America. I called St. John, we met for drinks at the Taj."

Brady turned and took a small wooden box perhaps six inches on a side from the walnut serving table behind him. He lifted the lid of the box and extracted a white velvet bag nestled in packing foam. He carefully picked off pieces of foam from the bag, then untied the drawstring on the back. He withdrew an object which he set on the table. It was perhaps three inches high, a vividly lifelike and life-sized cutting from an exotic garden. It consisted of a stem, three oblong leaves and a cluster of bright purple flowers. He flattened the velvet bag and placed the piece on it. He gingerly pushed the velvet to a position in front of Lee.

"Look, but please don't touch. This is the work of Leopold and Rudolf Blaschka," Brady said with a hint of reverence in his voice.

"Just don't ask me what plant it is. There's a number on the underside of one of the leaves and it ties to a catalog. The Botanical Society has two thousand of these. The Harvard Botanical Museum in Cambridge has the rest of them – around four thousand pieces though more than half of those are segments rather than complete flowers. Together, they represent the pinnacle of glass as art. Tiffany couldn't do this. Steuben doesn't do this. The art is lost. It took two generations of artists to create six thousand pieces of perfect botanical art and, until now, not a single piece of it is has ever been in private hands."

"It's all at Harvard and the Botanical Society?" Lee asked.

Brady nodded. "The two groups negotiated the exclusive rights on botanical glass through the Blaschkas' U.S. agent. These were done as teaching tools – imagine that for a moment. Leopold Blaschka and his son drew every flower on paper and determined how they would be created in glass. The drawings are at the Corning Museum, and they're marvels all by themselves. The Blaschkas worked with no assistants, year after year in their studio in Dresden. Harvard eventually put the cream of their collection out on display. The New England Botanical Society put theirs in the basement."

"In the fifties, Harvard loaned four pieces to the Corning Museum," Brady continued. "They were destroyed in a flood. It was twenty years before another piece left that museum. In the seventies, a few pieces went to Japan for an exhibition, and several hundred were couriered in a hearse for a display at Steuben in New York. But none of it has ever been sold. That's why it has the mystique."

"St. John contacted you?" Flynn asked.

"I called him and offered my services as an intermediary," Brady said. "A few days after we had those drinks, St. John invited me over to the Castle. It was about seven o'clock in the evening, and he took me down into the basement. He had opened a dozen of these boxes – and these are the original shipping containers from Dresden though the pieces were originally packed in straw. Very theatrical, a tiny spotlight on each one. I thought my heart was going to pop out of my chest. I had seen the couple of hundred Blaschka pieces at Harvard, but they're behind glass. There, I was holding them."

Brady positioned the glass piece to be in front of Flynn.

"St. John proposed that we start with twenty-five pieces of my choosing," Brady said. "He wanted half a million dollars – twenty thousand for each piece. I told him the figure was too high – that he'd be lucky to get half that amount from any dealer. He thanked me and said he'd speak with someone who 'recognized their worth'." Brady smiled. "Two weeks later, he called and said he would like to do business. He apparently didn't get any bites at half a million."

"How did you know he was authorized by the Society to make the sale?" Lee asked.

Brady made a face. "He had letters. Wonderful, authenticating letters from the trustees and lawyers acknowledging that he was acting with the full consent of the Society. I should have asked for copies. Hell, I should have demanded the originals. St. John was very smooth. He let me read the letters, then he put them back into his briefcase. That's the last time I saw them."

"But you had a buyer," Lee prompted.

"We worked out a plan," Brady said, tapping a finger on his temple. "The first twenty-five would be sold through Sotheby's to establish a floor value. Someone, or some small group of people, was going to own one of the rarest pieces of art in the world. Once those were sold, we would release another twenty-five and shoot for a price significantly higher than the first round."

"I heard there was a pre-emptive buyer," Lee said.

Brady nodded. "Sotheby put out the word that the pieces would be in the catalog for the February fine art sale. The buyer was in Dubai – a member of the royal family. I told Sotheby to say half a million plus buyer's premium. The guy didn't flinch. That's the value of the mystique."

"But you were paying only two hundred thousand," Flynn said.

Brady nodded again. "Only for the first group. I knew that from then on, my commission would be ten percent or less. Or, the Society, having established a relationship with the auction house, could also cut me out completely. This was my one opportunity to make a decent return.    Remember also that I was fronting the deal.    St. John demanded a certified check; not a promissory note payable after the sale. And, the sale was three months away. Like a fool, I agreed."

"Who was the check payable to?" Lee asked.

"The Society," Brady said. "All very up and up. I didn't suspect a thing. Well, except that it was fairly obvious that the Society needed the money. Otherwise St. John could have worked a better deal. But then the catalog came out in late December. I was listed by Sotheby's as the seller because I technically owned the pieces, and that was the way St. John wanted it. But you don't keep something like that quiet. I had agreed to not answer any questions – which ought to have set off alarms in my head. Harvard fielded a couple of hundred calls the first day asking if it was part of their collection. They, of course, said 'no' and so the Botanical Society's phone lines lit up.   St. John apparently tried to deny it at first – said it was a private trove and said it publicly, including to a couple of reporters. That façade lasted about half an hour."

"The trustees had no knowledge of the sale," Flynn said.

"Precisely," Brady said, nodding rapidly.    "It caught them completely by surprise. One trustee said exactly that to the *Times*, and then it blew up. The trustees couldn't publicly admit the guy who had the keys to the place was selling off the family silver without their knowledge. They closed ranks and said it was all perfectly fine but, by that time, the damage was done."

"The initial denial was what stuck," Flynn said.

"Right again," Brady said.    "The Dubai prince didn't want something with a dubious provenance on his hands. Sotheby's has been stung by looted art too many times. They sent me a nasty letter by registered mail saying they never wanted to see my face again, and that I was no longer welcome either as a buyer or a seller."

"You tried to return the pieces," Flynn said.

Brady smiled. "You know the story well, Detective. Yes, I tried to return the twenty-five pieces and get my two hundred thousand dollars back. St. John wouldn't take my calls. So, I went to Mel Dawson. She said she'd see what she could do. I think that's when the trustees found out the cupboard was bare. St. John and his small army of recent Seven Sisters graduates had gone through every dime. Payroll. Fund raising expenses. The Society would be broke until the Garden and Flower Show. My lawyers are prepared to garnishee the proceeds of the show to repay me."

"You can't sell these pieces?" Lee asked.

Brady slowly shook his head. His face bore a pained expression. "In a year, perhaps. In two years, certainly. I've already had offers. But the offers have been for less than a hundred thousand for the lot." Brady paused for a moment. "I am a gambler. I am willing to buy your grandmother's antique silver and give you cash because I believe that someone will buy it from me for a fair price. If the market for antique silver is strong, I make a decent profit. If the market collapses – or if, like at present, people spend money very carefully – I sit on your grandmother's silver for as long as it takes."

Brady continued. "But this is also a business that has more than its share of vultures. Everyone knows what I paid for the Blaschka pieces because it's been in every newspaper and art chat room in the civilized world. Vultures know these pieces will sell, and they also know that I don't have two hundred thousand dollars to lend, interest-free, for two or three years. Because of this incident, my reputation has taken a hit from which it may never recover." Brady indicated the contents of the room with his hand. "In the ordinary course of events, the items you see in this house would have sold during the Christmas season. You would see bare walls. Instead, this merchandise is a ticking time bomb because every dime I had is tied up in this inventory, and no one wants to buy from Raymond Brady."

"It would seem that St. John's death helps clear your reputation," Flynn said.

Brady laughed. "I wish you were right, Detective. I'm afraid you're wrong. Now, you've got a double tarnish on these beautiful pieces of glass. It is assumed that St. John died because he tried to sell them. Plus, they have that blemished provenance. Had the Society bought them back from me, all would have been forgiven. Now, it's clear that the Society may be forced to sell its entire collection, which depresses prices. Twenty five of something is extremely rare. Two thousand of the same things are a commodity."

There was silence in the room.

"We'll need to know where you were Friday evening," Lee said.

Brady tilted his head, his finger on his chin. "Certainly not at the Flower Show party. I was at the American Repertory Theater."

"Alone?" Lee asked.

"Alone," Brady said. "But people saw me."

"The theater gets out at – what – eleven o'clock?" Flynn asked.

Brady shrugged. "Yes. I suppose so."

"And what did you do after the theater?" Flynn asked.

"I didn't go to see St. John, if that's what you're suggesting," Brady said. "I came home. I had a drink. A medium tumbler of an inferior Cognac. I went to bed. And I live alone."

"One last question," Lee said. "How is it that St. John picked you to handle the sale of the glass?"

"Reputation, I imagine. It's how anyone chooses a broker or a dealer." Brady's eyes were off to the side, looking at a piece of Chinese jade.

"Mr. Brady, we're in the process of going through St. John's office and his computers," Lee said. "This isn't the time to withhold evidence. Did you offer – or did St. John demand – some kind of a personal inducement to give you such a lucrative deal?"

Brady looked uncomfortable and did not respond.

"St. John looks like the kind of guy who kept meticulous records," Lee said. "If I find something in his notes, it's just going to make me question everything you've told us…"

"Twenty percent," Brady said, his gaze returning to Lee. "St. John wanted me to kick back twenty percent of whatever I earned off of the pieces."

"Sixty thousand dollars," Lee said.

Brady nodded. "In cash."

As they left Brady's house, Flynn said, "I wouldn't have thought of the kickback question."

Lee gave a rueful smile. "That's because your father wasn't a Hong Kong businessman. You don't just hand somebody the right to more than double their money for fronting a transaction. Especially not someone like St. John. He probably shopped around for the highest kickback and chose Brady because he'd play ball."

"So, is he a suspect?" Flynn asked.

They got into Lee's car. "His alibi isn't worth squat," Lee said. "He no longer has a silent partner, so he just saved himself a lot of money. He's right that the glass will be harder to sell at a profit if a lot of it comes on the market at once. But I've never heard of a taint because of a death. If anything, that makes it more glamorous. The glass flowers now have an additional bit of history."

"You saw those little boxes," Flynn said. "Those are about as portable as things get. And, at twenty thousand a pop, they're more compact than cash. If I were Brady, and I suspected St. John was going to cut and run, and was taking along more of those glass figures as a going-away present, I'd want to preserve the value of my own inventory. Like Brady said, 'twenty five of something is extremely rare'. More of them around lower the value."

"He's a suspect," Lee said, starting her car. "Let's both go see Kosinski."

**Chapter 6.**

Jason Alvarez, the grandson of Cuban émigrés and the first person in the family's thousand-year lineage to bear the name 'Jason', sat in the tiny den that he and his wife shared in their Charlestown condo. The room was six feet wide and eight feet long and was just large enough to hold a desk, chair and a pair of filing cabinets topped by a piece of half-inch plywood to create a work surface. The room had been painted a cheerful yellow in an effort to make it appear larger.

The desk, in turn, had two laptop computers sitting side by side, each flanked by stacks of papers and file folders. On the plywood surface behind him were multiple printers and computer accessories. One printer was perched atop a box of paper. An external hard drive crowned a spindle of blank CD-ROM disks.

The pile representing Terri Alvarez's school work anchored the right-hand side of the desk. Notes on students, lesson plans and parent-teacher conference records were each assigned neat, color-coded folders. Until six months ago, Jason Alvarez's left-hand-side stack had consisted entirely of downloaded articles on cystic fibrosis and physician reports on their four-year-old daughter's prognosis.

When he earned his detective's shield, Alvarez had expected a file of pending cases to begin growing on his side of the desk. Instead, a few, slender folders represented his entire workload. What had appeared, instead, was a meticulous set of notes, updated daily or weekly as necessary, documenting the unworthiness of one Vittorio Mazilli to hold the rank of detective. Starting two days after Mazilli had been assigned as his partner, and the older detective had 'ran out to grab a pizza' and not re-appeared for four hours, Alvarez had vented his frustration by chronicling the sloth and ineptitude of the man who was supposed to be his mentor.

There was Mazilli pretending not to hear a call because the rape victim was in a public housing project known for sporadic gunfire. There were frequent robberies that went un-investigated by the pair because the call came within two hours of the end of their midnight-to-eight shift, and Mazilli never, ever worked unpaid overtime. In one folder were Alvarez's three formal written requests for transfer or re-assignment. Mazilli's poor work ethic was never cited. Instead, the reasons given were to be closer to home or a desire to lend his expertise to specific kinds of projects.

Alvarez's specialty, though not recognized by the department, was computers. Had it not been for the fact that his father, grandfather, and great-grandfather had been policemen, Alvarez would be making a multiple of his Boston PD salary analyzing data at any of dozens of companies that coveted such an ability. The skill came naturally, and the pleasure he derived from it was immense. His specialty was database creation and the mining of information from within those databases.

He built databases for fun in his spare time. One, he had built in earnest. It tracked the study of and search for a cure to cystic fibrosis. It daily culled and collated reports of research and treatments and delivered a synopsis of those results to his desktop. And, each day, the results were the same. Scientists actively sought a cure and had identified proteins and genes that advanced or retarded the genetic disease. But the prognosis remained the same. Unless a cure was found, their daughter, Abby, could not look forward to a normal life. Already a serious problem, mucus would accumulate in her lungs at an accelerating rate. By Abby's mid-twenties, either opportunistic disease or the wear and tear on her body would likely kill her.

This afternoon, though, he turned his skills to the computer that had been used by St. John Grainger-Elliot. Getting past the system's passwords and encryption algorithms had been simple. Even data sent through a digital shredder has been resurrected with comparative ease.

What had been disappointing was that this was apparently neither St. John's only computer nor his primary one. Files created on this computer had been transferred to another system on a regular basis, and those files were retrieved and re-assembled by Alvarez. But certain files on this computer were linked to that second computer and the transfer of data was one-way.

That second computer was likely located in the Grainger-Elliot residence. Getting it would require a subpoena, and subpoenas were seldom served on the families of victims of brutal killings. Unless Cynthia Duncastle was prepared to willingly hand the computer over to the Boston PD, large swatches of information about the life and times of St. John Grainger-Elliot would be missing.

Fortunately, the resurrected material on the digitally shredded computer hard drive Alvarez had copied was highly instructive. There was a complete forgery kit with high-resolution copies of law firm stationery, sales invoices, and signatures of dozens of people. Some names, such as those of trustees, he recognized. The meaning of others revealed themselves with a few taps of a touchpad to connect into the database he had created earlier. These were identified as auditors and partners at law firms serving the New England Botanical Society.

A chain of letters stored as high-quality digital images, purportedly dating back more than a hundred years and showing appropriate wear and tear, described and attested to the ownership of rare botanical plates. Thus, at least one of the charges leveled against St. John was true. He had removed plates from the Society's rare book collection and sold them, creating an ownership trail as needed. In the process, according to notes in the files, he had pocketed approximately $75,000.

Another file, also heavily encrypted and password protected, provided the relevant background of Grainger-Elliot.

St. John Grainger-Elliot, née John Spense, had entered the United

States in 2002 and almost immediately began constructing an American identity. There were driver's licenses in various names as well as other forms of identification as Spense moved around the country. By the time he applied for the executive director position at the Atlanta Horticultural Society, he had already been in the United States several years, contrary to his 'official' resume showing him as a recent émigré. His educational credentials and five-year-old letters of recommendation from the Royal Horticultural Society and managing director of Kew Gardens were all there, masterpieces of both forgery and humble appreciation for services rendered.

Another file showed that Cynthia Duncastle has been born Cindy Duncan in St. Paul, Minnesota thirty-four years earlier. Documents included forged British birth and school records, a British passport and European Health Insurance card. Scanned into the computer were also a set of genuine documents, including a GED obtained by Duncan while incarcerated at the Minnesota Correctional Facility in Shakopee and original birth certificates for two of the couple's three children, except that the father listed for Edward and Julia Duncan was one William Kassel. With a liberal use of Photoshop and considerable imagination, Duncastle's education had been upgraded to a fine arts degree from a minor college in London, and their children now showed both proper parentage and original nationality.

The file showed the creation of the couple's current identity approximately two months before he applied for the Atlanta position. How long the two had been together before they presented themselves as a couple was not documented. But the ruse worked beautifully. Here was a family man with an adoring wife and two beautiful children. His background and educational credentials were impeccable.

There was also tantalizing evidence of the ongoing creation of new identities for the family. The main work was being done on a computer elsewhere – presumably in the residence adjoining the

Society's headquarters. Snippets of older documents had been cut and pasted together, then copied off the computer. Texas driver's licenses in the name of Hugh and Anna Simmons has been scanned at varying resolutions. Work on this new identity had started in mid-January, and the most recent transfer was less than a week old. If Grainger-Elliot believed he was about to be unmasked, and if he had amassed or was amassing the funds to flee, then an alternate identity to begin a new life was a requirement.

There was, however, nothing on this computer to show the creation of a 'Government Center Garden Fund' or the transfer of stock or cash to any accounts. If there was a digital record of that activity, it would have to be found in the residence.

Now, knowing Cynthia Duncastle was a full accomplice to her husband's activities, Alvarez began to think of how he might gain access to that second computer.

\* \* \* \* \*

*"If I can come in on Sundays through the ice and snow to do these %$#&~\* favors for you, the least you can do is get your scrawny ass over here so I have a few hours of daylight to myself. LO"*

Medical Examiner Lois Otting's text message detoured Lee and Flynn from their planned appointment with Donald Kosinski to the Boston Medical Center and Otting's autopsy room where the glare of bright lights on white tile was, at first, blinding.

Otting looked up with surprise at the sight of Flynn. "Ye gods, a sight for sore eyes." Then a broad smile came across her face. "The Lone Ranger and Tonto ride again."

Flynn walked over and gave Otting a kiss on the cheek. "Just visiting, he said. "Vicki wanted some weekend backup, I'm still nominally on the job, and I work cheap."

"Well, the place won't be the same without the two of you cluttering up the joint with dead bodies. I'll take my thrills where I can get them." Otting walked the two detectives to the lone, occupied autopsy table.

"I think I can wrap this one up with a bow," she said. "Official cause of death: asphyxiation; means of death: a length of three-eighth-inch nylon cord. I found some fibers imbedded in the neck and the cord you found in the office has enough DNA on it to make a match to the victim, though that will take a few days. No water in the lungs, so he was dead before he was dumped. He took about fifteen kicks to the abdomen which, if he hadn't been strangled, would have likely killed him from internal bleeding in a couple of hours. He had already lost a quart of blood, and his liver, spleen and kidneys were barely recognizable. I think the scientific term for the person who did this is 'one mean bastard'."

Otting pulled Grainger-Elliot's clothing from an evidence bag. "Being in the water didn't help us a lot. There was dirt from the killer's shoe on your boy's shirt and some coarser-grained woody material that I would classify as mulch. However, don't ask me to swear that the mulch was transferred from the shoe. From what I saw of that exhibit floor, the whole damned place is one giant pile of mulch."

"Man or woman?" Flynn asked.

Otting shook her head. "There's nothing here to rule one gender in or out. The person who kicked him did so with his or her right foot. I can't tell you the exact shoe size, but I can say it was a fairly good size one and that the toe was rounded. It was someone strong enough to deliver those kicks. I could have done it if I hated someone enough. But, what I said from yesterday stands: the person who did this knew they were killing someone. This wasn't a beating that went bad. It was a slow, painful death. From the time of that first kick to when he died was about twenty minutes. I would not want to have been in that room."

"Blood alcohol came back negligible," Otting continued. "Couple of drinks in his system. No way he was inebriated. And, the tox screen was negative. When he died, he was capable of giving the perp whatever information the perp wanted."

Otting opened Grainger-Elliot's mouth. "He was gagged in addition to having had his mouth taped at some point. I found some cotton fibers on his tongue. Oh, and by the way, if you had any questions about nationality, these teeth tell you all you need to know." She pointed to his molars. "This is the British National Health at its most pitiful. If you ever lose a tooth or a crown in England, beg to be flown home for the dental work."

Otting looked over the rest of the body and sighed. "What else can I tell you that's helpful? His hands were bound with duct tape. He weighed one-fifty-five. Anyone with reasonable upper arm strength could have dragged him the fifty feet from the office to where you found him."

"So, let's put it all together," Otting said, ticking off points on her fingers. "I can tell you how he died, and I can say that the murderer intended for the victim to suffer. If the prosecution wants to hear that this was an excruciating death, I have no problem testifying to that. However, I have very little to offer you on identifying the perp except that he or she owns rounded shoes. There ain't no smoking gun here. In short, I can sound convincing on the witness stand that the perp deserves life without parole for murder one. But, there's nothing here that helps me to say, 'yes, it was Joe Schmo'. Any questions?"

Lee and Flynn looked at one another. Both shook their heads.

"Then I'll release the body and have a report for you Monday afternoon."

"Not so fast," Lee said. "We need you to take your time on this."

Otting gave an incredulous look. "I'm in here on a Sunday afternoon and now you want me to take my time?"

"Slight change of plans," Flynn said. "Grainger-Elliot's widow told us she wants to fly the body back to England for burial. She's tied into whatever scam he was pulling. There's a better-that-even shot that she's buying a one-way ticket. We need a couple of days."

Otting squinted. "A couple of days or a couple of weeks?"

"A couple of days," Lee said with confidence in her voice. "We just don't want to lose Cynthia Duncastle, and all that's keeping her here is her husband's body."

Otting shook her head. "What I do for you people."

\* \* \* \* \*

Donald Kosinski sat in a La-Z-Boy chair that gave every indication of having been rescued from a curbside trash pickup. It had once been plaid but the red had long since run to a muddled orange and yellow. Brown blotches riddled the arm of the chair and, in several areas, cigarette burns had left scorched fabric. The chair, in turn, was in keeping with the rest of the contents of the apartment.

*Major donor my ass*, Lee thought. The shabby chairs in which she and Flynn sat had once likely belonged to a dining room set. The coffee table in front of them was two wooden planks set on four milk crates. Everything in the room looked to have been found in a dumpster.

Kosinski looked to be in his early twenties, and he was visibly nervous. He wore a pale green sweatshirt that was once a much brighter color and khaki slacks that showed no evidence of ever having had a crease ironed into them. The conversation had barely begun, and beads of sweat were already forming on his brow. He crossed and uncrossed his legs and leaned back in the chair only to immediately re-position it bolt upright. The chair squeaked noisily every time Kosinski moved in it. His eyes continually darted left and right.

"I don't have to talk to you," Kosinski said.

"You were one of the last people to see St. John Grainger-Elliot alive," Lee said, keeping her voice both pleasant and conversational. "You can help us catch the person who murdered him." She smiled as she spoke.

"I don't know anything about it," Kosinski said. His voice was cautious and defensive.

"Well, we usually find that people know more than they think they know," Lee reasoned. "If I may ask, how did you come to be at the preview party?"

"What makes you think I was there?" Kosinski's hands gripped the arms of the recliner.

"Well, you're in quite a number of photographs, including one with St. John Grainger-Elliot taken about one-thirty in the morning." Lee's lie was told smoothly and with a slight tilt of the head as she smiled.

Kosinski looked down at his lap.

"Could you tell us how you happened to be at the party?" Lee asked again.

"My aunt gave me her invitation," Kosinski said. A bead of sweat ran down his sideburn. "She couldn't go."

"Ummm, no, that might have been true of some other event, but your name was on this particular invitation," Lee said. She was almost but not quite apologetic in telling Kosinski she had just caught him in a lie. "Also, it was what the Society calls a 'comp invite'." She shifted her position in the chair to lean forward. "Please, Donald, we have a number of people to see this afternoon. A man was murdered. We don't want the trail to get cold."

Sweat broke down Kosinski's forehead. He wiped it off with a sleeve of his ratty sweatshirt.

"Look," Kosinski said. "I'm just a graduate student. I don't know anything about what happened Friday night. Mr. Grainger-Elliot wanted to hire me to do some consulting for the Botanical Society. He said it would only be for a week or two but that the money would be very good. He said there would be an invitation for this thing waiting for me at the door. He said I should come, get a free meal, enjoy the show and that we could talk."

"What kind of consulting?" Flynn asked.

"Computers," Kosinski said. "I'm at Northeastern. I'm getting my Masters in computer science."

"How did he find you?" Flynn asked.

Kosinski shrugged. "I'm registered with the placement office as being available for consulting projects. I've also got a website."

"And what kind of consulting project was it going to be?" Flynn asked.

"We never had time to talk except a few minutes as the party was winding down," Kosinski said. His eyes darted left and right again. "I never found out."

Flynn and Lee looked at one another. *Lie.*

"You get one more chance to answer the question," Flynn said. "St. John Grainger-Elliot, the head of the New England Botanical Society, wanted to hire you for a short-term consulting project. What was the project?"

"I told him I couldn't do it," Kosinski said. Sweat was now running down both sideburns and into his eyebrows.

Annoyed, Flynn started to rise from his chair. "You need to let someone know you're going to be tied up for the next couple of days," Flynn said. "Get your coat and let's go."

"He wanted me to hack into a computer system," Kosinski said quickly. Sweat was pouring off him now, and he furiously wiped at it with the arm of his sweatshirt. "The Botanical Society's. He wanted me to nuke the thing."

"Nuke the thing?" Flynn said, returning to his chair.

"Mess it up so badly that it would have to be re-built from scratch."

"When did he want you to do that?"

"This weekend," Kosinski said. "He said he wanted them to walk in on Monday morning and find every file folder was empty."

"How much was he going to pay you?"

"Five thousand," Kosinski said, his voice dropping to a whisper. "In cash, as soon as it was done."

"So you started bright and early Saturday morning?" Flynn asked.

Kosinski looked surprised. "No. I heard that the dude was dead. But I was never going to do it. I told him he needed to find someone else, that I didn't do illegal stuff."

Another look passed between Lee and Flynn. Another lie.

"Am I in trouble?" Kosinski said. "I didn't do anything."

"Grainger-Elliot gave you administrative pass codes?" Lee asked.

Kosinski started to nod. Then he stopped. "No. He didn't give me anything. I told him I wasn't interested."

"Let's see, the guy was dead and, just a few minutes earlier, he had tried to hire you to crash his employer's computer system." Lee asked. "And it never occurred to you that this might be something the police would want to hear?"

"I didn't want to get involved," Kosinski said. "I didn't do anything wrong."

As they left the apartment, Flynn said, "St. John knows he's going to get fired the next morning. Is this a going-away present to the trustees, or is it the digital equivalent of arson to cover up another crime?"

"Arson, I think," Lee said. "You don't spend five thousand of your own money just to spite someone. You use it to cover your tracks."

Flynn listened to Lee's comments and added, "What makes you think planned to pay Kosinski? When that bill came due, he was planning to be long gone."

* * * * *

Alvarez, Lee and Flynn compared notes over coffee at a restaurant adjacent to the precinct.

"It isn't like we don't have enough suspects," Alvarez said. "Or enough motives."

Flynn winced at Alvarez's words. "Jason, quantity isn't everything it's cracked up to be. I think we can say with some degree of certainty that St. John was getting ready to fly the coop. We also now know that he felt compelled to hide whatever trail of evidence he was leaving behind, and that there is something – or several things – in the Botanical Society's computers that he didn't want discovered."

"Inventories," Lee offered. "I'm certain that the Society has everything in its basement catalogued on its computers. Destroy the data and they'll never know what he took with him."

"All the Society's finances," Alvarez added. "What's really in the accounts? What about the endowments? There's always a backup file somewhere, but the restore point may be weeks or months old, especially in a non-profit."

Alvarez fiddled with his spoon, looking at the table instead of his companions. "I want to get at the computer inside the townhouse. I have some ways…"

"If they're not perfectly legal, forget it." Lee said. "I don't want some defense attorney screaming, 'tainted fruit' at every judge in the courthouse."

"Hear him out, Lieutenant," Flynn said.

Alvarez gave Flynn a look of thanks. "Assuming Cynthia Duncastle goes online, we can plant a Trojan Horse on her computer. Unless she has some incredibly sophisticated security software on that computer, she'll never know we're there. I can transfer the contents of that computer onto one of ours in a single session."

"It's illegal search," Lee said.

"What if we have a search warrant?" Alvarez said.

"A search warrant for the computer files of the widow of the freshly deceased head of one of Boston's most revered institutions?" Lee asked. "Every judge I know would call it 'blaming the victim'."

"What if a third party – like this Kosinski guy – planted the Trojan Horse and then we seized…"

"Forget it," Lee said. "This isn't television. We have real Massachusetts judges who look for every opportunity to buff up their

ACLU credentials by sticking it to detectives who step over the line. We have ample cause – and permission -- to go through the Society's computers based on Kosinski's statement that St. John wanted to hire him to – what did he call it? 'Nuke the system'. If what we find on those computers gives us probable cause to go next door, then fine. But let's don't undercut our case. And, we're still looking for a killer. We're still looking for motive."

Lee drained the last of her coffee and looked at her watch. It was nearly three o'clock. "Alvarez, you're the expert," she said. "Call Mel Dawson. Get her IT guy over to the Society this afternoon and get complete access to the system. Don't assume you know what you're looking for. I'm going to bring the brass up to speed on what we're doing, and I'll catch up to you later."

"I'm headed back to the show," Flynn said. "I think the crime scene has more to tell us."

## Chapter 7.

Liz Phillips packed the last clipboard into a plastic bin and looked around the judges' room with a combination of satisfaction and unease. Her work, at least as far as the Northeast Garden and Flower Show was concerned, was done. Fifty containers filled with supplies were ready to be taken away and stored at Botanical Hall until next year's show.

She had been given this volunteer job – Judges Chair for Landscapes – three years earlier when its previous holder, a Back Bay doyenne, had announced that at age eighty, she was "too old to herd cats" and would henceforth be spending January through March in Florida. Phillips had apprenticed for two years, cataloging the hundreds of judges who polished their professional horticultural credits by agreeing to spend half a day evaluating landscape exhibits.

Phillips initially had thought her own role as second-in-command would be to match judges with specialties – rhododendron experts with rhododendron awards. That turned out to be the easy part. The infinitely more difficult aspect of her internship was getting to know personalities. Judge 'A' could never be on the same panel as 'Judge N' because of some long-running feud. 'Judge G' was a bully who would tolerate no dissent from his opinion. Judge 'O' was incapable of reaching a conclusion in the allotted three hours.

Each judging panel comprised three individuals. Two were horticultural or botanical experts. The third was what her mentor had called, 'the Pigeon'. 'Pigeons' were current or prospective Botanical Society donors who were *thrilled* to be asked to judge in such august company. And, immediately following judging in the two previous years, St. John Grainger-Elliot had descended like a bird of prey, collecting checks and pledges from well-heeled matrons who felt as though they had actually had an equal say in the awarding of the Frobisher Trophy for Outstanding Use of Succulents in a Landscape of Under 1,000 Square Feet.

Phillips had been surprised Friday morning when the Society's executive director made only a quick, token appearance at breakfast. A year earlier, he had devoted forty-five minutes to charming little old ladies; flattering them for possessing wonderful design judgment and encouraging them to use their skills wisely.

She was completely baffled when Grainger-Elliot did not appear at the judges' luncheon. This was where the "pigeons were cooing" in her mentor's acerbic phrasing. Two years earlier, Phillips had watched as a Marblehead woman wrote a check for $10,000 to the Society, all because she had been assigned to a panel with Kevin Doyle, a particularly charismatic landscape designer. It was very much unlike St. John to miss an opportunity to stroke prospective donors.

Not that St. John had any idea of who she was, or suspected she could have written such a check. To the Boston Botanical Society's executive director, all volunteers were functionally invisible. If they weren't smart enough to demand compensation for their labor, St. John likely reasoned, they weren't worth paying attention to or getting to know. Phillips had sat through four flower show committee meetings at Botanical Hall in the preceding months. Based upon the look on his face when she said 'hello' to him, Phillips was certain St. John had no idea who she was or what role she played.

Now, she wondered what assistance she could offer to Lieutenant Lee. *"You understand how this place works, and I frankly don't trust a lot of what I'm being told,"* Lee had said. *No,* Phillips thought to herself. *I know how landscape judging works. And I know exactly three staff members at Botanical Hall.*

Since yesterday, she had racked her brain for clues. Had anything out of the ordinary happened on Friday? Not really. When Phillips first arrived she had walked the landscape exhibits, making certain all identifying signage was covered. She had paused to admire some of the exhibits, especially those of Blue Hills Gardens and Sunrise Gardens. Oscar McQueen always created a stunning entry. The bridge over the pond would be a crowd-pleaser and would also sway judges' opinions toward his exhibit because of its unique design value. She had paid special attention to the clutch of small speckled shrubs, *weigela* 'Seurat' that had never been displayed at any flower show.

Stuart Wells' Sunrise Gardens display was also a knockout with its meandering stream and waterfall. She remembered his exhibits from earlier years; smaller and less ambitious. Now, he was stepping into the big leagues. At both exhibits – indeed, at all of the larger exhibits – dozens of employees or volunteers still touched up kickboards or groomed plants. The blue daylilies, *Hemerocallis* 'Carolina Blue' according to the Sunrise Gardens signage, had her entranced, and she had mentally attempted to calculate what it would cost to have a dozen in her own garden.

It was odd that Wells had chosen to pull them before judging, but it was hardly an unprecedented decision by an exhibitor. They looked fine to Phillips at 6:30, but Wells or the grower who supplied them may have deemed the display too small or the flowers insufficiently open. It all came down to what the judges would see later that morning. 'Peak of horticultural perfection' was the judging criteria; not what it would look like two days hence. For hybridizers exhibiting new plants at one of the major flower shows, the goal was to walk away with an award, not just merely be seen.

At 6:45, Phillips and two clerks had swept through the landscapes, warning that any exhibitor still on the floor would be disqualified. Oscar McQueen had shouted out to his crew, "finish what you're doing and pick up your tools." Other exhibitors had grumbled. Stuart Wells had looked at his watch, winced, and given her a pleading look, silently asking for more time. She had shook her head, no.

At seven, her head clerk had reported all exhibitors were out of the hall. A few minutes later, the first judges had begun appearing in the building. From that moment until the awards were posted in mid-afternoon, her day was a blur of competing demands. Ten out-of-town judges called to say their flights had been cancelled; forcing Phillips to re-configure panels. Clerks came back with blank comment pages while others were indecipherable. Panels could not find plant material in exhibits or, in one case, were mistakenly evaluating the plant material on a demonstration stage.

And, when the awards were tallied, it was obvious there would be an unending chain of complaints. Blue Hills Gardens had garnered the bulk of the major awards, and Phillips' attempts to subtly call judges' attention to the merits of other displays went unheeded. Linda Cooke had come to the judges room as part of her rounds, taken a look at the results, and said, to no one in particular, "I am going to be paying for this for the next six months."

Phillips left as soon as the last award was posted – fifteen minutes before exhibitors were allowed back in the hall – and went to her hotel room to change and rest. Over the next few hours, exhibitors had vented their anger on Cooke and Tony Wilson. At the Gala, she had paid scant attention to St. John, and St. John had made no effort to single her out. It was further evidence – not that any was needed – that the executive director had no inkling of what Phillips had done for the Society during the past three months. By ten o'clock, the day's exhaustion had taken its toll and she went home.

It all added up to being a bystander to a crime to which she had no connection. Why was St. John's body found in Oscar McQueen's exhibit? She had no idea. Who would have wanted to kill him? She drew a blank.

\* \* \* \* \*

Flynn sat in the office where the killing had taken place, absorbing the surroundings. Over the course of an hour, Flynn methodically reviewed everything he knew about the case and the circumstances of

Grainger-Elliot's death. He read his notes from his interviews with principals, Lois Otting's autopsy observations, and his doubts about whether Cynthia Duncastle grieved for the loss of her husband.

Now, he assessed the scene of the crime. *We have no way of knowing if Grainger-Elliot came here willingly and, therefore, had known his killer, or was overpowered and dragged here,* he thought. *But the killer knew that this area would be empty Friday evening and that this particular room commanded a view of the exhibit floor. Moreover, the killer or the killer's accomplice had taped open the emergency exit to facilitate ease of entry.*

Access to and knowledge of the room in which he now sat was a critical factor. A finite subset of people would have known of the existence of this area, how to gain to access, and been comfortable that twenty minutes would go by without discovery while he or she sought information from Grainger-Elliot, he thought.

Which led back to the Botanical Society staff. That group knew the facility the best and was aware that, after midnight, anyone could walk in and have the place to themselves – as evidenced by the panties found in the room nearby.

Both Alvarez and Alice Shelburne thought Linda Cooke should be high on the list of suspects. Flynn was not so certain. It was a brutal beating followed by strangulation. Brutality is primarily a male province.

*Even if Cooke had a male accomplice to administer the beating, she would have needed to be in the room if, as Vicki believes, the beating was intended to obtain information. It takes a special kind of personality to watch that kind of a beating,* Flynn thought. *Unless Cooke is one hell of an actress, I can't visualize that she would have witnessed that level of carnage and not shown it the next day. Also, if the beating was not to obtain information and was just a sadistic murder, then Cooke's accomplice would have needed an exceptionally strong motivation – passion or greed chief among them.*

Flynn had arrested hundreds of women for felony crimes, including more than a dozen for murder. But the brutality of this particular killing was matched by a requirement of physical strength. It would have been easy to simply leave Grainger-Elliot here and wait for his body to be discovered in the morning. Whoever did this took a risk and deliberately dragged the body into the exhibit hall and dumped it into the pond of Blue Hills Gardens' exhibit. Granted, the hour in the water may have washed away some potentially useful evidence, but very few killers think that far ahead.

*The body is sending someone a message,* Flynn thought. *The killer wanted to make a point. We just don't yet understand that point or to whom it was being made.*

He considered another staff member – one he had not yet met – Tony Wilson. Vicki had quickly ruled him out, calling him a 'nice guy' who was more upset about the murder than some of the other staff members. But Wilson had the strength, knew this facility and, for all Flynn knew, may have passionately hated Grainger-Elliot.

*Get to know Tony Wilson,* Flynn wrote in his notebook.

Wilson – or, for that matter, anyone on the Botanical Society staff – would certainly have known about the Expo Center's lack of security. But taping open an emergency exit would be a calculated risk for someone at the Gala. The person who did it had to be absolutely certain, first, that no alarm would be set off when the door was opened and, second, that guards would not check the doors regularly. The only way someone would know the doors were not alarmed would be if that person had seen other people open and close them…."

A thought forming in Flynn's mind: *The killer didn't even have to be at the Gala – provided he or she had entry to the building earlier. The killer could have entered at midnight or later, kept watch through the office's windows for the crowd to thin, and made an approach to Grainger-Elliot, all without being seen.*

He closed his eyes, imagining the scenario. It worked provided the killer already knew the door alarms had been disabled by the building owners and had taped open the door some time earlier in the day, or had an accomplice to relay that information.

Which re-opened the suspect pool to a wider group, including Raymond Brady or Cynthia Duncastle. For Brady, revenge was an ample motive. Duncastle may well have heard her husband complain about the building's lack of security. Flynn did not yet see much of a motive on Duncastle's part but, then, her life was one of deception.

*Someone at the Gala could also have taped open the door, left with the crowd, and then come back in with an accomplice as the party was ending*, Flynn thought. *Oscar McQueen is a braggart. He thinks he's better than everyone around him, and that's the kind of mindset that can lead to murder. McQueen also has a couple of incidences of violence in his past. There was also Stuart Wells. According to Vicki, beneath a pleasant exterior he is an angry man and, on Friday, much of that anger was directed at Grainger-Elliot. Vicki said Wells was hiding something. I guess one of my assignments is to figure out what he's hiding. Secrets are the root of motives.*

In his notebook, Flynn wrote, *Get to know Wells. Why was he angry?*

Flynn tapped his notebook. *Trustees.* Both Mel Dawson and Duncastle said one or more trustees had motive. Dawson said the Botanical Society – meaning its trustees – would go through a protracted public humiliation if Grainger-Elliot declined to go quietly. And, someone among the trustees violated the Society's ethics by feeding information back to St. John. That person had more to lose than anyone else among the group when his or her identity was discovered.

*Find the mole*, he wrote in his notebook.

Finally, there were the mysterious donors that Duncastle says were lined up to fund the Garden at Government Center. Flynn mentally ruled out Alice Shelburne. She believed in Grainger-Elliot. She says she was told there were several other multi-million-dollar donations either received or in the wings. In all likelihood, Grainger-Elliot intended to pocket that money as he made his escape.

*Find the other donors*, he wrote.

This morning, sitting at the donut shop table with Lee and

Alvarez, Flynn had heard only a jumble of unorganized facts. Now, he finally had a sense of the players and their motives. It did not make the investigation easier or simpler; all it did was to provide a road map. In theory, there would now be fewer dead ends or blind alleys.

* * * * *

Because it was the Sunday before a holiday Monday, Lee had expected to go into a deserted precinct where she could quietly compose an email to the chief of detectives, then follow it with a message left to his voice mail indicating that the status update was on his desk. Instead, she found an urgent message to call Captain Frank Abelson at home.

*So much for peace and quiet*, she thought.

"I'm glad you got Flynn involved," Abelson told Lee after she recounted the progress to date. "The two of you were quite a team."

"Speaking of teams," Lee said, "you've got to get Alvarez a new partner and a way to make use of his computer skills. This guy does stuff with databases I've never seen from anyone in the department."

"Let me work on that one," Abelson said. "In the meantime, get me more progress. I'm counting on you. Otherwise, the media are going to eat us alive on this thing."

The takeaway from the call was simple: solve the murder quickly with the resources you have and, if the sky falls in, you'll be blamed. At least she didn't need to write a progress report.

Lee looked at her watch. It was three o'clock. This was the afternoon Matt had set aside to get together with some old Carnegie-Mellon buddies at a *dim sum* restaurant in Chinatown. She had been to one of those luncheons a month or so after they first started seeing one another. It had stretched to three hours and consisted of equal parts economic one-upmanship and reminisces about keg parties and girls. Though sitting next to Matt, she had been treated as though she were invisible, her transparency extending to Matt's waxing nostalgic about multiple dorm room assignations.

Calling him would be an intrusion. She decided, instead, to leave a text message. She composed, *'How's it going? Find anything worth buying yesterday? Say 'hi' to the guys for me.'*

To her surprise, she received a reply almost instantly.

*'Busy. Later.'*

It was only two words, but her heart sank.

\* \* \* \* \*

The New England Botanical Society's head of information technology was a severe looking sixty-two-year-old woman named Lucretia Clarey. She was incensed at being called out on a Sunday afternoon but had acceded to Mary Ellen Dawson's personal appeal.

"I never liked him." It was said as a blunt statement to Alvarez by Clarey as she logged into the Society's administrative system. "I can say that now. It isn't good to speak ill of the dead, but he was sneaky. I wasn't allowed to touch his computer. He insisted on knowing everyone's passwords yet he never gave me his. I would come here in the morning, look at the log-in records, and see that he had spent his evenings looking at everyone's email and files. What he was doing may have been legal, but it was certainly not ethical. In an organization built on trust, rules of ethics trump the rule of law."

"He read everyone's email?" Alvarez asked, making certain he had heard correctly.

Clarey nodded. "He'd log onto the system with their password and dive right into the email accounts."

"Did he look for anything in particular?"

Clarey drummed her fingers on her desk for a few moments. "Let's see." She tapped keys and called up Grainger-Elliot's account.

"You said you didn't know his passwords," Alvarez said.

Clarey wrinkled her nose. "I said I wasn't allowed to touch his computer, and he never gave me any of his passwords. I didn't say I didn't take the trouble to learn them. He was sneaky, so I was sneaky right back." There was a look of satisfaction on her face.

Clarey pressed an 'enter' key and a screen of data appeared. "These are the emails he opened in the past thirty days," she said.

She scrolled through two hundred emails with Alvarez watching over her shoulder. Some were on the subject of fund raising; verification of interest on the part of a prospective donor. Grainger-Elliot, apparently, did not trust his staff to report the outcome of all contacts. Others were clearly personal messages sent by people on the development staff to friends outside the Society. One carried the header, *'ick factor'* and was dated three weeks earlier.

"May I see this one?" Alvarez asked.

"She's not here anymore so it doesn't much matter," Clarey said.

Two paragraphs into a rambling email to a friend with an 'slc.edu' address came this passage:

*SJ is on the prowl again. At least 3 of us got individual invites for a 'private 1-on-1 dinner' to discuss 'long term Society goals'. Accompanied by leers, of course. I guess Winona isn't fresh enough meat anymore. The worst part is that wifey comes around to look us over, dropping in for little 'chats' to see how we're doing and probably make certain we're ok for birth control and STD prevention. The ick factor is pretty high right now.*

"She quit two weeks ago," Clarey said. "She's in some bank's training program. I expect she's happier there."

"In terms of morale, are all the people in 'donor development' like this one?" Alvarez asked, indicating the email.

"They come in bright-eyed and full of confidence," Clarey said. "Six months later, they're not so sure. Some of them work very hard. Others just go through the motions until they find something else. St. John didn't fire any of them, though. He'd wait for them to leave on their own."

*To avoid lawsuits and motions for discovery*, Alvarez thought.

"I went through his computer this morning," Alvarez said. "I found a Botanical Society email account but it was all very straightforward. Did he have a second account?"

"Aren't you the clever one," Clarey said. "Yes, and he also had his own computer which he kept in his briefcase except when he wanted to use it. He was very careful never to log in through our network. He tapped into the Wi-Fi connection from his house next door for that computer."

"You didn't happen to get a password for that network, did you?"

Clarey smiled ruefully. "It wasn't for lack of trying."

For the next two hours, Alvarez copied off files of the Society's finances. He printed off current financial statements and found them cursory, at best. The most recent audited report was three years old. The accounting manager's computer contained detailed histories of the Society's multiple endowments and restrictions placed on the use of those funds. These, Alvarez both downloaded and printed off.

Clarey was still in her office, reading a book, when Alvarez finished. "I didn't find an inventory of the contents of the Society archives," Alvarez said. "Am I looking in the wrong place?"

"It isn't computerized," Clarey said. "It's a ledger. And, until all that business with the books started, there was just the one ledger. After that brouhaha, I sent it out to be scanned." She typed at her own computer for a moment, then inserted a blank disk into a slot. A minute later, she put the disk into a jewel case and handed it to Alvarez. "Your very own copy."

"Where's the original?" Alvarez asked.

"St. John kept it in the house next door," Clarey said. "For security."

"What would happen if your computer system crashed?"

"Well, there are copies on several computers here…"

"No, I mean, what would happen if someone managed to corrupt the entire network – trash every file?"

Clarey paused for a moment. "We'd have to go to the system backup."

"How long ago did you scan that ledger?"

"In early December," she said. "Less than three months ago."

"When did you last back up the full system?"

Clarey did not answer immediately. She tapped at her keyboard. "November 10. A little more than three months ago. But no one could ever corrupt this entire network. No one could be that malicious."

"Mrs. Clarey, I strongly suggest you take the rest of the afternoon and back up the system, then take home a copy on whatever you use for a storage medium."

* * * * *

Lee returned to the Harborfront Expo Center. On a Sunday afternoon the parking lots were filled to capacity, and it took Lee showing her police ID to get into the parking lot. Even the handicapped spaces were filled, and she was reduced to parking in a fire lane.

Inside, the crowd was far more dense than on Saturday, with movement difficult. Lee made her way to the Show Office where Linda Cooke gave quick commands to a group of young men and women wearing Garden and Flower Show aprons. When Cooke saw Lee, her face visibly fell.

"I don't need this right now," Cooke said, giving Lee an annoyed look.

"I don't need it either," Lee said. "Give me five quality minutes."

Cooke rolled her eyes, then motioned to her office. Inside, she closed the door. Even with the door shut, Lee could still hear the buzz of people outside.

"How close were you to St. John in the fund raising area?" Lee asked.

Cooke shook her head vigorously. "I had nothing to do with it. I run this show. I do other events at Botanical Hall. That doesn't leave me time to get involved with fund raising."

"There was a ticket for the opening party Friday night left for a guy named Donald Kosinski. You told Detective Alvarez he was a prospective large contributor."

Cooke closed her eyes and pressed her fingers to her temples. "He was on St. John's list. The list was big-ticket contributors he wanted to pull out the stops for. Private tours, somebody from development at their side all evening. That sort of thing."

"How many names were on that list?"

Cooke began looking on her desktop, pushing aside pieces of paper and folders. "Fifteen names, maybe. I thought I still had the list…"

"Was it handwritten or computer generated?"

"It was printed off. St. John's handwriting was terrible." She continued to look, opening drawers. "Here it is." She handed the list to Lee.

Lee scanned the page. Kosinski's name was in the middle. The list was in alphabetical order. "Did all these people show up?"

"Did they show up?" Cooke repeated, drumming her fingers on the desk. "I really don't know. Winona might. Shall I page her?"

"Not necessary," Lee said. "Look at the list – is there anyone on it that St. John talked about with any frequency?"

Cooke took back the list and read through it. "Alice Shelburne, of course. St. John said he was very excited about her interest." She looked at the list more closely and shook her head. "Clark and Julia Fowler are names he mentioned. The rest of these are just names, and I'm reasonably certain I've never met either of the Fowlers."

Lee pulled her cell phone from her pocket and tapped in a number. "Jason? Lieutenant Lee. Do you have that chart of people from Friday night? Can you check what you have for 'Clark and Julia Fowler'? Uh, huh." Lee listened for a few moments as Alvarez read her information. "Let's you and I go see them this afternoon." Lee disconnected the call, and Cooke looked at her expectantly.

"The Fowlers were here, or at least their name tags were picked up, but they left before midnight," Lee said. "He runs… well, he runs one of the big college endowments. The way those guys get paid, he definitely could be a donor."

"What about Donald Kosinski?" Cooke asked.

Lee shook her head. "Just a prospective contractor."

* * * * *

A hundred feet away, Flynn stood by the emergency exit that had been taped open on Friday night. Black temporary curtains on steel poles hid the door from scrutiny by anyone inside the exhibit hall. On Friday evening, the person who disabled the door could have come and gone as he or she pleased.

Once inside, it was a fifteen foot walk behind those curtains to the Show Office. Flynn knew from the security guard that the offices had been left open throughout the evening and were locked only when Linda Cooke, the last Botanical Society employee in the building, left after 2:00 a.m.

*The murderer could have come to the party, taped open the door, and left with the crowd,* Flynn thought. *Sometime after midnight, the murderer returned, went into the management area and watched until the crowd thinned. When he or she saw Grainger-Elliot alone or near the Show Office at 1:45, that person made an appearance just long enough to entice Grainger-Elliot into the area. Grainger-Elliot was held there until Cooke left, then beaten, killed and dragged out to the exhibit area after the night watchman made his 2:30 a.m. round. The killer then left through the emergency exit.*

The theory made sense. The office was not one being used by the Botanical Society staff. No one would have had reason to go into that particular office. The view of the exhibit area was ideal.

*The killer had to know all this in advance,* Flynn thought. *He or she brought rope, duct tape and gloves. They knew the layout of the management offices and had pre-selected the perfect one.*

Flynn left the office where the killing had taken place and found Winona Stone.

"During the week the exhibits were being put together," Flynn asked, "did St. John have visitors here in the building?"

"A fair number," Stone said. "It's considered quite a treat to be able to watch what we call 'the build'. All of the landscape exhibits go up at once. On Thursday there were probably two hundred people working on displays with trees and shrubs coming in enclosed trucks. St. John used it as a selling tool. He was talking about charging admission next year – twenty dollars to watch the build for two hours."

"So, major contributors came through here last week," Flynn said.

"I'm not sure who they all were. I imagine some of them were contributors. I saw several of the trustees."

"Do you remember which ones?"

Stone paused, thinking. "Mr. Zimmer – Bob Zimmer. Richard Durant. They were both here on Thursday. Ellen Slater. She was here."

*Robert Zimmer and Richard Durant had also been two of the last people to be seen with Grainger-Elliot*, Flynn though.

"Lieutenant Lee told me Zimmer is a man in his seventies," Flynn said. "What about Durant?"

"He's like you," Stone said. "Fifties. A bit on the chunky side, though. He's a big developer."

*Right*, Flynn thought. *With a couple of hundred empty condos at a project in Lexington.*

"But he was here on Thursday," Flynn said.

Stone nodded. "A couple of days before that, too. He and St. John went to lunch on, like, Monday or Tuesday."

*The mole?* Flynn thought.

"I need an address and a telephone number for him," Flynn said. As she wrote the address, Flynn asked, "Your boss -- Linda. I heard she showed up Saturday morning dressed – well, not looking as though she had been dragged out of bed in the middle of the night like everyone else."

Stone looked up, recalling the moment. "Afterward, she was so embarrassed. And more than a little miffed at the police."

"What do you mean?"

"Linda is really self-conscious about her appearance." Stone lowered her voice and looked to make certain no one was within hearing distance. "She's fifty-one but she gets facials and Botox and has a million creams. Even liposuction – twice. And it works. Everyone thinks she's thirty-five or forty. But she won't go out *anywhere* unless her face is done and she's dressed just right. She was the one who called us, but we all got here twenty minutes ahead of her because she had to do her hair and face. She said she had expected to be doing television interviews about St. John's death, and she was a little put out when Lieutenant Lee said no one could give interviews except for that police PR woman. By the time the PR woman said it was OK, the camera trucks had all left. Linda was really mad."

"Is she married?"

Stone shook her head. "Divorced."

"In a relationship?" Flynn saw the confused look on Stone's face. "The interest is purely professional. I have to get background on all of the principals."

Stone nodded slowly. "There's this one guy she sees. A real body-builder type. He's a lot younger than her. I think it's why she's so conscientious about her appearance."

Flynn thanked Stone and went back into the room where the murder had been committed. One red flag raised by Alvarez had been addressed. Some women did not go out into public unless every hair was in place. Linda Cooke was one of those women. Fine. But now there was a new flag: a younger boyfriend, 'a real body-builder type'. Steroids produced rages. Rages produced beatings like the one Grainger-Elliot had endured.

Flynn pushed the thought to the back of his mind. He looked at the suburban address he had been given and headed for his car.

\* \* \* \* \*

The Residences at the Mandarin Oriental rose a dozen floors above Boylston Street at the edge of the Back Bay neighborhood. For those who lived in Back Bay, the oversized, imposing bulk of the new building offered one undeniable benefit. However otherwise unwelcome, it blocked the view of the monstrous Prudential Tower.

The tenth floor residence of Clark and Julia Fowler, however, inexplicably included a bank of windows in the living room that faced onto the universally hated office building. The room itself was impeccably furnished with antiques and art.

"Camille Pissarro," Lee said, standing in front of one painting. "I've never seen one outside a museum."

"A lucky find," said Clark Fowler. "My wife loves the Impressionists. I believe you had some questions about St. John Grainger-Elliot."

Fowler was perhaps forty, perhaps younger. He was lean and full of kinetic energy, standing rather than sitting and rising onto his toes every few seconds. He wore a pale yellow cashmere sweater and tan wool slacks, his hands in his pockets. Tortoiseshell glasses complemented the ensemble.

Lee turned and tried her best smile. "You're aware he was killed sometime early Saturday morning."

Fowler nodded and rose on his toes again. On his feet were perfectly polished wingtips. Beneath the wingtips, an exquisite Oriental rug. "I read the articles, yes."

"You were at the Botanical Society's Gala Friday evening," Lee phrased it as s statement.

"My wife and I were both there, yes." Each answer was clipped and perfunctory, as though giving a deposition.

"Grainger-Elliot had approached you about a contribution for his Garden at Government Center." Again, Lee phrased it as a statement.

Fowler's feet stayed level. "Yes."

"May I ask the status of those discussions?"

"We hadn't committed to anything." There was caution in Fowler's voice. The hands went deeper into his pockets, limiting his ability to make any telling gestures.

"But those talks were well advanced," Lee said.

"I don't know what gave you that idea," Fowler said. "I requested a list of other donors and amounts and the right to contact them. That's not the same as giving money. I requested that list three weeks ago. St. John never supplied it."

"Did he say why not?" Alvarez asked the question.

"He said he needed their approval – it was a matter of confidentiality. I could understand that, but three weeks seemed odd given that the list should have been half a dozen people, most of whom I probably know anyway."

"Did he say how many names were on his list or just imply that it was half a dozen?"

Fowler's hands squirmed in his pockets. "He used the phrase, 'a handful'. Julia and I would be 'one of a handful of people' with naming rights to parts of the garden."

Alvarez asked, "Was there any discussion of how those funds would be collected?"

Fowler nodded rapidly. "He wanted to keep the funds segregated until the announcement. To make sure everything went to the garden. Yes, he spoke of that. But I hadn't committed to anything. Not until I saw his list."

"You asked him about it Friday evening?"

"He said I'd see it on Monday." Fowler smiled for the first time in the meeting. "I guess that deadline is by the boards, too."

＊ ＊ ＊ ＊ ＊

"What do you think?" Alvarez asked as they rode down the silent, oak-paneled elevator.

"That St. John was pushing for every dime he could get into his special account," Lee replied. "That he was planning to fly the coop Saturday or Sunday with everything he could lay his hands on. He got money out of Alice Shelburne and maybe one or two other people. But his other marks were people like Fowler who demanded to know who else was contributing and then would have had accountants get tax ID paperwork before transferring a dime. I think he was up against smart – or at least cautious – people."

Alvarez nodded agreement. "So, with the axe getting ready to fall, he was going to vaporize the Society's computer system, cover his tracks, and be gone long before the start of business Monday morning."

"But somebody murdered him first," Lee said.

"Somebody murdered him first," Alvarez repeated.

\* \* \* \* \*

The driveway was a quarter mile long, winding through a thick stand of rhododendron and mountain laurel under a canopy of hundred-year-old pines. One side of the driveway was a dry-stone retaining wall that probably took a crew of half a dozen men two months to build.

The gray colonial house at the end of the driveway stretched eighty feet with a flanking four-car garage meant to look like a carriage house. Flynn rang the doorbell and was rewarded with a snippet of *The Ride of the Valkyries*.

Richard Durant met with Flynn by the home's indoor pool, housed in a massive glass gazebo at the rear of the building. While snow lay more than a foot deep outside, the poolside temperature was eighty degrees, and the humidity was uncomfortably high. Durant, attired in shorts and a green Boston Celtics tee, smoked a cigar. He was a large man in his mid-fifties with an ample belly. A barely visible scar on his thick head of hair made Flynn suspect surgical intervention.

Durant settled his ample body into a lounge chair and, with his hand, indicated a nearby empty chair. "How can I help?"

"You are a trustee of the Botanical Society," Flynn said, choosing to stand.

"For five years now," Durant said, blowing a smoke ring.

"More than any other trustee, you were seen as being close to Grainger-Elliot." Flynn didn't know it for a fact, but it was worth seeing what kind of response he would get.

Durant shrugged. "St. John had his shortcomings. But he also had a vision. I was ready to resign before he showed up. The Society had been doing nothing for half a century."

"Then why did you become a trustee?"

Another smoke ring, followed by a long pause to admire it. "I build high-end housing, Detective Flynn. My homes start at around two mil. I've got a project in Lexington that has taken me six long years to get out of the ground. Now, I could tell you that it's altruism; that it is giving back to the community. And that would be a load of horseshit, and you would know it. I became a trustee to sell houses to other trustees. I bought my way in with a hundred grand contribution. That turned out to be a lousy bet because most of those trustees haven't moved out of the family mausoleums on Beacon Hill or in Back Bay in six generations."

"The real question is why I stayed," Durant continued. "And the reason is that I felt sorry for the sons of bitches. The trustees had managed to run the Botanical Society into the ground. But, they had a franchise. The Garden and Flower Show. They had a beautiful location on Comm. Ave. The world didn't know what kind of sorry shape they were in because they kept reaching into their wallets and pulling out just enough money to keep the place afloat. Plus, they kept their dirty laundry in-house."

Durant tapped some ash into a tray. "St. John was the breath of fresh air the place needed. A dynamo. Somebody who recognized that lighting a fire underneath those fossils was the only way to save the place. Enter the Garden at Government Center. One of the most brilliant ideas to come out of a not-for-profit in the past hundred years. Everybody in Boston hates City Hall. It's consistently ranked as one of the most reviled buildings in the world. People stopped making excuses for those eight acres of brick three decades ago, but it took St. John to come up with the right idea to replace a good chunk of them. He didn't wait for the pols to sign on. He just announced the damned thing and let public sentiment do the rest. The *Herald* did a poll: ninety-two percent of the people *love* the idea and can't wait for the thing to get built."

"Do you think any of the trustees have pledged money for the garden?"

Durant laughed. "That crew? They live off of trust funds. They don't 'dip into principal'. They can write a check for ten thousand to help the Society balance its books, but that's the limit of their largesse. Remember: I tried selling them houses."

"Have you contributed any money toward building the garden?" Flynn asked.

Durant blew another smoke ring while considering his answer. "This house notwithstanding," he said, "my business is built on leverage. Every dime I have is wrapped up in my projects. People like Alice Shelburne can give away millions in stock that didn't cost them squat. I don't have that luxury."

"You knew Mrs. Shelburne was a contributor?"

Durant nodded.

"Grainger-Elliot told her there were several other contributors, some who had pledged even more. Did he tell you who they were?"

Durant shook his head. "St. John told me the same thing, and that he was close on the rest of the funding. He didn't mention any other names."

"You were aware of Mary Ellen Dawson's private investigation," Flynn said.

Durant made a scowling face. "Hell, yes, I was aware of it. I was at the meeting where she read the thing aloud for ten minutes."

"It was fairly damning," Flynn said, keeping the statement mild.

"It was garbage," Durant said, anger creeping into his voice. "I don't have an MBA from Harvard. I didn't go to Yale Law. But I've managed to build a successful business from the ground up."

"But you never claimed those things, did you?" Flynn said.

Durant forcefully ground out his cigar into the ashtray. Sublimating anger, Flynn thought. Durant looked at Flynn. "I'll bet you a hundred bucks you grew up in Dorchester."

"Cushing Avenue," Flynn said. He didn't think the accent was that pronounced.

"Savin Hill," Durant said, pointing at himself. "I cringe at what's happened to the place. I never got a fancy degree. I was never invited to become a member of the right clubs. But I made my money in construction, where nobody gives a damn where you went to school. Pedigree is more important than brains to people like Dawson and her crew. They would never have looked at St. John if he didn't have the right background. So, he invented the background. He was getting the job done."

"You gave St. John a copy of Dawson's report," Flynn said.

Durant didn't answer for perhaps fifteen seconds. He stared at Flynn, then took out another cigar from a box on the table beside him. He rolled it with his fingers next to his ear, listening to the crinkle of the tobacco. Finally, he said, "Yeah. I gave him the report, or at least the synopsis that Mel gave to us trustees. I tried to borrow the full one, but Mel wouldn't let it out of her sight. The bastards were going to just fire him with no warning. I gave him the ammunition to fight back."

"You visited him several times last week while the show was being set up," Flynn said. "You must have talked about strategy."

Durant nodded. "He wasn't worried. He knew the pressure points. He planned to stay or to go on his own terms."

"But somebody killed him first," Flynn said. "Who would be at the top of your list of suspects?"

Durant clipped the end of the cigar and lit it. He took several puffs. "The paper said he was found in a pond at one of the exhibits. Did he drown?"

"The death was violent," Flynn said. "There's no chance that it was an accident." Flynn had no inclination to offer more information to this man.

"You talked to Raymond Brady?" Durant asked.

Flynn nodded.

Durant blew a smoke ring. "I'd give odds that's your guy. He's a real piece of work. He figured he was stealing those glass flowers at the price he was paying, and he was going to turn around and flip them at auction a couple of weeks later with a two hundred percent profit. Nice work if you can get it."

"What's his motive?" Flynn asked. "He owns the pieces. All he has to do is wait out the market." Then, a fishing expedition question: "Is there some information that Grainger-Elliot might have had that Brady wanted?"

Durant smiled. "St. John was no saint. Saints don't succeed in business and, while the brass plate on the entrance says 'Botanical *Society*', St. John understood he was running a business. St. John had some bargaining chips – a whole basement full of bargaining chips. If I were Brady, I would have been very worried about what St. John was going to do with those other flowers. Those things are like houses. Their price is measured by their cachet and their scarcity."

"St. John could have flooded the market?" Flynn asked.

Durant leaned back in his chair. "That's why they're called 'bargaining chips'. My guess is that Brady's back was against the wall financially. Desperate men do desperate things."

\* \* \* \* \*

The Dawson home – more properly, a compact estate – occupied a site adjoining 'The Country Club' in Chestnut Hill, so named because it claimed to be the first country club in America and therefore needed no further identification. Simple stone pillars, one bearing the house number, marked the entrance, and a blue stone driveway took Flynn to a large, rambling stone and half-timbered home dating from the 1920s. He rang the doorbell and, somewhat to his surprise, Mary Ellen Dawson opened the door.

"I didn't expect to find you at home," Flynn said. "I just came by for the report."

"My shift is in two parts today," Dawson said, gesturing with her hand that Flynn should come in. "Seven to three and then back at six for another four hours, followed by supervising the gate count." She turned and walked into a formal living room, the walls filled with art. To Flynn's untutored eye, the art looked very good and very old.

"You're taking your responsibility seriously," Flynn said.

"I've got nervous vendors, nervous exhibitors, and a staff that's walking on eggshells," Dawson said. "I can calm the vendors and exhibitors and, thank God, the gate is up nicely this year." She paused, gave a hint of a smile and shook her head. "While it's horrible to say, St. John's murder is the best publicity the show has ever had. We may have had our highest one-day attendance ever today."

She continued walking. "But, as to the staff, no one knows what to expect and, frankly, I don't know what to tell them. It may take weeks just to get through the books." Dawson took a thick, legal-size manila envelope from a table and handed it to Flynn. "If you have a minute, sit with me and tell me where you are in your investigation and what else I can do."

Flynn followed her into a book-filled study, a pair of overstuffed chairs and a tea table the lone furniture in the room. The tea table, with a pie-crust edge, looked like something he had seen appraised for several hundred thousand dollars on *Antiques Roadshow*. Afternoon sunlight poured in through a large window. Dawson sat in one of the chairs and tucked her feet underneath her. She leaned forward and looked at Flynn expectantly.

*How much to tell her?* Flynn thought.

"We think Grainger-Elliot died after someone either beat – or attempted to beat – information out of him," Flynn said, surprising himself because he had just declined to offer this explicit a level of detail to Durant. "To say the beating was savage would be an entirely accurate characterization."

In response, he heard Dawson's sharp, involuntary intake of breath.

"Ultimately, he was strangled with a nylon cord, but not until someone with a lot of strength had worked him over in that office. It was a very painful death."

Dawson looked out the window, her eyes misting. "No one deserves that," she said.

"Grainger-Elliot had information someone wanted," Flynn said. "What kind of information either at that show or around the Botanical Society is worth killing for?"

"St. John controlled the finances," Dawson said, her gaze still fixed on something beyond the window. "Brenda Carr was the nominal financial officer, but she's been there since the seventies, and St. John more or less rolled over her as soon as he got there." Dawson shook her head, a sad look on her face. "We should have replaced her years ago…"

"Detective Alvarez is going over the books," Flynn said. "By now, he has downloaded everything on every computer in the place. If there's something in the numbers, he'll figure it out." Flynn paused. "You also need to know that, based on everything we've found so far, Grainger-Elliot was getting ready to run. And, when he left, he was going to do the computer equivalent of burning down the place. He had hired someone to erase every file on every computer on the Society's network. The only reason it wasn't carried out was that the person who was going to do it heard about the death and figured he wasn't going to get paid."

Dawson's gaze returned to Flynn, this time with a pained expression. "You're certain of that?"

Flynn nodded. "Yes, I'm certain. There's also evidence that he may have collected at least one very large contribution – from Alice Shelburne -- for the Government Center Garden and had it deposited into an account he controlled."

"My God," Dawson said. "I had no idea."

"You found out you hired a con man," Flynn said. "You found out who he was and you forced his hand. He was pulling what is called a 'long con' on the Society. But he died before he could make his getaway. You also should know that the person who killed him broke into his room at the hotel as well as into Winona Stone's room, obviously looking for something. We don't think they found it, or at least they didn't find the specific thing they were looking for."

"Winona was his..." Dawson seemed to struggle for a word. "...Paramour. I've known about it for perhaps a month. From everything I could see, it was consensual. But we shouldn't have permitted it. It would have made sense to search her room given that he spent so much time there."

"Can you think of what someone would expect to find?" Flynn asked.

"An account number?" Dawson suggested, weariness in her voice. "If it was a very large contribution, I would think that would be worth killing for."

"It might explain why he was killed," Flynn said, "but it doesn't provide the reason he was dragged out of the office area and dumped into that pond. Either the person we're dealing with is particularly sick or else something about the pond is important."

"It can't just be to get rid of evidence?"

Flynn grinned. "You assume the killer was thinking ahead. This may have been pre-meditated, but the planning was probably measured in hours, not days or weeks. The person who killed Grainger-Elliot took a risk in dragging the body out into the exhibit area. Otherwise, it was just a walk behind a set of curtains to get out an emergency exit."

Dawson buried her head in her hands. "I feel like I set this all in motion. Commissioning the report. Dragging the trustees into taking action. Setting up the meeting for Saturday…"

Flynn sensed where Dawson was headed. "If you hadn't done those things, Grainger-Elliot would have played out his complete con. My guess is that one day in the next few months, you would have gone to some big press event where he was going to unveil twenty million dollars of funding for the Government Center garden. He'd be fifteen minutes late and then half an hour late. After about two hours, you'd realize that he wasn't going to show; that all the money benefactors had given him was in some personal account wired to an offshore bank, and he was on a plane to someplace beyond the law's reach. He would have drained the Society's accounts – including the endowments – and erased the files. You and the other trustees would be left to explain how it happened."

Dawson closed her eyes and slumped back in her chair. "Yes," she said. "I can see it."

"You did the right thing," Flynn said. "Someone realized Grainger-Elliot was getting ready to skip town. That person may have demanded a share of what he was taking. Grainger-Elliot may have taken something of value from that person – grabbing one last handful of jewelry on the way out of the store after a robbery is not an uncommon instinct among robbers – and the person may have wanted that item back. It may also have been a simple falling out among thieves. Those things happen, too."

"You have suspects?" Dawson asked.

"I have people I've spoken with that I know aren't telling me the truth. Lieutenant Lee, who is twice as smart as I'll ever be, is working the case, and she also has Detective Alvarez, who is also exceptionally bright, helping her. No, I don't yet have a suspect. I have leads. I welcome anything that you remember about Friday that you haven't told me because it may be a lead." Flynn held up the manila envelope, noting its heft. "I'm going to read this front to back this evening. This may have the clue we're looking for or it may point us in a new direction."

As he was leaving, Flynn had one more thought. "The Society owns the townhouse where Grainger-Elliot lived. I understand there was no lease arrangement."

Dawson nodded. "It was vacant and had been so for more than a year when St. John arrived. He asked if his family could use it."

"Lieutenant Lee or I may ask you for a letter authorizing us to enter that building. I think Lieutenant Lee will want to feel out the D.A. first, though."

"I'll have a letter ready for you at the show at seven o'clock tomorrow morning," Dawson said.

Flynn had no doubt but that even with today being Sunday and tomorrow a national holiday, the letter would be ready.

* * * * *

Lee, Alvarez and Flynn re-convened at the Dunkin' Donuts where they had met that morning. At four o'clock, the sun was low in the west and clouds were thickening, a portent of another snowfall. Each person gave a synopsis of what they had learned and what areas they felt needed further investigation.

"I've got an evening's worth of data to go through," Alvarez said, tapping his stack of folders and CD-ROMs. "I warn you that I'm not a forensic accountant. All I can do is look for things that stick out. I'll send around anything of interest tonight. I'm working from the assumption that St. John had his hands in the till and that the question isn't 'whether' but 'how much'."

"Everything comes back to motive," Lee said. "Was it Alice Shelburne's donation the killer was after? Was it something he had pilfered from the Botanical Society archives?" She shook her head. "We probably still don't know all the ways this guy was dirty."

"Or Cynthia Duncastle," Flynn said. "If he was getting ready to cut and run, so was she. She knows where the money is, she knows what else he may have stolen. And, having spoken with her, I'm not ready to rule her out as a suspect."

"There was something in one of the emails I saw at Botanical Hall," Alvarez said. "One of the development staff wrote to a friend about St. John's wife dropping around the Society to check out the young women there and to see if they had protection against sexually transmitted diseases."

"It could be hyperbole," Flynn said. "Or it could be that casual an arrangement. They're both using false identities. Two of the children aren't his. Maybe she wasn't part of his escape plan."

"Cynthia was at the show during the 'build' several times last week," Lee said. "She certainly knows the building and its weaknesses. St. John may even have told her about them."

"Maybe we've got it backward," Alvarez said. "Maybe St. John wasn't part of *her* escape plan."

Lee cocked her head. "Now, that's an interesting thought. Normally, women don't kill their young children's fathers. It's hard-wired into the species. But Cynthia Duncastle is anything but normal."

Flynn turned to Alvarez. "You may be right in wanting to look more closely at Linda Cooke. She has a boy-toy body-builder boyfriend, according to Winona Stone. Steroids and testosterone can be a fatal combination. On the other hand, that dress-for-success look at three in the morning is just the way Cooke is." To both Lee and Alvarez he added, "And we've got Raymond Brady. The one person who we already know benefits from St. John's death."

"But he's also St. John's accomplice," Alvarez offered. "A high-class fence. We know he agreed to kick back part of the sale price of the glass flowers. It's likely he also had a role in selling the botanical prints. He'd know who was buying and how to sell them quietly. Along with anything else that was down in the Society's archives."

Flynn nodded. "But killing St. John cuts off the income stream. St. John was a golden goose."

"Unless, in killing him, Brady got hold of enough things to fund a quiet retirement," Alvarez replied.

"Tomorrow, we bring in Brady for formal questioning," Lee said. "Jason, you're going to go through his finances with a microscope. I know you're not an expert. But, if he's our guy, I want to know it now, not later."

**Chapter 8.**

Lee walked to the Harborfront Expo Center and into the crush of the Northeast Garden and Flower Show. In the vendor halls, she looked at exotic plants and statuary, garden books and little signs offering wisdom such as, 'Chipmunk Crossing' and 'Gardeners know the best dirt'. She watched as people bought seeds and gardening implements, blissfully setting aside the overnight forecast for 'three to six inches of fresh accumulation' and certain knowledge that no seeds could be planted for at least three months.

In Hong Kong, gardens had been for the ultra-wealthy. Even flowers in public parks were admired at a distance from concrete sidewalks. In Vancouver, winter was a brief, wet interlude and flowers grew abundantly nine months of the year. Her family, apartment dwellers all their lives, had no experience with flower gardens. Upon buying their home in the largely Chinese suburb of Richmond, her father had commissioned the construction of a tea house and a koi pond, but it was surrounded by austere, Asian greenery rather than flowers. For Lee, there was simply no connection to flowering plants; no history.

Here, though, in a region where the first frost could come as early as September and nothing reliably flowered until May, thirteen thousand people were preparing for the next 'snow event' by purchasing trowels and gardening gloves.

Guiding Lee was Liz Phillips. For the better part of ten minutes, Phillips had stayed at Lee's side while Lee, in her own words, "got a sense of the show." Finally, Lee spoke. "All these vendors," she said. "Can they all make a living selling garden gadgets?"

Instead of answering immediately, Phillips picked up a red-handled pair of pruners from a vendor's table. "These are called

'Felcos'," she said. "This happens to be a 'Felco #2'. It's the basic tool for the serious gardener. I own three of these. I use my oldest one, which has to be fifteen years old, for grubby work – bushes with sap, that sort of thing. I have another pair for everyday pruning and save my newest one for when the cut has to be perfect. Does that make me a fanatic? Hardly. Felco must make two dozen different pruning shears, and I know people who have a dozen different ones. I have a friend who will use one of her three Felco 100s for pruning roses – and only for roses. She has two Felco #7s for pruning branches in trees and two #4s dedicated to trimming annuals. And that's in addition to a whole collection of #2's for her 'regular' garden work. That's five or six hundred dollars of tools just for pruning. Can these vendors make a living selling things for the garden? Oh, yes."

Lee glanced at the price of the pruners as Phillips replaced them. *'Show Special: $53.50'.*

The two walked a hundred yards to the main exhibit hall, and Phillips guided Lee to the floral displays in the rear of the area. "This is what is called a 'standard flower show'," Phillips said. "'Standard' means it adheres to a very thick manual providing every detail of how the show will be judged and what floral and non-floral material may and may not be included." She indicated four extravagant arrangements, each filled with at least a dozen different kinds of flowers and likely comprising a hundred or more stems.

"These are done in what is called the 'Dutch-Flemish' style. It's one of more than forty recognized styles in flower arranging. There are probably five hundred dollars of flowers in each one of these arrangements and, before entering the competition, you can bet that the designer put this together at least once and maybe twice or three times over the past few weeks to 'get it right'. Each day, the designer is required to come in and freshen up the arrangement so that you and I are seeing it just like the morning it was judged."

Phillips swept her hand across the banks of floral arrangements.

"There are fifty-six arrangements in two divisions and three different entry days. Every one of these designers has a basement full of vases and other containers, frogs, plant stands, dried materials and boxes of Oasis. Everyone who ever took a floral design course has bags of special materials they know they're going to need one day. I have friends who conspicuously leave out the receipts for their clothing purchases so that their husbands know to the penny what they spend on shoes and blouses. Those same women have secret checking accounts their spouses know nothing about – that's the money they use to buy flowers. This is a huge business."

"I'm beginning to understand that," Lee said

The two walked to the VIP lounge, where they sipped tea and Lee spoke. "I'm trying to go back over every detail. You told me that St. John gave a talk to the judges around eight-thirty. Someone else said he was out in the vendor halls until about eleven-thirty. How long did he talk for?"

Phillips answered immediately. "Less than five minutes. It was just a standard 'thank you'. Very perfunctory. He had nothing prepared. Then he was gone."

"And the judges went out right after that?" Lee asked.

"Oh, no. We still had some panels to assemble and rules to go over. I sent a couple of panels – the ones that had to look over every exhibit – at about ten minutes before nine. The rest went out starting at nine."

"And you didn't see St. John again until the Gala?"

Phillips nodded.

"Three hours in the vendor halls," Lee said, more to herself than to Liz. "But no one was allowed in the exhibition space between nine and four?"

Phillips shook her head. "Remember, we kicked out everyone from the exhibit halls at seven in the morning. And, everyone knew if I caught an exhibitor in the hall while the judges were there, I declared that exhibit ineligible for any awards."

"Why couldn't the Botanical Society staff be in the exhibit area all morning?" Lee asked.

"Perception of bias," Phillips replied. "I don't care if the staff cuts through the exhibit area on their way from one place to another, but if judges saw St. John or Linda Cooke hanging around an exhibit, they would conclude that exhibit was of some special merit. The same goes for anyone else on staff."

"What if a tree fell over or one of those retaining walls collapsed?"

"That happened last year," Phillips said. "A wall gave way during the judging. The judges walked around it. It got repaired after the last judging panel came back in. It was ready for the Gala. Four other exhibitors pitched in to help with the work."

Lee nodded. "And what if something isn't blooming or a plant has wilted leaves?"

Phillips poured another cup of tea for both of them. "These exhibitors are here all night on Thursday. They might have a crew of three or four grooming every leaf. I've watched them: they pull out and replace plants right up until the last minute. At seven in the morning, they clear out, they go back to their hotels, and they get the sleep they didn't get the night before."

\* \* \* \* \*

Flynn, too, returned to the Harborfront Expo Center. Like Lee, he attempted to piece together Grainger-Elliot's movements as well as his state of mind. Less than a hundred feet from where Victoria Lee and Liz Phillips talked, Flynn encountered Linda Cooke in the Show Office. She was checking bills against a computerized list.

"Long day," Flynn said.

Cooke looked at her watch. "And only another four hours to go."

"I heard that the staff is very upset."

"We are," Cooke said, pushing the bills to one side. "We also have a show to run. That is, if Mel Dawson doesn't drive us crazy first."

Flynn smiled. "She's the one who told Lieutenant Lee the staff is upset. She's worried about all of you."

"We'll be less upset if she lets us do our job. If you can pass along that message, we'd all appreciate it." Cooke took a drink from a coffee cup. "What can I do for you?"

Flynn found a chair and sat across from Cooke. "I'm trying to get inside St. John's head on the day of the Gala. By now it's no secret that there was a background investigation report floating around…"

Cooke nodded. "His résumé was a phony, and he was using an assumed name. Yeah. We've all heard that."

"Did he seem preoccupied that day?"

Cooke shook her head. "No. Not at all. He was full speed ahead, business as usual. He was psyched. Very excited. Looking forward to the future."

"Nothing that would have indicated he wouldn't be around much longer?"

"Nothing at all. He was working vendors and exhibitors, promising them a big, well-attended show and pressing them to be back next year."

"Take me through his schedule," Flynn said. "I understand you already did this with Detective Alvarez, but I need to hear it for myself."

Cooke took another sip of coffee. She unwrapped an energy bar and took a bite of it while she thought. "St. John and I had breakfast at the hotel at around six. We walked over here, together, before six-thirty."

"What did you talk about?"

"Details," Cooke said. "How many volunteers we had signed up to work the registration booth for the media. Whether the press kits were assembled. That sort of thing. We did a fast walk of the exhibit hall and had a very quick staff meeting."

"How quick?"

"Fifteen minutes. It was more like taking attendance. He made certain we all had our marching orders for the day. Asked if we were all ready. That sort of thing. Then, he and I cleared out the exhibitors. They're not allowed to be in the building once the judges start arriving. The judges aren't supposed to know whose exhibit they're looking at."

"And his mood was still very good?"

"Very bouncy. But that's the kind of person he was. He communicated enthusiasm. We had the last exhibitor out the door by a quarter past seven. He went to his office and did some work. A little before eight-thirty he called everyone together and said he was going to go give his annual pep talk to the judges. He said that, while he was gone, he wanted us to stay together and come up with a list of twenty fresh promotional ideas to boost attendance at the show this year."

"Everyone?"

"St. John believed that everyone had ideas worth listening to. If Tony Wilson had a good idea about how to improve accounting or Brenda Carr had an inspiration about maintenance, St. John would hear them out, then put the two of them together in a room to hash it out. He didn't believe people should be pigeon-holed."

"So, everyone got together and came up with promotional ideas," Flynn said.

"Right. St. John came back about half an hour later, asked if we were done, and said we'd discuss it at the twelve-thirty staff meeting. He warned us that the judges were on the floor and that we shouldn't linger by any specific exhibit until the awards were posted. He said he was going over to the vendor halls to 'chat them up' – his term. I did the same, and we crossed paths two or three times over there."

"His mood was still good?"

"He displayed terrific enthusiasm to the vendors," Cooke said. "He told them that if we didn't hit 125,000 paid admissions, he'd give them free space next year. He said he hoped they had brought in extra merchandise because he hated to see an empty booth with two days left on the show. That sort of thing."

"They believed him?"

"With that kind of salesmanship, they had to. I know he had lunch by himself because I heard him in his office on the phone. We had our staff meeting at half past twelve."

"And you discussed the promotional ideas?"

"Yes. He had read them all. He dismissed a couple as 'routine' but said half a dozen had real promise and assigned people to work on them. By that time, he had switched gears to the Gala and went through the checklist to make certain everything was ready."

"Nothing on his mind from those phone conversations?"

Cooke shook her head. "You never met him. He was one of these people who exude optimism."

*Like all good con artists*, Flynn thought.

"And, after the meeting?"

"More calls. I know he and Tony had a meeting with the union rep. Later on, he was back with the vendors. It was a little awkward because we had to stay out of the exhibit areas, and I think we were all anxious to get started on the mechanics of the Gala. I saw St. John briefly a couple of times around noon and during the early afternoon. He was meeting with people in his office."

"Anyone you recognized?"

"Just his wife, Cynthia, because she stopped to say 'hello' and wish us good luck on the Gala and apologized that she wouldn't be here. At about three o'clock, St. John told us the ribbons were going up in a few minutes. We all went out and watched that happen."

"With Blue Hills Gardens getting most of the ribbons," Flynn said. "How did St. John react to that?"

"He just said Oscar had put a lot of work into his exhibit. Then, he looked at his watch and said it was going to be a long night and he was going back to the hotel to rest up. I didn't see him again until a little after six." She hesitated, then added, "I understand from talking with people that he wasn't alone..."

Flynn nodded. "I spoke with Winona Stone. I take it that was fairly common knowledge among the staff."

"We had all figured it out a couple of months ago. It was Winona's business. It didn't affect how St. John worked with the rest of us."

"Do you think trustees and exhibitors knew?" Flynn asked.

Cooke nodded. "Trustees, almost certainly. I had one come right out and ask me more than a month ago, and she's one of the least involved people in the Society. Exhibitors? Why not? We did a number of planning meetings with them, and they'd see St. John and Winona together. They've also watched the two of them together for the past week while we did the build. They weren't obvious, but it didn't take a genius."

"So, when the killer searched St. John's room at the hotel, it didn't take any magical insight to know that they should also search Miss Stone's room."

Cooke gave a slight smile. "When you put it that way. Anyway, St. John was back here a little after six, all dressed up in that god-awful white tux. He went through the Gala arrangements, and then went into his 'meet and greet' mode."

"No change in demeanor?"

"Still just as 'up' as he had been all day. He was really looking forward to the Gala."

"I heard that some of the exhibitors were very unhappy about the awards," Flynn said.

"I think Tony had soothed most of those people before the party. I heard St. John make nice to several exhibitors, including some who got nothing but a Society ribbon."

"As the evening progressed, did you notice anything else about St.

John?"

"My job was to make certain everyone on staff was doing their job. St. John gave me a 'thumbs up' once or twice during the evening. There were a lot of people in the building. I wish I could say I kept closer tabs on him."

"The party started thinning out at about one in the morning, though," Flynn said.

"And I told Detective Alvarez who I saw him with toward the end of the evening. The very last person I can remember being with him was Donald Kosinski. He was on St. John's comp list as a prospective large donor. I had never met him before, and I only know it was him because I looked at the name badge after they talked. That was around one-thirty. I didn't see St. John after that, and I assumed he had left the party."

"You were the last person to leave?"

Cooke nodded again. "I supervised the clean-up, saw the caterers out the door, and went back to the hotel and crashed. That was about a quarter to two. The building management people called me about three-fifteen."

Flynn paused before continuing. Up to now the questions had been easy. Now, they were about to get difficult. "A couple of people have mentioned your boyfriend to me."

He saw Cooke visibly stiffen in her chair. "Who mentioned him?" she replied, wariness in her voice.

Flynn shook his head. "Several people and it isn't important who. They describe him as very athletic looking; someone who works out a lot..."

"What does he have to do with this?" Cooke interjected sharply. "He wasn't at the Gala. He's been here maybe twice all week." Her voice rose; defensive.

"May I know his name?"

"No. He has nothing to do with this."

"Please, Ms. Cooke. He's been described as 'a real bodybuilder type'. I need to eliminate him as a suspect."

"And I'm telling you he wasn't here!" Cooke slammed her hand on the desk. "Leave him out of it."

Cooke's response was irrational, Flynn thought. Most people would quickly provide the name. "So I'm going to be forced to ask everyone his name until they tell me…"

"Jean Claude wasn't here, dammit!" Cooke said. "I know where he was, and I know he wasn't here. Please leave him out of it."

*Well, at least I have a first name,* Flynn thought. "How do you know with such certainty?"

Cooke closed her eyes and exhaled. In that moment, Flynn saw the youthful mask with its creams and injections fall away. For an instant, there was the face of a woman in her early fifties, with all the experience and heartache that came with half a century of life.

"Because while I was here, working my ass off and cleaning up the glasses and plates after the party, he was off in the South End, screwing some twenty-year-old."

\* \* \* \* \*

Jason Alvarez massaged the back of his neck with his hands. It was after midnight, and he had been in front of his computer for more than five hours. His wife, Terri, had long since gone to bed. In front of him, stacks of printouts and folders were arranged across the desk.

On the computer screen were the digitized images of the ledger that itemized the contents of the storage rooms of the New England Botanical Society. The earliest entries in the handwritten ledger were from the 1880s. There were listings for seeds gathered on expeditions to South America and original plant drawings from African journeys.

In the 1920s, the Blaschka Collection began arriving. Each flower has been tagged with a tiny, almost invisible number written in gold ink. In the journal, that number became a description, *'#0213 - Malus domestica, representing April flowering, stem plus two emergent leaves'.* The handwriting was careful and never hurried. Alvarez imagined each batch of flowers arriving and the librarian, or whomever was charged with maintaining the ledger, carefully matching numbers to descriptions provided by Leopold or Rudolf Blaschka. The earliest entry date was September 1921. The latest was October 1935. For fourteen years, the glass flowers had been delivered at regular intervals, each batch of roughly twenty flowers diligently catalogued.

The storage room abounded in rare books. An entry from 1901: *Pierre-Antoine Poiteau and Joseph Antoine Risso, 'Historie Naturelle des Orangers' Paris 1818. 5 1/2 inches by 9 inches, app. 250 pages containing many hand-colored engravings. Gift of Mrs. George Dowling. Acknowledged April 29, 1901.*

Was the book even still in the basement? Did it still contain 'approximately 250 pages' and were the engravings still intact? The Society held thousands of such objects. For a thief with keys to the storage rooms, it was a dream.

A few items fairly jumped off the page. A 1913 expedition to 'French Equatorial Africa on the upper branch of the Ogowai River' had brought back not only seeds and leaves encased in waxed paper, but also 'app. 20 native artifacts including wooden animal representations' which had been summarily handed over to the Society by one J.W. Rippington, who had been sent an appropriate thank-you letter on December 2 of that year.

The commercial value of the seeds and preserved plant materials was likely slender. But, if the 'Ogowai' was the Ogooué River and the 'upper branch' was the Ivindo, then genuine, nineteenth century African animal carvings from Gabon – beautiful wooden creations handed down across generations intended to ensure a successful hunt -- could be worth tens of thousands each. An old *National Geographic* in the barber shop frequented by Alvarez had carried an article on the subject, emphasizing the scarcity and rising value of such carvings to collectors and museums.

The place was an incipient trove for a museum. Or, for someone with sophisticated tastes and no moral compunction, a gold mine.

Grainger-Elliot's nocturnal email reading had careened between the prurient and the gossipy. He had apparently used an email filter looking for the word 'sex' in any outgoing message and had been rewarded with a fairly detailed and sometimes graphic chronicle of the love lives of several staff members.

His second interest, though, was of his employees' opinion of him. Some of those messages were scathing – along the lines of, 'I met with him this afternoon, and all he did was stare at my chest while I talked'. But others were more hopeful. 'St. John is sweet and attentive,' wrote one. Another likely botched her chances for career advancement by noting that, 'St. John reminds me of my father'. The woman's email account was closed a few weeks after the message was sent.

Alvarez tried to focus on finances. Had Grainger-Elliot succeeded in hiring someone to wipe clean the computers of the New England Botanical Society, it might have been interpreted as an act of mercy on the income statements of the Society and its several endowment accounts.

Checks were written but recorded only after they cleared. Checks marked 'destroyed' in the Society's check ledger had a habit of being cashed. And, checks made out to 'cash' were routine and on the rise in terms of amounts. Reconciliation of checks to departmental accounts or to budgets was done, at best, quarterly. In some cases, checks dating back a year or more were still categorized as 'miscellaneous – to be determined'. There were digitized images of checks, but the handwriting of the person who had signed the check was invariably an illegible scrawl. Alvarez noted the banks involved. As to an audit, there was no sign of one ongoing or preparation for one.

There were deposits. Membership renewals were added to the

account regularly. The two hundred thousand from the sale of the glass flowers was there. And, as the Society's attorneys said in their letters to Raymond Brady's attorneys, the money had already been spent to meet payroll obligations. But there was no sign of a large deposit representing Alice Shelburne's contribution toward the Garden at Government Center. It was not in the main account. It was not in some segregated, tagged sub-account. It simply did not exist, nor was there any indication that any other patron had made a contribution to the project.

The endowments were relatively modest. J.W. Rippington, the man who had given the Society the African animal carvings, had left a trust that was now worth a few hundred thousand dollars and earned roughly two percent interest per year. The Cicely Applegate Endowment had briefly topped half a million dollars but its holdings were in low-yielding Treasurys. It earned the Society a few thousand dollars each year in dividends.

The lone, successful endowment was the Joseph and Mary Pitt Charitable Trust, which totaled $1.8 million. The fund was professionally managed by a Boston firm with the Society limited to two actions: to receive the steady stream of dividends and interest generated by the trust, and to borrow against the principal of the trust for 'appropriate cash flow purposes'.

For the two previous years, the Society had borrowed the better part of half a million dollars in the three months leading up to the Garden and Flower Show. The amounts had been promptly repaid from gate receipts and the ten percent of vendor sales collected by the Society. This year, the borrowings from the trust were six hundred thousand dollars. The funds had been disbursed months earlier, starting in September rather than November. Check notations, always exact in prior years, were now hazy references to 'food deposits' or 'Gala expense'. The signatures on the checks were illegible scrawls.

Part of the problem might be the Society's accountant. Brenda

Carr, according to the personnel file, was seventy and had been with the group since 1970. She possessed no degree in finance and held no certifications. She was also in increasingly frail health, taking forty or more sick days in the preceding twelve months.

The perfect accountant to be manipulated by a professional thief, Alvarez noted. St. John had left her in place.

But the larger issue was a lack of oversight. There were no financial controls. The books were unaudited and probably un-auditable because of the absence of supporting records. It was as though everyone in a family had a credit card, and no one was expected to produce receipts for their charges. Financial ruin was the inevitable, foreseeable result.

With the clock on the computer nearing one o'clock on the morning, Alvarez typed up his notes into an email and appended a few telling documents.

*It is clear,* he wrote, *that anyone with a mind to do so can steal the New England Botanical Society blind, and may already have done so. It isn't so much that the books are a mess than that they are non-existent. Though I will investigate further, I cannot tell who has written checks or taken money. It might be St. John. It might be any other employee who understands just how poor the recordkeeping is.*

*There is no account for the Garden at Government Center. There is no Alice Shelburne deposit. There are no contributions earmarked for the project from anyone else.*

*What I can say is that, as of three weeks ago, the New England Botanical Society had roughly two thousand dollars in its checking account and had borrowed heavily against its endowments. Last year's Garden and Flower Show brought in $550,000 over expenses. Based on the borrowings to date on this year's show, it will, at best, break even.*

*In short, the Society is bankrupt. It just isn't official yet.*

# Chapter 9.
# Monday

Lee awakened at 5 a.m. with a lengthy mental list of things to do. How early could she approach the Suffolk County District Attorney's office for an opinion about searching the Society's townhouse? How early could she bring in Raymond Brady for questioning?

Packaged waffles warmed in a toaster as she read through Alvarez's synopsis of the Society's finances. It confirmed what they already suspected about Grainger-Elliot, but it offered no new clues as to who had killed him.

They needed to get into the basement with an archivist to match the contents of the ledger to the objects that should be in the Society's possession. The discrepancies could point to the size of Grainger-Elliot's theft and possibly provide a stronger link to Brady. As she read reports and constructed her team's to-do list for the day, the list on the yellow legal pad beside her lengthened to two, and then to three, pages.

On the coffee table in front of her were three law books and a stack of Xeroxed cases. Her criminal law class met Tuesday evening, and she had hoped to use the time on the train to and from New York to catch up on her reading. Instead, she had been thrown into a murder investigation. She sighed, wondering when she would find the time to do the assignments and familiarize herself with the case laws.

There were also her parents to call. She dreaded making that one. *When are you coming to see us? Why haven't you written? What's happening with that nice boy you're seeing?*

That nice boy. There was no call from Matt. Not even a message. Just those two cryptic words: *Busy. Later.* No, they weren't at all cryptic. They were a flashing neon sign that said, *It's over. He doesn't give a damn. He can't even be bothered to tear himself away from his friends long enough to call you and ask if anything's wrong. You've wasted six months of your life.'*

She could have called him. But the thought of him looking at his phone, seeing her name, and letting the call go to voice mail was more than she could bear. If it was going to end, it was better to let the relationship die of natural causes. She was busy, he was busy. Wrong time, wrong person. At least it was only six months.

*Am I destined to be a stereotype: the too-smart, too-career-minded, not-pretty-enough and therefore un-marriageable professional woman, Chinese edition?* she thought. *Did I choose this career path to make certain I would be alone for the rest of my life?* Then she pushed the questions out of her head. She picked up her three-page list of things to do in the investigation and began adding additional avenues of investigation.

* * * * *

John Flynn was also awake at 5 a.m. For him, the morning rituals were governed by a need for speed. Shower, shave, and eat, all with an eye to the clock. His goal was to be out of the house before 6:15. It was not traffic that was his concern, though that was what he told others in explaining his perpetual early arrival. It was Annie.

Annie's overnight shift ended at six, and it was only a five-mile drive from the Longwood Medical Center to their house in Roslindale. While she generally lingered after her shift to talk with co-workers, there was no guarantee that she would not leave work immediately. He preferred to be gone when she arrived home.

He did not try to explain his home life to anyone. He doubted anyone would understand it, much less sympathize. He had been married for the better part of four decades and, while he lived under the same roof as Annie, he saw her infrequently. It was a choice each of them had made; a pattern that had evolved because of events that had transpired long ago. Now, it was irreversible. A cascade of history that led to an unspoken, mutual decision codified by silence and practice. They lived separate lives and communicated, when they communicated at all, by notes on the refrigerator. *At my sisters for the weekend. Took care of gas bill. Siding by garage door is peeling.*

It was why his 'retirement', which ought to have been finalized weeks earlier, was still 'pending' while he 'cleaned up case files'. As a senior detective for the Boston Police Department, his long hours and weekend work was expected and went unremarked upon by all except his partner. When Vicki Lee had been promoted to lieutenant after working with him for five years, he agonized over the decision but felt it was time to move on. Breaking in a new partner after Vicki would be too mentally and emotionally taxing.

But moving on involved filling those days when Annie might be home. From six-thirty in the morning until eight-thirty at night on weekdays and all weekend, he had to be somewhere. That 'somewhere' was not his home. He did not yet know where that 'somewhere' would be, but there was no chance in hell that it would be at home.

There were options. Every suburb around Boston had its own police department. Every police department had a detective. They pay was lousy but it was on top of a generous police pension. He was keeping his ear to the ground for openings.

The call from Vicki had been unexpected but welcome. The case was interesting. More important, it was challenging. Instead of being the kind of senseless, motive-free killing that was solved only when someone got mad enough at someone else to turn them in, it was a crime that would require both intuition and shoe leather to crack.

He liked working with Alvarez. The kid was bright, and the computer skills he brought were the kind that police work increasingly demanded. Alvarez had made detective just about the time he retired. If only he had known…

The clock read 6:20. Time to get moving.

\* \* \* \* \*

Jason Alvarez silently ate a bowl of cereal as coffee dripped through a filter. His laptop was in front of him, open and trolling for information. He carefully set each machine – computer and coffee maker -- to perform its task without beeping or clicking. Upstairs, Terri was finally sleeping soundly after a rough night with their daughter. The worsening symptoms of cystic fibrosis weren't supposed to come for as long as a decade, but Abby's lungs, never strong, seemed to fill with fluids on a schedule no specialist had been able to explain.

They had talked quietly as they worked the high frequency chest compression vest that allowed Abby to cough up mucus. Terri, the circles under her eyes dark from lack of sleep, stressed that she understood the demands being placed on him and that, because this was a school vacation week, he could devote the hours needed to the case. Alvarez, in turn, promised that when the case was solved he would take off as many days as were needed so that Terri could have recuperative time to herself.

It was a partnership, they agreed. They had to sacrifice now to give science time to find a solution. The alternative was never discussed.

Alvarez also reflected on working with John Flynn and Lieutenant Lee. Flynn was the partner Alvarez had hoped to get when he earned his shield. He was the antithesis of Vito Mazilli, always looking for the next, hidden clue and never being satisfied with statements offered by witnesses. Lieutenant Lee was a dynamo, continually forming and testing conclusions. He realized with something of a surprise that he and the lieutenant were likely the same age. Lee seemed infinitely more experienced.

That Flynn had mentored Lieutenant Lee was well known around the department, yet Flynn treated her with the deference you were expected to show to a superior officer, referring to her as 'lieutenant' in his presence even though they had worked as partners for five years.

It was no wonder he was retiring. How could you top being the person who shaped the career of the youngest woman lieutenant in Boston PD history?

His computer blinked an incoming alert. Alvarez put down his spoon and peered at the screen. He kept dozens of key words and tags related to work, friends, and his daughter's illness, but a feed at this hour of the morning was very unusual. It came from Boston.com, a website that was a continuously updating version of the Boston *Globe*. Alvarez tapped the screen, activating the feed.

*BROOKFIELD – Brookfield police are investigating an early-morning shooting death on Old Concord Road. The body of an as-yet unidentified man was found following reports of multiple gunshots at approximately 4 a.m. The address is that of Brookfield antiques dealer Raymond Brady, though police will not confirm that it was Brady's body that was found. Further details are pending.*

**Chapter 10.**

"Four shots with a .22. The shooter went for the chest and figured that if he or she fired enough bullets, they'd eventually hit something vital."

Brookfield Police Detective Martin Hoffman, solidly built, roughly fifty years old and with a full head of black, curly hair, lifted Brady's hand with its manicured nails. "No defensive wounds so we can be reasonably sure he wasn't expecting it. We can also be fairly certain about the time of death. The first 911 call was at 3:51 from the folks at the bed and breakfast next door. We found the open door at 4:02, and the blood was already coagulating. Brady likely bled out in about five minutes."

Lee, Alvarez and Flynn looked on; only Alvarez made notes.

Hoffman noted their downcast look. "You liked this guy for the murder of the head of the Botanical Society, right?"

Flynn nodded. "We were going to bring him in this morning."

"And your guy was popped at about two in the morning?"

Flynn nodded again.

"Then our shooter – assuming one person did both Brady and your guy – has a day job and the ability to come and go during the witching hour," Hoffman said. "He – or she – is no marksman. Brady was plugged with the first three bullets at a distance of ten feet, and the shooter didn't get the heart or even the two bullets within six inches of one another. The neighbors heard three shots then a fourth after five or ten seconds. I have to figure that the last one was to make certain he wasn't going to identify anyone."

Hoffman looked at Lee. "Your guy was drowned?"

Lee shook her head. "Bound and gagged, kicked hard in the midsection fifteen or more times, then strangled with a rope. His body was dumped in an artificial pond. We theorize the killer wanted information."

It was Hoffman's turn to nod. "With forty-eight hours between killings, I'd say your perp didn't get what he wanted the first time and figured out Brady was the likely answer. Do you know what he was looking for?"

"We can't be certain," Lee replied. "What we know is that Grainger-Elliot was dirty. He was looting the Botanical Society." She indicated Brady with her chin. "This guy was his accomplice in moving botanical prints Grainger-Elliot stole from the society, and was the go-between in selling a collection of glass flowers."

"You may want to make certain those glass flowers are still here," Flynn added. "Twenty-five small wooden boxes, six inches on a side. When we came to see him yesterday, they were in the dining room. He showed us one of them."

Hoffman beckoned over a uniformed policeman and asked Flynn to repeat the description. The policeman disappeared into the back of the house.

Lee knelt down next to Brady's body. "Robe and pajamas," she said. "He wasn't expecting his killer. It definitely wasn't a meeting." She looked up at Hoffman. "You're pulling phone records?"

Hoffman nodded. "We already did. Nothing incoming to the home phone since seven last evening; nothing to the cell phone since mid-afternoon. The last two outgoing calls were to the U.K. I'll get you a complete list. It's interesting that this guy made lots of calls but received very few in return."

Flynn looked around the area, a look of confusion on his face. "Shouldn't the state police be here?"

Hoffman grinned. "Presidents Day," he said. "We called them as soon as we found the body. That was four hours ago. They'll get here eventually but, until they do, I actually get to do some real police work."

"You've done homicides?" Flynn asked.

"Twenty-five years on the job in Cambridge," Hoffman said. "I had my share."

For the fifteen minutes, the four talked, exchanging notes. Neighbors heard no car; only the gunshots. The overnight snow had ended as a slushy rain, leaving no footprints or tire tracks. The confrontation had taken place in Brady's front parlor and there was no struggle.

"Try this theory, Flynn said. "Brady is awakened by someone ringing his doorbell. He comes downstairs to find someone he knows. It's late, certainly, but the person visiting is sufficiently well known to him that Brady invites him – or her – in. The visitor wants information – information Brady either doesn't have or won't give. The visitor produces the gun. Brady either gives up the information or doesn't have it. Brady, of course, has now put together the fact that his visitor is Grainger-Elliot's killer. The visitor's parting gesture is to shoot Brady, silencing a witness."

Alvarez, silent through much of the conversation, jumped in an alternative version. "Brady is awakened by the doorbell and opens the door to find someone he either doesn't know or barely knows waving a gun at him. Brady has no choice but to let him in. The visitor assumes Brady has the information he wants but intends to kill Brady even if he gets it. The important thing, to us, is that the killer concluded that Brady had possession of whatever thing St. John was killed for."

Flynn shook his head. "People don't open their doors for strangers at four in the morning. They look through a window and, if they see someone waving a gun, they retreat to somewhere safe and call 911. Brady had to know the person at the door, even if that person was unexpected." The admonition was delivered quietly; a correction rather than a put-down.

Lee listened to the exchange. It mirrored dozens of incidences in their early years together when she had leaped to a wrong conclusion, and Flynn had spoken in the same, patient way. "St. John didn't have what the killer wanted or wouldn't provide the information," she said. "It wasn't in St. John's or Winona Stone's hotel room. The killer is still looking for it."

"The 'it' is something physical," Hoffman interjected. "Just listening to these scenarios, your killer wasn't after an account number or anything like intellectual property. We're talking a safe deposit box key or something that would go into that box – cash, or something portable and very valuable. It's something your St. John guy was expected either to have had on him or have had ready access to, like in a bag in his room."

"Fresh perspective," Flynn said, a tone of admiration in his voice.

They were interrupted by the uniformed policeman carrying in a handful of small wooden boxes. "These are what you were looking for?" the policeman asked Hoffman.

Hoffman indicated Lee. "Show it to the experts. I feel like I've walked into a scene from *The Maltese Falcon*."

Lee took one of the boxes and removed the velvet bag. Inside it was a glass flower.

"Say hello to twenty thousand bucks," she said to Hoffman. To the policeman, Lee said, "You should find twenty-five of them. Any fewer and the killer may have taken some as a souvenir."

Hoffman held the flower. "Pretty thing. Definitely worth killing for. Except that Brady's killer didn't snap them up when he or she had the chance."

"So much for the theory that the Blaschka Collection was a bargaining chip," Flynn said.

"The Blass...?" Hoffman started to say.

"*Maltese Falcon* talk," Flynn said. "The glass flowers. Thousands of them."

"You big city guys lead interesting lives," Hoffman said.

\* \* \* \* \*

They reconvened at a noisy sandwich shop a block from the Harborfront Expo Center.

"I read Mel Dawson's report on St. John," Flynn said. "It's overkill, but it confirms what we're already learned. The really interesting parts are about Cynthia Duncastle, and the material is buried back in the appendix. The investigators apparently prepared it as an afterthought because they were being paid to get information on St. John, not her. I suspect Dawson never got around to reading that part of the report – I think she told me it was 'too depressing' – and it's not part of the synopsis that was handed out at the trustee's meeting. So, neither St. John nor Cynthia knew that her cover was blown."

"What does it say that we don't already know?" Lee asked.

"Sorry," Flynn said. "The report says she is as much a work of fiction as St. John. Just as Alvarez found in his computer search, her real name is Cindy Duncan and, under that name, she was pulling scams at the ripe old age of fifteen. Her mentor was William Kassel who, as Alvarez also found, is the father of her two older children. He was five years older than Cynthia, which would make him forty now."

"They grifted their way through the upper Midwest, conning gullible people out of money, mostly in ten-thousand-dollar chunks," Flynn continued. "She and Kassel were arrested when they upped the ante and walked out of a Minneapolis jewelry store with about three hundred thousand in engagement rings. Apparently, in Minneapolis, it isn't unusual for a fetching young couple to want to see a diamond ring out in the sunlight. Jewelers draw the line when you snatch a dozen rings with big stones while the sales clerk's attention is diverted. For that one, she got five years in the state's women's prison. Kassel got fifteen years – there were lots of outstanding warrants – but he managed to walk away from a work detail last year and hasn't been seen since."

"Don't rule out Cindy getting back together with Kassel," Lee said. "Shared parenthood is a powerful pull. I'll bet a tall latte that they've kept in touch."

"Noted," Flynn said. "When Cynthia got out of prison – she served two years – she held down a job just long enough to get custody of her children back from her parents. Then she was off. The detectives found a string of scams run by a woman answering her description, frequently with two adorable children in tow. She didn't get rich, but she paid the bills – or rather, skipped out on the bills. She's smart, and she learned how to fly under the radar of the feds."

"Then, about five and a half years ago, she acquired a new partner," Flynn said. "Six months later she was Cynthia Duncastle with an educated British accent and a degree in fine arts from the Guildhall School. And, of course, John Spense became St. John. Several visitors to their home while they were in Atlanta said they remembered seeing a 'colorful' marriage license hanging framed in their kitchen, but the investigator could find no evidence of a marriage license being issued to them under any of their various aliases. Not that she was ever married to Kassel, as far as the investigators could determine. We wouldn't want her going down for bigamy."

"She certainly was keeping up her act when I spoke with her Saturday morning," Lee said. "She had a rather nicely cultured accent; not quite Received Standard English, but it fooled me."

"She's had years to work on it," Flynn said. "Plus a good teacher. The reason I'm relatively certain that Cynthia thinks she's in the clear is that, when I met with her yesterday morning, she readily acknowledged the parts about St. John's identity, but talked about how 'we' left England. I think she's still working under the impression that we've never heard of Cindy Duncan."

"Then let's keep that as our little secret until the time is right to spring it on her," Lee said, looking at her watch. "We've got to get in that house  Seven-forty-five. How mad could he be?" The words were spoken aloud but to no one in particular. She looked around the coffee shop and said, "I'm going to find a quiet corner and call O'Connell. Be back in a few minutes."

Alvarez and Flynn sipped their coffee.

"So, is being a detective everything you dreamed?" Flynn asked, a smile on his face.

Alvarez gave a short laugh. "Actually, I was getting ready to ask to go back to a squad car before this case."

"Vito Mazilli," Flynn said, slowly shaking his head. "The man is a legend. The department really screwed you over on that one."

"And, I'm stuck," Alvarez said, grateful that he could speak honestly with another detective.

"That's where you're wrong," Flynn said. "This case is going to get you noticed. Assuming we find St. John's killer and we have sufficient proof for a conviction, Mazilli is going to find himself with no one to tell him to dust off the powdered sugar from his sports coat."

"I need to work nights for the next few years," Alvarez said. "We have a sick daughter at home. My wife's a teacher."

Flynn shrugged. "Some of the best crimes take place at night. I admire that you're working it out with your wife."

"It hasn't been easy," Alvarez said.

Flynn felt a twinge of sorrow.

"I have the story on Linda Cooke's boyfriend," Flynn said after a moment. "Your instincts were good, but he's not involved. He was with another woman when St. John was being murdered."

"You talked with him?" Alvarez asked.

Flynn shook his head. "I didn't have to. Sometimes, people tell you things in a way that you know they're telling you the truth. I can't explain how it works. You just know. Linda Cooke is a fifty-something-year-old woman trying to look and act thirty-five. She got herself the man of her dreams – a young stud. Sometime Saturday, that world came crashing down when she found out that her young stud was doing what young studs do."

"How can you be so certain?"

Flynn clasped Alvarez on the shoulder. "You're going to get the right partner in a few weeks. He or she is going to be someone with a lot of miles on the odometer. But they're going to teach you a hell of a lot and one of those things is how to be certain that someone is telling you the truth. Intuition is a gift. Human nature and spotting the way someone breaks down when they finally tell you the truth is something you learn."

Lee returned, a perplexed look on her face.

"I just got yelled at by Sean O'Connell," she said. "The man is a piece of work. 'We don't put victims on trial,' he said. 'Don't even *think* about asking me to go to a judge looking for probable cause.' And I thought I had a working relationship with this guy."

"You do," Flynn said. "It just doesn't extend to him doing things for you. Just wait until *he* needs a favor bright and early on a Monday holiday morning. How did you ask him?"

Lee shook her head. "I said that there was likely evidence inside the townhouse used by St. John that could either tie Cynthia Duncastle to the murder or rule her out, but that our investigation into her showed that her whole identity was a construct. That's as far as I got. Sean started screaming that we don't do inquisitions on widows when their spouse is still on the autopsy table..."

"Jesus Christ, of course," Flynn said, his hand slapping the table. "Roy Halliday and Sharon Tucci's case. The woman out in Wellesley that O'Connell put on trial for murdering her husband last year. It's the reason O'Connell is still a D.A. instead of Attorney General, and two first-rate detectives are doing puppet shows for school kiddies. If Duncastle is involved, O'Connell isn't going to touch this unless you bring him an airtight case."

"The bar just got moved on the burden of proof?" Alvarez asked.

"Sky high," Flynn replied. "And the problem is that the more I learn about Duncastle, the more I'm convinced she's in this up to her ears. Linda Cooke told me she was at the show Friday afternoon. She met with St. John. That doesn't square with a woman who couldn't go to the preview party because one of her children was sick."

Flynn looked at Alvarez. "You made a terrific observation yesterday afternoon. You said something along the lines of, 'maybe we've got it all wrong and that St. John wasn't part of Duncastle's escape plan.' I think we need to give that more serious consideration."

He turned to Lee. "We know St. John has – or had – five million from Alice Shelburne. We know about botanical prints and God only knows what else he may have purloined from the Botanical Society. We also know that St. John and Cynthia knew the scam was going to blow up as of Saturday morning. Why would he stick around? Because he expected to ding the trustees for a hundred thousand more as a severance payment? Shelburne's accountants were after him for a tax I.D. number he couldn't supply. As soon as that became apparent, Shelburne would demand her money back and, with her retinue of lawyers, I don't think they'd pull any punches in going after it."

Flynn continued. "Could St. John have been holding out on Cynthia? I can't believe she didn't know where every dime he had stolen was hiding. She's too smart to trust anyone that explicitly. Could she have murdered St. John Friday evening? I don't know. We're missing something – something major – if she did the first murder. But *if* she did that first murder, she would have had no compunction about plugging Brady, even if it was just to keep him quiet."

Lee listened intently to Flynn's theory, then said, "Jason, I want you to go back over your timeline for St. John. Re-interview everyone you can and try to get his movements for the entire day." She turned to Flynn. "John, you and I are going to see Duncastle. We're not going to search the place. We're just going to keep our eyes open."

"Start with Linda Cooke," Flynn said to Alvarez. "I know she's not your favorite person, but she saw more of him on Friday than probably anyone else there."

\* \* \* \* \*

The townhouse next to the Botanical Society headquarters now sported black bunting on the massive oak entry door. Perhaps, Lee thought, it was the gift of a thoughtful friend. Or, a shameless attempt to provoke sympathy and inhibit unfriendly questions.

Cynthia Duncastle met with the two detectives in the same front parlor room that she had used when speaking with Flynn a day earlier. The door to the room was directly off the entry foyer, allowing Lee and Flynn no glimpse into the private parts of the house. There was no sound of children or of any other activity. Duncastle had traded Sunday's black cashmere sweater for a dark gray one. She pointedly did not offer them anything to drink.

"You may have heard that Raymond Brady was killed early this morning," Lee said.

Duncastle nodded. "It was on the news. He was a wretched man." Her voice was somber. "I had thought it full likely he had murdered my husband. I still think it more than probable, and I suspect his death is a matter of a falling out among thieves. When you find Mr. Brady's murderer, you will also find the person who killed my husband."

"Ms. Duncastle, we're following a number of leads," Lee said. "All of them stem from the manner of your husband's death. The way he was killed suggests someone attempted to extract information from him, or to get him to tell him the location of something. What might your husband have known that was worth killing him for?"

Duncastle shook her head. Much too quickly, to Flynn's trained eye. The words that followed were rote. A well-rehearsed speech. "My husband was killed by someone who intended to bring down the

Botanical Society." Addressing herself to Lee, Duncastle said, "I told you as much Saturday morning. Find the person who benefits from the death of the Society, and you will find the person who killed my husband."

"We were told you were at the Harborfront Expo Center on Friday," Lee said.

Duncastle said nothing. She started blankly at Lee. *Never volunteer an answer to an unexpected question until you know exactly how much information the questioner has*, Flynn thought.

"May we ask what took you there?" Flynn asked.

"My husband called and asked me to bring some file folders from his office," Duncastle said carefully. "He asked for the red folders, I took them to him. He glanced at their contents – I imagine to make certain they were the right papers he wanted – and he thanked me."

"He said nothing else?" Lee asked.

"I was doing him a favor. I didn't know it was the last time I was going to see him alive." Duncastle pulled a tissue from her sleeve and dabbed at her right eye.

It was a nice touch, Lee thought, but it would have been more realistic if Duncastle's eyes had been even slightly moist. The tissue came away from the eye bearing only a speck of mascara.

Lee pressed on. "There is also considerable question about the status of at least one major contribution to the Government Center project."

"I don't know anything about that," Duncastle said, also much too quickly. "My husband did not discuss those details with me."

"One contributor told us she turned over stock worth five million dollars to your husband," Lee said. "Yet there is no record of it in the Society's financial records."

"The Society has an accountant on staff," Duncastle replied. "A little woman named Brenda Carr. Have you spoken with her?"

"We will have spoken with her by the end of today," Lee said.

"What we were wondering is, did your husband keep a computer here? A laptop, perhaps?"

It was another question Duncastle had anticipated. "Yes. He took it with him when he checked into the hotel Wednesday. I would appreciate its return after you've examined it as that is the computer he used to maintain our household finances."

"We found no computer in his office at the show," Flynn said.

Duncastle showed surprise. "I know he took it with him. He packed it up on Wednesday morning. I helped him." A dramatic pause. "You said his murderer wanted something from him. Could it have been that computer? Its passwords?"

"Perhaps it is still here in the house," Lee said. "Might we look for it in his study? Just in case he changed his mind?"

"No," Duncastle said stiffly. "I do not want policemen intruding into my home and upsetting my children. They are already quite distraught."

"But it might help us find you husband's murderer," Lee said.

"I believe I made myself quite clear," Duncastle said.

"We would prefer not to have to get a search warrant," Lee said. "That would…"

Duncastle cut her off. "And I would request that you *do* get one. And, when you serve it, you will do so in the presence of television cameras and newspaper correspondents, all of whom will record that you tore apart the home of a grieving widow and frightened her fatherless children, all for no good reason. I am telling you there is no computer in this home. Please accept my word for it."

There was a look of satisfaction on Duncastle's face.

"May I at least use your wash room?" Lee asked.

"There is one next door at the Society." Duncastle's voice was cold. "I wish to be left alone now. Also, given that you have long since established the cause of my husband's death, I request that you release his body so that I may give him a proper burial. I have made that request of the office of the medical examiner this morning and will make it again to your chief of police if I have not received word that my request has been honored. I should hate very much to have to tell those same reporters that you have done things to ensure that those same children cannot reach closure with their murdered father."

The tissue came back out of the cashmere sweater sleeve. It again was dabbed at non-existent tears. The interview was over.

* * * * *

"Feel like you've been set up?" Lee said as they walked down the front steps of the townhouse.

"Snapped, been put on a tee, and kicked through the uprights," Flynn said. "She saw us coming. However, I couldn't help but note the absolute lack of curiosity about Brady's death."

"Neither could I," Lee said. "Which gives me a nice, warm feeling inside. Let's go see how Jason is doing."

* * * * *

Alvarez dealt with the reality that people were becoming annoyed with him. When he had first asked questions on Saturday morning, the responses he got incorporated a kind of electric excitement that witnesses feel when they know they are helping to solve a crime. Now, those same individuals, having repeated their stories to two and sometimes three detectives, were becoming convinced that the Boston Police either didn't know how to take notes or else kept losing them. Worse, memories that were crisp and distinct forty-eight hours earlier now had two days to become clouded.

"It's important that I pin down his activities over lunch," Alvarez said to one of the development staff.

"We had a meeting," the staffer said. "I don't remember whether it was noon or twelve-thirty. I don't see what difference it makes."

Alvarez put down his pen, exasperated.

Linda Cooke was as helpful as Flynn had suggested. But she was also running a show and dealing with the multiple, conflicting requirements. Though the show had been open for the day less than fifteen minutes, her information was given between resolving crises, including that there were too few lunches for a garden club group, a tour bus had broken down in front of the main entrance, and a woman with a twisted ankle in the vendor halls was screaming for an ambulance.

"Yes, St. John was back here at about a quarter past six," Cooke said. In the background, a walkie-talkie blared the progress of a tow truck moving a disabled bus. "We did a final check of the catering stations, which took about twenty minutes. The Gala wasn't supposed to start until seven but we already had a lobby full of people at half past six, and he told me to open the bars and let them in. I didn't see him for the next hour except to nod."

Tony Wilson, the head of facilities for the Botanical Society and person in charge of ensuring that exhibitors and vendors at the Garden and Flower Show had the attention of the union hands on duty, was even more laconic. "Like I told you on Saturday. We met with the union rep at one-thirty. The meeting lasted maybe forty-five minutes."

"What did you discuss?" Alvarez asked.

"I had a punch list," Wilson said. "One hundred and thirty-two items that were still open. Little stuff, mostly. Lumber left in an aisle. Pipe and drape still needed. We went through every one. When we finished, St. John headed back for the vendor area."

"When did you see him next?"

"Three-ten, three-fifteen, as the awards were being posted. He said he needed to go rest up for the Gala. Which left me to deal with the chaos when exhibitors found out McQueen got all the big awards. He was out of the building when that hit. That was one nasty hour."

"Why didn't he handle that himself?" Alvarez asked.

Wilson shrugged. "Maybe because I'm only person on the payroll who's bigger than some of those landscapers. A couple of those guys weighed twice what St. John did."

"They were really that angry?"

"You shell out fifty grand for an exhibit. It looks good. And all you have to show for it is some dinky ribbon that everyone else has. You'd be plenty pissed off."

"Did any exhibitor give you special problems?"

"Oh, Stu Wells. At least at first. Sunrise Gardens. He was ready to tear St. John's head off if he had been here. Stood there screaming that someone had stolen his blue daylilies out of his exhibit. He cooled off. Came back a while later and apologized. Said he realized he had taken them out himself because they weren't going to be in bloom, but it was five in the morning, and he hadn't slept in two days."

"Anyone else?"

"Everyone had something nasty to say about the unfairness. I calmed them down best I could."

"And you saw him when he came back at a quarter past six?"

Wilson nodded. "A little after that. He asked how it went. I told him everything was cool."

"How did he react?"

"He looked relieved. He really didn't want to be here when those ribbons went up."

\* \* \* \* \*

Stuart Wells was not at the Sunrise Gardens exhibit when Alvarez went back to speak with him. The owner of an adjoining space, Eco-Solutions, said Wells typically came in at seven in the morning, checked his exhibit, then left for a few hours until traffic built to heavier levels. The exhibitor's name was Paul Steele, according to his name badge. Steele looked to be in his late twenties, dressed in earth tones and Birkenstocks.

Alvarez noted that Eco-Solutions had only two ribbons, a blue Botanical Society ribbon and a trophy for 'Superior Demonstration of Energy Conservation Techniques" from a state agency.

Steele smiled. "Hey, it's our first year." He pointed to the small wind turbine set in the middle of a vegetable garden, a row of black composters set against the back wall. "We've sold fifty of those babies in two days and put a couple of hundred people on an email list. As far as I'm concerned, the show is already a success."

"But Stuart Wells wanted ribbons," Alvarez said.

"He's writing his share of business," Steele said, a note of disdain in his voice. "I see him over there. Ladies with very expensive purses and good haircuts sit in that little patio of his and fall in love with the idea of making their McMansion in Wellesley look like an English estate. The guy is a hell of a salesman."

"You saw him Friday afternoon," Alvarez prompted.

"Oh, sure. We're all kept out in the lobby until just after three-thirty. Then, it's like the running of the bulls. We all rush back to our exhibits and look at the Lucite panels. I saw my two, I shrugged. And, yeah, I know one of them is just for playing nice with the other kids."

"What about Wells?"

"We came back at the same time. He looked and saw he got — what? — five ribbons. Then he did this double take and started walking though the exhibit. He was screaming, 'where the hell are they?' over and over at the top of his lungs. That's when he stomped off to find someone to strangle."

"I guess he cooled down. Half an hour later he was in his exhibit, sitting in that chair. He was making phone calls. Back to normal."

"You saw him at the party that evening?"

Steele laughed. "No, I didn't go to the Gala. Nobody who was at that wing-ding would have wanted to talk to me. I'm looking for the couple from Winchester with a quarter acre who believe in saving the planet. Not some rich people from Manchester-by-the-Sea who could finance their own nuclear power plant."

"How about Saturday morning?" Alvarez asked.

Steele pursed his lips. "Pretty mellow. He and two other guys went through the exhibit pulling out and replacing anything that looked wilted. He definitely got over whatever was bugging him Friday afternoon."

"Did you watch his exhibit get put together over the course of the week?"

Steele laughed. "You've obviously never been here during 'build' week." He shook his head. "You don't have time to watch what everyone else is doing. I did this with my partner, and we pretty well worked four days solid to get it looking like this. Wells had more than a dozen people working on his exhibit on Thursday and Thursday night. One lady did nothing but go over the kickboard with a cotton swab and a can of paint, re-doing anything that got nicked."

Alvarez left the Eco-Solutions exhibit and walked to Sunrise Gardens. Sixty feet long and twenty feet wide, it was easily twice the size of its neighbors. The waterfall with its moss- and fern-filled grotto attracted an admiring crowd. The grotto became a brook that wound the length of the exhibit.

It was a beautiful display, Alvarez thought. Pods of color from hundreds of plants emerged with each twist of the watercourse. The house façade seemed to grow naturally from the landscape, and the brick patio fringed with ground covers was the most inviting he could imagine. The trees, though small, were in full leaf and bloom. It was mid-May in the middle of February.

Alvarez tried to put himself in Stuart Wells' position, having worked through the night and then been barred from the building, along with other exhibitors, for nine hours. According to Steele, Wells went immediately to the Lucite stand in front of the display and saw his five awards. Then what did Steele say Wells did? *Then he did this double take and started walking though the exhibit. He was screaming, 'where the hell are they?'*

Alvarez walked to the Lucite panel. He looked back at the exhibit. Twenty feet to his right, the stream meandered close to the walkway.

At the bend of the stream, the color scheme of the perennials changed from gold to blue. Tags identified the clusters of plants. *'Campanula 'Blue Chips'', 'Veronica spicata 'Nana'', 'Lithodora 'Blue Star'', 'Geranium 'Johnson's Blue'*.

Alvarez imagined Wells expecting to see the Lucile Grassi Cup on the panel, not seeing it, then looking to the spot where his prized cultivar ought to have been readily visible to the crowds but just out of reach: *Hemerocallis 'Carolina Blue'*. The blue daylily.

Gone.

Alvarez raced through the crowds back to the management area where he found Linda Cooke. Riffing through his note pad, he said, "The judges' lady. Phipps…"

"Liz Phillips," Cooke said.

"Is she here?"

"I saw her earlier," Cooke said. "There's no judging today, but she… I have a cell phone number for her." Cooke picked up a clipboard and then dialed a number. She waited while the phone was answered.

"Do you want to meet her here?" Cooke asked.

Alvarez nodded.

Five minutes later, Cooke, Phillips and Alvarez were in the office that had been used by Grainger-Elliot.

"I want to make certain I have this timeline straight," Alvarez said. "Ms. Phillips, you said St. John spoke to your judges at eight-thirty but did so for only about five minutes and then left."

"Exactly right," Phillips said.

Alvarez leafed through pages of notes. "You also told me Saturday that every exhibitor gave you paperwork telling you the names of the awards they believed they were eligible for and the plants that judges should look for."

"That's also correct."

"And Sunrise Gardens listed itself as eligible for the Grassi Cup, citing the blue daylily, is that right?"

Phillips nodded.

"Can exhibitors change their minds? Can they come to you and say, 'no we didn't get that plant so take us off the list'?"

"The conscientious ones do," Phillips said. "They'll track me down the night before or even the morning of judging. I appreciate it."

"You told me on Saturday that when the judges couldn't find those blue daylilies, you went out on the floor to try to find them in the exhibit," Alvarez said. "Do you remember what time that was?"

Phillips thought for a moment. "Probably between ten and ten-thirty. The Grassi Cup judges had only five or six exhibits to judge. It had to be the morning because the same panel judged for another award in the afternoon."

Alvarez nodded and wrote quickly. "Ms. Cooke, you said St. John called everyone together just before eight-thirty, said he was going to talk to the judges, gave everyone an assignment and told them to stay here. Is that right?"

Cooke nodded.

"And St. John came back half an hour later," Alvarez said.

Cooke nodded. "Yes."

"And when did the first judges go out on the floor?" Alvarez asked Phillips.

"Roughly ten minutes before nine…"

"So, for at least fifteen minutes, St. John had the exhibit hall completely to himself," Alvarez said. "Ms. Cooke, would anyone else have been out among the displays?"

"The staff was all here, the exhibitors were told to leave before seven," Cooke said. "There was no reason for any vendor to be in the exhibits area."

"When St. John came back, were his hands dirty? Was he carrying anything?"

Cooke shook her head. "No, he was in a suit and tie. Very neat appearance."

It was only a theory, Alvarez thought. But it was the first theory with a sufficient motive for murder.

Alvarez called Lee's cell phone. The first time he had done so was to awaken her from a sound sleep to draw her into this case. Now, he thought, he might be offering a solution to it.

"Lieutenant, I may have caught a break," he said. "Can you and Detective Flynn get down here as quickly as possible?" As he spoke, he glanced down at Grainger-Elliot's desk. A stack of purchase orders were on one corner, awaiting a second signature that would never come. The first signature on the forms was that of Brenda Carr, her name typed below. Alvarez glanced at the scrawl, then looked again more carefully. Cooke and Liz were talking softly, their attention on one another. Carefully, Alvarez folded two of the purchase orders with one hand and slipped them into his breast pocket.

\* \* \* \* \*

Flynn, Lee and Alvarez sat in the VIP lounge. With them was a slightly puzzled Oscar McQueen, the owner of Blue Hills Gardens, the exhibit that had swept the bulk of the awards at the show. McQueen sprawled out of the office chair he had been offered, his legs splayed out at odd angles.

"Speaking completely theoretically," Lee said. "Let's say you came in tomorrow morning and found that someone had removed all six of the plants that won you the Grassi Cup."

"Weigela hortensis 'Seurat'," McQueen said. "And, it's a shrub. No one can steal them because I'm the last person out of here at night and I'm the first person here in the morning. And, while the security here is half-assed, I doubt that someone carting half a dozen flowering shrubs would get out the door unnoticed."

"When did you bring in those particular shrubs?" Alvarez asked.

McQueen grinned. "Friday morning about 2 a.m. They were the

last thing to go into the exhibit. I even had the space filled with a decoy shrub in case anyone had the time to look around to see if I had anything special."

"You had them someplace safe before that time?" Alvarez asked.

"They were under lock and key at my greenhouse," McQueen replied, nodding. "Like I said, no one is going to steal something like that from me."

"But let's say they did," Flynn pressed. "Let's say they got them out the door. What do you do with something that rare?"

McQueen leaned back in his chair. The chair groaned under his weight. He tilted his head and scratched his beard. "Propagate it. Get a couple of thousand tissue cultures going in some secret laboratory. The problem is, it wouldn't do you any good."

"Why not?" Flynn asked.

"Because the plant's DNA is registered. There are patents on it. Every step in the creation of 'Seurat' is documented thirteen ways from Sunday. Sonja Johanson – the breeder – this is her life. Go to a nursery sometime and pick out the really expensive plants. Look carefully at the label and it will say, 'not for propagation' and have 'PPAF' on its tag. That means 'plant patent applied for,' and Sonja would sue the ass off of anyone who tried to sell a 'Seurat' knock-off. These plants are worth a fortune."

Flynn pressed on. "So, let's say someone knows this. But they steal it anyway with the intent of making those ten thousand tissue cultures you talked about. What kind of person would buy it from whomever stole it?"

McQueen laughed. "You're making this hard. OK, I'd look for someone in China. Intellectual property and patents don't mean a damn thing over there. And, someone really smart would start tinkering with the DNA – add in a couple of traits that aren't in 'Seurat' so it isn't an exact copy. As long as you're in China, you can also fabricate the complete development history of the cultivar and phony up documentary evidence, including photographs going back ten years. The government would probably help you – supply all the document stamps, create the paper trail. In two years, you'd be able to sell it across Asia. In three years, you'd introduce it in the U.S. and Europe. Sonja could sue and try to have the plants impounded and destroyed, but with the evidence at hand, the Ag Department's enforcement unit would have its hands tied. By the time you proved it was a sham, it would be five, six years. By that time, whoever stole it would have sold four or five million dollars' worth of premium shrubs and the *real* 'Seurat' would be selling for ten bucks a gallon pot."

"A buyer in China," Flynn said.

McQueen nodded. "A buyer in China."

**Chapter 11.**

"Stuart Wells," Alvarez read from his computer screen. "His record is clean. The guy even pays his parking tickets promptly." He tapped the screen to scroll down a document. "Not married. Never been arrested. Never sued anyone. This guy is the most unlikely murderer I've ever seen."

"How about the business?" Flynn asked.

Keys were pressed. Screens refreshed. "Sunrise Gardens did four million in sales last year and was sufficiently profitable that they paid the state taxes at the statutory rate. No liens. No outstanding lawsuits. Wells is the sole proprietor and runs it as a Massachusetts-chartered company, not even a Subchapter S corporation."

"Whatever that means," Flynn said.

"It means he's a straight arrow," Alvarez said. "He isn't dodging taxes. He pays his share of his employees' FICA, offers health insurance, and contributes to their 401(k)."

"He figured out that St. John stole the plants that were going to win him the big award," Lee said. "In fact, he figured out that St. John *planned* it. A week before the show, St. John moved Sunrise Gardens' exhibit from front and center in the landscape area to a corner where it was out of sight in case somebody came along unexpectedly."

"But it doesn't add up to murder," Flynn said. "This is the way it ought to have happened: Wells comes back and discovers his plants are missing. He runs screaming and learns St. John isn't there. Instead, it's just Tony Wilson. And Wilson obviously isn't the guy who stole the plants. So, when St. John comes back at a quarter past six, Wells corners him and demands that St. John return the plants or else he'll have St. John arrested for grand theft. Equilibrium would have been restored before 6:30."

"Unless St. John told Wells he didn't have the daylilies," Lee said. "Swore on a stack of bibles that it had to be someone else but offered to get right on it and find out before the end of the evening. Knowing, of course, that this was his last night as St. John Grainger-Elliot, Botanical Society executive director."

"And, at one in the morning, St. John hasn't done squat," Alvarez filled in. "Wells was one of the last people at the party, talking with St. John after one-fifteen."

"I still don't get murder," Flynn said. "I get a call to the police and a demand to arrest St. John. This guy is a straight arrow."

"Then why didn't Wells make that call?" Lee asked. "Wells was entrusted with plants worth a couple of million dollars. He had them stolen out from under his care. Even straight arrows are capable of murder when they're under that kind of stress."

"The guy at the adjoining space – Steele – said Wells went back to his exhibit and started making calls," Alvarez said. "Give me an hour and I can find out who he contacted."

"Do it," Lee said. "That just became your top priority."

"St. John did a handoff," Flynn told Lee when Alvarez left to pull up phone records. "Fifteen minutes wasn't time to remove the plants, get to his hotel room, and get back to the staff meeting."

"The grieving widow?" Lee suggested. "Or the crooked antiques dealer?"

"Or someone else," Flynn said. "I have to tell you, though, I'm still bothered by Wells as a murderer."

"I learned a long time ago to listen carefully to you when something bothers you," Lee said. "But I don't see another suspect here. Means, motive and opportunity. Wells had all three, and especially motive."

"When we dumped St. John's calls, were any of them to the kind of people who could have done what McQueen suggested?" Flynn asked.

Lee took out her notebook and began flipping pages. "Let's see, I'm looking for calls to Tong Enterprises, unscrupulous Chinese specialists in mass-producing tissue cultures from stolen plants. Nope, not here." She looked up at Flynn. "A day ago, we were looking for contacts who might fence glass flowers. Now we're looking for people who can clone real ones."

Lee went back to her list. "No calls before nine in the morning. After that, there were half a dozen to nursery owners, but they're all local. Two calls to Cynthia. The rest were to people we've identified as donors or likely donors, making certain they were going to show up. And one to Richard Durant, his mole among the trustees."

"Which means that the handoff of the daylilies to the accomplice was pre-arranged," Flynn said. "And, who was making the getaway arrangements?"

They looked at one another and both grinned. "Cynthia," they said in unison.

* * * * *

Alvarez has been asked to obtain cell phone records for Wells' phone, which took less than twenty minutes. It was not in his nature to do the minimum required for any assignment. All through school he had turned in voluminous reports even when the request was solely for a two-page document. His innate computer skills allowed him to set up databases that mined other databases for deeper insights, collating and organizing that data in real time. When he said he could have the cell phone records in an hour, he intended to return in fifty-five minutes with a full dossier. It was, he figured, probably the only time he would have an opportunity to impress Lieutenant Lee with his true worth, Flynn's kind words that morning notwithstanding.

While Stuart Wells' calls were processed through his relational database, he thought of other tasks that he might accomplish while he awaited those results. He could re-process St. John's calls now that he knew they were looking for plant breeders. He could also pursue his belief that Cynthia Duncastle had more of a role in the affairs of the New England Botanical Society than she let on to Flynn and Lee.

Alvarez was also mindful of the pained expression on Lee's face following her phone call with the district attorney and the D.A.'s repeated comment that the police did not do inquisitions on widows. But obtaining, say, three days' worth of calls placed to or from the home of the deceased was not the same as a search warrant served on a widow. It was a way of helping find the killer even if some of those calls were made or received after St. John was dead.

Alvarez began tapping his screen.

\* \* \* \* \*

In the Brookfield home of the late Raymond Brady, Detective Martin Hoffman sifted diligently though hundreds of emails sent and received by the antiques dealer. Mr. Brady, Hoffman was rapidly concluding, was a first-class bore, but also a man at the end of his moorings. The story, as told in notes to anyone who would open Brady's messages, was fairly straightforward. Brady had scraped together every cent he either had saved or could borrow in order to purchase the glass flowers three months earlier. It was a can't-lose proposition because there was already a willing buyer from Dubai in the wings, and Sotheby's listing of the pieces would only whet the appetite of the market for more of them. Brady would net three hundred thousand dollars. Even after paying Grainger-Elliot a sixty-thousand-dollar kickback (or 'finder's fee' as it was delicately expressed in the emails), there was nearly a quarter million dollars of profit for Brady.

The outcry when the glass pieces appeared in the auction house catalog caught Brady by surprise. His demands to cancel the sale were answered by curt, 'we agreed the sale was final' responses from Grainger-Elliot. The Dubai prince was not interested, even at a lower price, after Sotheby's demurred on further representation of the pieces. This set off a furious search for other buyers… who, if they responded at all, did so with offers as low as fifty thousand. Worse, Brady found that the rest of his inventory was similarly assumed to be tainted. No one wanted goods that had passed through the hands of Raymond Brady. Each day, Brady sent out dozens of emails with photos, offering his inventory to other dealers with whom he had apparently worked cooperatively for decades. Few answered his queries. None wanted his goods.

On Thursday of last week, Brady had written one final email to Grainger-Elliot:

*St. John,*

*It is with considerable regret that I inform you that, if we cannot reach an amicable solution to the issues separating us on the return of Blaschka pieces Nos. 1 through 25, I will be forced to escalate our disagreement. There are two issues in particular that I suspect may cause you some professional discomfort.*

*In the course of our discussions concerning the Blaschka inventory, we agreed on a contingent finder's fee payable to you aggregating 20% of the net proceeds less original purchase price of the goods. A cursory search through the websites of both the Association of Art Museum Directors and the Association of Science Museum Directors, both of which you claim membership, finds numerous guidelines representing their Code of Ethical Conduct. Both organizations are in agreement that the payment of any finder's fee to any staff member in the deaccessioning process is explicitly unethical and grounds for expulsion.*

*The AAMD is particularly rigorous in this regard, stating in its position paper,* Art Museums and the Practice of Deaccessioning *(November 2007) that to 'either solicit or accept' such payment is 'antithetical to the public trust placed in museums as caretakers of artifacts'.*

*I have compiled a complete history of our dealings in the matter of the Blaschka collection, including authenticated, dated emails from you to me spelling out a flagrant disregard for that canon of ethics.*

*I have further compiled a set of emails setting out our proposed arrangements for certain other artifacts held by the Botanical Society. If we cannot conclude a financial arrangement for the return of Blaschka pieces Nos. 1 through 25 by the* end of the Northeast Garden and Flower Show, I will have no choice but to personally hand over authenticated copies of this evidence to the Trustees of the Society.

*Sincerely yours,*

*Raymond Brady*

Hoffman read and re-read the letter. If Grainger-Elliot hadn't already been dead for forty-eight hours, he would have been at the top of the list of suspects in Brady's murder.

He printed the email and continued sifting the contents of the computer.

\* \* \* \* \*

The windows began popping up on Alvarez's computer screen, first one or two, then in clusters of half a dozen. The windows faded and were replaced by new ones in green and red. After five minutes, Alvarez typed a few commands and the windows dissolved and neatly merged into a color coded list.

Stuart Wells' first call, at 4:14 on Friday afternoon, was to First Growth Farms, a plant breeder in Lancaster, Pennsylvania. Alvarez skipped over ownership and personnel information and went straight for an associated article from the January issue of a trade journal:

*'Carolina Blue' May Be Ready for Prime Time*

*The holy grail of the Hemerocallis development fraternity, Quentin Young's 'Carolina Blue' may be getting ready for a public debut this spring. A source at the Pennsylvania Hort Society says judges at the Philadelphia Flower Show have it on preliminary paperwork submitted by Estabrook Gardens for its landscape entry at the March show. Estabrook, a perennial top award winner at Philadelphia, has been the favored conduit for previous First Growth Farms introductions, including last year's Rosa 'Montego Bay'. If 'Carolina Blue' is headed for the Pennsylvania Convention Center, it could also put in an appearance at a handful of other prestigious shows, starting with the Northeast Garden and Flower Show in February…*

The call to First Growth Farms – presumably to Quentin Young

– had lasted ten minutes. Two incoming calls from the same number followed, each lasting about fifteen minutes. Wells' phone was quiet for the next hour. Then, at 6:30, Wells again called First Growth Farms, this call lasting ten minutes. At 11:30, Wells called Young's home phone, and Alvarez's computer displayed several profiles of the plant breeder. The phone was silent for the rest of the evening.

Wells called Quentin Young at 6:49 on Saturday morning – about the time word would have spread that the reason exhibitors were being kept out of the display area was that St. John Grainger-Elliot's body had been fished out of somebody's pond. That call lasted just a few minutes was followed by several more over the course of the morning, both incoming and outgoing.

The pattern of the calls settled one question even as it raised other, equally disturbing ones. Clearly, Wells had brought in the blue daylilies. Just as certainly, they had been stolen from the exhibit. Yet, after the initial discovery of the theft and his angry outburst to Tony Wilson, Wells said just a few hours later that it had all been a mistake – he had declined to display *Hemerocallis* 'Carolina Blue' because it wasn't in flower for judging, and had forgotten that fact in the whirl and exhaustion of last-minute preparation.

The answer tied to what the head of judges, Liz Phillips, had told him. Exhibitors groomed their displays through the night, pulling anything that was not in peak condition. 'All that counts is how it looks when the judges see it on Friday,' she had said. 'If the bloom of the world's most spectacular rose is still shut tight when the rose panel sees it, it doesn't win, even if it opens an hour later.'

The flurry of calls proved Wells had lied, first to Wilson and then, Saturday morning, to the police. Had he lied because he had he had killed Grainger-Elliot, or because he had been told by First Growth Farms to say nothing? If the latter was true, why would the plant breeder who had entrusted a million-dollar plant to a landscaper tell that person to lie about its disappearance?

Alvarez's computer beeped again. The summary of calls made from the Botanical Society's townhouse began to assemble themselves on the screen.

\* \* \* \* \*

The young woman cleared her throat. Lee looked up from her conversation with Flynn. The woman was in her early twenties, with impossibly straight honey blonde hair, blue eyes and a perfect complexion. She was dressed in wool slacks and a sweater that looked as though it was designed solely to be worn in front of a fireplace at an exclusive Aspen ski lodge.

"You're Lieutenant Lee?" the woman asked. When Lee nodded, the woman added, "May I speak with you privately?" Her eyes indicated Flynn.

"I'm going to get something to eat," Flynn said to Lee, rising from his chair. "Can I bring you back anything?"

The woman sat down, smoothing the flow of her slacks over her legs.

*Part of St. John's 'estrogen palace guard'*, Lee thought.

"You haven't arrested anyone, yet, have you?" the woman asked.

"Maybe you want to start by telling me who you are," Lee replied.

The woman nodded and bit her lip. "Missy – Melissa – Clifford. I work for the Society as part of the development staff."

"You have something you want to tell me?" Lee said. She lowered her voice, keeping it gentle, as though Missy Clifford might be frightened off otherwise. She also pulled her chair closer to that of the young woman. Their knees almost touched, and they could speak in soft tones.

"I've heard… people here are saying that St. John didn't drown in the pond. They say he was killed back here in the management area – one of the offices – and then dragged out to the Blue Hills exhibit."

"That's correct," Lee said.

"I may have seen something," Clifford said, her voice nervous.

She only glanced at Lee as she spoke. Otherwise, she spoke to the floor. "One of the other detectives started asking me more questions this morning and so I figured out that you must not have made an arrest…"

"What did you see, Missy?" Lee attempted to gently guide the conversation.

Clifford took a breath. "I was… back here in the management area a little after midnight. I saw a guy…" Now, she looked only at the floor, without even a glance up at Lee.

"What brought you back to this part of the building?" Lee asked.

"Is that important?" Clifford looked up briefly at Lee before allowing her gaze to return to the floor.

"Let's say that, if I don't know, your story is less credible."

Clifford continued to look at the floor. Several seconds went by. "I hooked up with a guy…"

*The black panties in the other office*, Lee thought.

"And it wasn't something you felt comfortable telling Detective Alvarez this morning," Lee said, touching Clifford's arm. Clifford looked up at Lee, and Lee gave her a wide smile. "We've all been there, Missy."

*Or not*, Lee thought. *When was the last time you met a guy in a dark office for a quickie? Other than Matt, when was the last time you met any guy, anywhere?*

Clifford looked grateful. She closed her eyes, remembering. "He was just a guy I met at the Gala. Good looking, I don't know, late twenties. He just came on really strong…"

"The two of you were in the third office on the left," Lee said, smiling. "You left behind a souvenir. Black. Victoria's Secret."

Clifford nodded. There was even a hint of a shy smile on her face. She no longer looked at the floor.

"You said you saw a guy," Lee prompted. "Did your friend see him, too?"

"No," Clifford said, shaking her head quickly. "He thought we shouldn't… leave together. It wouldn't look right. So I stayed behind a couple of minutes." She shrugged. "I also had to get myself together."

"So you went out into the hallway," Lee said.

Clifford nodded. "And there was a man. I only saw him for a second or two. Because it was awkward, and I just wanted to get back to the Gala. He was at the other end of the hallway."

"Can you describe him?"

"Older. Closer to forty. Brown hair. Short – the hair, I mean. He was probably six feet tall. Fairly lean build from what I could see. He had a moustache – just a small one. He was wearing a black turtleneck. He just stood there when he saw me, like he was startled. But I turned and walked away. I don't know what he did after he saw me. I heard a door open."

"What makes you think he wasn't just someone from the party?" Lee asked.

"The way he was dressed. And, he was wearing gloves and holding this coil of white rope. It really stood out against the black turtleneck."

\* \* \* \* \*

"Close to forty, short brown hair with a moustache. Around six feet and fairly lean build." Lee repeated Missy Clifford's description of the man in the hallway with the white rope.

"And she didn't bother to come forward with this information two days ago," Flynn said.

"These kids are convinced they're going to be let go any day because the Botanical Society is broke," Lee responded. "She had sex on a desk in a glorified closet at a party where she's supposed to be being nice to major contributors. She's going to admit this to a male detective?"

Flynn shrugged his shoulders. "Maybe the guy she had sex with is going to turn into a major contributor. But I see your point. The description doesn't tie to anyone we've spoken with."

"My conclusion, too," Lee said. "But the rope is one of those details that make my day. The guy was setting up for St. John."

Alvarez rapped on the door frame to announce his presence. "I've got a lot to show you," he said, holding up his computer.

"And we may have just found our first eyewitness," Lee said. "One of the sweet young things you've been peppering with questions just told me she saw a guy back here in the management area a little after midnight. Close to forty, short brown hair with a moustache. Around six feet and fairly lean build."

"Why didn't she tell me that?" Alvarez had an astonished look in his face.

"Because you're male. Does that description sound like anyone you've spoken to?"

Alvarez shook his head. "Wells is the right height but no moustache. McQueen is a lot bigger. Cooke's boyfriend is younger. It's no one I've seen around the exhibit area. And it's nobody on the Society's staff. Maybe a vendor?"

"So, we have either a murderer or a murderer's accomplice," Lee said. "Show us what you've got."

Alvarez ran through Wells' phone calls with First Growth Farms and its owner, Quentin Young. He showed them the articles. "I don't think there's any question but that 'Carolina Blue' was in the display at seven o'clock that morning and gone at eleven o'clock."

"Theory number one," Flynn said. "Wells calls Quentin Young and says, 'the lilies are gone, what do I do?' Young tells Wells to calm down and get hold of St. John, but don't raise a stink. That isn't the way to solve the problem. Wells goes back to Tony Wilson, who can't help him anyway, and says it was all a mistake. Wells sees St. John as soon as he gets back from his *cinq au sept,* and St. John says he'll find out who did the dastardly deed. At midnight, he tells Wells he'll have them back by morning. And, by morning, St. John is dead."

"Theory number two," Flynn continued. "Same as theory number one except that, when St. John puts off Wells at midnight, Wells comprehends that the guy who stole the plants has no intention of returning them. Wells, his reputation on the line, and an accomplice – name to be filled in later – lure St. John back to the office with the intention of beating the information out of him. It goes too far. They toss his body into McQueen's pond as a statement, intentional or subliminal, that McQueen got the award Wells should have had; he can clean up the mess."

"Do I hear a preference?" Lee asked.

"We pursue both," Flynn said. "I think a tag team, though. Two of us talk to Wells, the third one simultaneously gets this Quentin Young guy on the line and gets his story before the two – or their lawyers – have the opportunity to rehearse them."

"There's more," Alvarez said.

Lee and Flynn looked at him expectantly.

"I ran the phone for the townhouse," Alvarez said. "Most of it is pretty cut and dried, but there were some calls that are worth looking at."

"Jason, I really don't feel like being kept in suspense," Lee said.

Alvarez turned the computer to where the two detectives could see the screen. He tapped the screen.

"The green is when St. John was likely in the townhouse. The red is when he was probably here at the show, in his hotel room, or in the office." Alvarez tapped the screen again. Six green phone numbers pulsed. "These are all calls to people associated with the Botanical Society, three of them to Cooke." Another tap and four calls to two numbers were highlighted. "Richard Durant. Trustee mole. Home and cell."

"They had a lot to talk about," Lee said. "Some of those midnight calls lasted nearly an hour."

"Here's another set of calls," Alvarez said, tapping at the screen. Five numbers were highlighted. "Other trustees," he said. "No call over ten minutes. No late calls."

"Taking the temperature of the trustees," Lee said. "Polling them. Seeing if he still had any support. Probably finding out that he didn't, and the Botanical Society cookie jar was about to change its locks."

Alvarez nodded. "I can circle back to those trustees and get a gist of the conversation. But let's look at the red calls. These are after nine in the morning and before six on weekdays, plus all calls between Wednesday, when Linda Cooke says St. John checked into the hotel here, and Friday night."

There were far more of them – nearly fifty calls over a five-day period before Grainger-Elliot's murder. Alvarez tapped the screen and approximately thirty calls blinked in red. "These are the easy ones. Hairdresser, the children's school, restaurants, and residential numbers, mostly in Back Bay."

Another tap of the screen. Eight rows blinked the same number. "St. John's cell phone. They spoke twice on Friday. Once just after nine in the morning, then again Friday at about two o'clock."

Another tap. Six calls blinked in blue. "Raymond Brady, home and business."

"Good lord," Flynn said. "Did she have her own fencing operation going?"

"I'm sure if we ask her, she'll have a perfectly acceptable explanation," Lee said. "She wanted to buy something, she needed decorating services. And, of course, Mr. Brady isn't talking these days. But I'd give odds either she was St. John's back channel or else she was moving goods independently."

"And here's the grand finale," Alvarez said. He tapped the screen. Eight calls to or from the same number blinked red. "A pre-paid cell phone. An eastern Massachusetts overlay area code. All the calls were brief – always one minute. I can find out where it was purchased, and

I can pull up records on calls to and from that number, but I want you to pay special attention to the last two entries."

He pointed to the bottom of the screen. Two calls, both from the cell phone to the townhouse. One at 1:12 a.m. for one minute.

The other at 2:18 a.m. for one minute.

"I think that maybe, just maybe, we're getting into probable cause that might pass the Sean O'Connell sniff test," Lee said.

"Do you want to see the calls since Saturday morning?" Alvarez asked.

"You mean there's more?"

Alvarez nodded. A screen flipped. Alvarez pointed to the sixty-plus calls. "These are both incoming and outgoing. White are friends or what I assume are friends based on who the phones are registered to. I'll assume those are condolence calls. Green are non-suspicious, including several from trustees. The red numbers are to the pre-paid cell, and those get interesting. There are two on Saturday morning, then the calls almost stop. One on Sunday. None since."

"Reason to be filled in later," Lee said.

Alvarez pointed to the last group of calls, highlighted in yellow. "Cynthia Duncastle was on the phone to a pair of funeral homes Saturday afternoon."

"Too bad it wasn't Friday afternoon," Flynn said. "Then we could rest our case. Saturday afternoon is pretty much out there on the bell curve, but it's not proof of anything."

Alvarez's finger moved down the screen. "Virgin Atlantic Airlines. Also Saturday afternoon."

"Get the body home and buried," Flynn said. "I would have liked it a lot better if she was making those calls last week. Lieutenant Lee and I are in agreement that Cynthia was in charge of the getaway."

"Except that there isn't any evidence of a getaway," Lee said. "If they were planning to leave Saturday morning, there ought to be dozens of calls to make arrangements…"

"Unless they were all done online," Alvarez said. "Using the 'missing' computer. What we have is the 'official' paper trail which shows a woman making arrangements for her husband's funeral – after he died. You show this to a jury and they'll say, 'so what?'."

"Except for the pre-paid cell phone," Flynn said. "And the calls to her just before and after St. John died. Those are the calls the jury will have trouble with."

**Chapter 12.**

"We need a dump of numbers from that phone," Lee said, ticking off items on her fingers. "Everything the issuer can give us on when and where it was purchased. Video surveillance from the store where it was purchased. Interview with whoever sold the phone. Check credit card records. St. John had three or four of them in his wallet. If Cynthia is doing her getaway planning on the internet, maybe she slipped up somewhere. And, let's get our eyewitness with a sketch artist. This is an opportunity to make our own luck."

"What about Wells?" Alvarez asked.

Lee stopped. She chewed her lip. "Damn." She looked at Flynn. "We've got to rule him in or out. John, you talk to the plant breeder. I'll take Wells as soon as he shows up. Join me if you can." She shook her head from side to side slowly and sighed. "I could use a couple of extra hands on this one. For once, even Vito Mazilli would be welcome."

Flynn found an empty office and keyed in the number for the Lancaster plant breeder. It took just one transfer to reach Quentin Young. Flynn introduced himself.

On the other end of the line, Flynn heard Young sigh. "I figured it was only a matter of time before the police called."

"Why is that?" Flynn asked.

"Carolina Blue went missing. St. John Grainger-Elliot is dead. All in the same day. I told Stuart to just wait and keep his eyes open."

"I'm still not following you," Flynn said.

"Stuart Wells went to the police. You said you were with the Boston police."

Flynn scratched his head. "Actually, he hasn't come to us yet. If you told him to wait and to keep his eyes open, then that's exactly what he's done."

"Then, why are you calling me?" Young asked, sounding confused. "How did you know…"

"Because we need to know what Wells told you over the course of several calls on Friday, starting with the one around four o'clock."

"Is he a suspect…"

"Please, Mr. Young, we have a lot going on up here. He made a call to you around four on Friday afternoon. You made a pair of calls back to him shortly after that. Around six-thirty, he called you again and then a final time a little before midnight. Let's start with those calls."

Flynn heard the hesitation on the other end of the line. "Stuart called me as soon as he discovered the daylilies were missing. He was hysterical. I can only imagine what he was going through. This was the first public showing of a daylily that is going to change the way people think about daylilies. Pale blue and a repeat bloomer, mid-June to frost. Does that mean anything to you?"

"I've had it explained to me," Flynn said. "I didn't know the part about repeat blooms."

"Take my word for it," Young said. "This is a plant people will be talking about for years to come. Stuart lobbied for it. Said he'd make it the star attraction of his exhibit. As I said, he was hysterical. And, he was convinced that Grainger-Elliot stole it, right from the start."

"Why?"

"Because his display got moved to the back of the exhibit hall at the last minute. Because of that business with the Blaschka Collection and the Botanical Society prints. That kind of activity doesn't happen in a vacuum."

"What did you tell him to do?"

"My first thought was to have him go to the police. Then I talked it over with our people here." There was a pause on the line. "This is probably alien country to you, Detective. This is an industry that has worked on trust for decades. I wholesale my plant to you and you nurture it for months, then sell it at retail. When the stakes were low, it's how we did business. Plant genetics changed everything. Instead of looking for the interesting sport, we…"

"Sport?" Flynn asked.

"Mutation. Your hosta develops a leaf unlike any other. You nurture it along and see if you can cultivate more like it. Usually it reverts. Once in a while, the mutation sticks. Presto, you have a new hosta variety. Plant genetics is different. It's a whole new – and more expensive – ball game. You have laboratories and tissue cultures and you're injecting DNA from other plants, all in pursuit of something unique: the rose that has a particular scent or a color or one that lasts longer or opens so far and stays that way."

"Or a blue daylily," Flynn said.

"Yes. Carolina Blue. We've been working on it for ten years – and I mean ten years of serious development. We're racing everyone else out there who is after the same product. And now, this. Put yourselves in our place: this is Carolina Blue's first public showing, and the executive director of the New England Botanical Society steals the lot of them. What do you do? Shout from the rooftops that they're missing? You'll get everybody and his country brother looking for them or claiming they've found them. Or do you try to find them, quietly?"

"I see your point," Flynn said.

"We told Stuart to speak to Grainger-Elliot as soon as he could, tell him that we knew it was him, and offer to pay a ransom to get the plants back."

"A ransom?"

"Yes. Isn't that a kick in the head? You can ransom plants."

"There were other calls on Friday and Friday night," Flynn prompted.

"Right," Young said. "I had Stuart repeat his story to a couple of people here. They couldn't believe it until they heard it first-hand. When Grainger-Elliot showed up, Stuart did talk to him and offered to buy back the daylilies. Grainger-Elliot was astonished that someone had stolen them and said he would put out the word – quietly, of course. He also asked the size of the reward."

"How much were you offering?"

"A half a million dollars."

Flynn was speechless for a moment, absorbing the number that Young had tossed out so readily. "They're worth that much?"

"They're worth ten times that much to the right party. That's why we wanted to keep everything quiet."

"How many plants were there?" Flynn asked.

"We had seven specimens that were in bud. We gave all of them to Stuart."

"How many daylilies could you grow from those seven?"

"Using tissue cultures, somewhere in the low thousands," Young said. "In the right lab and with the right equipment, those tissue cultures would grow into plants that could be sold next year. If you culture from individual cells it would take longer but you could produce an order of magnitude more plants."

"Stuart Wells spoke with St. John – Grainger-Elliot – just before midnight, and then called you. What did he say?"

"That Grainger-Elliot believed he could have them back by morning and that no ransom payment would be required. I was dubious but I told Stuart to wait until morning. Stuart called the next morning to say the police had just found Grainger-Elliot's body."

"How did he sound?"

"Like a man who was watching his credibility get destroyed. 'Distraught' is not too strong a term to describe how he sounded."

"What do you intend to do about the daylilies?"

There was another pause on the other end of the line. "We listen and we wait. In the best scenario, we get a call that someone found them and that they're all safe with no clippings taken. In which case this will all be a nightmare that ends happily. The next best outcome is that St. John hid them somewhere, and they'll be found in a week; frozen, dead and unusable to anyone. It means we can't use them for additional tissue cultures, but then neither can anyone else."

"We talked with another exhibitor – without mentioning your daylilies," Flynn said. "He mentioned China."

"That's the nightmare that doesn't end," Young said. "But it would take a thief of extraordinary skill to make that connection. We understand no exhibitors or vendors were allowed in the display area between seven in the morning and the time awards were posted."

"We've been assured that was the case," Flynn said. "Only judges and the Botanical Society staff. If St. John stole your daylilies, he used a unique window of opportunity when the staff was in a meeting and the judges hadn't yet been released. It was only about fifteen minutes."

"He could have done it in five," Young said. "I can't believe a responsible non-profit hired a guy like that. Do you know who killed him?"

"We're getting close," Flynn said. He hoped he was right.

\* \* \* \* \*

Lee spotted Stuart Wells as he came back into the exhibit area. She asked him into the VIP lounge, invited him to sit in the most comfortable chair and offered tea or coffee, both of which Wells declined.

"We've established that you weren't completely honest with us about the daylilies – 'Carolina Blue', I think they're called," Lee said. Her voice was neutral, her approach, professional.

"They were stolen," Wells said in a low voice. His body flinched, a certain sign of nervousness.

"You believe they were stolen by St. John Grainger-Elliot," Lee said, observing the perspiration beads forming on Wells' forehead.

"He was the only person who could have done it," Wells replied. "I knew it as soon as I saw they were missing."

"Why didn't you say anything to the police?"

Wells paused before answering and, when he did, his gaze was to his hands, not to Lee. "I was told by the people who supplied the daylilies that I should approach St. John and buy them back. I did what they asked me to do. At first, he said he had no idea they had been stolen. Then, he said he was fairly certain he knew where they were and who had taken them and he could have them for me in the morning. The next morning, he was dead." Wells' hands were shaking by the time he had finished speaking.

*Lying?* Lee thought. *Or hiding something?*

"You were observed speaking to him around one-thirty as the Gala was breaking up," Lee said. "By that time, it was nearly six hours since you first spoke to him. What did he say that last time?"

Wells wiped at the sweat on his forehead with the sleeve of his shirt. "He said he had talked with 'some people'. He said he was 'ninety-nine percent certain' he could get them back."

"And you knew he was lying," Lee said.

"Yes. I knew he was lying through his teeth. I knew he was stringing me along, and I didn't know why. I said the plant breeder would pay half a million dollars to get them back. And I knew that regardless of how it turned out, it would ruin my reputation." More sweat, more nervous shaking. Anger seeped into Wells' voice.

"How would it ruin your reputation?" Lee asked. "He was the one who stole them."

Wells gulped air. "I went out on such a limb to get 'Carolina Blue'. I put fifty thousand into my exhibit. That's twice what I've ever spent before. I promised them 'Carolina Blue' would be the first thing people coming into the show saw. And, instead, I got dumped into the back of the hall with the propeller-heads. And St. John stole the damned daylilies. When it gets around – and it will – no one is ever going to trust me again."

"From talking with the exhibitors around you," Lee said, "they seem to think you're doing well. Lots of traffic. Lots of expensively dressed people spending a lot of time with you."

Wells closed his eyes. His fists clenched. "That… isn't… the… point. The point is that for the first time in ten years, an exhibitor – me – at one of the big shows – here – had a prize cultivar stolen out from underneath his nose. And not just any cultivar. The next huge thing in the plant world. And it was stolen from me because I wasn't doing my job."

The anger was out in the open now, surprising Lee. She asked her next question gently. "But no one was allowed in the hall when they were stolen, and St. John said he'd get 'Carolina Blue' back for you."

Wells smiled slightly. "He said, 'See me in the morning'. He made it sound like he had it all under control. He was just trying to put me off."

"So, what did you do?" Lee asked, her voice gentle, almost conversational.

Wells said nothing.

"Did you confront him again?" Lee asked. She was tiptoeing up to the subject.

Wells swallowed. "I went to the hotel. I went to my room. And I got angrier. The man had ruined my reputation." Wells looked at his hands again. "I went to his suite. He wasn't there."

Not the answer Lee had expected. "You knew where his room was?" Lee asked.

"He had the exhibitors in for a cocktail party Wednesday night. A lousy case of booze and some store-brand mixers. He wasn't there. Everybody knew he was sleeping with the little redhead – Winona. I figured he was spending the night in her room."

"What did you do?"

"I got the key to his suite."

"From where?"

"From the front desk. That rat hole of a hotel will give out the key to anyone who asks. They don't care."

"So, you went into the suite?"

Wells nodded. "I figured that's where I'd find 'Carolina Blue'."

"You really turned the place upside down," Lee said. "It was a mess."

"I was angry. I wanted him to know I knew he was lying to me. But they weren't there."

"You had the foresight to wear gloves," Lee said.

Wells shrugged. "Garden gloves. Work gloves. I stopped back at my room after I got the key."

"You expected the police to dust for fingerprints?"

"I expected St. John to press charges. The bastard may have stolen my plants but he'd have me charged with breaking and entering. But they weren't there. He hid them somewhere else."

"You never invited St. John back into the management area to talk at around a quarter to two?"

"No. I listened to his last lie. I did what Quentin Young told me to do. I tried to find them on my own." Wells' voice was far away now. He started into a space over Lee's shoulder. "I'm ruined. St. John ruined me."

"You went through Winona Stone's room, too?"

Wells looked at Lee, surprised, but nodded. "After they wouldn't let us into the exhibit hall and I heard St. John was dead. I went back to the hotel. I said I misplaced my key and a maid opened the door. I didn't think anyone would know I had been there."

"You didn't do any damage," Lee said. "But Ms. Stone noticed some things out of place."

Wells shook his head. "No. He hadn't spent the night there. But I thought he might have given the daylilies to her for safekeeping.

They weren't there."

"Do you have an idea of what St. John may have done with the daylilies?"

Wells exhaled. "If they're not in the hotel, they could be anywhere. And, that's the problem. If St. John wanted them for the ransom, he'd have pocketed the money and that would have been the end of it. If he got them to someone else – some intermediary – Friday morning, they could be anywhere in the world now. And no one is ever going to trust me with an important plant again." Wells finally looked at Lee. "I assume you're going to arrest me."

It was Lee's turn to smile. "No. I don't think so. I wish you had come forward. If you had been honest when we first talked with you, we might be a lot further along with our investigation. But I think those daylilies may still be the key. If you hear something, please don't keep it to yourself."

Lee reached out and took Wells' hand. It was an instinctive move. There was no motivation behind it other than to connect with this man who had gone through a private hell for nearly three days. To her surprise, Wells neither flinched nor withdrew his hand. Instead, he seemed to be comforted by the contact. "Like a lot of other people, you got played by St. John," Lee said. "We're also looking for "Carolina Blue' because it will likely lead us to his murderer."

The palm of her hand continued to lay atop his, her fingers curled around his, softly and lightly. It was something she had done with some frequency with women, especially those who had been victims of a crime. In five years as a detective she had never once made such a physical contact with a man.

"At this point, we know St. John was a con man…" Lee began talking about the case and what they had discovered about him. She did not know where to begin and where to end; only that she wanted to keep the physical contact. As she spoke she looked at Wells directly, taking in his rugged good looks and intelligent eyes. She kept talking and, as she did, she saw a gradual change in Wells' face, a relaxing of the muscles around his eyes and mouth.

*What in the hell are you doing?* a voice in her in her subconscious asked, even as she continued talking to him. *This is an investigation, not a singles bar...*

Suddenly, Wells' head jerked to the right, and he put his hands on his lap. Lee followed his gaze to see Flynn standing in the doorway, preparing to knock on the frame. He seemed not to have noticed anything, or else his face gave away nothing.

"I think we're finished for now," Lee said, rising from her chair. "If I have any other questions, I'll call you or come by the booth." Her heart was racing and she felt flushed.

Wells nodded quickly. "I...." He seemed to change his mind about what to say. "Thank you," he said after some hesitation. "Thank you for hearing my side of it."

Wells left the VIP lounge. Lee and Flynn remained behind, waiting until he was clear of the area.

"I wasn't going to push him," Lee said. "And, besides, he isn't going anywhere."

"He's still a suspect?" Flynn asked.

"He said he's certain St. John stole the daylilies from his exhibit Friday morning. He owned up to breaking into St. John's and Stone's room. And he acknowledges he wore gloves when he did it. That's worrisome. But I didn't hear a lot of evasion. I'm not crossing him off the list, but I think he was being straight."

"You're the boss," Flynn said. In his mind, however, he replayed the glimpse of interaction between Lee and Wells. She was leaning across the table, one of her hands seemingly caressing his. Flynn could not see her face, but Wells' expression was somewhere between bliss and relief. That Wells had pulled back his hand the instant he saw Flynn was telling. The look on Lee's face when she turned was one he had never seen before from her: complete surprise at being caught doing something unexpected. It wasn't his place to say anything. If she raised the subject, fine.

Lee was speaking, and he had missed the first words of what she said. "...problem is, if Wells isn't our guy and this isn't about blue daylilies or something else St. John stole, then we've been looking at the case all wrong," Lee said. "St. John was bound and gagged. We assumed -- no, *I* assumed — that someone wanted information from him and the daylilies made perfect sense. They kicked the crap out of him. When they didn't get the information, they killed him and then tossed his hotel room looking for the daylilies. Except that Wells readily admits to having been the person who went through both rooms. Maybe it wasn't information the murderer was after."

"Or, maybe we just haven't hit on the right information," Flynn said. "We didn't know about daylilies until a few hours ago. St. John could be dirty fifteen ways from Sunday. We've got a pre-paid cell phone calling Cynthia just before and just after the murder. We need to focus on her and find the person who made those calls."

* * * * *

In Brookfield, Hoffman rubbed his back against the chair in Raymond Brady's cramped, overflowing office. Detective work, he thought, that was once a matter of following physical clues and reading people's body language, had devolved into the pursuit of electrons and reading emails. Who called whom, who wrote messages to whom. Even who subscribed to whose Twitter stream.

The state police had come and gone. They were Old School; taking measurements of the body's position and determining the angle at which bullets were fired. They had collected all of the physical evidence of the crime and photographed the scene extensively. They had not bothered with Brady's computer and so Hoffman felt no compunction to, as the state trooper put it, 'stay the hell out of our case.'

Nominally, Brady's house was sealed. Hoffman heard talk of

troopers coming back to make a thorough inventory of Brady's shop to determine what might have been stolen – a process that could take weeks.

Hoffman turned back to the computer. There were multiple folders for saved emails within Brady's ancient – five years old, probably – desktop system. Hoffman methodically looked at message headers and, if the topic sounded fruitful, the full email. The tenth such folder he opened had the innocuous legend, 'pending items'. The folder contained perhaps thirty emails, all from a single Gmail account. The email titles bore titles such as *'missing u'*. He opened the most recent, dated just four days earlier.

"Jesus Christ," he muttered.

Hoffman reached into his wallet and found Lieutenant Lee's card, then pulled out his cell phone and tapped in her number.

\* \* \* \* \*

Lee looked at her phone and scanned the caller ID line. "Hoffman," she said to Flynn. She tapped the phone to connect the call.

"What do you know about Herr Doktor Friedrich Carl von Faber?" Hoffman asked.

"I hope you're going to tell me," Lee said.

"You're probably at the flower show, right?"

"Yes, and feeling sorry for ourselves."

"If I say Cameroon Grasslands Kingdoms, does that ring any bells?"

"For crying out loud, Hoffman, what are you talking about?" Lee said, annoyed.

"Let me print this stuff out," Hoffman said. "I haven't been to the flower show in years. Hell, it's President's Day. I'll bet there's nobody on the Pike, I can be there in half an hour, forty minutes tops."

"You're going to tell me what that was all about, right?" Flynn asked after Lee had ended the call, a perplexed look on her face.

"Your Detective Hoffman is coming down to see us, all the way from Brookfield. With printouts. Something about grasslands and Herr Doktor Faber."

"Animal House," Flynn said.

Lee looked at him blankly.

"Faber College. Blutarsky, Larry Kroger, Otter, D-Day, Dean Wormer. It all takes place at Faber College. The movie. *Animal House*."

Lee shook her head. "I ought to record this stuff and play it back to you. Working with you every day is like being on some trivia edition of *Jeopardy*. He asked if, in the course of our investigation, we had come across any references to someone called Doctor Faber. He's coming down to see us. He sounded fairly excited."

There was a knock at the door. Alvarez was grinning, his entire body animated with excitement.

"I'll bet you've found something," Lee said.

"The pre-paid cell," Alvarez said. "Purchased four weeks ago at a Wal-Mart in Framingham."

"Tell me there's security tape footage," Lee said.

"I've already uploaded it."

"God, I love computers," Flynn said.

Alvarez tapped an icon. A program started and, a few seconds later, the screen was filled with a twenty-second sequence of a tall, brown-haired man in a ski parka buying the cell phone. He paid cash for the phone and for an airtime card. The sequence ended and Alvarez replayed it.

"Freeze it there," Lee said.

The image was of a man, about forty years old, roughly six feet tall with short brown hair and a hint of a moustache.

"Missy Clifford's mystery man in the hallway," Lee said. To Alvarez, she said, "Figure out a way to get six or seven other clips from that same store. Give me men with brown hair…"

"You want a video lineup," Alvarez said. "I'll get on the phone to store security."

Lee and Flynn watched the video clip three more times. "Civil libertarians scream about this stuff," Flynn said. "Invasion of privacy. We're looking at a film of a guy who may have committed a murder or at least been complicit in one. All because he bought a cell phone and a transaction number from a register was tied to a digital camera recorder and Wal-Mart saves its tens of millions of videos on some server farm in deepest, darkest Arkansas."

"I'm looking at his hands," Lee said. "Long fingers but small hands. This guy doesn't work with his hands for a living. What does he do?"

"You can ask him when we catch him," Flynn said.

Ten minutes later, Alvarez was back. From his computer, he displayed a dozen downloaded video clips. Lee looked at each one, telling Alvarez whether to keep or delete it. After a few minutes, she had settled on six videos and the sequence in which they would be viewed.

"Let's go get Missy," Lee said.

Five minutes after that, Melissa Clifford sat before Alvarez's computer.

"We're going to show you six clips of a man making a purchase at a store," Lee said. "I want you to tell us if any of them is of the man you saw in the hallway Friday night. You can ask us to repeat or freeze-frame anything that you'd like to take a longer look at."

"I only saw him for a few seconds," Clifford said.

"Then, if none of them look enough like the man to identify him, just say so," Lee said.

The clips began. She made no comment on the first or second one. She asked to repeat the third one. She watched the fourth one, saying nothing.

Ten seconds into the fifth one, she said, "Oh, my God, that's him!"

"Let's watch the sixth one before you say you're certain," Lee said.

Clifford watched the sixth video, shook her head, then asked to replay the fifth. She froze one frame and jabbed her finger at the screen excitedly. "The ears," she said. "I forgot he had these funny ears. They kind of stuck out."

Flynn looked at the image. "Attached lobes, slight protrusion. Jug ears. Like Prince Charles."

"You're certain?" Lee asked.

"It isn't just the ears," Clifford said. "It's also the shape of the face and the eyebrows. How did you get this? Where was it taken?"

Lee smiled. "That's what we do for a living. Miss Clifford, there may come a time when we have to ask you to identify this man again, and we don't want having seen these images to prejudice you. Go back to work, keep the image of the man you saw in the hallway that night in your mind."

"But that's the same guy, isn't it?"

Lee quickly shook her head. "All I can say is that what you've done is enormously helpful. For now, go back to work."

Clifford left the room, the look on her face indicating she was uncertain if she had been of any help.

Alvarez had been sitting on the far side of the room, observing the video lineup but not participating.

"What's the matter, Jason?" Lee asked.

Alvarez exhaled and gritted his teeth. "She's the closest thing we have to an eyewitness. I talked to her twice, and she wouldn't say anything to me. Blew me off. Then, she spills everything to you. And all you tell me is that she wouldn't talk to me because I'm male."

Lee looked up at the ceiling and gave a sigh of frustration. "Jason, Missy Clifford didn't talk to you because she was too embarrassed. The reason she saw our perp is that, a little after midnight on Friday, she and a guy she barely knew came back into one of these offices and had sex." Lee used finger quotes to add, "They hooked up."

Lee continued. "She's twenty-two years old and has her first professional job – a job she's afraid she is going to lose any day because the New England Botanical Society looks like it's going to sink without a trace. You're a good looking guy with a wedding ring on your left hand. She's supposed to be establishing a career but, instead, she's still acting like it's spring break back at Duke or Brown or whatever incredibly expensive private college she went to."

Still seeing a downcast look on Alvarez's face, Lee said, "Get used to it, Jason. People are going to lie to you. Or else they're going to not tell you stuff because of how they perceive you. Believe me, it happened to me, too. Guys would open up to John – brag about things they had done – and they'd treat me like I was invisible. You're a detective. Look for the subtle clues – they're universal -- and work around whatever gender, race or nationality issues the interviewee has. It's why you have a partner."

"But I've had Vito Mazilli…"

"Not for much longer," Lee said. "Maybe not even for another day. Jason, you're good at what you do. You are stunningly good on that computer. The Department needs two dozen of you. After we get past this case I am going to go to the mat to make certain you're reassigned. But you've also got to work on reading people and pulling out information. Computers make detectives more productive. They don't replace interviews or intuition."

Alvarez was silent. Finally, he said, "Thank you."

"But you had something else to say," Flynn said. "Before Missy Clifford distracted you."

"Right," Alvarez said, a look of chagrin on his face. "Calls from the cell phone. There aren't any, apart from the ones to Cynthia Duncastle."

Flynn whistled. "This guy is good. One phone for one contact. He probably has a bag full of them."

"No way to create the web," Lee added. "Single points of communication with no way to connect them."

"And all calls are quick," Flynn said. "Plausible deniability. 'Wrong number'. 'An answering machine picked up'. 'There was no one on the other end of the line'."

"So, who is he?" Alvarez asked.

"That is the question we had better answer very soon," Flynn said.

"Could he be a pro?" Alvarez asked.

"I've considered that," Flynn replied. "If we assume that he did the work on St. John, then he's somebody who can inflict pain – and kill – without compunction. But, in thirty-five years I got to know all of the local talent and his face isn't familiar. Also, the up-and-comers were usually the guys hanging around in the background, waiting for their big break. You may not have known their names but their faces registered. Not this one."

Lee's phone rang. She looked at the incoming number, and held up a finger, asking for quiet.

"Hi, Lois… yes… no… no, of course I didn't know… oh, crap…. no, there's nothing you could do… OK…."

Lee put the phone back in her purse. She closed her eyes, her jaw was clenched.

"Sean O'Connell just ordered Lois to release St. John's body."

"With everything we've got, you can't take that to O'Connell and tell him we're close?" Alvarez asked.

"Jason, we've got five things that point straight to Cynthia Duncastle," Lee said. "But we've got nothing that even vaguely looks like proof. Cynthia isn't big enough or strong enough to have killed her husband, and we've known about the guy with the phone for less than an hour, and we have nothing that ties him specifically to all this. And, Sean O'Connell is a political animal. He's had one high-profile case where going after the widow blew up in his face. He isn't going to touch another one without a confession."

"How long do we have?" Alvarez asked.

"It depends on whether you have to embalm a body before you put it on a plane."

## Chapter 13.

"I don't think I've ever seen a more discouraged set of people in my life," Hoffman said. "I mean, I've seen football teams that were down three touchdowns in the fourth quarter that looked more hopeful than you three."

"Tell me you have something," Lee said, her chin resting on her hands as they sat in the VIP lounge. "Our chief suspect is about to go put her husband's body on a plane, and the chance that we'll ever see her after that is just about zero."

Hoffman walked into the room and looked around, noting the tasteful furniture and good lighting. "I could do with a place like this for interrogations. They don't happen to keep any good single malts in that sideboard, do they?"

Lee looked up. Sounding as tired as she felt she said, "Either tell us what you've got or else go back to the 'burbs."

Hoffman took a sheaf of pages from the pocket inside of his jacket lapel and unfolded them. "And I thought you were a fun bunch. I was going to ask if I could hang out and play with you guys."

He spread the pages across the coffee table.

"Let me take you on a little trip," Hoffman said. "And I ask you to bear with me because the payoff is pretty good on this one. It's 1916 and staid old Boston has just burst into the world headlines because of the anti-war riots in the North End. Now, the rioters are all those immigrant Eye-talian riff-raff and the like but, over in Germany, the Kaiser likes both what he hears and what his spies report. What they tell him -- rightly or wrongly -- is that the Brahmin set might have the clout to keep the U.S. of A on the sidelines while Europeans slaughter one another."

Hoffman looked to see if he had everyone's attention. He did.

"What the Kaiser needs is some trustworthy feet on the ground who can get a sense for who among the rich and powerful are really opposed to sending over American doughboys, and might get enlisted to the Hun's cause.  And so the Kaiser dispatches one Doktor Friedrich Carl Von Faber to Massachusetts to talk to the locals.  Faber, for those of you who may have let your subscription to *Who's Who in Germany* lapse, is one of the world's pre-eminent botanists who spent six years picking up interesting plants in Africa in the early years of the twentieth century.  He spent 1907 in German West Africa, specifically, a place called 'Kamerun' or, as we call it today, Cameroon, which will become important in just a moment."

"Faber loaded up a trunk with trinkets – interesting plants and knick-knacks--and delivered a series of lectures at the New England Botanical Society that were very well attended.  During the intermissions, he felt out the well-dressed attendees for their sentiments about the Great War.  Those who muttered that it was barbaric and that it was jolly good that America was sitting this one out got stroked in the form of nifty African plants for their greenhouses.  My understanding is that they also got follow-up visits from intelligence officers."

"When Faber had done his job – fourteen lectures over twelve days – he bade his hosts goodbye and left behind a present.  A genuine Kamerun Grasslands Kingdoms helmet mask.  Because I know you're dying to know, these masks were ceremonial in nature and the province of tribal chiefs who were part of the Kwifoyn, which was the Kamerun equivalent of the Supreme Court and Congress rolled up into one.  Above them was the Fon, the chief of the Grasslands Kingdoms."

"The Germans came through in the 1880s and did a quite thorough, typically Teutonic job of slaughtering the Kwifoyn, and they collected a fair number of these masks, most of which ended up in various German museums.  The Kaiser went through his attic and found one that reportedly belonged to the Fon himself. Brass, copper, glass beads, cowrie shells, and the image of the royal spider. The Kaiser thought it was plug ugly and told Faber to give it to the Americans. Faber did. The head of the Botanical Society, who apparently thought no more highly of it than the Kaiser, promptly consigned it to the basement where it was forgotten about."

"Fast forward ninety-plus years. Someone has been poking around in that basement. They find this mask. They do some research. They find out that one of the Rockefellers gave a similar mask to the Metropolitan Museum of Art, and it's the pride of the African collection. There hasn't been one at auction in more than a decade but, when that last one came on the market, museums and private collectors bid the thing to $1.7 million. And what's down there isn't just *a* mask, this is the *head guy's* mask. This is a retirement plan."

"One evening about two months ago, the mask was taken out of storage, and someone began creating a *provenance* for the mask. From Jesko von Puttkamer, colonial governor, to his wife, Henrietta, to their niece, Anna, to the Stürman Gallery in Antwerp, regrettably destroyed in 1944, et cetera, et cetera, until it comes to its present owner."

Hoffman smiled.

"You're going to keep us in suspense, aren't you?" Flynn said. "That, or else you don't know, and we're going to strangle you."

Hoffman produced the top sheet of his stack of papers with a flourish. "Cynthia Duncan," he said. "Who I assume is also Cynthia Duncastle." He handed two sheets, one of them a photograph of the mask, to Flynn, the other a document attesting that the Hennepin County Probate Court had named Cynthia Duncan the rightful owner of the Kamerun mask.

"And so we come full circle," Flynn said, reading the printed sheet. "And you know all this because?"

"A thorough search of Brady's computer coupled with a well-rounded liberal arts education plus an hour on Wikipedia," Hoffman said. "We've got a wonderful email trail between Ms. Duncan and the late Raymond Brady. He was helping to create that provenance and to find a buyer. All in return for a one-third cut of the proceeds, of course. And, while I'm no expert, I suspect there was a little hanky-panky going on, to judge from the 'adult' content of some of those emails. Apparently, while your Mr. Grainger-Elliot was plundering the Society, the mizzus was getting a little on the side from her friendly antiques dealer. I think they used to call that an 'open marriage'."

Flynn turned to Lee and handed her the two sheets. "Are we getting closer on motive?"

Lee laughed. "We have all of the motive we need. We've *had* all of the motive we need for a day now. It's tying Cynthia to the murder that's the problem."

"Do you want to enlighten me?" Hoffman asked. "Please remember, I have a murder to solve on behalf of that lovable group of Keystone Kops we know as the Massachusetts State Police. I sort of thought in the interest of inter-agency cooperation…"

"We have a guy," Flynn said. "At midnight on Friday, one of the staff people here saw 'Mister X' in the hallway outside the room where St. John was killed. We also have a dump of phone calls to and from Cynthia's and St. John's home – during the times when St. John wouldn't have been there – that show a pre-paid cell phone calling the home over the last few weeks. The phone was purchased out in Framingham, for cash, but we have video of the purchase. What's more, we have a positive ID of 'Mister X' on the video by the young lady who saw him in the hallway that night."

"God, you are one industrious set of detectives," Hoffman said. "And you're not busting down the doors of the adulterous widow because…?"

"Because Sean O'Connell is scared silly he's going to look like a heartless bastard on the six o'clock news," Lee offered. "No search warrant, no formal questioning. Not without unequivocal proof."

"But he *is* a heartless bastard," Hoffman said. "Why should a gutless D.A. hide his true colors? We don't do that in Middlesex County. Our D.A.'s own right up to their…"

"Got it!" Alvarez shouted. He had been on his computer since Hoffman's appearance and had not been part of the conversation.

"Got what?" Hoffman asked.

"'A corpse being repatriated to the United Kingdom, if recently deceased and properly refrigerated in transit, need not be embalmed or otherwise preserved, if interment is indicated within a reasonable period following the arrival of the corpse at a recognized international gateway.'"

"Who is this fountain of macabre information?" Hoffman asked.

\* \* \* \* \*

Two calls to the funeral homes contacted by Cynthia Duncastle produced the information that a Batesville Persian Bronze casket had been selected by the widow – a floor model, so to speak – and that a hearse had been dispatched to pick up the body of St. John Grainger-Elliot from the Suffolk County morgue. Because no public viewing or memorial service was planned, Cynthia Duncastle had asked that her husband be buried in a plain dark suit and that not even makeup be applied to give the body a better appearance. On the whole, the funeral director with whom Alvarez spoke sounded annoyed that the death of such a prominent local figure should yield only the mark-up on the cost of a casket and the mileage charge for the hearse.

A call to Virgin Atlantic Airlines confirmed that space for a casket had been booked for the 8:45 p.m. flight from Boston Logan to London Heathrow. Another call confirmed that Duncastle and her three minor children were booked on the same flight, with a return scheduled for two weeks hence.

Lee looked at her watch. "We've got eight hours to make a case."

\* \* \* \* \*

Hoffman agreed that the man in the video was not a 'player' in the local muscle-for-hire market. "It took four bullets to kill Brady," he said. "The first three weren't even close to being kill shots. Professionals don't waste bullets."

"So we just put out an APB?" Flynn suggested.

"Needle in a haystack," Lee said. "We also have the interesting fact that he hasn't called Cynthia since Saturday morning."

"He could have finished the jobs and moved on," Flynn said.

"Or finished the jobs and then Cynthia could have gotten rid of the only witness," Alvarez said. "I think Detective Hoffman has probably concluded Cynthia has ample motive for killing Brady."

"God, you're a bright kid," Hoffman said. "As a matter of fact, my leg has been twitching ever since I read those emails. With Brady dead, Cynthia doesn't have to pay out a third of the take from the sale of the mask. That's half a million reasons to kill the guy, at least."

"So why haven't you been on the phone to the Middlesex D.A.?" Alvarez asked.

"Don't get too bright all of a sudden," Hoffman replied. "My evidence is fresh and uncorroborated. I've got a D.A. who, except during fair week, couldn't find Brookfield on a map if he tried, and then only during election years. And, once he's presented with the evidence, he's going to demand more, because that's what's safe. Oh, and I'm not even on the case because I'm just the stupid local LEO in the eyes of the state police. Compared to what I have to go through to get a search warrant – and especially one on a widow lady – you guys are in cop paradise over on this side of the Charles."

"The emails certainly show an intent to defraud the Botanical Society and the probability of grand theft," Alvarez offered. "Isn't that enough?"

"No," Hoffman replied. Look at it from my D.A.'s point of view. Has anyone actually been down into this treasure-filled basement? Does anyone know if this mask is missing? Or was it ever there? I'm going on Cynthia's emails to Brady. She could claim she's writing the screenplay for the next Indiana Jones movie."

Lee looked sheepish. "That's on our 'to-do' list. From back when I thought we could keep the body for a few days."

"Got it!" Alvarez said, staring intently at his computer screen.

"More instructions on removing bodies?" Hoffman asked.

"An entry from 1916: *Kamerun Grasslands Kingdoms helmet mask before 1880, represented as having belonged to the Fon of the Grasslands Kingdom. Gift of Prof. Friedrich Carl Von Faber. Acknowledged October 3, 1916.*"

"Who *is* this guy?" Hoffman asked.

* * * * *

The decision to go to the Castle was as much to see what might be going on in the townhouse adjacent to the Botanical Society headquarters as it was to determine what items might be missing from the Society's archives. Hoffman and Alvarez stayed upstairs to make a further examination of Grainger-Elliot's office and those of other staff members. With Lee and Flynn was Linda Beckett, the Society's curator. She was a white-haired woman of at least seventy with a pronounced dowager's hump.

"Who has access to the downstairs storage area?" Lee asked as they descended the stairs.

"Only me," Beckett said.

"It's kept locked at all time?" Lee asked.

"That's right," the woman said. "I have the only key."

"Where do you keep the key?" Flynn asked.

"In my desk. And my office is locked."

"Is there a master key?" Flynn asked.

"Well, of course."

"And, who has a master key?"

Beckett stopped at the bottom of the stairwell and cocked her head. "Well, St. John had one. And Tony Wilson, of course. And…"

"Thank you, Mrs. Beckett," Flynn said. "I think I understand." *I understand that anyone who wanted to could readily gain access to the storage area.*

Beckett opened a sturdy wooden door and reached for a light switch on the inside. A bank of bare, incandescent bulbs came on in the low-ceilinged room. An intense, musty smell coupled with that of spice, like a potpourri that had been in a drawer too long filled the air.

Banks of wooden cabinets lined the room, which was perhaps forty feet long and twenty-five feet wide. Most were flat file drawers, all with brass pull tabs and ivoried cards with brown spidery handwriting. Oddly, there was no dust. The cabinet surfaces all gleamed. In the center of the room was a large oak table. It, too, looked to have been recently polished.

*Fingerprints? What fingerprints?* Flynn thought as he opened a random drawer. Inside were glass jars filled with seeds, some of them the size of golf balls. Affixed to each jar was a description of its contents. *Collected January 1904 Fleming Amazon Expedition. V6 04-122.5.*

"What does this mean?" Flynn asked, holding the jar for Mrs. Beckett to see.

Beckett adjusted her glasses. "That would be the expedition led by Jonathan Whitehall Fleming to the upper Amazon in 1904. The plant associated with the seeds is sketched in volume six of the expedition papers as plate 122.5."

"The Blaschka collection," Lee said. "Where do you keep it?"

Beckett indicated with her hand the floor-to-ceiling cabinets at the far end of the room.

"We're looking for an African tribal mask," Flynn said. "It wasn't part of an expedition. It was a gift to the Society from a German who visited the Society in 1916…"

"The Faber lectures," Beckett smiled approvingly. "One of the Society's more noteworthy achievements. "We have the complete original transcription of them in the archives; three stenographers working in tandem."

"What about the mask?" Lee asked. "Dr. Faber left it behind as a gift."

Beckett nodded. "We have several cabinets for things such as that." She tottered toward a mahogany case against the left wall, then changed her mind and headed for one in the center of the room. Her fingers traced down a set of descriptions on cards, and she leaned over to open the bottommost drawer.

Beckett turned to the group. "I have trouble leaning over too far. Would one of you be so kind?"

Flynn opened the drawer. A nest of yellowed paper occupied the center of the otherwise empty drawer.

Beckett gasped.

"I take it you expected the mask to be here," Flynn said.

"Who would take such a thing?" Beckett asked, clearly dumfounded. "It's just a mask."

"When do you last remember seeing it?" Lee asked.

Beckett shook her head. "Oh, at least five years ago, during the last inventory. No, make that seven years ago."

"Mrs. Beckett, I couldn't help but notice that there's no dust down here," Flynn said. "Everything looks like it's been kept polished."

"Well, I try to keep it neat…"

"When was the last time you or anyone from the staff was down here to dust and polish?"

"Oh, around Christmas time, I should think," Beckett said. "When we had that awful business with the Blaschka Collection, I asked Tony Wilson to send down a cleaning crew."

Flynn looked at the surfaces. Nearly two months had elapsed since that cleaning. With people walking on the floor above, there should be a fine layer of ceiling dust on every surface. Someone had cleaned here in the past week, wiping away fingerprints in the process.

"There are other objects in the Society's collection like the mask," Lee said. "Could you check some of those?"

Beckett, visibly still shaken, turned her head left and right, uncertain where to begin. She opened a drawer and breathed an audible sigh of relief. One below it was opened. She nodded, her face again showing relief. She went to another cabinet a few feet away. She pulled open the second drawer. She murmured, 'Thank God.'

"Can we try the Blaschka collection?" Lee asked.

Beckett slowly walked to the back of the room and unfastened a pair of covering armoire-type doors. "These were custom made to hold the collection," she murmured. Finding the mask missing was clearly a blow from which she would not soon recover.

Behind the two doors was the standard array of drawers, each about seven inches deep. Beckett pulled open the one at waist level and shrieked. Lee and Flynn rushed to her side.

"Someone's been in here," Beckett said, her hand to her mouth. "These were packed solidly. There are three missing from this drawer." She closed that drawer and opened the one below. "And one from here. Oh, this is horrible. I don't want to go through this again. And they've been opened. Someone opened the packing cases to look at them. We put everything back together in December…"

"I know you had several thousand of these," Lee said. "If you could just open the drawers and give us a quick estimate…"

"I hate this," Beckett said. "Everything ran so well for so many years. And now this."

"Just a rough idea," Lee said.

"It will take a while," Beckett said, her voice filled with dread.

"We'll leave you alone," Lee said. She looked at Flynn and her head and eyes made an 'up' motion. Without another word, the two left the room.

When they were on the main floor, Lee shook her head in disbelief. "It was like a candy store down there."

"And up here, too," Flynn added. "You have two people in their seventies – one in charge of the books and the other in charge of God only know how many millions of dollars' worth of highly portable trinkets. St. John had this place figured out from day one. All he had to do was stay in the job and he could retire a wealthy man."

"Until he started making mistakes," Lee said.

"Making mistakes," Flynn agreed. "Or getting tired of it all. Even the best con artists get bored of the game. Mel Dawson's report just accelerated an exit strategy that was probably well underway."

"But a con artist can learn to love the life that goes with the con, too," Lee said. "St. John and Cynthia had it pretty easy here."

"Except that it was coming apart," Flynn countered. "St. John got everyone excited with his City Hall garden idea, but he either couldn't or else never had any intention of delivering on it. When he finally got his big donation from Alice Shelburne, he pocketed it. From that point, there was no turning back. Mel Dawson's background report was the straw that broke the camel's back. He couldn't fight it. All he could do was get out with everything he could grab."

"But Cynthia certainly had it easy," Lee said.

"Unless she was also getting tired of St. John. If there is, say, a one-in-four chance that Stuart Wells had a hand in St. John's death, there's a three-in-four probability that Cynthia was calling the shots Friday night. The woman I spoke with Sunday morning was not a grieving widow."

"She could have been planning it for years," Lee said.

"If not for years, then for months," Flynn said. "I think the Blaschka Collection sale was the tipping point. If St. John had gotten away with that, he and Cynthia could have pocketed a lot of money. But the sale of the first pieces attracted attention – forcing St. John to put the money back. We still don't know if Cynthia was the brains of the operation or just a willing participant. She and Ray Brady were working together on the sale of the mask. Was she doing that on her own? Or was it at St. John's behest?"

"Hoffman said the emails suggested that there was an affair going on between Cynthia and Brady. I doubt St. John would have suggested that kind of a perk," Lee said.

"Are you so sure?" Flynn countered. "Alvarez showed us that one batch of emails St. John had collected from snooping on his staff. I remember one to the effect that Cynthia came over to the Castle to look over the development staff. 'Dropping in for little chats', I think was the way it was put, and making certain that anyone St. John might be thinking about sleeping with was on birth control. Did she know St. John was carrying on with Winona Stone? Everyone else did. That's a rather permissive attitude on her part. Who's to say St. John didn't encourage Cynthia to use her body to advance their plans."

"Well, whatever it was, it was mercenary," Lee said. "And, Cynthia is probably packing next door with that mask carefully stowed in the luggage, and there's nothing we can do."

"Nothing who can do?"

Lee and Flynn turned to the sound of the voice. It was Hoffman, striding down the hall, a wide grin in his face. Alvarez was directly behind him, trying to keep up despite holding his computer and a sheaf of papers.

Hoffman jerked his thumb at Alvarez. "Your detective is a damned genius." He turned to Alvarez. "Tell 'em, kid."

Alvarez caught his breath. "I started thinking about our 'Mister X' and what the three of you were saying about him not being local talent. Cynthia had to have gotten him from somewhere so I started thinking about 'known associates'…"

"Just show them the computer screen, Alvarez," Hoffman said, impatience in his voice.

Alvarez turned the screen so that Flynn and Lee could see it. The photo was black and white but was unmistakably the same man who purchased the cell phone in the Wal-Mart video. The ears were right, the eyebrows were as described by Melissa Clifford.

Below the photo was a name, assembled from the kind of snap-in letters police departments kept around for booking shots.

The name, created from block letters, read 'William Earl Kassel'.

**Chapter 14.**

"Courtesy of the Minnesota Department of Corrections," Alvarez said. "Of course, the photo is five years old…"

"It all makes sense," Flynn said. Turning to Lee, he added, "You were the one who said they'd still be in touch. The father of two of her children and her mentor. You were absolutely right."

"Kassel walked away from a work detail a year ago," Alvarez said. "Disappeared completely, without even one sighting in the intervening time. It doesn't seem right, though. Kassel's rap sheet is con games and grand theft. I don't see 'murderer' in that."

"He's been a fugitive for a year, plus he was in prison for – what – seven or eight years," Flynn said. "You can learn a lot of bad habits in that time, some out of necessity."

"Don't forget revenge," Lee added. "Cynthia and Kassel were together for more than five years. She bore him two children. When they split, it wasn't because of 'irreconcilable differences'. They were headed off to different prisons. Cynthia got out first. She went on with her life and hooked up with John Spense. They had five years together, living high as St. John and Cynthia. I can imagine that Kassel did not take kindly to knowing that his long-time girlfriend and mother of his children was with another man."

"Or having a child by him," Flynn added. "But note that she kept his name – 'Duncastle'. She could have stayed 'Duncan' or become Mrs. Grainger-Elliot. My guess is that Kassel was always in Cynthia's mind."

"So, we could have a pair of revenge murders," Hoffman said. "Kassel kills Grainger-Elliot for having 'stolen' his woman. And Brady for having had an affair with her. And for the money Brady was demanding."

"Kassel wasn't trying to get information out of St. John," Lee said. "Kassel was just trying to inflict the maximum amount of pain before killing him. Lois Otting said I ought to consider that when she did the autopsy. I was so focused on St. John as someone who held information everyone else wanted, it never occurred to me that it could be a revenge killing. That was stupid…"

Flynn cut her off. "Which also explains why Kassel pretty much kicked St. John to death around the midsection," Flynn said. "A little something he picked up in prison. You leave the wounds where they won't show unless the victim rats you out. As far as Cynthia knows – or is supposed to know – it was a quick and relatively painless strangulation. No nasty facial lacerations to make her feel sorry for St. John. It makes me wonder how she'll react when she finds out how badly Kassel mutilated her guy."

"But why put the body in the pond?" Alvarez asked.

"To give us a false trail to follow," Lee said. "If I were guessing, I'd say that Cynthia and St. John started seriously planning their disappearance a month or more ago. They'd take Alice Shelburne's five million and any operating funds they could pocket plus whatever they could steal from the Society's treasure chest downstairs. Whether St. John's demise was planned from the start is an interesting question, but I would bet that Cynthia goaded St. John into stealing the daylilies. She probably collected them from him when she came to the Expo Center Friday afternoon, knowing full well that was the last time she'd see him alive."

Lee continued. "As far as St. John was concerned, they were going to be gone forever as soon as the Society's party was over, and he was confident he could hold off Stuart Wells until Saturday morning. By putting St. John's body in the pond in Oscar McQueen's exhibit, it made the murder appear to have something to do with the exhibits or exhibitors. Cynthia not only stole the daylilies, she set up Wells to be framed for St. John's murder."

"Nice trick," Hoffman said. "Now, all we have to do is catch them and prove it."

"The phone calls," Alvarez said. "There were no more calls after Saturday morning. When we thought it was a professional job, I thought the calls stopped because Cynthia had no more use for the guy who did it. But, since it's Kassel who was making the calls, it's more likely that the calls stopped because he's with Cynthia."

"I think we ought to find out," Lee said. "And the nice part is that we're right next door. We also have a letter from the Society's lawyer telling us they have no problem with us going into the Society's property. I'm going to give Sean O'Connell a call, bring him up to speed, and tell him it's time to issue that search warrant. The three of you go ahead."

"I'd better stay behind," Hoffman said. "I'm Town of Brookfield, Middlesex County. I don't want Cynthia getting out of this on a jurisdictional technicality. I'm just an observer until my D.A. is ready to file charges."

Flynn held up a finger. "Remember, I'm officially a short-timer about to be put out to pasture. I can stand there beside Jason, but it looks like Detective Alvarez gets to make the arrest."

"Hell of a collar, kid," Hoffman said. "And you certainly pulled your weight. Go get 'em. I'll keep an eye on the alley in case Kassel tries an end around."

\* \* \* \* \*

Ten minutes later, Alvarez returned with Hoffman and Flynn.

"She's not there," Alvarez told Lee, disappointment apparent in his voice.

"And no one went out the back way," Hoffman said.

"Could she be inside and just not answering?" Lee asked.

"No noise from inside," Hoffman said. "And with three kids and either one or two adults, that's a tough act to pull off."

"Sean O'Connell is still uncomfortable with the whole thing and he demands kid glove treatment," Lee said. "We can detain her for questioning but, unless there's clear evidence of flight once we get inside the townhouse, no arrest." She looked at her watch. "It's still six hours to flight time. Where do you go with three kids?"

"I expect she's traveling light," Hoffman said. "Passports, bank account numbers and a claim check for a coffin don't take much room."

"No one travels light with three kids," Lee said. "Does the family even have a car?"

"No car registered," Alvarez said. "The Society has a van, though. She could have access to that. There are also things like ZipCar."

Lee squeezed her eyes tightly, trying to fight off the tension. "We're going to have to split up. Jason, go to work on your computer and the telephone: could she have taken a different flight? Could the coffin go separately? Is she booked on any other flight under any name? It could be Kassel, Duncan, or who knows. But there will be three kids in the party. She isn't going to leave them behind."

"John, get airport security to check the lounges for everyone who has a non-stop to London. Is Cynthia there now or could she have been there today? Let's get a photo circulated of her and of Kassel to the airport police."

"Detective Hoffman, I can't order you to do anything…"

"I've got a plan of my own," Hoffman said. "I know some people in a couple of federal agencies who might be able to help."

"Then do it," Lee said. "I'm going to get the warrant and get inside the townhouse. It will tell us how long she's been gone and if she's coming back. I don't want to have to chase this woman around the world. Let's get her and let's get Kassel."

\* \* \* \* \*

Alvarez's queries turned up both comforting and disturbing information. The coffin bearing the remains of St. John Grainger-Elliot was traveling to the United Kingdom under a 'return-of-deceased-national' provision in the IATA codes. The coffin's passage had been booked and paid for independent of the tickets for the widow and her children. Because there was a 'receiving mortuary' at the other end of the flight – a funeral home in Brighton – the coffin's accompaniment in its trans-Atlantic journey by an escort was not a pre-condition of its being allowed on the aircraft. Cynthia Duncastle, the consignor, could claim the coffin at Heathrow or meet it at the funeral home. All that mattered was that the coffin was sealed by the Boston funeral home, bore appropriate customs declarations, and that the appropriate fees had been paid.

The second discovery was that there were six daily flights between Boston and various London airports, including a pair of morning flights that would land within the next two hours. Because Flynn and Lee had met with Duncastle at approximately 8:30 that morning, it was unlikely she could have been on either of the morning flights. Still, it was at least possible that she was already out of the country and that the instructions to the funeral home for the preparation of the body had been given via phone or even in advance.

A third discovery was that Cynthia Duncan and three minor children were still booked on the evening Virgin Atlantic flight. Less reassuring was that on a Monday evening in February, flights traveled with many empty seats. Anyone with a passport and a valid credit card could walk up to a ticket counter an hour before flight time and be assured a seat in any class of travel – or even four or five seats.

A check with Logan Airport's customs office showed that the coffin had arrived at the airport in the prior hour and was now in customs quarantine. The Virgin Atlantic flight was a turnaround -- scheduled to arrive at 5:40 p.m. and be back in the air two hours later. The coffin would board with other cargo as soon as the incoming luggage was disgorged.

The reassuring discoveries were that no families with three minor children boarded either of the morning flights. A follow-up phone call to the funeral home gave the information that Cynthia Duncastle had personally visited the funeral home several hours earlier where she had made final arrangements with the home's director and checked that the coffin was as promised.

The distressing part of otherwise reassuring conversation with the funeral home was that Ms. Duncastle had been accompanied by her children, though not by a man.

"Was she carrying anything?" Alvarez asked. "Luggage? Shopping bags?"

The funeral director said he didn't remember but had not paid attention to such details.

"Could Ms. Duncastle have put something in the coffin?" Alvarez asked.

"We make it a point to give families some time alone with the deceased," the funeral director explained. "We don't spy on the family. It's not uncommon for a family member to place something in a coffin prior to burial. A ring or a watch, for example. This is part of the grieving process; part of accepting death."

"Do you look to see what they put inside?" Alvarez asked.

"We close the lid," the funeral director said. "It isn't our business to pry."

Alvarez called Lee with the results. "Keep digging," Lee said. "In the meantime, I'm going to ask for a subpoena to open the coffin."

\* \* \* \* \*

Grainger-Elliot's office computer – his 'official' computer that had already been scrutinized by Alvarez – fortunately used a family portrait as a screensaver. Flynn showed print-outs of the portrait at each of the airline clubs in Logan's Terminal 'E' along with the Department of Corrections photo of Kassel. There had been – or there were – families with children in several of the clubs but none which bore a resemblance to Cynthia Duncastle or her children. Copies were also circulated to the airport police with instructions to report a sighting but not to stop or detain the family.

Airlines were asked to provide copies of their manifests for flights leaving Boston from noon forward. All said they would comply though none offered a guarantee as to when manifests would be forthcoming.

A warrant to search the Botanical Hall townhouse annex was issued at four o'clock. The hour's delay was because Sean O'Connell, the District Attorney, declined to have his name attached to the document and, instead, had requested that it be issued in the name of the junior-most member of his staff.

A second request, to open the casket containing the remains of St. John Grainger-Elliot, was met with a tirade of profanity.

"It was a non-starter," Lee told Flynn.

Inside the townhouse, Lee and Flynn found every indication that Cynthia Duncastle and her children had left without haste. Closets were tidy and filled with clothes. Cosmetics and toiletries were in their expected places in the master bath. The children's bedrooms were still filled with stuffed animals.

"Either she's planning to start a new life using a lot of someone else's money or else she's gone abroad for a week to bury her husband," Lee said. "There's nothing here to prove or disprove either theory."

Examining objects in the master bath, Flynn added, "Or any evidence that William Kassel was here. We could get Crime Scenes here to look for DNA evidence but I don't see the point, at least until we've caught up to them. And, all we've learned is that she's traveling with just a few suitcases, which makes her all the more invisible. Of course, I also don't see any sign of the Society's archive ledger. Which means she either has it with her or, more likely, it has been destroyed."

"So, we're nowhere," Lee said, dejection in her voice. "Even if she and the kids show up in the departure lounge at seven o'clock, all we can do is make her miss her flight for a day and give her a publicity victory…"

Lee's phone chimed. She looked at the caller ID. "Hoffman," she said to Flynn. She opened the clamshell.

"You guys anywhere near the airport?" Hoffman asked over a great deal of background noise.

"We're at the townhouse," Lee replied. "She's gone but she didn't leave in a hurry. She dropped by a funeral home for a final farewell. I asked for a subpoena to have a look inside. O'Connell nearly tore my head off."

"I don't think I've ever heard any detective sound so thoroughly beaten," Hoffman said. "I'm going to have to revise my opinion of you three. Maybe I can still brighten your afternoon. Get on over to the Virgin Atlantic freight office at Terminal E. I may be able to put a smile on that face."

* * * * *

At 5:15 p.m., the bustle in the freight office made conversation difficult. The 'office' was merely the corner of the freight operation, and lift trucks continually moved back and forth within feet of where Lee, Flynn and Hoffman stood. Next to them, on pallets to raise it waist-high, was a bronze coffin. Around the coffin was a thick mover's pad, strapping tape and customs seals.

"I had this inspiration," Hoffman said, a grin on his face. "I had a suspicion that no D.A. in his right mind was going to ask a judge to open a coffin. So, I took a chance and called some old buddies of mine at APHIS."

"AFIS?" Lee asked. "This has nothing to do with fingerprints."

"Right pronunciation, wrong agency," Hoffman said. "These buddies are with the Plant Protection and Quarantine Section of the Animal and Plant Health Inspection Service. They are charged with issuing and enforcing these wonderful things called Phytosanitary Certificates and Export Certification letters…"

"And you're counting on finding the blue daylilies inside the coffin," Flynn said. "Jesus Christ. What an idea."

"And, the best part is that there's no need for a warrant," Hoffman said. "PPQ – that's the Plant Protection and Quarantine Section – has the right to search any parcel being exported if they have a credible report that illegal activity is involved."

A minute later, two women in blue jeans and bright yellow windbreakers appeared at the far end of the cargo area. One of them waved at Hoffman.

"Maria and Emily," Hoffman said to the other detectives as the pair approached. "I once gave them a couple of hot tips that got them a bonus. I've been wondering when I'd get to use that chit."

The windbreakers worn by the two women had 'PPQ' emblazoned in green on both the front and the back of the jackets. The two women were in their mid-forties and wore their auburn hair in identical pony tails, a distinctive style for someone their age.

Hoffman made introductions and rapped on the casket. "We have strong reason to believe that this casket is being used to smuggle something other than standard funeral flowers. As I told you on the phone, the cultivar, Hemerocallis 'Carolina Blue' is not authorized for export and is, in fact, stolen property. The plants' developer is in Pennsylvania and can provide all the documentation you need."

As Hoffman, Lee and Flynn stood out of the way, one of the two women took out a handheld video camera and began circling the casket, recording it continuously from every angle. The bill of lading was opened and recorded. After the exterior of the casket was fully documented, one woman continued to record while the other took a knife to the plastic strapping that held the lid and the thick pad on either side of the casket in place. The pads were removed and videoed.

"The moment of truth," Hoffman whispered, as much to himself as to Lee and Flynn.

The casket lid was lifted. Everyone moved in for a closer look. One of the women began to provide a narration of what she was doing. "I am now lifting the casket lid…"

Seven daylily plants with intact foliage and roots lay diagonally across St. John Grainger-Elliot's chest. Their roots were encased in clear plastic bags with moist soil. Several of the plants had wilted flowers at their top. The flowers were a pale blue.

"Lieutenant Lee, I think you just solved your case," Hoffman said, his voice soft so as not to spoil the continuing narration.

The daylilies were removed and thoroughly videoed, again with a commentary explaining each step as it was taken. The entire process had taken just ten minutes.

"Now comes the nifty part," Hoffman said to Lee. "Emily, having found one set of contraband, would you care to explore the casket a little further just in case there might be something else of interest?"

Emily grinned. "Having found these, there may be all kinds of other plant material in there. You're welcome to look over my shoulder."

The camera again went to the casket interior where Grainger-Elliot lay in his dark suit against the satin walls of the casket.

"Do those legs look a little awkward to you?" Hoffman asked of no one in particular. "Aren't they supposed to be straight? I think St. John's knees are bent. That looks like an awfully uncomfortable way to go through all eternity."

Emily obligingly lifted one leg and felt with her hand underneath. "Got something," she said.

She pulled out a white velvet bag with drawstring. Then another, then another. In all, seven of the small bags were found. Emily opened one for the camera. From it she extracted a wad of cotton and, from the cotton, a two-inch long glass orchid, vividly yellow and red. On it was painted in gold, '1327'.

"I'm going to take a wild guess and say this is part of that Black Shaw collection you were going on about yesterday," Hoffman said.

"Blaschka," Lee corrected. "This is the same style as the one Detective Flynn and I saw on Saturday in Raymond Brady's home."

"But all twenty-five of those were accounted for," Hoffman said. "They were still in Brady's dining room. So these must have come from the Society's basement." To Emily, he said, "You don't happen to have found a mask in there, did you? It's about one foot by two feet and maybe ten inches thick."

Emily shook her head. "I think that would do more than just make the corpse's legs look funny."

"Cynthia will have it with her," Lee said. "It will be in the overhead bin. It isn't the sort of thing you check through."

"The daylilies stay behind but I can't seize these," Emily said, holding one of the velvet bags. "I examined them for the record but I'm obliged to put them back. They're outside my jurisdiction."

"Can you hold the entire coffin as evidence?" Lee asked.

Emily winced. "You understand there's a body in there?"

"Why don't we let it go on?" Flynn asked. "It's been documented by a federal agency. It has no evidentiary value to speak of. And, once it gets into the system, there's no control, meaning none of us can guarantee either refrigeration or that it might not stay in storage for a year."

Lee pondered the thought of a coffin, with a body inside, left in an evidence locker. "It's not going to screw up our case later on?" she asked Emily.

"We acted on a tip from a credible law enforcement authority," Emily said. "We did everything by the book. We found contraband and the fact that it ties to a murder doesn't alter its admissibility. It's thoroughly documented and it's the court-tested path. You don't need the coffin – or the body."

"Then let it go," Lee said. "Seal it back up and put it on the plane. We'll…"

Lee's phone rang. It was the distinctive 'William Tell Overture' snippet.

"Alvarez," Lee said to Flynn and walked to a quieter corner of the freight office.

"I found them," Alvarez said. He sounded as though he were out of breath. "They just flew out of Dulles, headed for Heathrow…"

Lee began mumbling obscenities under her breath.

"But you can beat them there," Alvarez added. "Do you have a passport?"

"What?" Lee said.

"If you have a passport you can be on a BA flight that will get you in ahead of them. There ought to be a cart coming for you…"

Lee heard the sound of a cart beeping as it entered the cargo area. It bore a British Airways decal and had an amber light flashing on a pole above it.

"If you're carrying a weapon, make certain you give it Flynn for safekeeping because you can't take it on the plane," Alvarez said. "Otherwise, get in the cart. I'll explain the rest on the way."

Lee looked at her watch. The time was 5:35.

**\* \* \* \* \***

"I started looking at aliases William Kassel had used across his career," Alvarez told Lee over the phone. "'William Foster Stanton' was one that recurred several times. I found a driver's license in that name issued in Minnesota and subsequent renewals, with Kassel's photo. Then I found a passport issued last month. It's a separate identity he built up over more than a decade; maybe one of several, but it's the one that he used to book a round trip to London from Washington Dulles yesterday. From there, I looked at the manifest and found a woman travelling with three children in the name of Cynthia Stanton, who connected to the flight from Boston. Apparently the Stanton identity is one they concocted together and kept active. United wouldn't give me the manifest until the door was sealed, which was ten minutes ago. They took off at 5:24 and land at

Heathrow tomorrow morning at 5:55 local time."

Alvarez continued. "The good news is that they have to fly almost over Boston to get to London which gives us the head start. You're booked on a British Airways flight that leaves at 5:55 p.m. but gets into Heathrow fifty minutes ahead of them. By the time you get there, I ought to have settled everything with the British police. I'm still working that part of it, but the first priority was to get you on the flight."

Airport Security met Lee's cart at a tarmac-level entry point at the rear of the international terminal. At the top of a flight of stairs was a second cart, also with a flashing light. There was both a driver and a woman who identified herself as a gate agent.

"We occasionally have VIP's that get this kind of treatment," the gate agent said as the cart jerked forward. "You're the first policeman. We can give you a complimentary upgrade to business class but I'm afraid first class is full. I just need your passport and a credit card…"

Seven minutes later, Lee was at the boarding gate, having bypassed all check-in, security and U.S. customs. As promised, she was shown to a seat in the business class section of the aircraft and offered an 'amenities kit'. *At least I get to brush my teeth*, Lee thought.

Her phone chimed. It was Alvarez again.

"I understand you're on board," Alvarez said.

"How did you pull this off?" Lee asked. "I can show up two hours early for a flight and still miss it. Of course, I usually have a change of clothes with me."

"I spoke with British Airways security a couple of hours ago and asked what they could do," Alvarez said. "I didn't know I'd need it, but I figured it was better to have a plan. Both flights should be on time and, like I said, you should beat them by about forty minutes. I'm talking with the Metropolitan Police, who have jurisdiction at the airports. United will pull their luggage as soon as the plane lands and segregate it. The plan is to get them at passport control. Legally speaking, they'll never be on British soil. We can have them back on a flight to Boston at 11:30 a.m. London time that lands in Boston at 1:45."

"And this works, legally?"

"Chief Inspector Tuchman of the Metropolitan Police says they do this a couple of times a year. They'll even provide a matron for the children. Based on what you found in the casket, I've asked for both an arrest and a search warrant to cover the mask, Grainger-Elliot's computer, any knick-knacks she may have pilfered from the Castle and papers they've created. The search warrant will be there when you get to Heathrow. If they've got the mask, I'll alert Hoffman and he'll have a separate warrant from Brookfield."

"You really have this planned," Lee said.

"You told me to dig deep and use my imagination. I've also done some signature comparisons on the checks to cash written at the Society. Some are St. John's, but I'm pretty sure quite a number were written by the Society's treasurer. I know we can talk about that later, but I wanted you to know before you talk to Cynthia. Get as good a night's sleep as you can, call me when you get in, and I'll give you an update."

"It will be midnight in Boston, Jason."

"Lieutenant, I remember calling you at three in the morning," Alvarez said. "Serves me right."

Lee stretched back in the business class seat and began sorting through the amenities kit. On the plane's public address system, preflight announcements were being made, including one to turn off all portable electronic items. As she reached into her purse, her phone chimed again, its red LED blinking. Over the din of the cabin announcements she did not hear the distinctive ringtone but assumed it was Alvarez.

"Jason, they're closing the door," Lee said.

"Hey, I just got back. I thought we might get together for dinner."

It was Matt.  Returned from New York.

"Vicki?"

"Matt, I… thought it was one of my detectives…"

"What's that commotion in the background?  It sounds like the inside of…"

"I'm on a plane, Matt," Lee said.  "It's getting ready to take off."

"Take off for where?"

"London."

There was a silence at the other end of the line, then, "You couldn't come down to New York for the weekend, but you can hop on a plane to London?"

A cabin attendant leaned over her.  "Miss, I'll have to ask you to put away the phone now."

"I'm going to pick up a murder suspect, Matt."  And then she thought, *why the hell do I owe you an explanation?*

"To England," Matt replied.  "You have to get on a plane tonight to go get a suspect, but you couldn't be bothered to…"

"Matt, I have to turn the phone off now.  Goodbye."

She closed the phone lid with Matt in mid-expletive.

*Well*, she thought.  *That settles that.*

# Chapter 15.
# Tuesday

"Chief Inspector Fay Tuchman, Aviation Security OCU." The tall, lanky woman with short brown hair, freckles though clearly in her thirties, and a winning smile thrust out her hand. "Please call me Fay."

Lee, working on three hours of sleep, returned the handshake. "Tell me you have strong coffee somewhere around here. The stuff on the plane was weak and lukewarm."

Tuchman smiled. "Terribly hot and wonderfully strong. We on the overnight shift like it that way." There was pride in her voice.

They were standing in the jet way outside the aircraft. Tuchman motioned Lee through a security door held open by a second officer. "I think we can bypass the niceties," Tuchman said. "It's a beautiful terminal but, with luck, you'll be here only about six hours."

The two walked down a flight of stairs to the tarmac where a police car waited. "We're going to Terminal 1, which serves United," Tuchman said. "That terminal also gives us a bit of a break because the queues for immigration get rather significant about now, and your friends aren't traveling on an EC passport." Tuchman walked to and stood by the driver's side and smiled as Lee made the disorienting mental switch to right-hand-drive vehicles. "Your Detective Alvarez told me you grew up in Hong Kong, so this should be familiar after a bit." She started the engine. "For someone I never heard of until twelve hours ago, Detective Alvarez and I are becoming quite good friends. He is enormously efficient. We have everything from fingerprints to family portraits and video of Kassel acquiring the mobile. And, we have arrest warrants awaiting your use, as well as a search warrant for their luggage."

They arrived at a cluster of offices that represented the

Metropolitan Police outpost in Terminal 1. Coffee was poured.

"Let me show you the layout," Tuchman said, guiding Lee to a wall of glass. She pointed to the vast space beyond. "This is the immigration hall. It's about half full now, but there are some twenty flights due in the next hour that will dump nearly four thousand people into here. There's no jumping queues; everyone waits. From the time they're off the plane, it will be at least forty minutes before they present their passports. We can watch their progress from here."

Tuchman indicated several conference rooms. "We thought you'd like to interrogate Ms. Duncastle and Mr. Kassel separately. I can supply a room monitor while you shuttle from one to another. That person will be stationed outside the door and you need only request assistance. We've a third room for the children. It's got cots and toys, and there will be a matron on duty. There's no telling what their mum has told them. I would suspect some adverse psychological implications down the road, but Ms. Duncastle ought to have thought about that before she decided to get into the murder business. There's also a vacant office where you can look through the luggage."

Tuchman turned to Lee. "You understand we can't be part of the interrogation. We can facilitate. We will video the proceedings. We can lend you all manner of assistance, but past experience says we best keep silent once the questioning begins. In theory, they're not in the U.K. until they're through that kiosk with a stamped passport. Some very sharp barristers have argued that if someone from the Met is asking questions, it's tantamount to having that immigration stamp and extradition rules apply."

"Alvarez said you've gone through this before," Lee said.

Tuchman nodded. "Including once last month for some fugitive financier from New York. Had him back on a flight in two hours. Something of a record." Tuchman looked at her watch. "The plane lands in fifteen minutes, and there'll be nothing to do for the better part of twenty minutes after that while we cull their luggage and bring it here.  I can arrange a cot if you'd like a lay-down."

"What I really want is a shower," Lee said.  "I know clean clothes are too much to ask."

\* \* \* \* \*

The baggage arrived half an hour later.  It was placed in an office and Lee, freshly showered, quickly went through the four pieces. William Kassel's luggage included eight thousand dollars in hundred dollar bills, rolled inside a small plastic talcum powder bottle.  Cynthia Duncastle's suitcase contained a laptop computer, carefully cushioned inside other clothing.  And, inside one of the children's suitcases, amid clothing and a few stuffed animals, were five more Blaschka flowers in velvet bags.  They apparently were too noticeable when placed in the coffin.  Also in the children's bag inside a stuffed giraffe was a manila envelope containing identification in the name of Cindy Duncan, Cynthia Duncastle and William Kassel.

Tuchman picked up one of the glass flowers.  "Incredibly beautiful," she said, holding it to the fluorescent light in the office. "Detective Alvarez said these were worth a small fortune.  Fifteen thousand pounds apiece. Is that right?"

Lee nodded.  "And someone's life.  We still don't know exactly how all the motives tie together.  I'm hoping there's something in this computer.  Right now, I've got them cold for grand theft, but they've covered their tracks fairly well on the murders.  I need a break to make this stick."

A patrolman stuck his head inside the office.  "They're about five minutes away from the head of the queue."

"We can watch from here, with sound, or I can station you out there," Tuchman said.

"I've met twice Cynthia twice before," Lee said.  "Seeing me would likely spook her.  Let's keep me out of sight."

The group of five people, two adults and three children, moved forward a foot or so every two or three seconds.  To the people in the immigration line, the wall to their right was smoky glass with bands of color. From the inside, the view into the immigration hall was crystal clear.

It was the first time Lee had ever seen Kassel. He looked alert, almost feral, with his eyes moving left and right as though trying to discern a threat he knew was there in the underbrush. His body was filled with kinetic energy, wanting to dart forward but unable to move because of the crowd in front of him. He was a man running on adrenaline. It made no difference how much or how little sleep he may have gotten on the flight. His instinct was to flee.

Cindy or Cynthia – with all her aliases it was time to settle on one name for her, and so from now on, she was simply 'Cindy Duncan' to Lee -- was preoccupied with the children. Lee had never seen these children either. A four-year-old rubbed her eyes and needed to be coaxed along. A boy and a girl, nine or ten years old -- the boy's resemblance to Kassel made it immediately apparent that he was now with his father -- looked sullen from lack of sleep. Whatever excitement they may have felt when they first left the plane had now dissipated in the slow movement of the line.

The vignette made Kassel seem like the tiger protective of its mate and cubs. Duncastle was too tired and preoccupied with caring for the three children to focus on external threats. Kassel, used to being the hunter, was now the apprehensive guardian, passing across unknown and dangerous territory.

Lee's attention, though, was drawn to the shopping bag on Duncastle's arm. It bore the name of Nordstrom but inside it she could see a single cardboard box. It was perhaps two feet in height, a foot wide and a foot deep. It was the size of the mask stolen from the archive of the Botanical Society. The bag did not sway as she walked, indicating it was heavy.

Ahead of them, a uniformed policeman efficiently moved travelers to vacant passport control stations. "Step left, please.

Straight ahead to number seven…" As the five reached the front, the policeman calmly said, "Step right, please, kiosk one," then immediately told a teenager with a backpack, "Straight ahead, please. Kiosk four."

Kassel pushed his and Duncastle's passports across the counter. Duncastle stayed behind the stripe on the floor, keeping the children together.

"Purpose of your visit?" the immigration clerk asked, opening the first passport.

"Family funeral," Kassel said.

"Ah," the clerk said, looking up from the passport. "So sorry." He scanned one passport under a barcode reader. He scanned the second one and frowned. "I'm terribly sorry, Mr. Stanton. You and the mizzus are fine, but I see three children back there." The clerk indicated Duncastle and the children with his chin. "One of them doesn't show up on the record."

"They're on Mrs. Stanton's passport," Kassel said, apprehension creeping into his voice.

The clerk shook his head. "That's right," he said, holding up the passport for Kassel to see. "I've just scanned it, but it keeps coming up with two little ones. I'm sure we can straighten this out." He flipped a switch and a light came on above the kiosk.

The policeman came over. "Problem?"

"Got a child who isn't coming up on the mum's passport," the clerk said. "Can you get it straightened out?" The clerk's voice was friendly, seeking only to expedite a trivial issue that threatened to hold up a very long line.

"If you and your family would step this way…" The policeman indicated the double doors into the area where Lee and Tuchman observed.

"No!" Kassel said, his mind sensing the trap and his body immediately tense and ready for a fight. "There's nothing wrong with the passports! Just scan them and let us through!"

Duncastle, distracted until that moment by the crying of the younger daughter, instantly recognized the danger.

"Please, sir, we can deal with this. If you'll please just…"

"My God!" Duncastle screamed, loud enough so that it instantly brought silence to an area fifty feet around her. "We've come to bury these poor children's father after he was murdered in America!" She was in full English accent, incensed and alarmed, stressing the word 'murder'. "His coffin is here, his children are grieving, not understanding where their father has gone. And these – people – won't let us through to bury him!"

The policeman moved closer to Duncastle. The youngest child screamed. The policeman reached for Duncastle's arm. "Please, ma'am, just come with me…"

"No!" Duncastle screamed. "Someone! Someone call the newspapers! Tell them what's happening! Tell them that the *fascist* police won't let these children say goodbye to their *murdered* father! His name was John Spense, and he was *murdered* in Boston on Friday! Someone, call the media. Alert them!"

"This is out of hand," Tuchman murmured. Then, loudly, she turned and barked an order. "Peters, Wilson, Parker, Urquart. Get out there, now. Get them inside here. You have five seconds!"

Four police officers, two of them women, rushed through the doors.

Duncastle pulled her arm away from the first officer and screamed. "Stop the fascists! Stop the Brownshirts! Let these poor children bury their murdered father!" Now, all three children were screaming, terrorized by their mother's sudden rage.

Two male officers seized Kassel by his arms and pulled him through the doors. The two women each took Duncastle by an arm and dragged her, screaming, toward the opening. The last policeman, the one who originally tried to persuade Kassel to enter the detention area willingly, leaned over to the three children and whispered, "You'd best follow your mum. She'll be worried."

The three quickly followed Duncastle through the door. No policeman ever touched them.

Inside the detention area, Duncastle immediately stopped screaming. It had been an act, calculated to draw intervention. Perhaps she thought that, in a melee or other confusion, she might flee through immigration and customs. But it had failed because the police had acted swiftly. On the other side of the glass, the lines were again moving smoothly. The ripple of Duncastle's screaming had left no trace except, perhaps, wonder of what the woman had done wrong that five police had been required to subdue her.

"I need to comfort my children," she said to Tuchman, noting the three pips on shoulders of the woman's uniform. Duncastle said it in such a way that it was implied that it was the police who had caused this dislocation.

"You have two minutes," Tuchman said. "Mr. Kassel, you are in this room." Tuchman indicated one of the conference rooms. "Wilson, you will make certain he stays in the room."

As Duncastle moved to gather her children to her, she saw Lee standing to one side. Initially startled, her look quickly turned cold. She turned to her children and cooed soothing words.

Ignoring Lee, Duncastle said to Tuchman, "They will require something to drink and a place to sit for a few minutes." The statement implied that this detention was only for a brief interval before they were allowed on their way.

"Officer Parker will see to their needs," Tuchman said. "A room has been provided for them."

As she gathered her children to her, Duncastle put down the shopping bag. Lee walked toward the bag. Duncastle immediately looked up, grabbed the bag and snarled, "You leave this alone."

"Your two minutes are up," Tuchman said, looking at her watch.

"They need me," Duncastle said. To the children, she added, "Don't you?"

"Your two minutes are up," Tuchman repeated. To one of the officers, she said, "Officer Parker, please take the children to their room."

"You can't do this," Duncastle said, tears streaming down her face. "I'm their mother. Let them stay with me." The children obediently began crying.

"Officer Parker." Tuchman repeated.

"Don't be inhuman," Duncastle said, clutching at her youngest.

"We are prepared to handcuff you if necessary," Tuchman said coldly. "Let go of the child."

Duncastle looked around her. A resigned look came over her face. The skirmish was over.

"Go with the policewoman," she said to the children. "I'll join you presently." She smiled. The children allowed themselves to be led to the office, looking back apprehensively.

"We'll talk in this room," Lee said, indicating the closest office.

"We'll talk when I have an attorney present," Duncastle said. "You can go screw yourself."

"Then I'll talk and you'll listen," Lee said. "But we go into this room. Or, would you prefer handcuffs?"

Holding the Nordstrom bag firmly in both hands, Duncastle walked into the room, which consisted of a small conference table and four utilitarian wooden chairs in an otherwise bare room with taupe walls. She sat down and looked around the room. She noted the unobtrusive camera mounted high in one corner.

Duncastle motioned to the camera. "Is this being recorded?"

"I thought you weren't talking," Lee said.

"Excuse me, Officer," Duncastle said. The English accent had vanished. "For the record, is this being recorded?"

"Let's assume it is," Lee said.

"Good. I demand an immigration hearing before a magistrate," Duncastle said. "I request that an immigration counselor be summoned and I want legal representation. Now." She crossed her arms. A slight smile crept across her face.

Lee shook her head. "There isn't going to be an immigration hearing, Cindy. And thank you for dropping the phony accent. I personally thought it was charming back in Boston, but I suspect it would probably make people around here giggle. There isn't going to be a hearing because you were never admitted to the U.K. Technically speaking, while you may have left the United States, you were on the legal equivalent of one of those cruises to nowhere. The ship sails for home in about four hours."

"Then I demand, in addition to an immigration hearing, a qualified immigration counselor and an attorney, a hearing at which I may request political asylum."

Lee shook her head again. "None of that is going to happen, Cindy. You aren't in Great Britain. You're on the wrong side of an immigration barrier in a never-never land that is, for all intents and purposes, a little bit of the United States. And I have a warrant compelling your return to Boston to face certain charges."

Lee opened a manila envelope and produced several sheets of paper. "This is a search warrant permitting me to search you and your luggage. I'd like to start with that shopping bag. Please hand it over."

Duncastle read the search warrant and made no effort to hand the bag across the table. "This warrant is issued in the United States and makes no reference to being served anywhere outside the United States. You want to conduct an illegal search of my property. Anything that happens as a result of that search is tainted fruit, not inevitable discovery."

"A jailhouse lawyer," Lee said. "Unfortunately, it appears the Minnesota Corrections Center at Shakopee was missing a few critical volumes. I assure you that the search is legal."

"You aren't opening the box," Duncastle said, her voice filled with defiance.

"Pardon me for a moment," Lee said. She rose from her chair and walked to the door, opened it. One of the policemen stood outside. "I need restraints for Ms. Duncan so that I may examine her carry-on luggage and purse."

The officer followed Lee back into the room, handcuffs at the ready.

"All right," Duncastle said, eyeing the policeman. "But it's an illegal search. She reached beside her and passed across the Nordstrom bag with two hands. "Tainted fruit," she said. Then, glancing up at the camera, added, "And it's all on tape."

"You have my word that it is not illegal," Lee said. She began unsealing the box.

"It's mine," Duncastle said. "I intended to declare it at customs."

Lee opened the box. Inside was the Kamerun mask, nestled in packing peanuts. On top was a file folder. In the folder was a raft of papers, some of them brittle with age. The last one attested to the mask's ownership by Cindy Duncan.

"Exactly how did you intend to square 'Cindy Duncan' with the name on your passport – 'Stanton' – I believe."

"Stanton is my married name."

"Not Duncastle?"

"John and I were never married."

"So, when you married William Kassel, you became Mrs. Stanton?"

She shrugged.

"Here's the problem, Cindy." From the manila envelope in front of her, Lee withdrew a printout of a page from the Botanical Society handwritten ledger and passed it across the table. "This mask came into the possession of the Botanical Society in 1916."

Duncastle did not bother to read the document. "*A* mask came into their possession. I inherited this one."

Lee next pulled out a printout of a photograph, emailed during the night from Alvarez. It showed Dr. Faber presenting the mask to the head of the New England Botanical Society. Lee pushed the photo across the table. "Cindy, it's the same mask."

Duncastle barely looked at the photograph. "I have all the proper documentation for this mask," she said.

"This mask's provenance was created on Raymond Brady's computer," Lee said. "We have all the interim steps he went through." Lee pulled out more sheets showing the mask passing through other, fictitious galleries.

"Then Brady stole the mask," Duncastle said. "He gave it to me with all proper documentation. It was a gift. I can't imagine he stole it."

Lee removed two sheets of paper and passed them across the table. "These are a few of your suggestions for 'improving' the mask's provenance. I have several other examples if you'd like to see them."

For the first time, Duncastle blinked as she saw the email traffic. But she said, "Then I suggest we let a court settle the matter." She shifted in her chair. "Look, what if I agree, right here and now before witnesses…" She pointed to the camera. "…To return to the United States. Let me bury John. Let the kids say their goodbyes. Give me three days. Then you can wrap me in chains. I just want to bury the man I lived with for five years. And the father of one of my children. Can we agree on that? I swear I'll come back."

"Bury him with or without the blue daylilies?" Lee asked.

Duncastle's intake of breath was audible. "What do you mean?"

"The casket arrives in an hour," Lee said. "Hemerocallis Carolina Blue stayed behind in Boston."

"You can't open a casket," Duncastle said. There was a look of revulsion on her face. "That's illegal."

"I didn't open it," Lee said. "Federal agents did. It seems you forgot to get an export license."

Duncastle sat with her mouth open, not knowing what to say next.

"They also found some other trinkets." Lee reached into a bag at her side and brought out one of the velvet bags. She pulled out a glass peach blossom.

"I have no idea how those lilies got into the casket," Duncastle said. "I suspect the funeral home did it. Someone probably had them delivered and, since there isn't going to be a service in Boston, they put them in the casket." Duncastle indicated the velvet bags Lee was lining up on the table. "And I have no idea how those got in the casket, either. Those are the glass flowers the Society sold to Ray."

Lee shook her head. "These weren't in the casket. These were in your luggage."

"Shit," Duncastle said. "So you did an illegal search of my luggage, too."

"Read the warrant, Cindy. It covers luggage. When the coffin arrives, customs police will open the casket and find the other glass flowers. They'll all come back with us to Boston. John Spense will get buried, however. The casket and body entered the country legally."

"I still have no idea of how they got there," Duncastle said. "It's obvious that the police planted them."

Lee shook her head. When she spoke, she did so bluntly. "Ultimately, though, this isn't about masks or glass flowers or even blue daylilies, Cindy. It's about murder. John Spense's murder. You planned it, Kassel carried it out. The rest of this? Compared to the top count, it's just little stuff. Grand theft, embezzlement. It's interesting, but it's murder I'm really here for. And now it's time that I read you your rights, American style."

Lee did so. As she did, she watched Duncastle's eyes looking for an exit strategy. The pretense of being in control was gone.

"William Kassel walked away from a work detail a year ago," Lee said. "He had been in prison for seven years. If you were like me, you never got over him in those seven years you were apart. You had two kids with him, and it wasn't his idea to be convicted. But your kids had to eat and John Spense – let's call him 'Spense' for simplicity's sake – was good at the con and so a decent provider. You prepped him for the Atlanta job and, when you saw what stupid saps they were in Boston, you said, 'go for it'. And, by that time, there was another kid, and Kassel was looking at another five years before he was even eligible for parole."

"But then he turned up," Lee said, "and all those years melted away. Here's the love of your life, standing at the front door, wanting you back. Any woman can understand that. Meanwhile, little by little, Spense is getting in over his head. He's got people like Alice Shelburne ready to give him serious money, but he's also been a little too brazen in dipping into the till. Not to mention his interest in the sweet young things he keeps hiring, which you find annoying."

"Kassel says the two of you can get away. One big, final score. Get Alice Shelburne's five million and disappear with the kids in some tax haven. Let Spense figure out how to explain it all to the trustees. But you have a better idea. Grab everything you can and, while you're at it, get Spense out of the way, cleanly. You started working on the Kamerun mask back in December. You were even willing to have a little pity sex with Brady to make certain he got you the best provenance money could buy. There were also the Blaschka pieces to pilfer. Then, last week Spense started talking about the incredible new plants at the show, and you realized there was one final multi-million-dollar opportunity right there. You told Spense when and how to steal them. He did, then you collected them Friday at noon."

"All this time, you were telling Spense you've got the perfect getaway plan. Saturday morning – before Mel Dawson can lower the boom – the family was going to be on a plane to somewhere beyond the reach of the law and the IRS. But in reality, it was a very different plan; one that reunited you with Kassel. And, all Kassel had to do was kill St. John and dump the body in a way that threw suspicion elsewhere long enough for you to make your getaway."

"The problem is, Kassel got spotted. One of those sweet young things Spense hired saw Kassel in the management offices at 12:30, with a rope in his hand. In the meantime, we were checking phone records and got curious about those one-minute calls from a pre-paid phone. Kassel bought the phone at a Wal-Mart in Framingham. Do you want to see the video of him buying the phone? He called you when he was in place at the Expo Center and then again when the job was done."

The look on Duncastle's face told Lee she had put together the story correctly. Now, it was time to deliver the blow that would spark a confession.

"Here's the part you don't know," Lee said. "Spense's death was neither quick nor painless, which is probably what you asked Kassel to do. Kassel really made him suffer, Cindy. Twenty minutes of pure, non-stop hell." Lee took three photos from the envelope. "You were going to see these autopsy photos at some point anyway, so you may as well get used to them. And there are lots more, some even more gruesome."

Lee lined up the photos in front of Duncastle where they could not be ignored. "According to the Medical Examiner, Kassel pulverized Spense's liver, kidneys and spleen with those kicks. They were expertly delivered, intended to inflict maximum pain without showing marks outside the clothing. It's a trick you pick up in prison if you're there long enough. Cindy, it may make you change your mind about whether you want that man around your children and especially around the one that isn't his."

Duncastle picked up the three photos, one at a time. She stared at them, a look of shock on her face.

"So, you were making plans to leave, but there was this one last loose end," Lee said. "Ray Brady knew too much and he wanted money. Kassel also doesn't care for anyone you've been intimate with. So, the two of you paid Brady a 4 a.m. visit. You had to be there because Brady would never have opened the door for Kassel. Four bullets later, Brady was dead and no longer in a position to demand money."

"The rest was supposed to be easy. A one-week trip to England to bury Spense that would turn into a life-long vacation. There's five million from Alice Shelburne, a couple of million from a Chinese plant breeder for 'Carolina Blue', one or two million for the Kamerun mask, and a dozen glass flowers for walking-around money, plus whatever else Spense stole from the Society's archives."

Duncastle continued to stare at the three photos, tracing a finger over the mass of red and black contusions on Spense's torso.

Lee continued. "If it hadn't been for Kassel getting spotted Friday night and those phone calls, you might have gotten away with it. But instead, you're both going to be convicted for first-degree murder. Twice. Once in Suffolk County for Spense, then again in Middlesex County for Brady. You'll probably never see your kids again. Or Kassel, of course. Being Massachusetts, the death penalty is off the table. So, you really have no bargaining position. And, having tried to flee the country once and with five million or more stashed somewhere, I wouldn't count on bail."

"That's the case, more or less, Cindy. There's a DA in Boston who really needs a slam dunk to restore his career. You and Kassel are perfect. I'm telling you this because, when they take you off that plane in Boston this afternoon, you're going to want to hug those kids extra tight. It will probably be for the last time."

"And, with that, you'll have to excuse me," Lee said, pushing her chair back from the table. "I'm going to go cut a deal with Kassel for testimony. He'll get twenty to life, but he'll plead out and he'll have provided the color commentary on how you were the brains behind it all and he was just the dumb schmuck who did your bidding." Lee looked at her watch. "The flight leaves in about three hours. You'll be locked in here until then. I'll have a sandwich sent in."

Lee rose from her chair.

"Wait," Duncastle said, pleading.

Lee smiled.

## Acknowledgments

I am far more familiar with flower shows than any author ought to be. For three years, I served as Chairman of Blooms! at the Boston Flower & Garden Show, organizing the activities of the venerable Massachusetts Horticultural Society at that event. As a consequence of my work on behalf of that organization, I can vouch that almost everything contained in the pages of this book related to the operation of the fictional Northeast Garden and Flower Show is drawn from personal experience. I will hasten to add that the plot of this book is entirely a product of my imagination.

But personal experience should also be leavened with professional expertise, and I can point to three individuals who have my thanks for sharing their long trade show experience. Carolyn Weston and Garry Edgar of The Paragon Group, which created the superb Boston Flower & Garden Show, have my gratitude for sharing their wisdom and anecdotes. And, Paul Miskovsky, head of the eponymous Falmouth-based landscaping company, lent his exhibitor's point of view. He also allowed me to gain invaluable experience by pitching in to build his award-winning landscape exhibits at half a dozen flower shows in Massachusetts and Rhode Island.

Over time, an author creates a large cast of fully realized characters and imbues them with specialized skill sets. At some point, writers must choose either to continue to invent fresh characters with new names and attributes, or else to take the same repertory and give them new adventures. In the course of seven mysteries, I've both populated my books with people that will live only within the pages of one story, and characters that continue from book to book.

As I began to write *A Murder at the Flower Show*, I realized that many of the specialized qualities required for my new story already existed in earlier books. Moreover, they all lived in and around

Boston. While the story's anchor is the newly minted Boston Police Department Lieutenant Victoria Lee, I already had a terrific amateur horticulturalist in Liz Phillips and a wisecracking, small-town detective in Martin Hoffman.

Readers of my other mysteries will recognize certain familiar names and faces from other stories. Detective John Flynn will, in a few months' time, come out of a too-brief retirement to take up the position of town detective in Hardington where he and Liz Phillips will solve several murders. In both *A Murder in the Garden Club* and *Murder for a Worthy Cause*, Flynn makes many references about (and even speaks to) his former partner. Careful readers will note that Liz and Flynn never cross paths in this story and neither Lee nor Jason Alvarez reference Flynn in Liz's presence or vice-versa.

Brookfield Detective Martin Hoffman is the same character who figures in both *The Garden Club Gang* and *Deadly Deeds*. This story predates the ones told in those two mysteries. And, very careful readers will recognize that District Attorney Sean O'Connell was also Kat's nemesis in *Murder Imperfect*, together with Detectives Roy Halliday and Sharon Tucci. Readers who were rooting for Kat will note that O'Connell is still smarting from his humiliating loss in that prosecution.

I am grateful for the 'technical support' I receive for each book. The multi-talented tag team of Faith Clunie, Marilyn Racette and Connie Stolow are superb editors who mask my inability to master the art of the use of the comma, among other, larger failings. Artist Lynne Schulte's cover perfectly captures what that night watchman saw on his rounds the night of the Gala. My wife, Betty, read and astutely commented on this manuscript until she was able to quote lengthy passages from memory.

Finally, I want to thank the dozens of garden clubs, book clubs, libraries and civic groups that have sought me out as a speaker this year. You are wonderful, appreciative audiences.

Made in the USA
Charleston, SC
11 November 2016